The
Second First
Chance

The
Second First
Chance
Blakely Bennett

TandemWriters

The Second First Chance

TandemWriters

Cover design by Happi Anarky
Logo design by Olivia E. Bennett
Edited by Harper Jewel

ISBN: 978-0-69264-330-3 (Trade Paperback)
ISBN: 978-1-94478-631-1 (eBook)

The Second First Chance is dedicated to the real Patrick (Paki) who made my first college experience an adventure. And like with Jayden's Packy, we lost touch for decades. Writing this novel jarred his last name from my memory, and we have reconnected. Some friendships are meant to last a lifetime just like ours.

With love and gratitude,
Blakely

PROLOGUE
JUNE 2015

"**D**o you think you'll make it through the eulogy?" Sweet Pea asked me on the second worst day of my life.

Sweet Pea was my kid sister Shannon, not that we were kids anymore by a long shot. At the overripe age of 48, I had lost my husband, my whole reason for living. My daughter Ashley might suggest to me I was being overly dramatic, and I couldn't blame her. I had told her that at least a thousand times during her childhood, and she was still in payback mode. Not that she would say it today. Not on the day we had the funeral service for her dad.

Even though Callahan and I considered ourselves agnostic, I had allowed his huge southern family to cajole me into an open casket viewing before the service, which I personally found barbaric. The love of my life would be cremated after the affair, half of his ashes would come to me, and the other half would be buried in a plot of his family's choosing. He was the baby with five older sisters and just taking on one of them at a time was daunting. All of them at once, I had no chance to win the fight. However, they had mostly stayed out of our lives, and I knew they needed to grieve in their own ways.

"Why are you the one giving the opening eulogy?" my sister Shannon asked me again. "I mean, how will you get through it?"

We were in a separate room from the rest of the extended family. I needed time away from all of the crying to gather myself together.

1

"It's usually the best friend who gives it, and I was definitely his. Plus, I owe it to him."

"I don't see how that's true but okay. I'll be standing by with the tissues."

"Please make sure the song plays at the right time."

"I'm on it."

The Pastor of the funeral home came in and told us to follow him. My bright outfit might put off the congregation of friends and family, however, Cally thought funerals should be a celebration of life, so I wore his favorite color: teal.

A cacophony of conversation and array of fragrances assaulted my already overwhelmed senses as we entered the chapel.

Everyone else wore the requisite black as I saw pew after pew filled with all the people who loved my husband of twenty years. They had to open the divider to expand the room, and people were still lining the walls because there wasn't sufficient seating for everyone in the already large space.

Shannon and I, with the eulogy clasped in my hand, sat with Ashley and my parents in the left front row as the Pastor began.

"Callahan East, father to Ashley, husband to Jayden, brother to Jeanie, Stacy, Susie, Sissy, and Frannie and son-in-law to Mr. and Mrs. Cooke, has passed safely into the loving arms of his already departed parents..."

My sister and I glanced at one another, and I did my best not to cringe. Callahan and his parents never saw eye to eye on politics or religion, and the last place I could imagine him would be in the arms of his parents. My mother squeezed my hand, and Ashley leaned against me, tears streaming down her cheeks.

The pastor continued, "This space, here today, is a testament to how many lives Callahan touched during his sixty years on this earth. On behalf of the Easts and the Cookes, we thank you for showing your love and support today. Callahan's wife, Jayden, will speak first, and then their daughter Ashley, and finally his sisters. Jayden?" He held out his hand for me to join him behind the pulpit.

I rose, not feeling at all grounded in my body as if the nightmare was reaching the pinnacle, which would jolt me awake. Once I reached the stage, the pastor took a seat behind me. I glanced at the golden wood coffin beside me, thankfully closed, and then out at all the people waiting for me to start.

My mouth dried up, and I tried to swallow down the lump that had lodged itself in my throat. I coughed, and the pastor must have sensed my distress or was used to it.

He poured a glass of water and handed it over to me.

After drinking a few sips, I set the glass on the podium and took a deep breath.

"Let's get this over with, love," I heard Callahan whisper to me as he had on many occasions when we felt obligated to attend a function but would rather be alone together anywhere else.

"Okay," I said to him and then the audience let out an audible sigh. I looked down at my notes and then pushed them to the side, deciding to wing it. "Shannon, my sister, asked me why *I* was giving the eulogy for Callahan and here's what I said." I paused, taking another deep breath and forged on, "Cally was my best friend, my soul mate, my life blood, the cause of my greatest joys along with our daughter Ashley. Our relationship, we believed, defied the odds and every day we re-chose our life together. Callahan felt that funerals should be a celebration of life and not a mourning of death. This dress I am wearing today was one of his very favorites although I looked much better in it ten pounds ago."

The congregation laughed.

"I often wished I could see myself through his eyes. For him to tell it: I was the most beautiful woman in the world. The best mother, the best wife, the best friend, but we all know love blinded him."

The audience chuckled again.

"Thankfully, I was the lucky recipient of his love and loyalty. Twenty years. It was, however, way, way too short. No time would have been long enough with him but this, this was the greatest love story interrupted.

"If he were here, he would say, 'Jayden, love, you're doing a great job, and you'll be fine without me. You were always the rock.' He would be wrong. He was the rock, and I was the roll, he was the stalwart who tethered my flighty airheaded balloon to the earth, which would have otherwise flown toward the sun and popped. He was the foundation, and I was the decoration. He made me feel safe in this crazy world, and with him at my side, I could conquer anything.

"He made friends wherever he went, fearless in the face of rejection. I envied the confidence he had in himself and his convictions even if I had to be the one to point out the flaws in his reasoning every once in a blue moon. And of course, we had our big rows on occasion, but he had the good sense to know I was usually right."

I heard mostly feminine laughter that time.

"Like any couple who has been together for a long time, you occasionally talk about what would happen if one of you dies before the other. We had those conversations. We both would want the other to find other loves and to continue to live, and yet we both admitted we probably would never love again. And how would that even be fair? No one could ever live up to what we created together. Our life..." I sighed heavily.

"So if you don't see me moving on as fast as you think I should, hold your tongue. Few have had a love like ours, and Callahan's love will always be with me. Thank you, Cally, for the best twenty years a gal could ever ask for. Shannon?"

My sister pressed start on the CD player and "Everything I Own" by Bread filled the space. I sat back down in our pew and held Ashley as we both cried.

Once the song finished, I helped Ashley dry her eyes and whispered, "Are you sure you want to—"

"Yes, Mama," she said as she rose. Looking tall and regal in black and so much like her Dad with her thick mane of rich tawny hair, Ashley walked up to the pulpit and spread her pages out in front of her.

She cleared her throat and began, "My father was the greatest man I have ever known. He could be hard on me, always believing I was capable of doing more, giving more, creating more and he was right. Although we had our trying times through my early teens, he never gave up on me. He held his expectations high, and I now know it caused me to strive to be a better student and a better person."

She glanced down and then continued, "For a girl with her parents so in love, it was hard at times. As a young child, I remember feeling jealous of their connection. Most of the girls I grew up with had divorced parents. My friends wished their parents were like mine. As I grew older, I realized that very few couples love each other like they do. Did..."

Her tears resumed as she continued, "I thank you both for showing me what real love is, and I promise you, Dad, I won't settle for less. Thank you." She stepped down and returned to her seat.

I managed to remain for her whole speech, and once I had her settled into her grandmother's arms, I left through the doors to the outside. Callahan's sisters would probably be pissed that I hadn't stayed inside to hear them speak, but I needed to be alone. I needed fresh air. I needed to breathe.

The large oak trees swayed in the light summer breeze, and I had to admit the sisters had picked a beautiful spot in Live Oak, Florida for half of Callahan to rest. Not that I really thought his ashes embodied him. I didn't. His wish was to have his ashes scattered on the beach in St. Augustine and into the ocean across from the very spot where we met. I had every intention of carrying out his request, just not right away. It was symbolic of letting him go, and it would be a long while before I'd be ready for that.

Love and hate broiled within me. I hated that he left me and not only on our vacation but also on our twentieth anniversary, marring the day we pledged to be together forever. How could that happen to us? Forever turned out to be mighty short by my estimation. I never spoke these thoughts to anyone. They wouldn't understand.

We had plans. Ashley was finishing her senior year in high school and had gotten into her first-choice school at Florida State University. We had saved up, which wasn't easy given the economy and our chosen careers: me a high school English teacher and he an insurance sales representative.

We finally had enough to pay for Ashley's college and chase our dreams, of me being a novelist and he a painter. We planned to sell the house and live simply. Now I was left to figure out another life for myself.

I wanted to beat on his chest with my fists.

Several times over the years, I had jokingly said to him that I would kill him if he left me early. Yes, I felt angry, although in light of everything the word was weak. Painfully weak. I had no recourse to expend my rage, no god to blame. His sisters repeatedly expressed how it was 'all in God's plan,' and I had to settle with clinching my fists at my sides instead of smacking each one swiftly across the face. No, *just* god would take my love away from me. No, I could never believe in one so cruel and heartless. If anything, Callahan's death reinforced that for me.

Just then, five white butterflies swirled around me, and I gasped. The white ones had always been our favorites. "Are you here?" I turned on the spot, seeking an answer. I received no response. As quickly as they appeared, the white flapping wings flew away. We had talked about having a sign as a way of communicating after death, only we'd never chosen one. Was that the sign?

A lady once told me that every time she found a penny, she knew her husband from the other side had sent her a message of love. Being the skeptic, I thought, *you should have made it a five-dollar bill and then you would have really known*. I still do think of her every time *I* find a penny, though.

Turning around, I saw that I had traveled far from the funeral chapel. I forced myself to head back to be present for the end of the service. I dreaded the line of all the condolences and people telling me it would be okay. It would never, ever be okay, and I despised hearing it over and over again. However, I couldn't abandon the rest of the family to cope with the line of well-wishers without me.

Reentering from the side door, I hovered along the wall as Frannie continued to speak.

"...charmin' everyone. I think it's because he had six mothers in our house. All of us girls took turns holdin' and carin' for him. I don't think his feet hit the ground for the first two years of his life. We loved him in life and will continue to love him in death." She tilted her head toward the casket and said, "I look forward to seein' you again in heaven. Callahan, you were the best brother a sister could ever want." She ended with a shuddered breath and descended the steps.

Once the pastor stood, I hurried back to my seat. He seemed relieved to see me. "Thank you all for your attendance. The burial ceremony will take place in a week, and all are welcome to attend. You can pick up a leaflet with the information on your way out. The family has requested that in lieu of flowers you donate to Doctor's Without Boarders or to the Arbor Day Foundation. These were important causes to Callahan, and this will honor his memory.

"Sissy has opened her home and will be receiving guests in thirty minutes time. Her address is on the placard by the door. Can the family please line up outside?"

I took Ashley's hand, and Shannon grabbed my free one. We did as bid and headed into the sunshine. *Where is a good thunderstorm when you need it?*

The condolences seemed endless, and once the final person, a work associate of Callahan's, hugged us, I turned to my mother and said, "Can you take Ashley with you to Sissy's? I want a few minutes alone with Cally."

"How will you get there?" she asked.

"I'll take her," Shannon said. "I'll wait outside for you."

"Thanks, Sweet Pea." I hugged Ashley and Shannon and closed the door behind them. To the pastor, I said, "When are they moving the body?"

"You have time."

I shook his hand and thanked him.

He closed the inner door, and I had the now cavernous space to myself. Well, Callahan's body and I did. I sat on the edge of the raised platform with my back to him.

"Forgive me, Cally, but I'm going to curse. I know you hate it, but if there was ever a time, it is now. How the fuck could you leave me like this? We had plans, lots of plans. We made a deal, and you broke it. I don't know how I'll ever be able to forgive you. I no longer know how to navigate the world alone anymore. Now Ashley is talking about taking a year off from college to stay with me as if I'm an invalid without legs. Don't worry, I won't let her, but you know there will be a battle ahead. You were always the one who knew how to handle her. Goddamn it, Cally. What the hell am I supposed to do now?"

I groaned aloud and continued. "What kind of asshole dies on his anniversary while on vacation? What happened to looking both ways? That was a really fine touch. Yes, I know. You didn't plan to have the car hit you as you ran back across the street after getting a flower for my hair to make the anniversary sketch of me perfect, as you said. But tell me what are the odds? None of it makes any sense. My life doesn't make sense anymore."

I closed my eyes, hoping to reach him on the other side. *Are you there?*

Warm, loving energy and the smell of cinnamon surrounded me, but somehow it didn't feel like Callahan. I opened my eyes and yelped, "Holy hell, who are you?"

A man I didn't recognize stood in front of me dressed in an expensive-looking, tailored white suit. His assessing white-blue eyes held mine.

"I didn't hear you come in. Are you a friend of Callahan's?"

"No. I'm here to talk to you."

I stood and stepped back, hoping to outdistance the profound sweeping energy that reverberated all around me. I touched the closed coffin as if my dead husband could assist me from the grave. "I ... this isn't a good time," I said, sweeping my hand around the room. "My sister's waiting for me."

"We have time," he said with a calm, assured voice.

"I don't know what you mean. I have to—"

"I'm here to give you a second first chance."

"Excuse me?" I said, backing up until my butt pressed against the casket.

"Please, don't be frightened. I mean you no harm and, in fact, I'm here to take away your pain."

"Oh, *great*," I said sarcastically. "Are you here to convert me? Help me find *God*? You're wasting both of our time. I really must go." Scared to pass by him, I used the door that led into the family waiting room and ran out the front to my sister's car.

"What's wrong?" Shannon said when I hurriedly got in.

"Please, drive!"

She pulled out of the parking space with the tires squealing, and headed down the road.

"Some odd man came into the chapel, and I think he wanted to convert me. He said something about chances and smelled like cinnamon."

"Cinnamon?" She glanced in my direction.

"It was very weird. Did you see anyone at the service with ice-blue eyes in a white suit?"

"No." She turned right at the light and headed east.

In a moment of impulse, I pulled my cellphone out of my purse. "Fuck."

"What, Jayden? Are you okay?"

"Yes, damn it. I was about to text Cally."

"Oh, one of those funny texts?"

Tears spilled down my cheeks. "Yeah. **Text to self:** *Don't trust men in white suits.*"

She chuckled, but it sounded painful, and I could totally relate. "He would have cracked up, given the circumstances.

Was the man a friend of Callahan's?"

"No. He said no."

"That does seem strange. Well, I wouldn't worry too much about it. I'd worry about the wrath of the angry sisters once we arrive at Sissy's."

I sighed. "Today of all days, they have to cut me some slack."

"Don't worry, babes, I'll run interference and be glued to your side."

"Thanks, Shannon. Did you see Del? I saw him standing at the side when I came back in."

"I can't believe he showed *and* took the kids home with him," she said as she parked her car a block away from Sissy's home. "Damn, the streets are crowded with cars."

"Good thing Sissy kept her parent's house in the divorce. She's the only one who could hold all these people."

"Yeah," she said, staring off.

"You and Del don't have to get divorced. You don't have to sign the papers, you know. You could try again."

"I've been thinking about it. Del keeps telling me he's ready to work on our issues."

"Maybe he means it this time." I unbuckled my seatbelt.

"And if he doesn't?"

"Better to be a fool for love than scared to take the chance."

"Yeah. Thanks, babes. Please think about you and Ashley staying with me for a while. I imagine it has to be hard to be in your house without him."

"I'll talk to Ash later and let you know. Please stay glued."

"I will."

Shannon didn't allow anyone to linger around me for long, and I spent most of my time on the flowery couch in the living room while picking at the plate of food my mother brought to me.

An uncontrollable sob threatened to erupt once the reason for the gathering fully sank in. I hopped up, almost knocking Ashley's plate over. I placed mine down on the coffee table and locked myself in the bathroom by the front door.

The doily that lined the top of the toilet along with the teacup and kettle wallpaper didn't help my mood. The bathroom catapulted me from 2015 back to the year I met Callahan in late 1994. The decor hadn't changed. After washing my hands and splashing water on my face, I snuck out the front door.

As I strolled down the street, I thought about Mr. and Mrs. East. They had never granted me permission to use their first names and forget about calling them Mom and Dad. Cally's parents had always been polite to me on the surface, but they couldn't hide their apparent distaste for my liberal persuasions. His mother would tell the sisters who would immediately pass on the unwanted information.

As I continued to reminisce, the smell of cinnamon hit me again, and I searched the street for the odd man cometh. Across the way, I saw him resting against a giant maple. Tucking my chin to my chest, I strutted down the sidewalk, leaving him and Sissy's house behind.

As I came around the block, the man with the very pale blue eyes had settled against an oak on my side of the street.

"Ahhh," I yelled. "How did you do that? This is beyond stalking." I folded my arms across my chest and stepped back. "Why are you following me? Do I need to call the police?" A wave of love eddied around me, and I looked behind me, expecting to see Callahan's ghost there.

"No. I'm here to help you. As I stated before, I just need a few minutes of your time."

"And then you promise you'll leave me alone?"

"If that's what you want, then yes." He stood up straight, and in the shade of the tree, I noticed the striking unlined features of his face. I couldn't place his age.

"Why do you smell like cinnamon?"

"I thought it would be pleasant to you."

I tightened my arms around myself. "You have two minutes, and then I hope never to see you again."

"Well then, let me get to the point."

"Please do."

"Callahan was not set to die on June tenth."

"Not set?"

"Excuse me. Scheduled."

"What the heck are you talking about?"

"I am not going about this at all well."

"Clearly," I said, stealing a look back in the direction of the house. I wondered if I could outrun him.

"When you are born, you are dispatched with an eternality group of souls. This is not unlike the friendships you forge during your time here on earth. However, the eternality group spans lifetimes and supports those within the group who are currently occupiers."

"Occupiers?" I unfolded my arms. I decided that if the man in the white suit meant to kill me, he'd have gotten to it already and wouldn't be wasting my time with his cockamamie bullshit.

"Souls within a body. Some never care to venture in, but most rotate from supporting the occupiers to being one themselves." His warm energy relaxed me. Plus, the smell of cinnamon reminded me of my grandmother baking apple pie and cinnamon rolls.

"What does this have to do with Cally and me?"

"Your husband's sentinel failed. Callahan crossing the street should have been delayed, and therefore, he would

13

not have come into contact with the speeding vehicle."

"If you're trying to make me feel better, you're failing miserably."

"I am here to possibly rectify a scathe."

I shook my head.

"Rectify a wrong."

"I see. So are you going to say a voodoo spell and bring him back to life?" Not that I believed he could. "Why didn't you do that in the chapel?"

"No, that cannot be done. Once a life has been extinguished, in any given timeline, it cannot be resurrected in his or her present state. However, there are other possibilities."

"Well, short of bringing him back to life, I don't see how you have anything to offer me." I turned to walk away.

When he touched my wrist, my heart skipped several beats, and I gulped at the air.

"You're not human!" I growled, yanking my arm away. I ran from him as fast as I could, back toward the house, but when I rounded the corner, he was there in front of me. *Shit!*

"No. That is true, I'm not human per se," he continued as if I hadn't run away from him like a bat out of hell. "You and I, however, are both souls just currently in different manifestations."

"Is that supposed to make me feel any better? Are you the one that let Cally die?"

"No. I am not of your eternality group. You may think of me as an overseer or advisor."

Something caught my eye, and I saw someone come out of Sissy's home. "We need to walk."

We strode down the sidewalk away from the house again.

"Why should I believe you?"

"You already do."

"If you aren't like me, why do you look human? Are

you God?"

"You don't believe in God, Jayden."

"Well no, I don't, but then what is all of this?" I wondered how he knew so much about me and what his name might be.

"I'm known as Toly."

"And you answered another question." He could hear my thoughts. "Please continue before I change my mind and run away again."

"We, all of nature and the universe, are connected. We are at once one large entity and separate. The connectedness is godlike but not the god of most religions. There is no masculine deity deciding the fate of people or answering their prayers. However, the will of the masses has the power to cause change for the honorable or the profane. Some special souls can heal outside the normal routes known to occupiers."

"Back up for a bit. Are you saying this is the first time anyone has allowed someone to die before their time?"

"No, however, in cases where soulmates find each other, there is special protocol."

"Wait. So there is no free will? Our lives are all prearranged?"

"That is not the case. Souls choose their biological mother and depending where on the stratus of development a particular soul resides, they may or may not set their occupying end date. You and Callahan hoped to meet in this lifetime, but there were no guarantees. The existence you created, the choices you have made, were all your own."

"Are you saying that people, who, say died of cancer, chose their exit date?"

"Some, yes, and others are assigned. However, because life is random, people do die outside of their designated slot."

I closed my eyes, shook my head, and opened them again.

Toly still stood there, gauging my expression.

"So according to you, I'm an occupier, and people are supposed to be watching over me, over Callahan too?"

"Not people like you, but souls, yes."

"So now what?" I shrugged. "What are you suggesting?"

"You can stay here in this present time and move forward. That is the simplest option to consider. However, given the structure of this particular timeline, you can be reinstated at thirty-eight, twenty-eight, eighteen, or eight."

I threw my hands up in the air and huffed. "What does reinstated mean?"

"You may be placed back into one of the age frames I mentioned."

"You mean I can go back ten, twenty, thirty years and start from there."

"Yes."

"Will the ... the—"

"Sentinel."

"Yes. Will he still be with Callahan?"

"No, not for this occupation."

"What happens to Ashley?"

"She will be born again once you get pregnant. However, since the circumstances may be different, she could be different as well."

"How do you mean?"

"Who inseminates the egg, when it happens, who you are at the time and many other factors."

"Will I remember me from now? Will I keep my memories?"

"That is something you can choose."

"Wow. I don't know. Cal and I have often wished we had met sooner in life. He was almost forty by the time our paths crossed and had already gone through a horrible divorce but— My head is spinning and like this entire day, I'm still concerned I might be hallu—"

"Who are you talking to?" Shannon said as she touched my shoulder.

I spun around in a circle, and Toly was gone.

"I'm either having a severe flashback hallucination from the few times I dropped acid in my twenties, or I've gone certifiably insane and need to be directly deposited into a padded cell."

"I think you just need some rest. Mom asked me to come looking for you. Guests are starting to leave, and Dad has had enough of the gaggle of sisters."

"Okay," I said, allowing her to lead me back to the house. I actually looked up into the trees lining the road, expecting to see Toly perched on a high branch like a hawk sitting in wait.

Ashley and I opted to go with Shannon to her home. Both of her kids, Chaz and Tamara, had gone home with Del after the service, so it was just us in the house. We climbed into Tamara's queen-size bed, and Ashley was asleep a few minutes later.

I, however, lay in bed wondering if I had crossed over into coo-cooville. I desperately needed to talk to Callahan. He would know what to make of it all. If Toly was real, could I walk away from the life we built and start over? There was so much I could and *would* do differently.

I could go back to the age of eighteen and hunt down Callahan, and we could start ten years earlier. I wouldn't drop out of college after my first year, throwing away my parents gift of four years paid tuition, room, and board. I could pursue creative writing from the start instead of waiting tables for years as I paid my way to earn my teaching degree.

If I couldn't convince Cally to love me straight away, I would have the opportunity to have more sexual experiences. He had so many more lovers than I did when we met that he felt like I had somehow missed out. However, having sex with another while still so deeply in love with Callahan might prove challenging.

I wondered if I could change my appearance, or if I would have to look the same as I did at eighteen. I was attractive enough, but if I could change a few things here and there... On the other hand, it would be amazing if Toly could hold off cellulite until I was, at least, sixty or make me one of those women who bounce back from pregnancy in a week and never look like they had a baby in the first place.

The only stumbling block—well two of them really—which stopped me from outright considering it: Ash lightly snoring beside me and whether or not my mind had fractured over the loss of Callahan and had decided to play trick or treat with me.

I slipped quietly out of bed and went downstairs to find some alcohol to help lull me into sleep. My racing mind would not shut up.

In the cabinet above the refrigerator, I found a bottle of Stolichnaya vodka. At the table, I poured an inch into a tumbler and knocked it back. The smell of cinnamon wafted over me just before Toly reappeared. "Back again, I see." I poured another shot into the glass.

"We had not completed our conversation." He bowed slightly. "My apologies for the abrupt departure."

"Understood. Shannon would have swift kicked you had she met you on the street. Of course, my sanity is still in question. Whether I believe you or not is simply beside the point."

"To answer your question, the only change I can make for you would be to retain your memory if you decide to go back. In addition, as soon as you make your choice, I will be gone. If you choose to remain here and now, I can wipe your memory of me."

"So you can't make me enjoy cleaning or have less of a sweet tooth?"

"No."

"Wait a minute," I bristled. "Do the collective of watchers or whatever you called them see everything I do? Even in my private alone time? Pick my nose? Touch my... Okay now, I'm an open-minded woman, but that's just—" I was about to say fucked up but instead said, "Creepy."

"Their purpose is not to judge or gawk, but to guide when necessary. The more closed off the occupier is, the less influence they have. You are considering eighteen for your insertion time," he stated, taking a seat at the table.

"Would you care for a drink?" I asked, my southern politeness overriding the fear of my apparent lunacy.

"I have no requirement of sustenance and prefer you refrain until our conversation has concluded."

"Fine," I said, pushing the glass away from me. "Yes, eighteen makes the most sense to me or really is the most appealing. I'm not sure I have any sense left. I would love an extra ten years with Callahan, and retracing the same steps I've already covered seems like a dreadfully boring prospect. I was always the dreamer and the risk taker of the two of us. I know, knew, know Callahan so well and yet, in this crazy scenario, I have no idea what he'd advise. I do know he would take any opportunity for a longer life together. But I feel like I'm abandoning Ashley when she needs me the most. I get that she wouldn't have been born yet, but she will still be real to me."

He watched me intently and waited for me to continue.

"If I'm going to go full-blown into this delusion, let's get down to business. Can I tell Callahan about all of this if I go?"

"Yes, but there are no guarantees he will believe you."

"I'm certain he won't initially, but I think I can get past that. And other people?"

"It would be ill-advised to share it with others, but there is no rule against it."

"Can you send me back with a lot of money?"

"No. You're financial situation will remain the same given the particular time you select. However, once in, you can manifest any changes you would like within the confines of natural law."

"Can I go back to the very day I arrived at Florida State University *after* my folks drive away?"

"That can be done."

"I know I already asked this, but please tell me again that I will definitely have Ashley if I go back."

"If and/or when you get pregnant, she will be your first child."

I forced out a breath and said, "Let's do it, but first I want to kiss her goodbye."

CHAPTER ONE
AUGUST 1985

In a burst of consciousness, I quickly scanned the three boxes and two suitcases that sat by the bed closest to the door in my small, two-person dorm room. I remembered, as if it happened minutes ago, my heated conversation with my mother over her wanting to help me unpack.

"I can handle it myself," I groaned.

My sister, Shannon who was always Sweet Pea to me, made a funny face over our mother's shoulder, and I had to fight to hold back the laughter. I shot her a dirty look as she mimed hysterical laughter, dipping forward and back, covering her mouth. "Cut it out," I mouthed when Mom joined Dad by the window on the other side of the room, overlooking Landis Green.

"Come over here." I hugged Shannon to me. "I'm going to miss you, kid."

"I'm not going to miss you a bit," my bratty twelve-year-old sister said, pushing out of my arms. "I'm moving into your room."

"No, you're not!" I yelled. "Dad?"

"She's just giving you a hard time because you're leaving. Sweetie, leave her be," Dad said, leading Mom back toward the door. "We're going to take off and let you get settled."

I glanced up at my mother, noticing her tear-filled eyes. "Thank you so much for everything, and as soon as I have the phone turned on, I'll call you." I hugged my mother first, breathing in her sweet perfume.

"I love you, and please be safe," she said, embracing me.

"I love you too, and I will."

"I'll lock your bike to the rack downstairs," Dad said, giving me a quick hug and a pat on the back.

"Thanks, Dad."

Shannon buried her curly-haired head against my chest and with her little arms squeezed my ribs as hard as she could.

"I'll miss you most of all scarecrow," I said, staring down at her and holding her face.

"You'd better," she said, peering up at me. Her eyes were wet as well.

"I'll see you in a few months, and you can call me anytime."

"Let's go," Dad said, pulling my sister along.

Although I intended to skip their departure and the pressure it placed on my heart, it was there with me anyway.

I looked around the dorm space and opened the closet on my roommate's side. As I recalled from the first go-around, I found her clothes already hanging there.

Mental note: *I will not steal any of her yogurts this time around from the refrigerator we share.*

I quickly unpacked my clothes and set up my stereo/record player right beside the door. I shoved my crate filled with records and cassette tapes under the bed. I set the box of school supplies on my side of the partitioned two-way desk and stuck the final box into my closet.

As I washed my hands at the sink in my dorm room, I hazarded a look into the mirror. I gasped. Then I pivoted from side to side, taking in my face from different angles. *It's amazing what another thirty years of perspective can give you. Wow, I'm hot!* I now appreciated the angle of my high cheekbones and my abundance of rich brown curls. I'd worn it long for so many years, shoulder-length with bangs wasn't nearly as bad as I recalled. The fullness of my lips, which I detested as a kid, looked incredibly provocative on my young face.

I stripped off my clothes and stepped into the cramped bathroom between my room and our suitemate's room. On the back of the door hung a full-length mirror. *Damn, girl, you had it going on and you never knew it.* I admired my high, round butt that I used to think was way too large and the narrow dip in at my waist. Callahan's love for my abundant cleavage caused me to appreciate my breasts on my younger self in a new way.

The jiggle of our dorm room door startled me. I yelled, "Just a second." I swept up my shorts and T-shirt from the floor of our room and practically dove back into the bathroom to dress. "Okay."

After putting my clothes back on, I came out to re-meet Debbie. "Sorry about that," I said, extending my hand to her. "I'm Jayden."

"I'm Debbie, and I don't plan to be here a lot," she said, shaking my hand.

"Oh," I said as if I didn't know why.

"I have a boyfriend, and my parents aren't ready for us to live together, so I'll be at his place a lot."

"No problem at all." I turned away and then said over my shoulder, "I'm going to go for a ride around campus and then finish unpacking in a bit. Catch you later?"

"Sure thing."

I grabbed my small purple fanny pack off the desk, placed my key with a few dollar bills and change in, and headed out the door. Downstairs, out front of Cawthon Hall, I bent over to unlock my bicycle. I heard a cluck of appreciation from my left and tilted my head up to say, "Hi."

"Hi yourself," said a cute gangly boy around Ashley's age.

"Well, I'm off for a ride," I said, pushing off and

leaving the jailbait behind. I may be eighteen in body... *No way am I going there! Ewww as Sweet Pea would say!*

I hadn't been on a bike in years and immediately lost myself in the pleasure as I roamed the streets of Tallahassee, Florida. I had forgotten the beauty of the campus with its lush trees, rolling hills, and brick buildings. Letting go of the handlebars on my white ten-speed bike, I held out my arms in victory.

I passed one of my favorite spots and came to an abrupt stop. With my feet on the street, I shuffled back a few steps and then dismounted. I propped the bicycle up against the glass storefront and entered The Sweet Shop to buy a decadent apple fritter. I stopped allowing myself to indulge in the future but planned to set that right again.

You might expect me to be pining for my husband and daughter, but truly, it felt like such a dream that I only felt elated. Physically, I felt better than I had in years. Gone were the chronic neck ache and the sore ankle from standing too long. Plus, I had this smokin' body that I had zero appreciation for the first time around.

I knew if I waited a few more minutes before heading back, Debbie would be gone for the rest of the day. The call to the phone company had to come first, which I had procrastinated on taking care of last time. Next, I had to figure out where Callahan might be living. This was his period of flux as he'd put it. I planned to check Gainesville first. The pay phone in the lower level of my dorm building, I recalled, had phone books.

Motherfucking shit! Just then, it hit me: no internet, no computers, no cellphones, or even Facebook. I'd have to use the computer center to type up my work for class. Then I burst into laughter, fritter in hand, leaning on the side of my bike. *Good thing I didn't think about that first, I might not have come.* I doubled over laughing, trying to catch my breath.

"You must tell me what's so incredibly funny that it's put you in a state of conniption hysteria."

"Psychology major?" I asked, lifting up my elbow for him to shake. I held onto my bike with my right hand and the partially devoured glazed fritter in my left. My eyes finally met his, and immediately I was taken by his dark, penetrating gaze and longish, wavy, light-brown hair.

He looked like he should be playing tennis in his tight blue-striped Polo shirt and short, white shorts with front pockets. "Travis," he said, taking my proffered elbow into his hand.

Behave, girls, I mentally snapped at my nipples. "Jayden."

"Nice to meet you. I'm a professor of literature and writing at FSU."

"Interesting. Well, maybe our paths will clash again."

"Let's shoot for cross. If they do cross, you have to promise to tell me what was so funny."

"Oh, I could never do that. You wouldn't believe me anyway. Listen, I should probably shove off. I still have some unpacking to do and..."

He stared at my mouth, which caused me to brush my lip, thinking some glaze or crumb had settled there. "Why don't you give me your number so—" he started.

"I don't have a phone yet. Gotta run." I kicked off and pedaled down South Copeland just past Eppes Hall. *God, he was hot, even in his dated clothing.* I took the sidewalk across campus to Convocation Way. *Get a grip! Don't forget you're on a mission, Jayden,* I berated myself as I stood on the bike pedals to increase my propulsion. I headed north past Reynolds and Murphy on my way to the door. I zipped to the front of Cawthon Hall to lock up my bike.

Before heading up to my room, I waited in line for my

turn at the payphone, shifting my weight from my left to my right foot, still impatient as I was at eighteen. I missed my cellphone already. Finally, I stepped up and called the phone company. They informed me my line would be live within forty-eight hours.

"Shit," I mumbled. "Does anyone have a pen?" I glanced over my shoulder to the students behind me.

"Here," said an adorable boy, holding out his hand.

"Thanks."

Just as our fingers touched, his face went crimson.

I smiled, liking how the new, old me had an apparent effect on the opposite sex. I tore off a piece of a page from the inside of the phone book, hanging underneath, and wrote down my new number. Noticing that the phone books were local only, I decided to call information.

"I have to make one more call," I said to the girl next in line.

After I had hit in 4-1-1, I waited as the phone rang. I wondered if people still used 411 in 2015. Me, I looked up numbers on the web. Numbers, addresses, restaurants, shops, travel; I used the internet for all that and more.

"Yes, sorry, Gainesville, Florida."

"And the name?"

"Callahan East. C-A-L-L-A-H-A-N."

"There is no listing for Callahan East."

"Oh, crap..." I thought for a second. "Wait. Can you check Live Oak for Callahan East?"

"Yes, ma'am... No, ma'am. There is no listing for a Callahan East in Live Oak."

"Okay, thank you." My shoulders dropped in disappointment. *I guess it's not going to be so easy to find him.*

Back in my dorm room, empty as expected, I sorted through the boxes and put everything in my suitcases away.

After I'd made the bed, I pulled out the crate filled with my record collection and various cassettes, some blank. I slipped Led Zeppelin's debut album on the turntable, starting at song four on side one: "Dazed and Confused."

While I lay in bed listening to my old records, which I had given away years ago, I remembered Patrick, my best friend in college. Packy, as I'd called him, lived on my floor on the other side of the building. At eighteen the first time around, I had wished quite often, he was straight. Closing my eyes, I recalled how we met.

He tugged a heavy, square refrigerator down the hall. His dark, floppy, straight hair fell into his face, and he kept flipping his head to get his long bangs out of his eyes.

"Want some help?" I asked.

"Sure," he said with a heavy sigh.

We manhandled the fridge to the end of his bed and then he flopped down onto the mattress by the window. "Upper body strength has eluded me all my life but don't expect me to be paying for a gym membership anytime soon."

The way he said it, with a flourish, caused me to crack up. We laughed together, and I started falling in love with him that very day.

After I'd dropped out of college, we lost touch.

No chance I would lose contact with him this time around. Hell, now I could give him my email address of the future, and we'd never be without a means to reconnect. Lying in bed, I tossed back and forth whether to wait for that exact moment again, two weeks from now, or meet him sooner.

The wonderful thing about Packy was his open mind. Although Toly warned me about sharing my second chance,

I knew immediately that I would share it all with Packy.

Still impatient at forty-eight, I scooted off the bed and headed down the hall to the other side of the building. The door to his room hung open, and I saw Jamie, his roommate, unpacking his clothes into the front closet.

"May I help you?" Jamie said in his formal speak, which he loses halfway through our freshman year. His girlfriend Lenore—they haven't yet met—who lives across the hall, greatly expands his narrow Midwestern horizons.

I have to admit, I was enjoying the knowledge of what awaited around the corner for those people.

"Hi, I'm Jayden," I said, stepping inside their room. "I have the last room on the left down the hall. I pointed to the right.

"I'm Jamie, and this is Patrick," he said, indicating the other side of the room.

Packy walked toward me, and I could have sworn his expression looked like he recognized me. *Wayward souls, spotting each other?*

"Hi, Jayden," he said with a slight smirk. "The pleasure is all yours."

As always, he made me laugh. "Of that I'm sure," I countered. "Feel free to drop by when you're greatness needs some appreciation."

"I'm in love," he said, gracefully circling back to his side of the room.

Jamie raised his right eyebrow, and that too made me chuckle.

"Later gentlemen," I said and practically skipped back to my room. I had a feeling I would hear from Packy soon.

From my desk shelf, I grabbed the course schedule. I had just helped Ashley choose her classes online for the fall in 2015. Back in 1985, instead of doing everything online, I had to get signatures from the professors of each class and then turn in the schedule to be processed.

My second time around, I planned to register for Freshman Composition 1101, Beginning Spanish, Sociology, Art History, and Mathematics for Liberal Arts I. Last time I took on Pre-calculus with trig for math, and the workload and complicated equations nearly did me in. I didn't need it to graduate and planned to focus my time and efforts on honing my writing skills. The second change would be finding a different Freshman Comp professor. The instructor on my first go around almost put me off writing altogether.

Tomorrow would be the day to get all the signatures and classes would start on Monday. After signatures, my sole focus would be to find Callahan. I hope that the ride-board in the student center would be the answer I sought in finding a ride to Gainesville over the weekend. Packy was a wiz on the bus system, so maybe he'd have some suggestions. However, I needed to wait for him to come to me. I didn't want to put him off by coming on too strong.

"Toly," I shouted when I realized that I had completely forgotten about my boyfriend, Rider. Somehow, I assumed all my memories would be crystal clear and readily available. Like where Callahan was currently living. Was this the period of time he shared a house with Port? I couldn't even recall his real name. Why didn't I ask Toly where I could find Cally? Would he have told me anyway?

Rider, my high school boyfriend, was currently living in Kissimmee, Florida, working for his uncle's rodeo. Like his name sounded, he was obsessed with horses and had no plans to attend college.

At least at eighteen, I had the good sense to say we should see other people while I was away at school. He was a complication I'd rather not have to deal with for a second time. He was an okay guy, but he lacked any real depth. I definitely planned to skip the on again, off again relationship of my first year away at school. I would call him once my phone worked.

I headed down to the school cafeteria for dinner. Groaning over the food quality, I remembered why we ordered in pizza a lot or bought subs instead of eating the already-paid-for meal plan.

I ended up crashing early that night, falling asleep to my favorite mixed tape from the past.

CHAPTER TWO

Walking through the campus, I had a sense of personal power that greatly eluded me at eighteen. I recalled being nervous as hell to approach my professors for signatures.

A huge smile spread across my face as I approached the Williams Building that housed the English department. Tables set out in the main lobby had long lines behind them. I had two options that fit my time slot for my composition class: a Professor Stratford and a Professor Solomon.

Standing on tiptoe, I looked over and around the students to see the teachers. Stratford was a man, although I couldn't quite see his face and Solomon was a woman. I decided to go male this time around. After waiting in line for thirty minutes, watching the students and fantasizing about what to say to Cally once I tracked him down, I got a good look at Professor Stratford, Travis Stratford. I debated for five full minutes about jumping out of the line to the other teacher.

He must have sensed me staring because he looked up and caught my eye. His huge smile showed off his perfect, white teeth, and he only looked away when the student in front of him tapped his shoulder.

So much for all my confidence and swagger. I believed the man could be dangerous. The class would probably be in one of those huge classrooms with stadium seating, so I decided not to sweat it too much. Maybe Packy knew something about him.

Once it was my turn, I stepped up to the table and slid my paper in front of him.

He peered up and said, "Criss cross, miss..." Looking down again, he signed the page and continued, "Miss

Cooke. I'm looking forward to having you in my class."

Unable to stop myself, I said coyly, "I'm sure you say that to all the girls."

He shook his head to the contrary and touched my hand as he handed back my class schedule. "I can see there's more behind your eyes than your age alludes to. I look forward to getting to know your talents."

A strong wave of lust struck my eighteen-year-old body, and I couldn't determine if it originated from him or me. "You're very perceptive, Professor."

"Soon," he whispered and then turned his attention to the next student in line.

One of my regular masturbatory fantasies included a teacher with a ruler. Maybe, just maybe my body cried, but my mind said, "Get a grip."

Text to self: *Stay away from the "young" and "old."*

Damn, it doesn't leave me much to work with. I'll have to convince Callahan quickly. I could tell that having a very horny eighteen-year-old body had its drawbacks. What was it I always said to Ashley? Think with your head, not your clit. She hated that adage.

Off I went to garner the rest of the signatures necessary to register for my classes and put Professor Hottie out of my mind. Once I turned in the schedule, I headed to the student union.

"Hey, Jayjay," Patrick said, sidling up next to me. "Did you get all the classes you wanted?"

"I did and you?" I said with a slight chuckle of joy knowing our friendship was on track.

"It's easier when you're a sophomore. There's less competition for each class."

"That's good to note. Do you know anything about Professor Stratford? I have him for English comp."

"I've never had him. Why?"

"Just curious. Hey, is there a ride-board around here somewhere? I'm hoping to make it over to Gainesville this weekend if I can."

"You're first weekend here? Boyfriend?"

"Well ... a ... not exactly. It's a long-winded, complicated story."

He clapped his hands together and slid them back and forth. "I love a good twisted story. Let's grab some lunch and you can fill me in. Here's the board and I don't see any notices."

Fuck! I thought. *Now what?* "You're from Gainesville right?"

"How do you know that?"

"It's part of the long story."

"Huh, now I'm really intrigued. I'd ask around the dorm for a ride. I always manage to snag a ride or borrow a car when I want to go home for the weekend."

"Thanks," I said as we walked to the cafeteria line.

I opted for a turkey sandwich and an apple, and he went with the spaghetti and meatballs with a side of fries.

We found two seats on the far side of the place and huddled close.

"So spill it," he said, twirling the spaghetti around his fork. His hazel eyes peeked out from behind his straight, brown bangs that hung past his brows and swooped to the left.

Trying to decide how to begin, I took a bite of my sandwich in the meantime. After swallowing the mediocre mouthful, I said, "Maybe this should wait until we know each other better. You'll probably just think I'm certifiably insane."

"I like a little insanity in my friends," he said, holding up his fork for emphasis.

"You asked for it. Just remember that when you go

running away in the other direction."

"You're stalling. Rip it off like a sticky Band-Aid."

I laughed and said, "Fine. I'm really forty-eight years old back in my eighteen-year-old body. The day before yesterday for me was June 2015."

"You're right. You're crazy, but as delusions go, this is an interesting one. Can you prove it?"

"Um ... that's a good question. Let's see... You ordered a refrigerator from housing and will get it in another week and four days. That's how we met last time. I helped you carry your fridge, and we became the best of friends. Oh, I thought of something better. Are you familiar with the Night Stalker in California?"

"Yes, he's been all over the news."

"He gets apprehended on August thirty-first in East Los Angeles." *Why do I remember that of all things? Toly, really?*

"That's still a few days away."

"If I think of something else, I'll share it."

"You're very odd, Jayjay, but I like that about you. So let's say for the moment that what you say is true. Why are you back?"

"My husband died, and if you think I'm odd, the man who sent me back makes me look like a straight arrow."

"You're married?"

"Was? Will be? I was in 2015 for twenty years. I think he, my husband, might be in Gainesville, and I'm hoping to track him down."

"Then what?"

"Then I'll do what I'm doing right now with you. The first time around, we didn't meet for another ten years."

He sat there, shaking his head back and forth.

I figured the jury was in, and he had decided the fate of my fractured mind: raving lunatic.

"I'm giving you the benefit of the doubt, but that's mostly because I find you undeniably entertaining. Are you hoping to get him to fall in love with you now?"

"Yes, that's the plan."

"Then *do not* start out by telling him this story. He will think you're a nut, and you might lose your shot altogether."

"What do you suggest?"

"Woo him and get him to fall for you before you unload your bag of crazy."

"Oh my god," I cried. I laughed so hard tears poured down my cheeks. "Damn, Packy, it's so good to see you again."

"Packy?"

"Yeah, that's my nickname for you and you call me Jayjay."

"I was thinking more along the lines of Craycray."

We both cracked up, garnering the attention of the tables around us. We dumped the rest of our food, and Packy walked me to my bike.

"So how does it feel to be forty in an eighteen-year-old body?"

I wondered if he actually believed me or was just playing along. "I am forty-eight, and it feels amazing. I never appreciated it last time. I really need to find someone local that does a Brazilian. Having a full bush in 2015 is very passé, and I'm not at all used to it."

"Do I even want to know?"

"Waxing, Packy."

"Ouch! I think I'll leave my pubes right where they are."

"You may feel that way now but wait fifteen years, and you might change your mind. Or your boyfriends might change it for you."

"I never told you I was gay."

"I assure you that doesn't make me a genius or a time-traveler." I smacked him on the butt and then rode away. "Come see me," I shouted over my shoulder.

He waved over his head as he walked in the other direction. If he thought me crazy, he would know the truth soon enough.

Back in my room, I sat on the bed and wrote down ideas for stories. Debbie suddenly blew past me and shouted a "hey" and "in and out." She threw a few items into a bag. "I see you've hooked up a phone. Can we share?"

"It should be working sometime tomorrow, and sure, we can split the cost."

"Fantabulous. Catch you on the flip." And out she went.

Last time it bugged me that Debbie was never around, especially when I read *The Shining* by Stephen King and freaked myself right out. This time, I considered it uber convenient to have the space to myself.

In the binder on my lap, I started a list for the next day:

1. Call Mom and give her the phone number
2. Give the number to my roommate
3. Set daily schedule
     a) Class
     b) Study
     c) Exercise
     d) Writing
     e) Find a part-time job?
4. Write a letter to Sweet Pea
5. Call Rider (Not looking forward to this one.)
6. FIND CALLAHAN!!

Then it occurred to me that I might have another way to find Cally. I turned off the music and kicked off my shoes.

Lying back onto the bed, I focused on remembering Callahan's parent's phone number. I knew it once, years ago, way before electronic phone books and cellphones. Sissy probably had the same number in 2015, but when you only have to hit dial, that information no longer needed to be stored readily in your head.

"Shhh," I said to myself. I focused on my breath and tried to summons a time I had to call The Parents, as we had dubbed them.

Callahan surprised me with what I thought was an impromptu trip to St. Augustine. We dropped our belongings at the Secret Garden Bed and Breakfast and then he drove us to the very spot where we had originally met. After driving onto the beach, the sand crunching underneath the tires, he stopped and popped the trunk to pull out a picnic basket filled with wine, cheese, crackers, and grapes. Once he spread out the blanket on the sand and poured wine into two plastic cups, he said, "You're the biggest surprise of my life. Do you know what today is?"

"No, should I?"

"We met on this very spot six months ago."

"Our six-month anniversary? Who knew you were such a romantic." I threw myself into his lap and wrapped my arms around his neck, nuzzling in close. "Of course, I remember. You were checking out my legs."

"That's not all I was checking out."

I laughed. "I love you, Callahan East," I murmured against his neck breathing in the scent of his warm skin mixing with the ocean breeze. "You sure were a hard nut to crack, but I'm profoundly happy for the six months we've had together."

"There's something else in the basket," he said, shifting it closer to us.

"Chocolate?" I asked, peering into his eyes with one brow raised in question.

"Go see."

I opened the wicker top and felt around the bottom until my hand clasped a velvet box.

"No way!" I cried out.

"Yes way." He shifted me off his lap. "I never thought I would love again, be able to open my heart to another. You, my crazy, flighty, adventurous spirit have stolen my heart. Will you do me the honor of marrying me and continue to keep me young and on my toes?"

"Let me think about it," I said, tapping my lip.

He pushed me over and covered my body with his. "I'll just kiss you until you decide."

When he stole my breath with his lips, I felt a new kind of possession settle over me, freely giving myself into it. Never for a second did I consider saying no. I knew from the moment we met that he had my heart. Every day since I had hoped he would choose to keep it for a lifetime.

When we finally broke apart from our steamy coupling, my body vibrated with need. "A thousand times, yes. Take me back now. I need you inside me."

"What about the wine and cheese and—"

"Pack it up or leave it for the birds."

He chuckled over my impatience. "And the ring?"

"That I definitely want to keep. Can I see it?"

"I hope you like it," he said, holding the box open. He removed the ring from the velvety folds and slipped the ruby floret onto my finger.

"It's gorgeous. I love it. I love you. I thought it would take several more years to convince you." I hurriedly tossed the food back into the basket, and he poured the wine from the cups onto the sand.

Once back in our quaint room with quilts and country furnishings at the Secret Garden, we stripped off our clothes and dove into the cushy bed.

"When should we get married?" he asked me.

"As soon as possible. Let's start practicing now."

With a deep belly laugh, he said, "Come here, you." When his lips touched mine again, I sighed into his mouth. With my head in his hands, he deepened the kiss, his tongue touching mine, coaxing it to come out and play. He nibbled my full lower lip and then sucked my tongue into his mouth. The lewd gesture sent more moisture between my folds. I yelped when he moved lower and tugged my nipple with his mouth. He slid his tongue across the tip, as he lightly grazed it with his teeth while he cupped the soft flesh of my breast. "I love how your buds get so hard and tight for me."

I groaned, as his fingers drifted down my stomach and into my wetness. He spread my legs wide, draping my left thigh over his thighs.

"You're a naughty man," I said when he plunged his fingers into my core. I felt him grow harder against my side.

"Let me show you just how naughty I can be." His lips found the pulse on my neck and nibbled and bit his way to my lobe. With one hand, he fingered my G-spot and with the other, he lightly circled my arousal.

My back arched over all the stimulation, and I soon found myself at the edge of release.

When he stopped, I momentarily pouted until he shifted himself down between my legs. His blessed tongue resumed our foray of passion. I held his head as he kissed and tongued me but not to guide him. He needed no such assistance, the advantage of dating an older, experienced man.

"Cally, let me play too," I said, rolling onto my side.

He maneuvered his body around so I could take him

into my mouth. I captured the pearl of moisture on the tip and savored his heady, musky taste. He hitched his hips, pushing himself past my lips as I hummed around him, sucking and breathing in his manly aroma, which made me dizzy with desire. With my mouth around his swollen head, I grasped his shaft and fondled his sac.

While he lapped at my growing wetness, he held my top leg up so he had easy access. I cried out when he fingered my center, inching me ever closer to my climax.

"Give it to me, Jayden, and make sure to take me out of your mouth before you soar."

I did as he suggested, and asked, "Are you worried I might bite— Ohhh, yes Cally, please don't stop."

"Not a chance."

I flew outside of myself for each release and back into my body for the subsequent contraction.

Floating in his arms, he held me, grounding me to the earth as my heart began to slow.

"Now, please," I murmured.

He didn't make me wait. On top of me, he gave me the penetration I had asked for on the beach, no longer merely my lover, but the man I would marry. He sought my eyes with his and mouthed, "I love you." The sensual ride of his hips against mine brought me to the edge once again. Together, we solidified our connection as we called out in shared abandon.

As we recovered, he spooned me to him and whispered, "I love you so much. I can't wait to shout it from the rooftops that you're mine forever."

"You never shout, Cally." I could feel the joy from the top of my head down to the tips of my toes.

He tickled my sides and said, "I'll make an exception this one time. We should call your folks and then The Parents."

I laughed and spun in his arms to face him.

He reached behind him and pulled the phone over to us, handing me the receiver. "My parents will be shocked that I'm marrying again. I swore I never would. My mother will be thrilled to plan another sweeping East event. Dad on the other hand... Actually, let's get mine over with first. That way we can end on a positive note with your people."

"Good idea. What's the number?"

I popped up in bed. It almost felt like I'd awakened from a dream. The lurch in my heart made me gasp for breath. Before I forgot it, I jotted their number down and changed number six on my list to call Callahan's parent's house.

Forcing aside the pain from Cally's death and all we had built together, I tried to focus on seeing his younger self soon.

After getting ready for sleep, I lay wondering what to say to his mom. I contemplated saying I was Cheryl Lyn, his old girlfriend from high school, but thought better of it. Cally's mom might know her family or have questions I couldn't answer.

CHAPTER THREE

As soon as I awoke, I picked up the phone in hopes of finding a dial tone and found none. On my way to the cafeteria for breakfast, the best meal of the day there, I noticed a few people I recognized from high school. I didn't go out of my way to make contact with them.

Back in my dorm—Debbie still a ghost roommate—I checked the telephone once again. My heart dropped into my stomach when I heard the dial tone. I dreaded dealing with Rider and worried I might screw up my one chance to find out where Callahan was living. Facing the situation, I dialed my high school boyfriend to get him off my list.

"Rider here," he said when he answered the phone.

"Hi. It's Jayden."

"Excellent! I didn't think I would hear from you so soon."

Don't be mean, I thought. For the first time in my forty-eight years, I had to break up with someone. Last time around, Rider and I called it quits because we both knew it wasn't going to work. I hated knowing I would be hurting him. And in a way I couldn't completely explain.

"You still there? Give me your number and I'll write it down."

"Yeah, I'm still here. Listen—"

"You sound funny."

"I've been thinking about us a lot and I think—"

"What the fuck? You met some guy in your first few days at—"

"No, of course not."

"So why you giving me the Dear John bullshit?"

"I just think it's best—"

"*You* needa think carefully about what you're doin'.

42

Call me back when you've got some sense going." *Click.*

Fuck, that went well!

Not sure I could fully cross Rider off my list, I went for something easier. I wrote my number down on a piece of paper and put it on Debbie's side of the desk. Number 2 crossed off my list.

I dialed my mother next.

"Hi, Jayden. I guess your phone's working."

"Yep." I gave her my number. "How's Shannon doing?"

"She's been sleeping in your bed. You should call back when she's home from school. She'd be thrilled to hear from you."

"I'm writing her a letter today."

"Oh, she'll love that!"

"Listen, Mom, I need to run. I'll call again soon."

"Love you, Jayden."

"Love you too. Tell Dad hi from me."

"Will do."

Other than setting up my daily schedule and writing Shannon, I had the phone call to make to Callahan's parents. I still didn't know what the hell to say to them.

I opted on getting the letter to Shannon out of the way first. Rolling on from my memory of last time, I wrote:

> *Dearest Sweet Pea,*
>   *I hear you're keeping my bed warm for me. Just remember that I'll be back in it for the holidays.*

Or maybe not. I wasn't sure I could make it through winter vacation back in my parent's house. I continued:

> *Is the house quiet without me? I bet you're making up for my absence. How's school? Any cute boys? Did*

Cindy apologize to you for being mean at the sleepover? Make sure to walk Skippy every morning, and tell him I love and miss him.

Mom has my phone number here, and you can call me anytime.

Do me a favor and give Dad a big hug from me. He probably misses reading the paper with me in the mornings.

You can borrow any of the clothes I left behind but not the sundress in the back of my closet. Make sure Scrappy Cat stays out of my closet if you take anything out of there.

Well, it's time for me to get going. I want you to know that I love and miss you and look forward to a trip home soon.

Your big sis,
Jayden

I sealed the envelope and addressed it. Expelling a huge sigh, I lay back on my pillow, trying to come up with something plausible to say to extract a number from Cally's parents. An idea struck me, and I bounded out of bed.

I slipped on my sandals, grabbed their number, and ran down the hall to the other side of the dorm. Pounding on Patrick's door, I yelled, "Get up, sleepy head! I have an emergency."

I heard him stumble out of bed and lean against the other side of the door. Mumbling, he said, "If you know me so damn well, you know never to wake me before noon."

"Yes, I know that, but it's close, and I need your help. Now!"

He opened the door. "Were you always this pushy?"

I laughed and joined him on his bed. "Nope. I have an

idea, and I couldn't wait to tell you."

"Next time I'll shun you for a week."

"You did that to me once, and it was horrible."

"What did you do?"

I turned a pretend key over my lips and shook my head.

"I'll tickle it out of you."

"No, you won't," I said, already laughing.

He tackled me against the bed and proceeded to tickle under my arms and down my sides. "Confess." He chuckled with me.

"Stop, stop!" I cried.

"No can do." Then he did his worst to my neck, and I gave in.

"Okay!" I cried. I had to give in. "Your breath, ewww."

He lifted himself off me and said, "Fess up, Craycray."

"Only if you go back to calling me Jayjay."

He held out his hand and shook mine. "Deal."

"This is embarrassing as hell."

"Procrastinate much?"

I stuck out my tongue, loving every moment with him. It felt like an extra gift from Toly that I had my college best friend back. "Fine! I got drunk one night and threw myself at you."

He burst out laughing so hard that he shook the bed. "Oh my god, that was good. So what? I got pissed?"

"Yeah, I guess. I begged, and you finally relented to be my friend again."

"I've kissed girls before."

I hit his shoulder. "You have? You never told me that."

"Sure and it's fun, but it doesn't rise the Johnson if you know what I mean."

I hugged him so tightly. "I've missed you so much."

"I'm not sure I can say the same," he said, pulling me off

him. He got up and brushed his teeth at the sink in the room.

"You'll get used to me. Trust me."

"Giving you the benefit of the doubt," he said with a huge smile.

I knew it was love at first sight just like last time.

"So?"

"I remembered Callahan's parent's number, and I want you to call them."

"Eh, no."

"Come on! You have nothing to lose. They don't know you from Adam, and I don't want to screw up my only chance to find my husband."

"You must know how completely weird that sounds, right?"

"Come on, Packy. Just say you're an old friend who heard he had gotten into the insurance business. Ask for his work number. Oh, and butch it up a bit."

"Fuck you," he said, lifting his phone off the top of the desk with flare.

I handed him the number, knowing he would do it for me. Patrick liked to piss and moan a lot, but he would bend over backward for his friends, even for craycray ones.

"Yes, this is Jim Banks," Packy started with an English accent.

I shook my head.

"I'm an old friend of Callahan's and heard he's working in insurance now." He made funny faces as he listened to the person on the other side of the phone.

I had a hard time not cracking up. I covered my mouth, shaking the bed myself.

"Yes, his work number would be much appreciated."

I breathed out a long sigh and fist-pumped the air that is until Packy put the phone on the cradle without writing anything down. "Where's the number?"

He pointed to his head. "I have a perfect memory."

"Don't fuck with me! Write it down before you forget!"

"I want something in exchange."

"Remind me again why I liked you so much last time?"

He chuckled and said, "I want to know what it's like to kiss a forty-eight-year-old broad in an eighteen-year-old body."

I tilted my head. "Get the fuck out of town."

"Seriously."

"Give me the number, and I'll consider it."

"Kiss first."

"Why are you doing this?"

He tilted his head and seemed to be considering my question. "Because I want to kiss you."

"But why? This makes no sense. You never did last time."

"Makes no sense to me either. Come." He beckoned me to stand.

I walked into his arms feeling the oddest mixture of curiosity and confusion. My eighteen-year-old-self had dreamed of kissing Packy for months, but the forty-eight-year-old me still felt like it was a betrayal to Callahan.

The soft touch of his lips felt more familial than sexual.

He stepped back. "Yeah. That was a stupid idea." He tore a piece of paper out of the student manual and wrote down the number.

"Hey, it was all you. I'm a great kisser."

"You're still a girl."

"You're so mean!" I laughed.

"Glad to have that out of the way."

"Phew, yeah me too. Thanks, dude. I have the number!" I jumped up and down.

"Leave me." He shooed me out his door.

"Are you going to brush your teeth again to get my cooties off?"

"How did you know?"

I stuck out my tongue. "Come get me when you're ready to go to dinner."

"Yeah, yeah."

Back in my room, I flopped onto my bunk and stared at the number. My heart pounded in my chest. I hoped the insurance company had a receptionist so I wouldn't have to hear his voice right away. I didn't know how I would cope with it.

I must have picked up my beige princess phone and put it back on the hook a half dozen times before I finally dialed the number and waited as it rang through.

A soft melodic voice answered, "Scarborough Insurance, may I help you?"

"Yes, can I get the address of your office, please?" I quickly wrote it down on my list page.

"Is there anything else I can help you with?"

I thought about asking about Callahan but decided against it. "Thank you. That's all I needed."

"You have a great day."

"You too."

I felt elated with my progress but also stymied about how to get to Gainesville. I couldn't wait until the weekend and expect to find him at work. Rummaging in my desk, I found my checkbook. Two hundred for the month wouldn't get me far, but maybe I could catch a bus.

By the time Packy came to get me for dinner, I was considering hitchhiking to Gainesville.

"That's the stupidest idea you've come up with yet,"

Packy said as we walked to the cafeteria.

"What do you suggest?"

"I'll drive you—"

"You have a friggin' car? Since when?"

"If you'd shut up a minute, you'd hear. No, I don't, but I have a friend who owes me a huge favor. You, in turn, will be indebted to me for life."

"Dramatic much? Fine, you can have my second born. We'll leave at nine, and that will get us there around lunchtime. Hopefully, he goes out to eat, or I'm fucked."

"I'm not sure I want kids, so that holds zero influence with me, and you can kiss off nine in the morning. Clearly, you *are* crazy, Jayjay, if you think I'm getting up at that ungodly hour."

"*Clearly,* I can't kiss you into helping me!"

He threw his head back and laughed. "Damn, woman, you *are* funny."

"We have to leave early, dude, please! *Please*!" I dropped down to my knees and clasped my hands together begging.

"Get up, Jayden."

"*Please*! I'd offer you sex but—"

"Ewww no!"

"I'll buy you expensive coffee, and you can crash in the car while I go out stalking."

"I'll wait for you in a swanky coffee shop. It must be swanky!"

I chuckled. "I do solemnly promise not to wake you early for a whole month."

"A whole semester."

"That's entirely impossible!"

"I'll take you up on the month then, and you have to accompany me to any parties I want."

"Oh, Packy, I've heard the stories. On one condition."

"Missy, I think you're a bit confused on how negotiations work. I have the car."

"Put your foot in your mouth for one second and shut it."

He lifted his foot up and bent over, pretending to try to reach his mouth.

"I'm willing to go to any party that doesn't get broken up by the police. I remember all the stories from the last time and have no interest in sharing a jail cell," I said, tapping my head with my finger.

He held out his hand and said, "Deal."

We shook on it.

I figured, this time, his parties might be good fodder for my stories. I was beside myself with elation and fear. Would I be able to get Callahan to talk to me?

CHAPTER FOUR

I knocked lightly on Patrick's door, worried that his roommate might still be in bed. Neither of them answered. I rapped my knuckles a bit harder and still nothing. *Fuck! Don't let me down, Packy!* I used the side of my fist to bang.

Dressed and ready, he jerked the door open. "Hold your horses, woman."

"Are you *trying* to stress me out?"

"Is that what you're wearing?"

"Don't fuck with me. It's too early, and I'm freaking out already."

"Seriously, Jayjay. Go put on a dress that shows off your legs. *You* are trying to get *his* attention, right?"

I looked down at my jeans and T-shirt. "Okay, you might have a point." I grabbed his hand and pulled him along with me. Unlocking my door, I waved him into my room.

"Roommate?"

"AWOL."

I unbuttoned my pants and yanked them down.

"What are you doing?"

"Changing like you told me to. Like you've never seen a girl in a bra and panties. Buck up, dude." I took off my shirt and pulled a flowered, red sundress over my head. "How's this?"

"You can see your bra straps."

"It becomes all the rage soon enough." I unhooked the bra from behind, slid off the straps, and pulled it out from the side. "How's this?"

"You can see the impression of your nipples."

"Perfect. Callahan always loved my nipples. Let's

boogie on out of here."

He swept his arm toward the door and said, "Your chariot awaits."

We took the stairs and moseyed to the parking lot on the other side of the campus.

"Do you know where you're going?"

"Yep," he said. "Just a little farther now."

"Okay."

We came upon an old, black, four-door Chrysler sedan. We climbed inside and belted in.

He started the car and opened all the windows. "Let's motor. It's early, and it's hot in here already."

"Sure is. Whoever thought a black car with leather seats was a good idea in Florida wasn't thinking past winter. Turn on the AC."

"No AC."

"Shit." I hoped I wouldn't be a hot, stinky mess by the time we got to Gainesville. "Do you know where the Scarborough Insurance office is?"

"Yeah, no problem. Your job is to keep me entertained while I drive. Tell me about the future."

"Let me ask you something first. Do you actually believe I'm from the future?"

"I believe you believe it."

"That's good enough for me. You'll know tomorrow for sure once you watch the news. What do you want to know?"

"Is there world peace in 2015?"

I guffawed. "Tell you what, you can ask as many questions as you want, and I'll try to answer them as honestly as I can. World peace, not even close ... less close than even today."

"Who's the president?"

"You probably won't believe me, but his name is

Barack Obama, and he's the first black president, which on the one hand is progress, but—"

"There's a black president?" He glanced at me, then back at the road. "Get out!"

"Yeah, well don't rejoice just yet. He wasn't my first choice for president. I wanted Hillary Clinton."

"A woman? Can gays run too? His name is Barack Obama?"

"Yeah, hard to believe, but yep, that's his name. Not much gets done while he's in office. However, health insurance becomes available to all, which is a huge win for the left. As I said, it seems like progress, but it just really emphasized the divide between the democrats and republicans. Very sad."

"That doesn't sound very encouraging."

"Sorry, sad but true. Me, I can't stand either party. It feels like nothing matters more than the ole mighty dollar and the one percent who keep growing their fortunes. Middle class barely exists anymore. Tax cuts for the wealthy, bailouts for banks and corporations, recessions ... sounds great, huh? I'll stop ranting now. Sorry."

"Way to go on the depressing news. Anything good going on in 2015?"

I chuckled and said, "Technology is booming. Everyone, and I mean *everyone,* has a cellphone and a computer. I've seen homeless people with cellphones."

"What's a cellphone?"

"Like mobile phones in cars but you walk around with them in your pocket. They get *way* smaller. They're really like a mini computer. You can go online—"

"Online?"

"Right. There will be this thing called the World Wide Web, and it's like this massive database of information, retail shops, government info, games, porn—"

"Porn?"

"Anything and everything you can imagine."

"Oh, girl, that sounds totally overwhelming and possibly awesome. How does that work?"

"You log in to your personal computer, yes, that's what I said, personal, and you have a browser and I'm certain, none of this means anything to you. Hmmm. It starts slowly, but then really takes off. At first, we had email. So instead of mailing a letter, which people still do, by the way, you send it electronically."

"Like a fax?"

"Sort of, kind of, not really."

"Darling, you're going to have to do better than that for an answer."

"Sorry. It's like when you go to the student computer center and send your document to the printer. Instead of using a cord that ties you to the printer, it sends it through the air."

"Like television."

"Yeah, but on different waves, I believe. You'll like this. In some states, it's legal for gay and lesbian couples to marry. The Supreme Court was set to rule on it for the whole United States later in June 2015."

"Now I definitely don't believe you. You're lying to me right now."

"Seriously. Trust me when I say there is still a huge faction of people against it. They say it goes against god and crap like that. What god, even if he/she existed, would want to limit love? You know what? Callahan was convinced that religion was becoming less prevalent in 2015 and maybe even less in years to come, but it didn't seem that way to me. I don't care if people choose to believe in god, but I abhor it when they use religion to be prejudiced or hurtful."

"You're preaching to the choir on that one, sista."

"Yeah, I know." I reached out and touched Patrick's shoulder. "It's so good to see you again. I hated that we lost touch after I dropped out of college. You were really the bright spot last time in a rather dismal college experience. We can't let that happen again."

"Okay, we'll pinky swear to stay in touch." He offered his pinky, and we locked fingers. "I solemnly do swear." He laughed. "Hey, let me ask you this. Why do you have all your memories and Callahan doesn't?"

"That one is harder to answer. Toly, the man, or whatever he was, who sent me back explained it a bit, but it doesn't really make sense to me."

"What did he say?"

"That I could go back in and be reinstated, but Callahan couldn't because he was dead. He did promise me that Ashley—"

"Who's Ashley?"

"My daughter."

"You have a daughter?" he asked, glancing at me with wide-open eyes.

"Had, but he promised that I would have her again."

"As delusions go, this is full blown. How old was she in 2015?"

"My age."

"Freaky."

"Yeah. Let's talk about something else. It's finally sinking in that I won't be seeing Ash in a few days. Mostly, this still feels like a dream, and I'm going to wake back up in 2015."

"I bet."

I leaned against the passenger door and stared out at the

scenery passing by along I-75. Sitting still with nothing to occupy me, the pain of my loss surged through me, and my tears spilled. I'd never fully grieved Callahan or Ashley, and I wasn't sure I could. I zoned out for a while until Patrick spoke again.

"What do you plan to say to him? Did that Toly dude give you any advice?"

"Don't laugh, but the only advice he gave me was not to share that I come from the future. It wasn't forbidden or anything, just ill-advised."

Patrick cracked up and hit the steering wheel. "Are you rebellious by nature? I mean, come on! A spiritual entity gives you advice, and you just toss it to the wind?"

"Something like that," I said, giggling along with him. "I just knew you would roll with it, and you have."

"Rollin' rollin' rollin' keep those doggies rollin'."

"OMG!" I cried.

"What the hell does that mean?"

"Sorry, oh my god! In 2015, there are a lot of shortcuts. Everything happens very fast. You'll see."

"Again what does 'OMG' mean?"

I laughed. "Oh ... my .... god. O for oh—"

"I get it," he said, shaking his head. "We're almost there."

"That was a short two and half hours," I said, feeling my stomach tighten. "Shit, I'm scared as hell."

Packy patted my thigh. "Breathe and be your flirtatious self." He made a left turn and pulled up next to a bus stop. "His office is across the street over there." He pointed toward Scarborough Insurance. "I'll be up two streets and over one to the right at the coffee shop on the corner."

I grabbed my fanny pack. "Thank you so much! I owe you big time."

"Yeah, you do."

I sat on the bus stop bench, swinging my legs in an attempt to counterbalance the tension fueling every cell of my body. *Maybe this was a stupid idea!* I looked at my watch and saw that it was just before noon.

Finally, the door to his office opened, and my heartbeat ratcheted up, but it turned out to be two women.

Fuck! I thought and then reminded myself not to curse in front of Callahan. *Oh, and don't say his name either.* I leaned back and continued to swing my legs. After another three false alarms, I thought I would die of a heart attack.

Then the door opened again and there he was, tall and striking as ever, only skinnier than I had ever known him to be. His gray suit hung on his body.

I stood, riveted to the spot, staring as he crossed the street in my direction. I quickly sat back down and turned my body away from him as I watched each of his steps reconnecting our worlds. The closer he came, the more my heart tore in two. I hadn't factored in how it would feel to see him so distraught.

His steely blue eyes belonged to someone else—sadness and longing etched there.

I hung onto the wood rungs of the bench so I wouldn't jump up and try to hug away his pain. Once he passed me, I hopped up and trailed after him to Leonardo's Pizza. I got in line right behind him, willing him to turn around and look at me. Thankfully, the line was quite long, and it gave me time to come up with something to do to garner his attention. I tried to edge my way to the side of him to get him to give me, at least, a glance. Finally, I couldn't take it anymore. When he stepped forward in line, I purposefully bumped into him.

"Sorry," I said, peering up at him.

He glanced down momentarily and dismissed me.

Hang in there, Jayden! Shit! Stop cursing! I sighed at

myself and then thought, *It doesn't matter if he can't hear me.*

Time to shut up and put on my lady balls as Ashley and her friends liked to say. I tapped his shoulder, and once our gazes locked, I said, "Your brooding silence is very attractive." As soon as I said it, my nipples peaked, and heat crawled up the back of my neck.

He smiled at me, but it didn't reach his eyes. "Do you go to school here?"

He speaks! I swallowed hard before I uttered, "No ... I go to FSU. I'm just in town for the day."

"You came all this way for pizza?" He ran his fingers through his golden light-brown hair as I had seen him do hundreds of times in an older version of himself.

"No, I came all this way to meet you." I blushed uncontrollably. I had never so blatantly thrown myself at a man and, even at forty-eight with the younger version of Callahan, it felt overwhelmingly frightening.

He stepped forward in line then looked back at me. "Do you make a habit of seducing older men?"

I had hoped he would notice that his presence caused my nipples to strain against my sundress, but he didn't even glance down. "Nope, you're my first. How am I doing?" I sounded much more confident than I felt. At least, I thought I did.

"Not bad." He nodded his head.

A bright smile overtook my face, and some of the tension left my shoulders. *Progress!* "Jayden." I held my hand out for him to shake.

"Callahan." He clasped my hand, and the contact jolted my being. He, unfortunately, seemed unaffected.

My younger body's response rendered me speechless. I imagined that my eyes dilated as I stared at him. *Please don't turn away,* I pleaded down to my soul.

He took another step forward, and I followed, stopping

just beside him. "What are you going to have?" he asked.

I glanced at the menu above the register. "I'm going to get a slice of the Florentine pizza. You?"

Just then, it was his turn at the counter, and he ordered a slice of the Greek, the sausage, and the Florentine.

For me?

"What do you want to drink?" he asked.

"A coke would be great." Internally, I danced around high-fiving everyone in the universe. My elation was short-lived, however.

He handed me the cup to fill at the dispenser and my slice of pizza. "Well, it was nice meeting you."

"Aren't you staying to eat?"

"No, I'm going back to the office."

Fuck!

"Wait a second." I searched around for a spot to put down my pizza and ended up resting it on top of the register. Reaching down, I unzipped my fanny pack and pulled out a piece of paper with my name and number on it. "One more second." I quickly filled my cup with ice and coke, grabbed my slice of pizza, and walked outside with him. "This is going to seem crazy but, well, today is a crazy day."

"Go on," he said, tilting his head to one side.

I held the soda and pizza in one hand and slipped the paper into his front pants pocket. "Here's my number. Before you crumple it up as soon as you walk back into your office and chalk me up as some silly girl, please just hold onto it. There might come a time you need someone outside of your daily life to talk to, and I'm offering."

"Do you always keep your number handy to give out?"

Heat infused my face, and the words caught in my throat. "I ... I ... no, of course not." Then I did something I rarely had with Callahan. I lied. "I had that in there for my suitemate. I just had my phone turned on."

"Uh huh." He scrunched his face in an expression I knew well. Disbelief.

I felt like my second chance was slipping away from me.

One of the things Cally always loved about me was how unpredictable I was. He often said I surprised him all the time.

Drastic times call for drastic measures. I leaned over and bit off the tip of his Greek pizza that hung over the edge of the plate.

His eyebrows shot up, and his mouth hung open. The shock on his face would have been hilarious any other time, like in 2015, but not here in 1985. "You just stole a bite of my pizza after I was kind enough to buy yours?"

In a reflex to our usual banter, I said, "I'm certain I deserve a spanking for it."

The surprise on his face morphed into something approaching desire. His breathing seemed to increase, and his eyes flared but then squinted. He shook his head and said, "You're something else."

"Don't forget me." I scanned his face one last time, committing it to memory, and stepped out of Callahan's way so he could cross the street. Watching his back, I willed him to turn around just once. *Come on, come on, come on!*

Once he opened the door to the office, he glanced over his shoulder.

I quickly shoved my soda into the crook of my arm and waved.

He nodded his head.

Phew!

The initial relief I felt soon fled, and dread took over as I walked down the street, my tears spilling. I had a second first chance, and I blew it. Passing a trashcan on the side of the road, I tossed the pizza and coke.

I shuffled my way the few blocks to the coffee shop, plummeting into a massive depression. I felt like the stupid teenager to which my body alluded. I plunked down into Packy's booth with tears still in my eyes.

"That good?"

"Worse."

"Sorry, Jayjay. Care to share?"

I shook my head and lowered it onto my arms resting on the tabletop.

"Did he talk to you?"

Without lifting my head, I nodded.

"Well, that's good. Did you give him the number?"

I nodded again.

"That doesn't sound so bad."

I peered up at him and rested my chin on my hands. "Fine," I said and filled him in on all the details. I watched him struggling to keep it in, but then, he just let it rip.

He laughed hysterically and slapped the table.

"See what I mean? I totally fucked it up!"

He continued to carry on and shake his head. "Jayjay, OMG!"

"Yeah, don't I know it?"

"Maybe you were weird enough that he'll call you."

I sat up and sighed. "Now you're just being nice. It's not like I can show up again without him thinking I'm some raving stalker."

"I agree with you on that, but you still have his work number."

"I guess that's a good point. Are you ready to rock and roll?"

"Let's do it."

We didn't talk much on the way back to Tallahassee. I spent my time dissecting my brief time with Callahan.

Sorry, Cally, I think I fucked up our chance. Oops, I mean messed up our chance.

Back in the dorm, I hugged and held onto Packy. "Thank you so much for taking me. I doubt I'll ever hear from him."

"What will you do?"

"Wait I guess, and try again. I don't know. If I don't hear from him within a month from today, I'll have to show up again or call him or ... I don't know."

He patted my back and said, "Don't be too hard on yourself. Like you said, he's not in a great place right now, so you have to consider the timing."

"Yeah, I know. It was just so hard to see him so ... so ... sad and not like himself at all."

"Write it all down. It'll make a great book, and if he ever believes you, you can show it to him."

Packy's words totally shifted my mood. "That's a brilliant idea! I'm going to start right now."

I hugged him again, kissed his cheek, and headed into my room with more pep in my step.

Bang ... Bang ... Bang!

"What the fuck!" I blinked my eyes several times, trying to remember where I was. *Damn!* I flipped on the light, and my dorm room came into focus. "What?" I shouted through the door.

"Let me in!"

"Fuck, Packy, what time is it?"

"It's after midnight." He flew through the door and collapsed on my bed.

"What if my roommate had been here?"

"She might have answered the door faster?"

I shoved him. "What is so important that you had to barge in here in the middle of the night?"

"I watched the news and the Night Stalker was apprehended just like you said."

My eyes shot open, and my adrenaline woke me fully. "So?"

"Truthfully? I believed you before, but seeing the arrest on the news? It was like holy fucking shit. Does that mean there's a god and all that crap?"

"According to Toly, not by religion's definition, no."

"Phew. Hate to think I got that all wrong. Thought I might have to stomach church and all the preaching. Good gawd!"

I broke out in giggles. "You are too funny."

"Okay, I'm off." He jumped up off the bed and twirled toward the door.

"Love you, Packy."

"Love you too, girl. Guess I can't call you craycray anymore," he said as he pulled the door shut behind him.

I fell back against my pillow and chuckled. "At least one person believes me." *I guess Toly didn't factor in Patrick.*

The rest of the weekend flew by. Every day I wrote and took in a long bike ride. I vowed to keep riding, even after college, to keep my legs nice and smooth into my 40s. I struggled not to berate myself continually over my contact with Callahan. Always the one to just jump right in, I wish I had taken more time to plan things out better.

Oh well.

Text to self: *Curb those unruly impulses.*

I imagined Cally's text back: *Definitely not on my account. Come here, naughty girl.*

Me: *One my way and don't forget you asked for it.*

My emotions ran the gambit from elation over seeing Callahan to dread over completely screwing up my chances with him. Every time the phone rang, my heart lodged in my throat until I heard the voice on the other side.

By Sunday, I was excited for my classes to start. I felt jittery and on edge and desperate for the distraction. That night, I tossed and turned until I finally fell asleep.

CHAPTER FIVE

Unlike Packy who scheduled his classes either later in the day or at night, I liked to get mine over early in the day. I figured it would give me plenty of time to write and get my homework done—very different from my first time around. I wouldn't hook up with the same group of friends who majored in pot smoking and drinking. I had no interest in going down that road again.

I awoke early, showered, and shoved the books for composition, sociology, and math into my backpack for my Monday classes. I rode my bike to campus for my first class with Professor Hottie.

I found a spot about midway across the second row of seats in the vast classroom. There had to be about 300 students in there with me.

"Your homework assignment is on the board." Professor Stratford pointed at the chalkboard behind him. "Make sure to write it down. You." He curved his index finger and beckoned me to the front of the class.

"Me?" I looked behind me and then back at him. My heart practically popped out of my chest. I stood up on shaky legs, my ninny knees giving me fits, and managed to make my way down the aisle, over to the front of the stage.

He leaned down and handed me a stack of papers to give out to the class. "Come see me during office hours," he whispered as his hand brushed against mine.

Cut it out girls, I internally hissed at my nipples. I scanned his deep, sultry eyes and whispered back, "Shouldn't you wait to see the rest of the pickings?"

"It's already decided." He stood up. "Hand out the syllabus to the class, and we'll go over it."

I turned around with as much grace as I could muster, feeling like a melted mess inside, and passed over a stack of the pages to each row for them to disperse down the line.

Once all the papers were distributed, Travis talked about the policies for late papers, late arrivals, absences, and due dates.

I scribbled the homework assignment down in my notebook as he spoke.

1. *Read chapter one on rhetoric in your composition textbook and be prepared to discuss on Wednesday.*
2. *To get a general idea of your writing style, pick one of the following topics and write a 500-word paper due on Friday.*
    a) *Describe your dorm room (make it interesting)*
    b) *Describe a pertinent event from your life*
    c) *Describe something you did over the summer*
    d) *Describe your ideal mate*

Come on, Professor Hottie, you can do better than that! I wondered if my time travel would count as a pertinent life event. Giggling, I covered my mouth to hide my revelry.

Travis raised an eyebrow in my direction, and I straightened up to listen, following along with the syllabus.

The first class of my rebirthed college life flew by, and I had just enough time to get to my sociology class. In a smaller classroom, where we waited for the teacher to show, guys on either side of me vied for my attention. How had I missed it last time? It was baffling. Maybe they could sense my complete disinterest and that made me more appealing.

I thought about visiting Professor Hottie between my sociology and math classes but wasn't sure what I hoped to accomplish. Maybe to set things straight? *Hmmm, maybe.* Maybe I just wanted to see him again. Then I rationalized that he could be a useful distraction until Callahan came around. He had to call. What would be the point of all of this if he never gave me the time of day?

Sociology was the same drill of going over the syllabus, and since I took it the first time around, I knew what to expect. We would have lots of debates and discussions on current social issues.

After class, I slipped into the women's bathroom, used the facilities, and checked my appearance. While looking in the mirror, I fluffed my brown curls and applied ChapStick to my lips. I swept my backpack onto my shoulders and headed to the English department. I found Travis' door locked, so I knocked and waited.

He opened the door. The phone cord stretched across the room as he continued to speak. When he looked up, he grinned and cocked his eyebrow. He closed the door behind me and flipped the lock. Walking backward, he waved me forward and pointed to the chair in front of his desk.

Something about his expression caused me to imagine unbuttoning his denim shirt and his khaki pants. I slipped off my backpack and sat down, shunning my wayward thoughts.

"Yeah, I have a student here now. No, no, we can talk about that later. Yeah, sure, eight o'clock works." He hung up the phone and sat down in his leather bound chair behind the desk.

"So," I said, scanning the walls lined with books. "Have you read all of these?"

"Most of them. You laughed again in my class."

"You noticed that?" I glanced up and took in his expression.

He had a teasing smile that tugged at all of my sensitive parts. "You're very hard not to notice."

"Wow, well. So how often do you do this?" I motioned with my hand, back and forth between us.

"I don't ... haven't."

"Bullshit." I crossed my arms and leaned back in the chair. *Yeah right, and I didn't just time travel from 2015.*

He just stared at me for a while with his eyes slightly squinted as if to assess me. "It's a rarity."

"Then why am I here?"

He rubbed his chin and then folded his arms on the desk. "I met you before you were my student."

"Way to rationalize."

"You're different, and I want to know why you seem to be laughing at the oddest times."

I had had a few lovers before Callahan, but they weren't men like Cally. Neither was Travis, but part of me wanted to throw caution to the wind. Cally thought I should've had more experience before we met. Compared to him, I hadn't, but I never felt like I had somehow missed out. However, being back in my horny eighteen-year-old body it was difficult not to consider the prospects. Especially when I couldn't be sure if I would ever hear from Callahan again. "If I tell you why I laugh, you won't believe me."

"That's the second time you've said that to me."

We sat glowering at each other as I evaluated him against Cally. Compared to him, Travis stood a few inches shorter and wasn't quite as broad. However, he seemed uber fit under his clothes.

I shrugged. "Let's just say, life's been interesting lately."

"That's your assignment for next week. Tell me about

the interesting stuff."

I shook my head and huffed out. "That's a really bad idea. You'll think I'm fucking with you or crazy. One or the other."

"You curse a lot."

"Yeah, sorry, bad habit. I'll do my best to refrain."

"Don't."

"Ummm ... don't stop cursing?"

"It turns me on."

Oh shit! "I'm in love with someone else," I blurted out.

He seemed to be contemplating my disclosure. "I see. Is he in love with you?"

I frowned. "Not yet."

"Is this part of the story?"

I sighed again. "Yes. How old are you?"

"Is my age an issue?"

I tilted my head. "Not in the least or not like you think."

"I'm thirty-two."

I'm practically cradle robbing. I chuckled lightly.

"You're doing it again."

I tried to hold back my laughter but failed miserably.

"Come here."

I stood and hesitated.

His brow furrowed and his mouth opened slightly. "I'm not going to hurt you."

"But I might hurt you." I stepped forward toward him.

He reached for my hand and said, "Doubtful." He brought my hand to his mouth and kissed my palm.

Heat shot down my chest and landed square on my most sensitive flesh.

"Are you attracted to me?" He placed my hand on his cheek, and he closed his eyes momentarily. When he looked up at me, I nodded. "I'm very attracted to you," he said.

"Aren't there rules against this?"

He wrapped his arm around my waist and held me close. "Yes, but only because you're currently my student. Relations between professors and students aren't forbidden."

"I think I see." I played with the wave of his hair along the collar.

"Mmm ... that feels good," he groaned.

His unique citrusy smell filled my senses and rattled my brain. He smelled good, felt good, and I wondered if he could take away my fear and loneliness.

"I am your student," I whispered.

He peered up at me. "I can't say I was disappointed to see you in my line the other day. I intended to track you down. You made it easier and harder for me."

I glanced down at his pants, opting for the literal meaning and wasn't disappointed either. "This is all very problematic. I could never live with myself if I cost you your job. Plus, you might not feel the same after you read my paper."

He surprised me by drawing me onto his lap.

I laughed and snuggled in next to him. "Plus, I'd be using you," I said boldly.

He laughed so hard he shook us both. "You're a bafflingly unique woman."

"You don't even know the half of it."

He hugged me tightly and then placed me back on my feet. "I have another class in a few minutes."

I checked my watch. "Shit, me too."

He chuckled. "Give me your number before you go." He slid a piece of paper and pen in front of me.

"Here you go." I held the note out to him.

His hand clasped my wrist, and he used it to draw me down to him. He gave me a warm, quick kiss that stole my breath.

"Ohhh." I stood up, hoping I wouldn't topple right back over. *Legs don't fail me now.* I swooped up my backpack, unlocked the door, and left without looking back. *Now I'm stuck waiting for two phone calls.* I smacked my forehead as I ran across the quad to my math class. *Get a grip woman!*

Math class was a breeze compared to last time, and most of it would be a review of what I took in high school. Fortunately, those memories were still fresh.

I grabbed a sandwich and chips to go and biked back to the dorm. Inside my room, I found Debbie on her bed talking on the phone. She pointed to the desk, and I found a note with a message from Shannon. I mouthed, "Thank you," sat down, and tackled my math homework first. Then I read the two articles assigned for sociology and the first chapter for English. Once done, I pulled my notebook out and started on my paper. I planned to turn it in early.

If you had met me a week ago, it would have been in the year 2015, and you would have found a forty-eight-year-old woman wondering what the fuck to do with the rest of her life. The love of my life was killed on our twentieth anniversary in another country. Getting his body back to the states, as my shattered heart struggled to beat, nearly killed me. If it hadn't been for my daughter Ashley and my sister Shannon, I would have walked straight into the ocean and followed my husband into death.

If I had to listen to my sisters-in-law say, "It's all in God's plan," one more time, I might have become a homicidal maniac.

So when this ... this ... man, for lack of a better term, approached me with a chance to come back and find my Cally sooner, maybe you'll understand why I said yes, why I abandoned my daughter and my whole life to come back to the eighteenth year of my existence.

Sometimes I think I'm still dreaming. I'll wake up, Callahan will be snoring lightly beside me, and all of our plans for the rest of our life will still be lined up in front of us. We'd still sell the house as soon as Ashley is safely tucked in at the university of her choice, downsize, retire, and I'd work on writing the novel I'd always dreamed of writing while Cally painted.

I didn't think it would really work. That's part of what you need to understand. I felt damn certain I had lost my friggin' mind and was fast approaching a padded cell. But who wouldn't want a second chance? Cally and I always wished we had met sooner, and I would have him back, in theory anyway.

So, once I found myself back in my eighteen-year-old body, I trotted off to Gainesville to find the younger version of Cally. He was so sad and heart broken. It practically killed me to see him that way. I know all the history of his devastating divorce and the loss of the baby Callahan and his first wife, Britt, never got past. I essentially made an ass of myself in front of him, and I might have severed the only shot I had at getting his attention.

Then you show up, and I want you and you want me, but my heart is tangled up in Callahan and always will be whether or not he ever comes around. I can't help holding out for the day we first met. Even if he never calls, ten years from now I'll still be sitting on that same beach hoping he notices me again.

Now you're left to decide if I'm certifiably insane or if you believe the story I've laid out for you. Toly, the man who sent me back, warned me not to share this with anyone. It wasn't forbidden but ill-advised, and I guess I'm about to find out if he was right.

Laugh #1: When we were at The Sweet Shop, I remembered all the technology I left behind. What I thought to myself at that moment was that if I had considered being without all the modern conveniences, I probably wouldn't have come. The thought was hysterical to me at the time.

Laugh #2: I wondered if my time travel would count as a pertinent event from my life.

Laugh #3: While in your office, just after I asked how old you are, I thought, I'm practically cradle robbing. You being 32 and me being 48.

I reread it several times, editing where it needed. I felt impatient to get it to Travis, not wanting to have to wait for his reaction. It felt similar to waiting for Callahan's call.

I hopped out of my chair at the desk, causing it to teeter on its back legs. I caught it just in time and righted it in place. My need for Cally overwhelmed me, and my breath became stuck in my throat.

"I'm going out," I called to Debbie and ran out the door. I straddled my ten-speed and rode through the streets of Tallahassee, tears trickling down my cheeks. I didn't want to do life alone anymore. I missed being Cally and Jayden. I missed being an "us" and knowing I no longer had to navigate life on my own. Just then, I felt eighteen again and didn't like it one bit. I had this illusion that my forty-eight-year-old self was so grown up, but without Cally, I was just the same silly girl I was when we met. The loss of my life, the loss of Callahan and Ashley, none of it seemed fair.

Mothering myself, I reminded me that life isn't fair. How many times had I said that to Ashley? Countless times.

I pushed myself to ride up the hills fast, fighting to combat the reality of my situation—the consequences of the

choice I made when distraught over my husband's death.
Goddamn you, Toly!

CHAPTER SIX

Day two of classes started with Beginning Spanish. Shrouded in a haze, it felt like I was going through the motions. Fortunately, I had already taken both Beginning Spanish and Art History. All the art slides I memorized last time still simmered on the surface of my brain.

Packy came and found me at lunchtime.

"You're up," I said.

He flipped his bangs out of his eyes. "Yeah, it's my early day. Party Saturday night." He pointed his finger at my chest.

"Ugh!" I groaned.

"Come on, Jayjay. We'll have fun."

"Fine, fine. Maybe it will distract me."

"No call."

"No, and now the loss of Callahan and Ashley has become real, and I can't seem to get away from the grief." I took off my backpack and extracted my wallet.

"A party will do you good. When was the last time you had too much to drink?"

"Decades."

Packy laughed and slapped his thigh. "Come on, Jayjay, let's go get some bad food." He swung his arm around my waist.

"Okay." I smiled up at him.

He kept me entirely entertained and after lunch, I went to the computer lab to type up my paper.

Back at the dorm, I quickly tackled my homework and continued to write down my experiences for Callahan and maybe a book someday.

My gut twisted when I paused between activities. The

typed paper in its folder sat on the corner of my desk. The temptation to rip it up and instead write about my dorm room plagued me all day. My anxiety rocketed so high I did something I didn't do the last time. I scrubbed the bathroom and vacuumed our dorm. I felt like a ball of nerves that even with riding to class and back, I could barely sit still.

Not wanting to cry again, I got up, shuffled down to the community TV, and watched the soap opera on the screen. After a while, even the drivel on the tube didn't help, so I went back to my room and pulled out *The Shining* and started rereading it.

After scaring myself silly, I managed to drift off to sleep, mulling over how Travis would respond to my paper.

CHAPTER SEVEN

I arrived at English class early and placed the folder with my paper in it on the table. My heart incited a riot in my chest, even though I knew Travis wouldn't be reading it for a while.

He entered the stage from the back, and I watched him search for me. Something like relief flashed across his face. His shoulders settled, and his eyes brightened. He pushed his leather briefcase under the table and flipped open my folder. His right eyebrow rose as he scanned my face. Something in his eyes compelled me to relax.

I sighed visibly and looked away.

"All right, class. How many people have started on their papers?"

I raised my hand, as did many of the students.

"Look around. Most of you with your hands up are lying."

The class laughed.

"Let's try another one. Who read the assignment for today?"

Up went my hand again, and about half of the other students raised their hands too.

He walked around the table and sat back on the edge of it. "Still not believing you."

We all laughed again.

He then paced away from the table. The blazer he wore fit his shoulders perfectly and over the jeans and button-down shirt, he looked sexy as hell. "Who would like to explain occasion, context, and purpose as it pertains to rhetoric?"

I glanced around at the other girls in the class and knew they too wanted him. Whether or not I could go through with it remained to be seen, but watching him strut across the stage—damn—I wanted to try.

After my three classes, I made it back to my room and found a note from Debbie.

> *We have a meeting on Thursday at 12:30 p.m. to discuss your paper.*
> *Professor Stratford*

Under it, she wrote:

> *You had a paper due already? Will be gone the next two days or so.*

I leaned over the sink and said to my reflection, "What the fuck are you doing?" I shook my head at myself. Without Callahan, I had no compass, no stalwart to ground me. *Why isn't he calling me? Shouldn't soulmates automatically recognize each other? Toly! You owe me!*

I put Journey's *Departure* album on the turntable and stretched out on my twin bed. "I'm Cryin'" played, and I bellowed along with it. After allowing myself to wallow in misery for one side of the album, I pushed myself up and swung my legs to the side of the bed.

Back at my desk, I managed to focus on my homework. I also wrote to Callahan.

> *I clearly hadn't thought out what traveling back in time would mean. I have all our memories, and you have none. Even though I intellectually knew you wouldn't know me right away, I didn't think through the ramifications. Will we even fit together now? Me at forty-eight and you at thirty.*
>
> *What would you have had me do? Stay in 2015 with Ash? God, I miss our daughter, someone you will never*

really know. Not like the daughter we already raised together. Right now, if Toly showed back up and gave me the option to go back, I'd probably jump at it. It's intolerable waiting for you to call, and part of me is still expecting sixty-year-old Cally to show up, not Cal the young, heartbroken version. The need to speak to you is so goddamn consuming it makes it hard for me to breathe, makes it hard for me to want to go on without you.

Part of me wants to be with Travis, so I can lose myself in another and not have to feel this unbearable anguish anymore, but it feels like cheating on you, cheating on our memories. And yet, there isn't even a "you" or "us" to cheat on.

I've put myself in this cage of my own making.

I'm so sorry for abandoning Ashley. You never would have. I have to stop writing you now, or I'll end up finding a tall building and flinging myself from it. I love you forever and always, my Cally.

I skipped dinner entirely and thought about Debbie's yogurts in the fridge but upheld my promise to myself. I left them untouched. When I thought I would lose my mind if I spent another second alone, I picked up the phone and dialed.

"Patrick, your humble servant, what say ye?"

"Can I talk you into a sleepover?"

"Debbie does Dallas *again*?"

I chuckled. "Or whatever her boyfriend's name is."

"Pajama party! I'll bring the drinks."

"And food if you have any?"

"On my way."

Yay!

I quickly changed into shorts and a T-shirt, and as soon as I heard him knock, I opened the door wide. "OMG, Packy!"

Packy stepped in wearing Pac-Man covered, long-sleeved pajamas with matching bottoms. "I've been waiting for the chance to wear them." He struck a model's pose.

Laughing, I fell over onto my bed. Calling Packy was exactly the right thing to do. "Damn, I love you." I sat up and hugged his waist tightly.

"Where should I put this stuff?" He held up a bottle of Boone's Farm Wine and a large bag of Doritos.

I moved aside my textbooks and pointed to the desk.

"What would we be doing differently if this was 2015?"

"We would have a laptop computer or tablet, and we could watch a movie together on it."

"Cool that!"

"Pick a song from any of the albums."

"What will I pick?"

I laughed, already loving the game. "That's easy. I'll write them down." I pulled my notebook onto my lap and wrote:

> "How Soon Is Now" by The Smiths
> "Please, Please, Please, Let Me Get What I Want" by The Smiths
> "People Are People" by Depeche Mode
> "Blasphemous Rumours" by Depeche Mode
> "Whole Lotta Love" by Led Zeppelin

I closed the notebook and set it on the desk.

Packy carefully extracted an album from its sleeve and placed it on the turntable. He set the needle on the song he selected. "How Soon Is Now" started playing. "Were you right?"

"But of course. Toss me the chip bag."

We sat on my bed and listened to music while slugging the bad wine and munching on chips.

"Albums are pretty obsolete in 2015." I wiped the wine from my face with the back of my hand.

"Get the fuck out of town."

"True, true, I promise you. Tapes too. Music moves onto these shiny disks about yay big," I said, using my thumbs and index fingers to make an O. "But those are quickly going out too."

"So how do people listen to music?"

"It's called an iPod, but in 2015, I had all my music on my cellphone."

He shook his head with his mouth and eyes open wide. He looked like a cartoon character.

I giggled. "Do you know how you save a file on the campus computer?"

"Sure."

"Songs become files like that, and they can be stored on a small device. Think of a very mini Walkman."

"Wow, that's cool. So you can store like a whole record collection on it?"

"Exactly."

He switched the song to "Please, Please, Please, Let Me Get What I Want." "Right again?"

"That was my number two."

"Damn, Skippy, this is *so* cool."

I smiled. "Thank you for coming to my rescue. I was contemplating a tall building."

"Still no call?"

"Nope. Given how I acted, what are the chances?"

"Slim, but you still have the beach in St. Augustine."

"Ten years, Packy. *Ten ... long ... years.*"

"Yeah, it rightly sucks, but I think it's way too soon to give up hope. We'll party until he comes around."

"I'd kiss you but..."

He laughed and handed me back the wine. "What about taking a lover in the meantime? You're a hot number. Probably every straight man's dream, right? A mature woman in the body of a babe."

"Thank you, I think, and I'm not that mature." I held the bottle up in a pretend toast to make my point and took a swig of the wine, cringing as I drank it down.

"Seriously."

"I'm considering it."

He spanked the bed between us. "You have someone picked out already? Fuck, girl, OMG." He did his wide-eyed, opened-mouth expression again.

"It's fucking hilarious when you say it. Pick another song."

He carefully returned The Smiths, *Hatful of Hollow*, back into the album sleeve, lifted the *Led Zeppelin II* album, and put on "Whole Lotta Love." "I tried to mix it up this time. Did this make your list?"

"Number five, dude."

"This is fun! Too bad we didn't keep in touch because then you could tell me how the rest of my life goes."

"That's true, but who knows how you knowing about me changes things. We didn't hang out on this night last time."

"Huh, right. And according to you, you never came to the party with me on Saturday night that you *will* be attending."

I smacked his thigh. "I already said I'd go. I keep my word."

"We'll dance all night and get shitfaced."

"I have a confession."

He rubbed his hands together with his sinister smile. "Fess it."

"I was very angry with you for going to your parties and

82

tripping on acid. We fought about it. Then later, in my early twenties, I tried it."

He cackled and rocked in the bed. "Oh my god. Were you this cool last time?"

"You seemed to think so."

"Huh. This is some really crazy stuff, don't you think?" He brushed his bangs aside and popped a Dorito into his mouth.

"Totally. Sometimes when I'm feeling sorry for myself and missing Ashley and Callahan, I wish I'd thought this through a little better."

"That's understandable. I'm not sure I'd have the balls to travel back. So who's the dude?"

"How do you mean?"

He tilted his head and shoved my shoulder.

"Top secret." I shook my head. "Plus, I haven't decided."

"Ahhh, a professor! Go get him, girlfriend. I'm so jealous."

"Shut up, Pakster! I mean it."

"Lips are sealed! I would think you would want someone older. That makes sense. It's kind of surprising you and I get on so well."

"Apparently, I never really grew up." I laughed. "My mother has always said she still feels twenty-five. Now I really know what she means. The body ages but the mind really doesn't."

"I'm always praying I won't get old and stodgy."

"Not a chance. You're the coolest cat I've ever known."

"Truly?"

"The honest truth."

Packy and I crashed in my bed together. His friendship helped ground me in just the way I needed. I would make it through another day.

CHAPTER EIGHT

In the morning, I had to climb over Patrick to get out of bed and get ready for class. I did my best to keep quiet. I slipped into the bathroom to shower and dress. I chose a loose-fitting, yellow sundress and brown sandals.

Packy groaned in his sleep a few times, rolled over, and then breathed deeply again.

With my backpack over my shoulders, I closed the door softly behind me.

Once in class, I had a hard time focusing on Spanish and Art History. My mind wandered to the upcoming meeting with Travis. Part of me hoped he would think me completely insane and the other half wanted him to lay me on his desk and have his way with me.

I trotted nervously across campus to make my scheduled meeting. In front of his door, I took a deep breath, stretched my neck to either side, and chastised my heart. *Stop beating so fucking fast. This isn't the principal's office!*

I tapped lightly and waited.

A girl with a huge smile on her face walked out, not even pausing to look at me.

I, in turn, frowned on my way into Travis' office. "She looked happy."

"Lock the door behind you. I told her she could retake a class she failed to drop in time last semester."

I flipped the bolt and said, "Uh-huh, right."

"Damn, you're cute. All forty-eight years of you. You have a way with fiction. It didn't exactly fit the assignment, but I'll let that pass because of the humor in it. Loved your reasons for your laughs. Come here."

I wasn't sure if I felt relief that he didn't believe the story or frustration. I definitely didn't believe the crap about the girl who just walked out. From the looks of it, she knew she would be getting laid soon by Professor Hottie. I'd stake my life on it. It did, however, simplify matters.

I stepped closer and said, "Just tell me you practice safe sex."

"You don't believe me?" His eyes widened and his mouth made an O.

"About as much as you believed *my* story." I couldn't help wondering if my eighteen-year-old self would have fallen for his tripe.

"Fair enough. So what's your plan?"

I knew what he was really asking but said, "Graduate with a degree in creative writing. I want to write novels."

"A lofty goal. Do you want to know what my goal is?" He clasped my hand and pulled me close.

My breath hitched. "What?" I squeaked out.

"You. I'm going to major in you."

I laughed hard, wondering on how many girls he'd used that very line. "You're such a player. What about the chippy who just walked out of here?"

He hugged me tightly. "I have no interest in anyone but you."

"If we're going to do this, can you pretend I'm an adult and cut the bullshit? You're hot and don't need to do all the wooing. I'm not looking to fall in love with you. Callahan, from my story, he's real. He doesn't know me yet, but—"

"I understand. I can help you bridge the gap."

"Perfect. Just don't pretend you love me and I'll do the same. I do have a question."

"Okay?"

"Why me?"

"I wanted you naked, underneath me, from the first moment I laid eyes on you."

"Honesty, I like this much better. What about your job?"

"We have to be careful here. Do you have access to a car?"

"No."

He pulled me onto his lap. "We'll sort it out." His warm hands cupped my face and brought my lips to his. When his heated breath mingled with mine, an intense need sparked within me, leaving me aroused and scared. He tasted uniquely himself, very different from the man I had spent twenty years loving.

I kissed him back harder, forcing my body tightly against his, wanting to rid myself of my thoughts.

The chair tilted back as our kiss deepened.

"Whoa," he said once our connection had morphed into raging sea of fervor. He lifted me off his lap. "Not here." His mouth parted in surprise as his chest rose and fell.

I laughed. "I promise you'll be fine once you stop thinking of me as a young girl."

He smirked. "I'll try. You can't tell anyone about us."

I straightened my dress. "No, of course not. I wouldn't."

"Can you come to my place for dinner?"

"You move fast." I stared at him and then said, "How will I get there?"

He sat upright and said, "I'll pick you up at the back of The Sweet Shop. Five?"

I grinned. "Okay."

"Are you a virgin?"

I glanced up and to the right, thinking. Chuckling, I said, "Technically, yes."

His brow furrowed, but then a huge smile broke over his face. "It'll be a first for me."

"In body only."

"All the better," he said with a wicked grin.

"Ha! You're funny."

"You seem so different than—"

"Than your usual fare?" I perched on the desk behind me. "Before we go further, there's something I need to say."

"I'm listening." He took my hand in his, stroking my palm with his thumb.

"I will not fall in love with you. If I feel like you're playing me, we will be short-lived. If Callahan comes around sooner than I expect—"

"How old is he?"

"Your age. I'm not trying to talk you out of it. However, I do want you to understand fully where I stand. What I have to offer."

"What are you offering me?" Travis asked.

"Me. Just as I am. I can't even promise for how long."

He nodded. "No one can make that promise. Me, least of all."

"I guess that's true. I do have a request, though, and I'm not sure it's even fair."

"I won't be spending intimate time with anyone else. If that changes for either of us, we'll talk about it."

"Seriously?" I asked, hoping he meant it.

"Yes."

"Ahhh, I think I see. One per semester? Okay," I sighed out. "It's a done deal then."

He gave me a quick kiss and led me to the door. "Thank you for stopping by," he said in a formal voice and then whispered, "Looking forward to unraveling you."

A huge grin broke across my face. "Yes, thank you for the help," I said and walked away. I felt a skip in my step as I made my way to my bicycle.

After eating lunch, I tackled my homework and wrote more to Callahan. My heart stopped when I heard my phone ring.

"Hello?" I asked.

"Hi, Jayjay," Shannon said.

I blew out the air that had caught in my lungs. "How's it going, Sweet Pea?"

"Your bed is *so* comfortable!"

Like a wave, I was flooded with the memory of our conversation. Last time we fought, but I wouldn't let that happen this time. "Make sure to leave my closet closed. Otherwise, make yourself comfortable."

"What?" she yelped.

"Sleep in my room if it makes you happy." Thankfully, I packed my vibrator for college and didn't leave it on the top shelf of my closet.

"You hate when I go into your room!"

"Would you like me to order you to stay out?" I leaned my chair back, balancing it with my feet against the desk.

"Well, no."

"Okay. Let's make a deal."

"What's that?"

"When I'm home, you go back to sleeping in your room."

"Deal!" she squealed into the phone. "You are the bestest sister ever!"

I laughed. "No, Sweet Pea. You're the best little sister anyone could have. I miss you."

"I miss you too. I think Dad does too."

"Oh yeah?" I moved over to the bed and sat down.

"He lets me read the comics in the newspaper at the table now."

"Have you figured out how to be quiet, so you don't bug him?"

"Most times. Sometimes it's hard to sit still."

"For you, it is because you're a jitterbug."

Shannon giggled. "I miss you, Jayjay. When are you coming home?"

"I'm not sure yet, but I'll let you know as soon as I do. You should have a letter in the mail from me soon."

"Yippie! Mail for me."

"Give Dad and Mom a big hug for me."

"I will. Love you!"

"Love you more. Call me again soon."

"Okay!"

I took another shower and got ready to see Travis. After dressing in jeans and an off-the-shoulder blouse, I thought about applying makeup but decided against it. Travis seemed to like me as is, and I hadn't worn a stitch of it since arriving back in 1985.

CHAPTER NINE

After closing my dorm door behind me and skipping down the stairs, I walked over to The Sweet Shop and found my way around back. Only a minute or two had passed before Travis pulled up in a maroon Saab convertible with tan leather interior.

"Wow, nice car."

He stretched across and opened the passenger side door for me. The front had bucket seats.

As soon as I slid in, he settled in next to me, his warm hand on my thigh.

"Are you nervous?" he asked as he pulled out onto the street away from the restaurant and the main drag near campus.

The breeze from the car ride blew my curly hair out of my face. "No, not really. I am feeling reckless."

"Your neck gets all red."

I laughed. "Yeah, that always gives me away."

He squeezed my thigh and said, "I'll be gentle."

"Who says I want you to be." I placed my hand on top of his.

It was his turn to laugh. "You're a feisty one." He made a right into a nice neighborhood of brick homes.

He flipped his hand over and wove his fingers through mine. "I haven't been this excited about a woman in a long time."

"Uh-huh. Would you have really searched for me?"

He nodded. "Absolutely. Fortunately, your name isn't common, and I planned to comb the student records if necessary. Have you ever had a lover?"

"No. Patrick says I should take a lover while I'm

waiting since it could be a long time."

"I like your friend. Why not him?"

"He'd be more interested in you."

"Ahhh. Gotcha. Well, we're here," he said as he pulled into the driveway of a two-story Tudor home.

"Nice. I didn't think professors got paid this well."

"Generous in-laws."

"Wait a fucking minute! You're not married are you?" I shot a look at his left hand as if I could have somehow missed the ring.

He hopped out of the car and came around to me. "Of course, not. She never appreciated the gift of the house from her parents, so I ended up with it in the divorce."

"Wow, okay." I breathed out, trying to rid myself of the adrenaline coursing through my veins.

He lifted me to my feet. "You're really upset. I'm sorry."

I stepped into his embrace. "No, no. I just would never consider an affair. I think I'm more invested in this distraction than I realized."

His smile brightened. "You're adorable. I've never known someone like you. You just say what you think."

"Yes, it's probably my worst trait. No filter."

"You're so wrong about that. After being married to someone who kept it all in, leaving me in the dark about where I stood, it's very refreshing." He took my hand and led me to the front door.

"I'll have to take your word for it."

He unlocked the door and pushed it open, waving me inside. "Why do you think it's your worst trait?"

"I've put my foot into it many times. My mother has said, on a number of occasions that I don't need to say everything I think." I strolled deeper into the house and scanned the living room area. "Wow."

"Her parents had it furnished too."

"I can see why it would have pissed her off. I mean, it's gorgeous. Love the large marble tile, but I'd hate someone to overstep me in that way. Plus, it's a bit formal, don't you think?" I brushed my hand over the perfectly polished mahogany table. "Maybe she thought it was all a bit too perfect?"

"Yes, I agree with that. She thought she had to be perfect too. I never wanted that of her."

"I see. Well, I'm far from perfect, so you have nothing to worry about with me. I'm very aware of my flaws."

"Silly you. You're perfectly imperfect."

I laughed. "I'm happy you think so." In my mind, as I paraded around the room, I was forty-eight in an adult conversation with a younger good-looking man, and then I saw my reflection and smiled. She smiled back at me. I was young, gorgeous, and needed to take advantage of the circumstances in which I found myself.

Travis led me into the huge kitchen with stainless steel appliances and granite counter tops.

I hopped up on the island, lying back and spreading my arms out wide. "This is bigger than my dorm bed."

He peered down at me. "You're giving me ideas."

"Have you christened all the rooms?"

He shook his head and came in close. "Who are you, Miss Jayden?" Then he whispered, "You are bafflingly alluring."

In an attempt to ignore my arousal, I quipped, "I thought adverbs were a no-no."

An uproarious laugh escaped him. "You're going to inspire me to dust off my novel. Or we could write one together."

"You're kidding right?"

"I have a feeling we'll inspire each other."

"Oh, I'm feeling inspired," I said, wrapping my foot around his thigh and pulling him in closer.

He buried his hands in my hair and schooled my mouth.

I tugged the tail of his shirt from his jeans, my hands seeking the warm skin underneath.

His mouth broke away from mine. He rested his chin on the top of my head and said in a voice deeper than before, "Dinner first."

I leaned back on my hands. "What's on the menu? I mean, other than you for dessert."

His grin lit up his entire face. He adjusted himself in his pants, the outline making it clear what I had to contend with later. His cock looked formidable. "Up here," he said, pointing to his eyes.

"Sorry, I got distracted."

"Damn, woman, you make it hard to stay focused."

"How hard?" I glanced down again.

"Someone's going to have to pretend to be the adult here."

"If you say so."

"I'm old-fashioned. At least, a meal first."

I jumped down off the counter. "Do you wine and dine all your girls?"

"They seem to like it."

"I'm enjoying myself so far. What's for dinner?"

"How do BBQ chicken, baked potatoes, and roasted veggies sound?"

"Like a feast. Sign me up! You should realize you're saving me from another horrible dinner at the cafeteria. What can I do to help?"

"I need to start the grill and let it heat up. I've got the rest covered. We can sit outside or wait in here."

"It's not too bad out. Let's sit out there."

"A glass of wine?"

"Sure. As long as you know you're providing alcohol to a minor."

He bowed his head in an exaggerated motion. "Sorry, officer. I swear she told me she's forty-eight and from the future."

I chuckled and made my voice deep, playing along. "And from this report, it says she's your student as well?"

"Yes, sir. She promised to drop the class, officer."

I raised my eyebrows and said, "You're in a whole lot of trouble there, buddy." Then I broke character. "Do you want me to drop the class?"

He opened the refrigerator and pulled out the vegetables, potatoes, and chicken. He stopped and glanced back at me. "We can talk about that later."

"Okay."

After he rinsed the chicken parts and prepped them for the grill, he cleaned the potatoes and vegetables, wrapping them separately in foil. Once we walked outside, he lit the gas grill and closed the top to let it heat up. "Come sit."

The raised brick patio had a circular glass table with a closed green umbrella attached.

He pulled out a chair and sat. "I have plans to redo the house, but it's not cheap. The location is perfect for the University. Not far, but far enough I'm not surrounded by college students."

"Do you let all your semester girls know where you live?"

"It hasn't been a problem."

I took my seat across from him. "Right. How long have you been living here alone?"

He changed chairs and sat next to me. "About a year and a half."

"Did you sleep with students before or during—?"

"No, definitely not. I don't want anything serious and—"

"I get it. Perfect," I said, scanning him up and down. Even without the blazer, in jeans and a dress shirt, he exuded sexual confidence.

"It wasn't a matter of lack of opportunity."

Obviously! "Of course not." I played with the light hair on his arm just above the wrist. "So we're both still recovering," I let slip. I traced over the bone of his wrist, never before realizing I could be turned on by that part of the body.

"Look at me," he said.

"Yes?"

Our eyes locked together, and I gasped at the intensity of his gaze.

"You aren't like the others."

Whoosh, I felt his desire surf across the contours of my skin. *Sorry, Cally, but I think I'm going to have to tap that!*

He stood up and put the chicken and vegetables on the grill. "Let's go inside. I want you closer."

He brought me into the formal living room, sat me down on the plush white couch, and held me close.

I melted against him, needing everything he offered me. Tilting my head up so I could see his face, I asked, "How long were you married?"

"Six years."

"How long was it good?"

"I'm not sure it was ever good for her. Her parents liked me too much. I was too accommodating. Blah, blah, blah."

"But for you?"

"I was under the delusion of happiness for about four years. At that point, the cracks started to show. She couldn't keep it up anymore."

"I'm sorry, Travis." I brought my mouth to him, to kiss away the pain for us both.

"Yeah," he sighed. "Me too."

When Callahan popped into my head, I pushed him away, letting myself sink into the kiss. My Cally didn't exist anymore. He died in 2015, and I had to give up on expecting the man I knew to show up.

Once back outside, Travis opened the grill and checked the food. "Potatoes need a few more minutes." He set the chicken and veggies to the side and stepped back into the house.

I scanned the expansive yard while imagining a pool and kids out back in the shade of the tall oak trees. "It's beautiful out here," I said when he stepped back out with butter and sour cream. "Trying to fatten me up, I see."

He chuckled. "You're perfect as is, Miss Sexy Legs."

"You think?" I stretched my leg out from under the table.

"I noticed those legs first and then you blew me away with your laugh."

I moved into his lap and said, "I noticed your legs, too, in those tiny shorts."

"Tiny?" His hand moved mine over the zipper of his jeans, and I felt him twitch under my caress.

"It wasn't a commentary on your package."

He chuckled. "Is that what they call it in the future?"

I laughed. "Amongst other things, yes. I thought you didn't believe me."

"Oh, I don't, but it's fun to speculate. What do they call this?" he said, cupping my breast.

"Breasts, boobs, tits, hooters, knockers, holy rollers, and tatas."

"Holy rollers?"

"I threw that one in there to make you laugh."

"It worked," he said, still chuckling. "Kiss me."

"Yes, sir." I saluted and then kissed him with ever-growing passion brimming in my body. My heart planned to stay out of it.

He pushed me off his lap and grabbed the oven mitt, using it to remove the potatoes from the grill. "Well? Hurry up. Let's eat."

We loaded our plates outside. Then he smiled as he waved me into the house. He was just too damn cute for my own good.

We clinked our wine glasses together.

"To new friendships," I said.

"To our new friendship."

"Even better." I took a sip of the tart, white wine. "This is yummy," I said, munching on a barbecue chicken thigh. "Do you cook a lot?"

"Eating out by yourself gets lonely."

"Yeah, I can imagine."

"I'm the master of the grill."

"You sure are and hopefully other things."

"I think you'll be pleased."

"Big talker." I laughed.

After dinner, we settled on the couch again, and the kisses flamed between us, raising my pulse and my need. His smooth hands held my face as his tongue dueled with mine, simultaneously revving my desire and prying my closed heart open just a bit more.

Then we were all hands, unbuttoning, pulling, and removing each other's clothes. I loved every inch of sixty-year-old Cally, but I'd forgotten the pleasure of a hard-as-steel thirty-two-year-old.

"Just let me look at you," I said, trailing my fingers down his cut stomach muscles. "Damn." A smattering of hairs led the way to his rock hard cock.

It twitched when I played in the precum crowning the

head. "Oh yeah, baby, that feels great." His fingers found their way to my labia, opening my folds and spreading my wetness to my clit. He plunged two fingers into me, causing me to gasp. "I want in there."

I froze, but my eyes flew wide open as I tried to catch my breath. "Can we ... I mean, maybe just ... play around? No intercourse?" I guided his hand away from me and said, "I'll be right back." I scurried down the hall and found the bathroom.

Leaning over the sink, I stared at myself. "Whoa, what the fuck was that?" *Shit!* It felt as if Callahan stood in the bathroom with me. Not like a ghost or anything like that, but his presence pervaded me.

"Get back out there!" I said to the younger version of myself. Out in the hall, I headed back to the living room.

When I approached, he asked, "Are you okay?"

I reached for my undies. "Yeah, but I'd like to take a rain check if that's okay."

He smiled. "Sure."

I assumed he was used to dealing with fickle eighteen-year-olds.

He held my hand as he drove and then dropped me outside of campus with a quick kiss goodbye. "Let's make plans again soon."

"Definitely," I said, but the jury was busy socializing in the lobby and not ready to cast their verdict.

Back in my dorm room, I found it empty and sighed in relief. I grabbed my phone, pulling the long cord over to my bed, and plopped down. After I had punched in the number, I lay back and listened to its ring.

"American Bandstand..."

I laughed. "Hi, Packy. I need my shrink."

"I charge by the hour."

"I'll order you a pizza, but I'm stuffed."

"Get me a coke too and you have a deal."

"Done."

"On my way."

I called in the order, and just as I was giving the guy the address, Packy knocked on my door. I waved him in. "Okay, sounds good. Thanks." I hung up the phone. "Should be here in twenty minutes or so."

He rubbed his belly. "Good thing you're a mess this time around. My stomach thanks you."

"Shut up and sit down." I patted the mattress next to me.

"Do you need to lie down?"

I giggled. "No."

"Sooo..."

"I went to this man's house—"

"Miss Jayden, are you telling me you met a new cock? I'm so jealous!"

I shoved Packy's shoulder. "It was a very brief hello."

Then he became serious. "What happened?" He rested his hand on my leg.

"Callahan happened. At first, it seemed so easy and so deliciously distracting, but the more..."

"The more what?"

"Exposed, literally and figuratively."

"Yeah, I get it. I can't imagine being you."

"Hell, I can't imagine being me, and yet, here I am." I sighed heavily and shook my head.

"Is he hot?"

"Ridiculously so."

"Are you going to try again?"

"I don't know. I'm thinking about ditching class."

"He's in your class?" Patrick gave me his wide-eyed stare and then nodded. "Right."

"Wait, Packy, don't say—"

"Never!" He jumped up and said, "Let's get this party started. Doctor's orders." Crouching down, he reached for my album collection just as a knock sounded at the door.

Packy, as always, managed to bring the fun into my otherwise crazy life.

The first time around, I felt so lost and unsure of what I wanted to do with my life. Back then, Packy knew how to cheer me up and lose the depression that hovered so close. Amazingly, at forty-eight, he still managed to bring out my best self and to direct me to a positive view of my circumstances.

After he had devoured the pizza and soda, we danced around the room like silly children.

"Did you hear that?" Packy asked as he stopped gyrating his hips.

I ran over to the stereo and turned it down.

Bang, bang, bang, came from the bathroom door.

"Come in," I said, collapsing onto my bed.

"Can you guys..." Tori said, leaning into the room and taking notice of Packy, "...keep it down? We're trying to study."

"Oops, sorry about that. We were just burning off some steam."

"I think that's my cue to go." Packy started toward the hall door.

"No worries," Tori said and then closed the door behind her.

Packy and I cracked up as I playfully pushed him out of the room.

"Thank you so much for lifting me up."

He bent over and cupped his hand to my ear. "If his appendage is as nice as you say ... if at first you don't succeed, try, try again."

"Ha! Is that the doctor's orders?" I asked with another laugh.

"Yes, and you'll need to provide full details later on."

"Off with you!" I shoved him on his way.

"You're my most pushy patient," he tossed over his shoulder and then waved. "Don't forget Saturday night."

"How could I possibly? You won't let me." I waved back.

CHAPTER TEN

The moment I awoke, a knot pulled tighter in my stomach. *Should I ditch my English class and avoid Travis?* I quickly nixed the idea and got ready for the day.

Instead of sitting in my usual spot in the second row, I took a seat in the top row at the back. When Travis sauntered onto the stage, I saw him scan his audience. He almost looked disappointed. Was he searching for me?

"Please pass your papers to the right, and the last person in the row bring them to the front." Travis leaned back against the desk with his arms crossed, still scanning the auditorium.

As I passed the stack to the right, I felt a chill crawl up my neck. I glanced back toward the stage and found Travis staring at me. My last swallow caught in my throat, and I felt myself blush.

He grimaced and then pushed himself off the table. "Your next writing assignment is on the board and is due next Friday. Today, we're going to cover how to evoke emotion with your writing. As you can see, that will be the goal of your next paper. Make it at least five hundred words. A cliffhanger is fine, but make sure the reader will want to read more."

I quickly scribbled the assignment into my notebook and then looked back toward the stage.

Travis was squinting against the lights and seemed to be looking at me again. "You, in the red top," he said, his finger pointing in my direction. "Please share with the class one way to move the reader to feel something."

Oh, shit! I had read the assignment for class, but it all just escaped my brain like a prisoner needing fresh air. Why had he called me out?

Deciding to wing it, I stood and cleared my throat. "From my experience, if I feel what I'm writing and adequately describe the sensations and emotions, then it translates to the paper and then to the reader."

As I made to sit down, he called out, "One more moment please, Miss..."

"Jayden." *So we're going to play it like that?* I remained standing, my heart racing a mile a minute, shaking and struggling to keep it together. *Fuck, I should have skipped this class.*

"Miss Jayden, can you give us an example?"

From their seats, the class had shifted to face me. If Travis' intention was to reduce me to feeling like the eighteen-year-old my body alluded to, he had done a banner job. All the examples that flashed across the screen of my mind came from my older self: Marrying Callahan, being pregnant with Ashley, our anniversary trip, Callahan dying, his funeral. However, the backbone Callahan had helped me forge, surged to the forefront.

So I began, "One day in English class, my professor called on me. Although I had read the assignment, all the knowledge fled once he put me on the spot. Why is he calling on me? I thought. My heart, completely disobeying, raced like a motherfucker."

The class roared with laughter, which only encouraged me to continue.

"I struggled to catch my breath, and by standing up perfectly straight, tried to hide the shaking that had started in my legs and threatened to take over my whole body. Since I had participated in class before, being singled out, clearly, wasn't for my lack of engagement in the course. Still, being forced to answer with all the students staring at me left me confused as to the professor's intention. Of course, I couldn't ask while the whole class watched my every move." I shot a glance in Travis' direction.

His mouth hung open, and he held a file on top of his lap. Had I shocked and aroused him?

Unsure of my own intention, I quickly sat down as the class erupted in laughter and applause.

"Well done, Miss Jayden. Would anyone else care to share an example?"

I didn't take in another moment of the class while waiting desperately for Travis to make eye contact again, which he never did. Just before the class ended, I slipped out the back and breathed for what felt like the first time since the class began.

As the rest of the students filed out, many patted me on the back or held a thumbs up in my direction. Somehow, I'd inadvertently put myself on the map instead of staying in the safety of my cocoon. "Brilliant," I muttered sarcastically to myself.

Text to self: *Follow gut instinct when it comes to skipping class.*

I barely paid attention in sociology and math class and just wanted the day to end. Hopping on my bike, I raced back to the dorm and threw my books down on the desk. I had planned to tackle my homework, but instead, I lay down on my bed and read more of *The Shining*.

When the phone rang, it startled the crap out of me. I didn't answer it right away. I had no interest in dealing with Travis, but it could be any number of other people, including my roommate's friends or Callahan. I contemplated letting it go into voicemail but gave in and answered.

"Yeah?"

"Jayden? Ya don't sound like yourself."

Shit! He must have gotten my number from my mother.
"Hi, Rider. Listen—"

"No, you listen here. I met someone—"

"Cassie?"

"How the hell do ya know about that?"

"Lucky guess?" *Fuck, Jayden. Will you ever learn to keep your foot out of your mouth?*

Text to self: *Keep foot out of mouth! STFU!!*

"I'm giving ya another chance to come to your senses."

"I think it's time for us to move on. I'm sure you and Cassie will be very happy together."

"Fuck that shit. I'm not calling you back."

"I understand."

"The heck you do!" he yelled and hung up.

Rider and Cassie married in the last version of my life and divorced in their early thirties. I lost contact with him after that.

"Well, at least, I got one person off my list," I said aloud to myself.

"Who is that?" Debbie said from the other side of the partition.

I stood up. "Holy shit, you scared me. I didn't know you were here."

"Yeah, Darin and I got into a fight, and I'm staying here for the next few days to teach him a lesson."

"Do I want to know?"

"Definitely not."

I had totally forgotten about the fight. If I remembered correctly, she takes off in the middle of the night on Saturday when they make up.

"Dinner later?" she asked.

Ah yes, the one meal we share together in my short college career. "Yeah, sure."

CHAPTER ELEVEN

S aturday morning, on my sanity bike ride, I pushed myself up the hills to get rid of the anxiety that plagued me. After stealthy snagging an apple fritter, I settled down at my desk to tackle homework. My composition assignment stated that the goal was to evoke emotion. It didn't say the story had to be true, but in this case, it was, based on my last go around.

During the second semester of my college experience, a new guy moved in across the hall with my drug supplier Paul. Paul and I had a mild flirtation with each other, occasionally making out but never taking it any further. He, in fact, introduced me to Tray.

"Hey, Jayden. Come in for a sec," Paul said, grabbing my arm and pulling me into his dorm room.

"Did you get the new stuff—" I immediately snapped my mouth shut and looked up at the darkly handsome guy towering over Paul and me.

"This is Tray, my new roommate."

"Uh, hey, Tray," I said, staring into his clear green eyes.

When he didn't look away or even blink, I felt my whole body blush as heat migrated up my neck. My heart pounded erratically with desire and fear.

Still locked in Tray's gaze, I asked Paul, "What happened to Stan?"

"He dropped out," Paul said.

I tore my gaze away from Tray and nodded toward Paul. "Well..." I swallowed hard and continued, "It was nice to meet you."

His deep voice took me by surprise. "Hope to see you around."

I pointed to my door on the other side of the hall, two doors down. "It's rather unavoidable." I scooted out of the room without looking at either of them but felt Tray's attention follow me out, causing a chill to creep up my back. I should probably stop reading *The Shining*, I thought. It's giving me crazy ideas.

Fast forward four weeks and I found myself watching a strip poker game on the opposite side of our dorm floor. Why I was there could only be chalked up to boredom. People drank and smoked, and I shared in the abundance.

Tray was there as well, and he too wasn't playing but watching and drinking. As the players began to remove more clothing, I got a clear sense of where the game was heading, and I didn't want any part of it. I slipped out the door, and Tray quickly followed behind me.

"It's not like I'm a prude or anything," I said over my shoulder. "It's just..." Why was I justifying myself to him?

"It's just?"

"Not my thing."

"Yeah, I get it. There's another party going on in the RA's room."

"Well, I—"

"Just come along and you can leave anytime you'd like."

"Okay, I guess." I let Tray pull me along to the RA's large single room. All my alarm bells were firing off, but I went along anyway.

He opened the door ahead of me.

When I stepped forward into the room, my hand shot up and covered my mouth. "Oh, I'm sorry," I said, taking in the naked RA and his girlfriend getting ready to take a shower.

"Not at all," the girl said, waving me forward. "Come join us."

Fuck! *"Sorry, not my scene." I tried to leave, but Tray*

blocked my way. The alcohol and pot churned in my stomach as I cursed my stupidity. It would serve him right if I vomited all over him. The initial attraction I experienced with Tray fled, and all I could see was another twisted Stephen King character in the flesh. I struggled to slow my breathing so I wouldn't pass out.

Tray held my arms at my sides. "You can leave at any time, and it's only a shower. It'll be fun."

I stood up as straight as I could muster. "Anytime is now. Please, step out of my way."

"Come on, Jaydenk, I won't hurt you." His grip on my arms told me otherwise.

Channeling the couple of classes of Tae Kwon Do I took as a kid, I twisted both of my arms at once, breaking his hold. I ran out of the room, down the hall as fast as I could, hurriedly unlocked my door, shut it, and slammed the lock into place.

Just reliving those moments again, stressed me out. I put on U2's *War* album and turned up the volume.

On that scary night from the past, Tray came to my door, over and over, alternating between sweet apologies, pleading with me to forgive him, and angry, threatening rants of what he planned to do to me once I opened the door. At 4 a.m. that morning, I heard scratching on my door and really freaked out. That was one of the many times I cursed my roommate for not being around. I called dorm security again, and they finally came to get me from my room and with my pillow under my arm, they brought me to an RA's room on a different floor.

They moved Tray off my floor, but that didn't stop him from coming by to torment me. So much for him being sorry. He thankfully dropped out of school soon after, and I never saw him again.

Bang, bang, bang, sounded against my door, causing my pulse to jump so fast and hard I thought I might keel over from a heart attack.

"What the fuck!" I cracked the door open almost expecting Tray to be standing there.

"Be ready to go by ten-thirty." Patrick leaned in against the doorframe.

"If you remind me again, Packy, I'm going to renege on our agreement."

"Like hell, you will. Just be ready." He smiled and said, "I can't wait to get you drunk and loosen you up."

"Save that for your male friend's lower half."

"OMG."

"OMG indeed."

At 10:30 p.m. on the dot, Packy obnoxiously banged again.

"Fuck, man, settle down!" I yelled as I yanked open the door.

He shook his head back and forth. "*You* are not wearing *that*!" He stormed over to my closet and pulled out a blue jumper. "This, unbuttoned, with a red tank beneath it. Don't you have any cool earrings?"

I pointed to the drawer of my desk and quickly shed my jeans and T-shirt. "Why do I have to dress up when you're in jeans and a tee?"

"Because where I have a P, you have a V."

"Sexist much? And by the way, we call it a cock where I come from."

"Cock-a-doodle-do. Now get dressed and let's boogie."

Patrick led me up College Avenue to the row of fraternities and sororities.

"This is where you go to party? Really? I figured *your kind* had your own parties."

He raised an eyebrow. "You'd be surprised at the numbers of *my kind* in fraternities."

"Huh, well, show me."

The minute we arrived at the party, I completely regretted my agreement with Packy. It was akin to crashing Ashley's graduation party, and it left me feeling like a dirty old woman. "I'm not sure how long—"

"None of that," Packy said, pulling me over to the barrel keg surrounded by stacks of solo cups. He filled two red cups and handed me one.

"I haven't had a beer in years."

"You'll survive. Okay ... casually look over to the right, just past the fireplace. Queer as a three dollar bill."

"No fucking way. That guy? He looks more like a football player or a lumberjack," I said, shaking my head in disbelief.

"Oh, he's way in the closet, and I'm certain his fratmates don't know a thing about it, but that didn't keep him from ... from..."

"Is the Pakster getting all shy on me? Sucking your cock or maybe getting acquainted with other features of your anatomy?"

"Let's just say as masculine as he appears—"

I shoved his shoulder and whispered, "He's looking at you."

Patrick glanced over at him, and they held a silent exchange.

"Double dipping? Do you do that?"

"I do tonight."

"Does that mean I'm free to travel?"

"Not yet. Let's dance." He yanked me toward the dance area as I searched for a place to get rid of my beer. As I leaned down to place it on the edge of an end table, a young man scanned my face.

"You're that girl from my composition class. That was classic." He smiled warmly.

I almost felt bad having to shoot him down. Not that he was my type or anything like that, but he seemed like a sweet kid Ashley would like. "Uh, thanks. I'm here with someone."

"Oh, well, let me know if that changes."

"Right." Where the hell were all these guys last time around? I might have enjoyed college more. I searched around for Patrick for a while, and when I couldn't find him, I made a beeline to the front door and let myself out.

The warm, humid air assaulted me, but I didn't care. It was better than staying trapped in an air-conditioned frat surrounded by jailbait.

Text to self: *Do not attend any more frat parties! Jailbait!*

I slowly walked the night streets, thought about my life and my recent stupid choices, and wished I sat on the couch with Ashely snuggled up close as we watched a movie. Instead, I lived trapped in a time warp of my making. Callahan was never going to call the crazy girl who stole a bite of his pizza, and I was destined to relive my life over again without him.

Tears meandered down my cheeks as I made my way back to my dorm. Feeling sorry for myself had become a torturous habit I needed to break. Instead of going back to my room, I settled on the couch in the common room to watch *Saturday Night Live* with the other social rejects. I did manage to laugh a few times but decided to cut out before the end of the show.

Back in my room, I flipped on the lights and felt

relieved to find Debbie gone. I used the bathroom and then brushed my teeth at the sink. Once I had changed into PJs, I noticed a note on my pillow. "Motherfucker. No, no, *nooo*! Goddammit, Debbie!"

The note read:

> *I forgot to tell you on Friday that you got a call from a Travis (is he cute?).*
> *Tonight, you got a very odd call from a drunk man (hopefully not your dad). He slurred his name. Calhoon, Calhill, maybe Callahan? Hopefully, this means something to you.*

It was a damn good thing Debbie had made up with Darin, or I might have thrown her out the dorm window or strangled her for not getting Callahan's number.

I paced back and forth, anxiety roaring through me, air trapped in my throat. I had lost my one and only chance to hear from Callahan. I took a few deep breaths, using the very same technique I had taught Ashley to get her occasional anxiety to subside. *I can always go back to Gainesville again,* I soothed myself. *I can call him at work if I get desperate enough.*

Tears erupted, and I crumbled at the end of my bed. I wallowed in self-pity, sobbing. Then the phone rang, and I froze. It rang again, and I prayed to the god I don't believe in, "Please let it be him!"

I pushed myself up and raced to the phone. "Hello?"

"You okay? I called bef—" Patrick whispered.

"Hey, Packy," I sighed out, dropping my shoulders.

"Where were you when I called earlier and are you okay? You don't sound like yourself."

"Where was I says the disappearing man? And I'm not the one whispering!"

"Yeah, sorry about that. Chuck wanted to show me his frat room."

"I'm sure he did. Are you there now?"

"Yes, and he's sleeping. Tell me."

"He called, and I wasn't here. My asshole friend dragged me to a frat party, and I missed Callahan's call. Can you believe that? And to make matters so much worse, my stupid roommate didn't get his number."

"What a tool! I'll have a talk with your party dragging friend." He chuckled quietly. "Don't sweat it, Jayjay. You still have his work number."

"I know, I just... I want *him* to be the one to call *me*, not the other way around."

"I'm sorry, babe, truly."

"Packy?"

"Yeah?"

"What about his roommate? The hot guy?"

"Home for the weekend."

"Be careful. I'd hate to see that beautiful face all smashed in."

He cleared his throat. "Come to think about it, I think I'll dress and take off."

"You're talking to me while you're naked? Ewww."

Packy erupted in laughter. In the background, I heard a muffled voice and then Packy said, "I gotta run. Yeah, for me too. Give it to me. I don't need a pen."

"I'll let you go."

"Okay, Jay. Don't beat yourself up too much, or me either. Keep in mind that he kept your number when he could have easily thrown it away. He'll call again."

"Yeah, yeah," I said and hung up.

Wishing I had the vodka bottle from Shannon's house to help me sleep, I, instead, tried to visualize my next step. Based on Debbie's note—that stupid fucking incomplete note—he sounded shitfaced. Would he even remember calling me? Should I catch another ride to Gainesville, sit on the bus bench across from his office, and wait for him? He did save my number... I forced out a deep breath and smiled. He kept my number!

"Toly, oh Toly," I said aloud. "Do something! Nudge him. Make him call—"

The phone rang again, and I held my breath, my pounding heart clearly audible to my ears. I cautiously lifted the receiver and said, "Yes?"

"Who is this?" a man slurred on the other end of the call.

"You called me!" I responded.

"I have tis num...ber on a pshiece of—"

"Where are you?"

"Huh?"

"Callahan, listen to me," I yelled. "Where are you?"

"Ummm..."

I visualized him looking around his current location.

"Place ... home ... bed."

I sighed out. It was the oddest conversation I could imagine with Cally. He hardly touched alcohol later in life, other than a glass of wine with dinner. "Good. Do you think you could sleep?"

"Whooo's this?"

"Jayden, your future, if you ever get your shit together."

"Nice girllls should ... n't say ... soap in mouse."

"Cally?"

"Nobody calls me that..."

"I do. Now listen to me."

"Okey dokey."

"Do you think you can sleep?"

"Bad, bad dreammmz."

"Is your roommate there?"

"Sleeping beauty..."

"Wake him up and give him the phone." I impatiently waited for a response.

Callahan breathed heavily, and I thought for a moment that he'd fallen asleep. A knock sounded and then a muffled angry conversation. A loud crashing sound reverberated through the phone. I hoped that Cally had just dropped it instead of his roommate smashing it to the floor in anger.

"Do you have any fucking idea of the time?" yelled a deep, gravelly voice I'd never heard before.

"Port?"

"Yes, who the fuck is this?" Apparently, it was okay for men to curse.

"Callahan called me, not the other way around. He sounds really drunk, and I was hoping I could talk you into making him a cup of coffee."

"At this time of night?" he yelled.

"If Cal drinks coffee at night, it knocks him out. Pretty please?"

"Fine," he grunted.

"Thank you so very much."

"You owe me, whoever you are."

"The pizza snatching vixen."

"Oh, I heard about you," he said with some enthusiasm. "I've been trying to get him to call you."

"While he's drunk?"

"No, of course not."

I could hear him shifting things around in the kitchen and running water. "My name's Jayden, and I have one more favor to ask."

"Good grief, woman!"

I laughed, deciding that I liked Port. I planned to give him a big hug and kiss if I ever got the opportunity to meet him in person. "Can I please get your number? Cal called earlier, and my roommate took the message without getting his number. There's a really good chance that he won't remember this in the morning."

"Oh, don't worry about that, I won't let him forget. He owes me." He gave me the number anyway, which I jotted down.

I made him recite it three times to make sure I got it right. "Thank you, Port. Truly."

"Hey, how'd you know my name?"

"A little birdy told me. He likes a little cream in his coffee but no sugar. Thanks again."

"Hey, wait!"

I didn't respond and hung up. Stunned by the sudden turn of events, I bounded up from my bed and jumped into the air. *Fuckin' A! He called!* Relief and panic fought for equal space in my brain and body. *I have his number, and I hope he calls again, so I don't have to use it. At least, Port is on my side.*

I had half a mind to camp out in front of Packy's door and wait for him to show up. It could, however, be a long night if he'd already made it back. Sure I couldn't fall asleep, I climbed back into bed with *The Shining* and shortly after that, drifted off.

CHAPTER TWELVE

"Come on! Go to lunch with me," Packy whined, leaning against the doorjamb of my room.

"He's got to call, and I don't want to miss it."

"That's why we have voicemail. Buck up bitch and let's boogie."

I crossed my arms over my chest and shook my head. "Can't you just pick me up a sandwich? You owe me for abandoning me last night."

"Fine but just remember, chippy, you don't want to seem too eager."

"Chippy?"

"Far better than CrayCray."

"Hey!" I shouted and leaned forward to stand up.

Packy must have sensed my intention to shove him out of the room because he quickly pirouetted and cackled his way down the hall.

I knew Callahan would be nursing a hangover, but really, how much effort would one quick phone call take?

After I completed all the homework I could drum up for myself, getting ahead in a few classes, I broke down and decided to call Travis, not Callahan. I wanted to avoid another awkward showdown during class on Monday.

Lying back on my bed, I listened to the phone ring. "Stratford speaking."

"Uh, Travis?"

"Yes, who is this?"

"Jayden. Last week's conquest."

His laughter echoed through the phone. "You were incredibly adorable in class on Friday."

Adorable? "Uh, I don't know how to respond to that."

"Say you'll come over and spend the day with me."

"I can't leave my room today. Long story." I twirled the phone cord around my finger, tugging it tightly.

"What are you wearing?"

I rolled my eyes and stared at the ceiling. *Really?* "I didn't call to get together."

"Why then did you call?" His voice sounded annoyed or maybe rejected.

"To make sure we're cool. You were ... ummm ... odd in class. Odd and obvious."

"I think your description made it obvious, but you overestimate your classmates' imaginations."

"You didn't answer the question," I said, shifting uncomfortably. I sat up and dangled my legs off the bed.

"As soon as I have you alone again, I'll be just fine," he said with a flirtatious tone.

The familiar butterflies tickled my stomach, and I cleared my throat. "Can we play that by ear?"

"As long as you sit in the front of the class in that cute sundress."

Can he be more boy and yet adorable himself? "I'll think about it."

He chuckled. "Looking forward to seeing your cute self tomorrow."

The phone chirped in my ear, warning of another call coming through. "I have to go." I didn't wait for his response and clicked over.

A voice cleared his throat and said, "Ummm ... this is—"

Hearing Callahan's voice, I became a sugar plum fairy, dancing across the stage. I floated outside of myself until he said...

"Callahan. Port says I called you last night."

"Twice."

"Twice?"

"And you don't remember either call?"

"No. I'm very sorry for anything I might have said. I don't normally drink and not to the excess of last night. I promise I won't bother you again."

"Hold on, wait!"

"Yes?"

"You kept my number. *You* called *me*. Now, three times. Shouldn't it be up to me whether I want to hear from you again or not?"

"Well, I just assumed—"

"How about we don't do that. Why did you keep my number?"

"I ... I'm not sure I have a good response for that."

"How about the truth?"

"Something about you struck me, and when I went to throw it away at work, I couldn't do it. It's been in my wallet ever since."

"You keep a girl waiting a long time. What made you call yesterday?"

"I don't know. Earlier in the night, I remember thinking about what you said to me across from my office."

"What did I say?"

"Don't forget me."

"And you didn't." My heart soared, and the mice from *The Nutcracker* joined my dance.

"You're anything but forgettable."

"That's what I was counting on."

"How do you mean?"

"Do you believe in fate?" I asked, already knowing the answer.

"No. Not fate or religion, which is a huge beef between my parents and me."

"I'm not talking about God or repentance or anything like that. More like people clicking, more like meant to be."

"After this year, I don't believe in much at all. Work, food, friends, that's about it. I don't want to keep you."

"I want to be kept."

Bang, bang, bang!

"One second, please don't hang up." I swung the door open, and Packy stood there with a lunch bag.

"Your lunch, madam." Then he noticed the phone to my ear and pointed. "Is that him? Is that your Callahan?"

"Will you STFU?"

"What?" he mouthed.

"Shut the fuck up!" I mouthed back.

He twisted an invisible key over his lips and plunked down on my bed.

"Sorry," I said into the phone. "My friend brought me some lunch."

"He knows about me?"

"He's the one who drove me to Gainesville the day we met, so yes, he knows about you."

"I don't know what to say."

"Then let me help you." Packy tugged on the sleeve of my shirt, and I shook him off. "Come to Tallahassee and take me to lunch. I promise not to eat your food this time."

Packy nodded his head in approval.

"I don't know..." Callahan said.

I sighed. "There's nothing to know. I want you to, and you need a friend." My breath remained locked in my throat as I waited for his response.

Packy held up his palms in question.

As if he had to force out the words, Callahan said, "Let me think about it, and I'll let you know."

Without thinking, I said, "Don't think too long. I have

other suitors."

Packy smacked his forehead and shook his head.

I shrugged and waited.

"Okay. You'll hear from me soon."

"Excellent. Have a wonderful day. *I* sure will." I squealed lightly. As soon as I hung up the phone, I danced around the room with all my pretend Nutcracker characters.

Packy killed my high when he said, "He might not call back."

I lowered my shoulders, but only for a second. "Listen, negative ninny, he told me I would hear from him soon. He keeps his word."

"He did when you knew him but—"

"Oh, just shut the fuck up. *He* called *me*! Three times! Count them. One, two, three!" I counted out on my fingers. "And he said he couldn't throw my number away. There was something between us. Who cares if he doesn't believe in fate! Maybe I'll change his mind."

"Okay, okay," Packy said with his hands held up as if I had a gun pointed at him. "He'll call."

"Thank you for seeing it my way." I plopped down beside him on the bed and hugged him. Then I held out my hand and said, "What did you get me?"

I spent the rest of the day on Sunday dealing with my laundry and finding myself lost in the fantasy of spending time with "young" Callahan. Clearly, depression sat as the focal point of his life, and I could totally relate. How could I not? The only difference between us was that I chose to restart my life to have him back and brought the loss of Ashley onto myself. The loss of his baby had irrevocably devastated his marriage and shaken the foundation of his life. None of that surprised me in the least. He shared many stories with me of that particular time in his life—his now.

I fretted over spending time with Callahan. Being me, fucking it up was a distinct possibility. Just my foul language alone could put him off.

CHAPTER THIRTEEN

Monday came all too soon, and as directed, I wore my sundress to class. Even knowing I shouldn't encourage Travis, I did it anyway. Somehow, it made my heart feel better, flirting with certain disaster. It was just a dress, anyway, I told myself.

Once settled in the second row of the large classroom, I pulled out my composition textbook and turned to the section I recently read for class and started to reread.

Travis took the stage, and once again, sat on the edge of the table. He stared down at me and said to the class, "Who would like to tell me the meaning of SOAPS in the context of the rhetorical situation?" He lacked subtly or guise.

The intensity of his attention seemed to reach inside me, causing my heart to beat faster. Although I knew the answer to his question, I didn't raise my hand. Instead, I raised my eyes and met his gaze.

"Everyone get out your books," he said and then mouthed to me, "Office after class." At the board behind the desk, he wrote: Subject, Occasion, Audience, Purpose, Speaker = SOAPS. "If I can't get some participation in this class, you will all write a five-page research paper on SOAPS."

Hands shot up in the room, and I started taking notes. I tried to ignore the twisting in my gut about Travis' request. Part of me thought I should blow him off, but knowing Callahan the way I know him—knew him—he would likely be more motivated by competition and possibly not as scared to see me and be friends if he thought I had other interests.

Class sped by too fast, and I had to decide. I collected my book and notebook and stuffed them back into my backpack.

I only had a few minutes between classes, so I decided just to go and see what would happen. After knocking on his door, I stood, waiting impatiently.

He came up behind me, pressing his rock-hard body against me, inciting a riot inside me, as he unlocked his office door. I, at once, felt warm and yet shivered.

As soon as he shut and locked the door behind us, I said, "You like living dangerously."

"You inspire recklessness." He brushed past me, propelling a frisson across my skin.

"Uh-huh." Doubting his words, I slipped off my backpack and stood with my hands on my hips.

"Truly adorable in that dress." He took my wrist off my hip and led me to his desk chair. Once he positioned me on his lap, he lifted the skirt of my dress.

"Hey," I said, smacking his hand. "What about no fraternizing in the office? Plus, I have a class to get to."

"I'd like to make an exception for you. I *need* to hear you come. I can barely think of anything else. And your smell..."

I shook my head and smoothed my dress over my thighs. "That's not at all a good idea."

"You're still on my lap," he pointed out.

"I'll take a kiss and then skedaddle."

"On one condition."

"What?"

He wrapped one of my curls around his finger and tugged, bringing my mouth closer to his. "You let me make you come soon, right here."

Text to self: *Sitting on a hot man's lap leads to risky behavior.*

"Uh ... ummm—"

"Tomorrow, between your two classes—"

"You know my schedule?" *Holy shit!*

"Yes, I do." Then he didn't wait for me to decide and kissed me. He held my face in his hands, softly caressing my lips until the dam broke, and we tangoed our tongues while hanging onto each other.

During the very steamy kiss, my panties got way too damp, so I pushed him away and hopped off his lap.

"See you tomorrow," he said with a cheeky smile.

I scooped up my backpack and rushed off to my next class.

After my third class, I ran into Packy. "Lunch? Chuck's been calling me."

"Is that a bad thing? Are you buying?" I asked with a wink.

We both got lunch on our meal plans and found a table for two by the back windows.

Packy took a huge bite of his burger and after swallowing, he asked, "What's going on with you? Dare I say you look effervescent?"

I spat out the coke in my mouth and started choking. "Effervescent? Good god!"

"You saw *him*, didn't you? Oh wait, did Callahan call? No, he couldn't have, you would've told me right away. Fess up!"

"Settle down, Pakster! Your turn first. What's up with up-Chuck?"

"Very funny. He wants to hang." He shoved fries, drowning in ketchup, into his mouth.

"Sounds tragic. What's the problem?" I pointed to his chin. "There's some ketchup— Yep, you got it."

"Well let's see, Jayjay, I'm gay. I don't have to wear a

placard around my neck for people to know."

"Yes, Packy, I'm well aware. Your pirouettes give you away every time. So are you worried his friends will beat the living shit out of you? Because I think, that's a realistic fear in this day and age."

"He wants to hang in my room, which is problematic because of Jamie. I'm not sure Jamie knows what gay is."

"I'm certain that's not true. However, I see your point. And his frat room doesn't work either." I looked up into his eyes and said, "Oh, no, don't give me that look."

"Well you know the nights Debbie *will* and *won't* be there, right?"

"Where the hell am I supposed to sleep? It's not like I can sleep in *your* bed."

"It wouldn't have to be all night."

"Not that I'm considering it, but you'd have to use your own sheets and put a towel down and bring air freshener."

Packy smiled knowingly.

"Don't look at me like that, dude!"

"You're a softy. You do know that, don't you?"

I stuck out my tongue, and he laughed. "You didn't ask this of me *last* time!" I said.

"Yeah, well, times are a changin' so you keep telling me. Now you fess up!"

"I went to see my mystery man, and he is very interested in hearing me come."

"Are you considering it?"

"Oh, trust me, you'd consider it if you saw this man. Hot is an understatement, and he seems to have a thing for, guess who? Yep, me. The good thing about it is that it'll be transient."

"Miss Thesaurus, do you mean short-lived?"

"Yep, I sure do. About the length of a semester."

Packy exaggerated a look to the left then to the right and slammed his palms down on the table. Leaning in toward me and with a drunken English accent, he said, "You're a hooker? Jesus, I forgot! I just thought I was doing *great* with you!"

I laughed my ass off, hiccupping and making quite the scene. When I could finally breathe, I said, "I love *Arthur*. It has to be one of the funniest movies ever. Oh, you know ... they remake it in..." I thought for a moment and said, "2011. Ashley liked it, but it's nothing like the original, trust me."

"Why do they always want to mess with perfection?"

I wiped away the tears from laughing so hard. "No idea. Frankly, it seems like they've run out of new screenplays in 2015."

"Back to your hot man and mine?"

"Fine, tell me when you need my place and do not tell Chuck about me."

Packy laughed. "No chance of that. Did you tell your guy?"

"Don't laugh, but yes. He didn't believe me and just thinks I'm a great fiction writer."

"Yeah, Jayjay, you should keep that stuff to yourself."

"Yeah, well. Shouldn't you be getting off to class?"

He glanced at his watch. "Shit!" He gathered up his tray of food and books and ran off.

Riding back to my dorm, I took the time to thank the universe for Packy. Without him, I'd most probably have gone insane, trapped in my new/old world. With him, I didn't feel alone. I found it so interesting that he was changing too. The Packy I knew last time didn't double dip. It was like a code of behavior for him. I wondered why it was different this time. Was it the knowledge of the future or closeness of our friendship? It baffled me, but it was also very cool.

Once back in my room, the usual feelings of insecurity rushed back in. The phone had become my nemesis. I shot it dirty looks, and when it rang, my heart stopped each time. A heart attack lived on the horizon, waiting to strike at will.

"What?" I screeched into the phone.

"Relax, Jayjay, it's just me."

"From now on, call, let it ring once, hang up, and call me again."

"What are we spies now?"

I huffed. "You'll be saving my heart from a near fatality."

"Gotcha. So your room..."

"That didn't take long. Is your dick a'twitching?"

"That's cock to you, missy!"

I laughed. "So when, dude?"

"Would tomorrow night work? Maybe you can play professor-student with your ummm—"

"None of that. Okay. I'll be scarce. How much time?"

"Two hours?"

"Tomorrow night it is, but make sure it's sometime after six and the coast will be clear."

"Cool beans! You're the bomb baby!"

"Just make sure I don't explode. Clean up after yourselves."

"Consider it done."

"Oh, and one more thing..."

He exaggerated a huge sigh. "What now?"

"I'm off the hook for all future parties."

"Jayjay," he whined. After a pause, he said, "Fine. I guess that's fair since I'm putting you out."

"Like a dog."

"You're too funny. See you around six-thirty tomorrow."

"Okay, Pakster, see you then."

CHAPTER FOURTEEN

Tuesday had arrived way before I was ready to deal with Travis, but I had made up my mind before I fell asleep the night before. To save my sanity, I would meet Travis in his office between Beginning Spanish and Art History. He, at least, could make the wait tolerable.

"You showed." Travis' sexy smile set my pulse racing.

"Did you have doubts?"

"You aren't like the others."

I stood up straighter, my confidence growing. "So you've mentioned. I'll take that as a compliment. I like knowing I'm keeping you on your toes."

"And I want to curl yours."

"Ohhh?"

"Lock the door and come sit on my lap." He waved me to him. "You wore a dress. I like this red, flowery one as well."

As soon as I stepped up behind the desk, all of my confidence fled, and I felt truly eighteen again.

"You're adorable when you blush like that." He pulled me up onto his lap, my back against his chest. His hard arousal settled between the globes of my buttocks. He then moved my arms up, so they encircled his neck. Softly, he touched his way down my bare inner arms.

I sighed and settled against him, happy to be facing away.

His mouth lowered to my neck while his hands traveled over my dress and teased my nipples, causing them to stand at attention. Then his palms made their way to my thighs, parting them, so my legs hung on either side of his.

I groaned when he bit between the nape of my neck and shoulder.

His hands trailed between my thighs and navigated

upward toward my growing wetness. "You smell so good," he hummed against my throat and nibbled up the side of my neck to the base of my ear. He slid his fingers along the elastic of my panties as he teased along the edge. They quickly saturated with my juices, reminding me how easily my young self could become wet.

"Ohhh," I cried out when his fingers ventured to my labia and clit.

"Shhh," he hushed. He kissed around my cheek, and I bent my head up and to the side, as his lips closed over mine. His fingers took their time, slowly circling my arousal, while his mouth passionately possessed mine. The taste of him, the touch of his tongue, propelled me further away from my predicament.

Grunting and groaning into his mouth, I couldn't stop the tsunami that rapidly approached. "Oh god, I'm getting close," I murmured.

He continued to tease all my sensitive places. "Let me have it," he whispered in a sultry voice, which pushed me over the edge.

The orgasm shot me out past my body and mind. For the briefest of moments, I was no longer Jayden at forty-eight or Jayden at eighteen, Jayden stuck in a dream, or Jayden in a nightmare. Instead, I came as a woman desperate for relief from it all, and I got it. However, mere moments don't last long.

"What was that?" I asked, floating in the aftermath of my first release since going back in time.

"Fuck, the door."

I clumsily climbed off his lap and raced to straighten my clothes. "Shit, I'm late for class."

"So am I."

"Ohhh," I said, and then broke out in laughter. "You

better get going then. Hopefully, that's not the dean waiting to see who stumbles out of your office. I grabbed my backpack and hid behind the filing cabinet. "You go first."

He stalked over to me.

"You need to go." I pushed against his chest.

"Not before I give you a kiss goodbye and tell you how hot that was and definitely not before I convince you to come—" The knock sounded again, and he ignored it. He forced me back to the wall and kissed me hard, rubbing his clothed cock against me. "Say you'll come over tonight."

"Yes, if you promise to go now. Pick me up at seven at the same place. Now go!" I shoved him toward the door.

"I like you," he said over his shoulder as he casually strolled away.

I shook my head and hid out of sight. A female voice greeted him, but I couldn't make out what she said. After a few minutes, I peered around the side of the cabinet, ran out of the office, and then darted across the quad.

After arriving late at Art History and apologizing profusely, then not taking in a word the professor said, I continued to vacillate between berating myself and getting lost in reliving my much-needed orgasm.

❤❤❤❤❤

On the way back to the dorm, I rode, standing the entire time because of my wet undies. I laughed again thinking about how our short tryst ended and then chastised myself for agreeing to meet up with him later. Oblivious to my surroundings, I almost rode right into Packy, who thought it wise to stand directly in my path.

"Hey!" he screamed, reaching out for the handlebars.

"Whoa!" I skidded to the side. "What were you thinking?"

"Uh, that you'd look ahead of you like a normal person?"

"Right, sorry for almost taking you out!" I laughed, jumping down off the bike. I threw my arms around Packy and gave him a big hug.

"What's that for?"

"For almost killing you, and you're just the person I need to see. Can you come up? I need to change."

"I'm off to get breakfast—"

"You mean lunch—"

"For the average Joe."

"Well," I said, raising an eyebrow, "there's nothing average about you." I took in his green-gray slacks and green T-shirt with a silhouette of a man walking a dinosaur.

"I take that as a huge compliment. Run along quickly, change— Why are you changing again?"

"That's part of the story."

"Well then hurry the fuck up. I'm starving!"

Walking away, I muttered loud enough for him to hear me, "Yes, sir, right away, sir." I could hear him laughing as I entered the dorm. I ran up the stairs, pulled off my undies, tossed them in the laundry bag, used the toilet, and slipped on a clean, dry pair.

Once I arrived, back down stairs, Paki said, "That was fast, Jayjay, but you look exactly the same."

"Let's just say I'm now nice and dry in my special places."

He pretended to retch into the grass.

I patted his back and said, "Get over it."

"Dish, woman." He held onto my hand and swung it between us as we walked to the cafeteria.

"I let Mr. Hottie shoot me to the moon." Remembering how good it felt, a blush warmed my cheeks.

"Is that some new modern way to say come?"

I squeezed his hand. "More like old-fashioned."

"Did you return the favor?"

"No time. Tonight, though."

"So we'll both be getting some?"

"Thankfully, not in the same bed." I laughed.

He chuckled along with me. "Indeed. I'd ask you for more details but have no interest in returning the favor."

I nodded. "That works for me too. I will say, I plan to make him feel good but—"

"Saving the V?"

"I know it's completely ridiculous because I'm not my body, and I certainly didn't save it last time, and frankly, Callahan won't care and yet..."

"Makes plenty of sense to me. You're still in love with him and penetration for girls can be more intimate."

"Are you saying you take it up the ass with no problems?"

"No comment." Packy made one of his silly faces.

"Fine." I tugged his arm. "Let's get lunch."

❤❤❤❤❤

After we had eaten, we parted ways and didn't meet up again until he pounded on my door at 6:30 p.m.

I whipped open the door. "Jesus H. Christ, do you always have to bang like the world is coming to an end?"

He flashed his cheeky smile and lugged in a large cloth bag behind him. "I have it on good authority the world is still here in 2015."

"Then chill the fuck out."

He bumped my shoulder. "What are you stressing about?"

"Oh, you know, this and that."

"I could give you some pointers."

I fell onto my bed in hysterics. "OMG. That's hysterical. Respect your elders."

"Listen, missy, I have the equipment."

"And I've been sucking cock for..." I had to think about it for a moment. "...thirty-two years."

"And I have owned a cock for nineteen years, which trumps all that noise."

"I appreciate it, but I've got that covered. What's in the bag?" I tried to peer inside, and he waved me away.

"Stuff. I promise your place will be pristine when you get back."

I scooted to the edge of the bed. "Do you like this guy?"

"It's hard to know."

"How do you mean?"

"We don't just hang out. I don't really know him. If he had your personality, then it would be a no-brainer."

I threw myself into Packy's arms. "That's the sweetest thing you've ever said to me."

"Don't let it go to your head!" He tried to peel my arms from around him.

"I'm not letting go."

"You're just procrastinating. Get in the shower, and I'll set up in here."

I relented and gathered my robe. "Okay, but I won't forget what you said." With a huge grin on my face, I closed the bathroom door behind me. If Callahan never came around, I knew I wouldn't be alone in the world. At the very least, I'd have Packy's friendship, which grounded me in a way I desperately needed.

Since all my sundresses needed washing, I chose a pale pink skirt that stopped just above the knee and a white crop top.

"That's cute. I approve. Now get lost."

With my hands on my hips, I said, "Jeeze Louise, show some appreciation!"

"Thank you, thank you, thank you, now bounce!"

"Bite me! Impatient much? You don't want our paths to cross? Fine. I'm out of here. Late lunch tomorrow?"

"I'll pencil you in. Jayjay?"

"Hmmm."

"I really do appreciate it."

Smiling, I said, "I'd say anytime, but I don't mean it." I winked, grabbed my fanny pack, and left the room.

The moment I stepped outside, my gut twisted and turned.

What are you doing Jayden?

Ummm, keeping busy, having fun?

Are you having fun?

The jury is still out.

Are you sure you want to go?

Shall I remind you that your room is ocupado, or shall I remind you to shut the fuck up?

Thankfully, that worked. *Breathe,* I thought as I waited behind The Sweet Shop for Travis to show. I paced back and forth for a bit and then settled my butt down on a parking stump. I kept checking my watch half-hoping he would show and half-hoping he'd forget. At 7:10 p.m., ten minutes past the time he should have showed, I stood and wiped the back of my skirt.

Once I shuttled to the front of the shop and didn't find him there either, I wandered around campus, trying to kill time. Depression crept along the edges of my psyche. Being stood up wasn't the cause, per se, because my heart had no investment in Travis. However, without the distraction of the new adventure, all I felt was the terrible loss I had yet to deal with fully. If I had been in my right mind when Toly approached me, I would have never considered it. I wondered if young Callahan would be angry that I abandoned our daughter. Would it compound the loss with which he was already grappling?

I struggled to fight back the tears when a sob caught in my throat. Looking left and right, I found myself outside the classroom for composition. I tugged on the door, but it didn't budge. After wiping the tears off my cheeks, I headed to the library. I stole to the bathroom and splashed water on my face. Catching my reflection in the mirror shocked me yet again. I still wasn't used to young Jayden staring back at me. The sadness in that young girl's face gutted me.

"We're going to be okay," I said to her. I washed my hands and headed back out of the library toward the dorm.

In my own world, I didn't notice the people walking by me until someone grabbed my arm.

"Thank god. I hoped I'd find you."

I looked up into Travis' face.

"You've been crying. Listen, my meeting—"

I knew he wouldn't believe me, but I said it anyway, "These tears aren't about you. Don't worry about—"

He brushed my curly hair away from my face and then hugged me to him.

I let myself sink in next to him for just a moment, wanting the surrounding warmth of another.

"Please let me make it up to—" he started.

I took a step back. "That's not happening tonight. Listen, truly, you're off the hook where we're con—"

"That's not what I want." He took hold of my arm again.

"I need to go. We're fine, okay?"

His mouth hung open, and his eyes winced when I yanked his hand off my arm and walked away.

My dorm room wasn't an option, so I went down the opposite hall to Packy's room and knocked.

The door opened, and Jamie stood holding it.

"Would you mind if I crash on Packy's bed until he gets back?"

"Well, ummm ... I'm not sure—"

I pleaded with my eyes. "I promise I'll be quiet as a church mouse and that Packy won't be angry with you. Please." As nice as I knew Jamie to be last time around, he could never say no.

"Okay."

I hugged him tightly and said, "Thank you."

He gave me an awkward smile and quickly moved away.

I slipped off my sandals, fanny pack, and watch, flipped Packy's pillow over, and climbed under the covers. Although my heart continued to break, I focused on the positives so I wouldn't bawl all over Packy's pillow and freak out Jamie.

Callahan had to call. He just had to. Not that Toly alluded to it, but soulmates must recognize each other on some level, or we would never end up together in the first place, and Callahan and I had. He didn't throw away my number when he had every reason to do so. What I didn't know at the time as I wallowed in misery in Packy's bed, was that Callahan was interrupting Packy's and Chuck's tête a tête with a phone call.

"Jayden," a voice whispered.

"What? Wait! Stop jostling my shoul—"

"Shhh!" Packy grabbed my wrist and tugged me up.

"Where am I?" I whispered in the dark as I sat up.

"You're in my bed. I've been waiting for you in your room."

I yawned. "Okay, I'll go to my room." I climbed out of bed, stumbling over Packy's shoes. "Where are my sandals and pack?" I quietly asked.

"I've got them. Go."

I stepped out into the hall and headed to the other side

of the building.

Packy unlocked the door to my room, and it looked just as I'd left it.

I tugged my dress over my head and climbed into bed in just my panties.

Packy sat down next to me.

"You're still here," I said, squinting up at him.

"I have a few things I need to tell you."

"I'm sure your sexual adventure can wait until tomorrow."

"Jayden, are you okay? Travis called."

I sat up in bed, tucking the sheet under my arms. "You answered my phone?"

"I didn't want you to be mad if you missed a call from Callahan."

Rubbing my eyes, I asked, "And a man answering my phone is the better of the two options?"

"Well, sorry, I hadn't really thought about that part."

"Yeah, well, so what happened?" Sleep had fled, and in its place, stress reigned. My empty stomach filled with an ever-expanding pit of dread.

"Travis called and assumed you'd hooked up with someone else. He wanted to apologize."

"Tell me exactly what he said."

Packy recited from memory:

"Hello."

"Oh, did I dial the wrong number? I'm looking for Jayden."

"No, this is Jayden's room. She's out—"

"Wow, she works fast."

"No, it's not what you think. I'm her best friend and she lent me her—"

"Oh. Oh! She mentioned you. Do you know where she

might be?"

"I thought she was with you."

"My meeting ran late, and I didn't make it in time, and then I saw her, and she was upset, and she ran off."

"Dude, that's harsh."

"I know, which is why I'm trying to find her."

"I don't know. I'll tell her you called."

"Thank you and tell her I'm sorry I screwed up tonight."

"Sure thing."

"He really sounded concerned," Packy conveyed. "Were you upset because of him?"

"No, of course not. I mean, I wasn't thrilled. I was looking forward to the distraction, but I wasn't really disappointed. How did your night turn out?"

"Well, your phone didn't stop ringing, so it was a bunch of starts and stops but, at least, we were laughing about it."

My mouth turned down in a frown. "Is there something else you'd like to tell me?"

"I'm getting there, just don't hit me."

I smacked the mattress instead. "Fuck! Cally called again when I wasn't here?"

"Yeah and he almost hung up."

"Goddammit, Packy! Get your auditory memory thingy going again and tell me exactly what he said."

"Hello, Jayden's room," I said.

"Ummm ... I'm sorry, this was a mistake."

"No, please wait. This is Callahan, right?"

He cleared his throat. "Yes."

"She will kill me, literally, if you hang up. She's out and should be back in a few hours. She sort of lent me her room."

"I'm not sure why I called."

"Because you'll be in Tallahassee soon and want to take her to lunch? Dude, help me out here."

"Well ... Port says I should, but I have nothing to offer anyone else."

"Jayden is the best person I've ever met. She has the biggest heart of anyone I know, and she has taken a liking to you. It's not necessary that you see it in yourself. I'm asking you, begging you really, to give friendship a chance with her. Trust me, she needs it as much as you do."

"You said that to him?"

"And I meant it, Jayjay."

"I love you, Packy." I reached over and hugged him tightly. "Now, tell me the rest."

Once we broke apart, he said, "I love you too. Okay..."

"I don't know," Callahan said.

"Tell me, what do you have to lose other than a bit of gas money?"

"It's not me I'm worried about."

"Then what day and time shall I tell her you'll be in town?"

"Shouldn't I just call back?"

"And make Jayden wait for another phone call? Help me out here."

"Saturday, noon."

"Kick ass! Excellent."

"Damn it, Packy, he hates cursing!"

"Yeah, well you failed to mention that little tidbit."

"Finish," I demanded, jumping up from the bed and starting to pace.

He cleared his throat again and said, "I hope I won't regret this."

"Your only regret would be not getting to know her."

"Okay..." He paused, and I prayed he wasn't changing his mind. "Have her call me to let me know we're on for Saturday."

"I will. Have a good night."

"Thanks, you too."

"Holy shit, Packy! You're the best. Better than the best. You're the bestest!"

Packy cracked up. "Don't forget to call him."

I picked up the phone, and Packy shouted, "Not now!"

"Right. What time is it anyway?" I searched around for my watch and saw it on the desk with my fanny pack.

"It's a quarter past a monkey's ass. It's late." Packy stood up and stretched his lower back from side to side.

"You were waiting all this time for me to show?"

"I feel asleep in your bed like you did in mine."

I chuckled. "That's kind of funny."

"My bed is much more comfy."

"Ha! I'm not sure I'm going to be able to sleep. I'm so damn excited."

"What are you going to do about Travis?"

"Shit, Travis, I mean shoot. I need to stop cursing. Did you tell Chuck about Travis?"

"No, of course not. He thinks it's another student."

"Phew, okay. I have no idea what I'm going to do about him other than blow him off until I see Callahan on Saturday." I twirled around and then collapsed back onto my bed. "You did good, Pakster. Really good."

He leaned against the dorm door. "Does that mean I can borrow your room again? Next time, I'm not answering the phone."

"Sure. You deserve it. I think I'll write to Callahan and

then try to get some sleep."

"Lunch tomorrow?"

"Perfect," I said with a radiant smile. "Sweet dreams." After the door had shut, I pulled my spiral notebook onto my lap and wrote:

Cally! You called. I can't help wondering how it would have gone had I been the one to answer the phone. Would you have asked to see me this weekend? From what Packy relayed, he cajoled you into having lunch with me. Not that I'm upset about it at all. I'm thrilled. If I could love Packy any more than I already do, I would.

I just hope I don't fuck it up with you, mess it up with you. The first time around, I worried about putting you off, and you were in a much better place than you are today. Why the hell didn't I ask Toly more questions? So like me, I just jumped without a parachute.

I need to practice not cursing for the next few days. That will be challenging enough. I can't fathom how I'll explain my interest in you without sharing our future.

I'm so excited but also on the verge of severe nausea at the same time. I can't imagine how I'll feel when you're standing right in front of me. If I screw this up, the life I came back for will be lost. I need you to recognize me. I need you to need me like I need you. Can you please do that for me? And Toly, if you're listening, you better use your magic to help make this work.

By the time I met you, Cally, at the end of 1994, just before your fortieth birthday, you had mostly recovered from the events of 1985. Still convinced you would never marry again, I never pushed it with you. With every fiber of my being, I knew I wanted to spend my life with you, and I was willing to do it on your terms if it turned out to be necessary. You never let on that you thought about proposing to me or that we had a forever future together.

Our intimacy continued to grow and blossom, but it never occurred to me that you had changed your mind. Years, in my mind, had to be lived before you might come around.

I sighed heavily and thought, *I must channel the same patience I had for him last time.* What I really wanted to do was lay out all the facts, as I knew them, but of course, that would just send him running in the other direction. *How do I not push my will onto him? How do I refrain from using the future as a way of controlling the present?*

Things would have been much better the other way around, Cally. You would have known what to do, what to say.

I tossed my notebook onto the desk, slipped out of my panties, turned off the light, and climbed under the covers. With my eyes still open, I lay on my back and stared at the dark ceiling, my brain still unwilling to shut off. *I love you, Callahan, and that is going to have to see us through.*

CHAPTER FIFTEEN

Wednesday started like any other day, but I felt completely different. My chest seemed to expand more with each breath, hope taking up residence in my heart instead of fear. Fate rested in my hands, and I intended to take the reins of my life and guide them the best I could. For starters, I wrote a note to Travis to bide me some time.

> *Travis,*
>
> *I'm sorry I ran off last night. It's true, I was upset but it wasn't about us, or you standing me up (although, don't make it a habit). Life has gotten a bit complicated, so I'm asking for some space. If you feel compelled to move along, I'll completely understand. The girl I crossed paths with at your office was rather cute and seemed uber-willing.*
>
> *If on the other hand, you can be patient, then I ask you to give me a week and we can talk/meet then.*
> *Jayden*

I made it to composition class a few minutes early, climbed the steps to the stage, and left the folded note on the desk. After finding a seat in the second row, I took out my notebook and reread my paper for class while making a few edits. I needed to make time to get to the computer lab to type it up.

Travis strolled out from the right corner of the stage and searched for me.

I smiled once his eyes lit on my mine, and then I tilted my head toward the desk.

He quickly skimmed the note and subtly nodded.

I sighed out the breath I hadn't realized I had been holding. For a second, I almost regretted the note. I had three days between now and Saturday, a long stretch of desert looming ahead without a sip of water. However, my rational brain chimed in: *There is no possible way you could be present for Travis knowing your date with Callahan awaits you.*

Text to self: *Send the drama packing and focus on the goal.*

I had said that a bunch of times to Ashley. She always hated when I did it. But then, I overheard her on the phone one day talking to her best girlfriend, and she'd said the same to her. That was a good day.

When we got scared or nervous, Ash and I, Callahan would always remind us: *Your true beauty shines from your willingness to be yourself. People love genuine.*

Travis had said something very similar to me too. He garnered my attention when he cleared his throat and began to teach.

I did my darndest to focus on the class by taking notes and marking places in the book to reread.

"Don't forget class, your papers are due on Friday, and you will be having your first test on the first three chapters."

At least, I'll have studying to keep me busy, I thought.

After my three classes, I met up with Packy for a late lunch.

"So did you call Callahan?"

"Holy shit, I totally forgot. Shoot, I meant shoot, dammit."

Packy cracked up. "There's no way you forgot to call, and you'll never stop cursing. Give it a rest."

"You know me so well. I plan to call after he gets off

work today. I didn't want to call too early, and I don't want him to know I have his work number. I'm trying to lay low on the stalkerish vibe."

"That's probably wise. Did you call Travis back?" Packy took a bite of his fried chicken sandwich.

"I left him a note."

He swallowed and asked, "Did you end it?"

"Not exactly. I asked for space."

He nodded. "That's a good idea."

"You think? Half the time I don't know what the hel ... heck I'm doing."

"You'll be less intimidating if you aren't throwing yourself at Callahan. Travis might be able to help you take your time."

"Packy, if I fu ... mess this up, how will I ever forgive myself?"

He tilted his head and wiped his mouth with a napkin. "Just focus on getting to know him. Forget the Callahan you knew and get to know this one."

"Thanks, Pakster. That's good advice. So how are you and up-Chuck?"

He pushed his plate away. "We're planning to hang out soon. We're talking about taking the bus and getting away from here. He's into art museums, so we might check out the LeMoyne Center for the Visual Arts. He wants to be an art major, but he comes from a family of lawyers."

I grinned. "You like him. I'd best stop calling him up-Chuck. Do I get to meet him?"

"I'll ask him, but he's not exactly out and he's ... touchy about it."

"I think I get it. Well, as long as you're having fun."

"Indeed. Time for me to take off."

"Thanks for lunch. Catch you later."

After a couple of more bites, I cleared away my salad, dumping the rest in the trash.

The computer lab bustled with students, but I managed to find an open seat. I quickly typed up my paper and printed it out.

After unlocking my bike, I rode back to the dorm. The short ride seemed to wipe me out. *I must not have slept well last night.*

Instead of jumping on my homework, I turned on my stereo and slipped in a Genesis cassette. I didn't take time to undress. I just threw off my shoes and climbed under the covers. Sleep found me almost immediately.

Banging on my door woke me up. "Packy, cut it out!" I pulled open the door and collapsed back in bed.

"Do you know what time it is?" He stood in front of me, staring down.

I squinted up. "No, no idea. Please close the door, the hall light is killing my head."

He reached down and touched my forehead. "Girlfriend, you've caught a bug."

I abruptly sat up, causing my head to swim. "Oh fuc ... fudge, I can't be sick."

Packy shut the door and flipped on the lamp at my desk. "Do you have a crock pot?"

"Yeah, it's here somewhere. Maybe in the box in my closet? Why?"

"My grandma's remedy. I'll need to do some shopping tomorrow. Is your throat sore?"

I sneezed three times in a row and groaned. "A little. I can't miss my lunch with Callahan."

Packy ducked into the bathroom and came back with a wad of toilet paper.

"Thank you," I said, wiping my nose with it.

"Do you have any supplies at all in here? Tea? Salt? Hydrogen Peroxide?"

"Uh, no."

"What about your roommate?"

"Definitely no. I made a promise to myself not to use any of her stuff this time."

He ignored me and rummaged under the sink. "Score!" In his hand, he held up a dark brown bottle. "Gargle with this before you go back to sleep. I'm sure your ghost of a roommate won't mind." He left it on the edge of the sink. "Oh, I have an idea. I'll be right back."

"Uh, okay. I'll be here," I said, pointing to my bed and sliding down the wall until I lay on my back. I couldn't recall the last time I was sick. Maybe when Ashley was younger and used to bring home every cold from Florida to Ohio, or at least it seemed. Callahan would make us homemade chicken soup with tons of garlic, and we swore it always made us better.

I rolled onto my side and imagined Cally spooning me from behind and rubbing my shoulders. Tears slowly trickled down the side of my face. I blew my nose into the ball of toilet paper and tried to steady my heart. "Whoever gave me this cold? I send a pox in your direction!" I wondered if Travis was sick too.

Packy, smiling, ran back through the door. "I got Chamomile tea and honey from Lenore and salt from Jamie. The only thing missing is lemon, and I can swipe some tomorrow from the cafeteria."

Slowly, I sat back up. "Above and beyond the call of duty."

"Oh, no," he shook his head. "Call it self-preservation. If you miss your date on Saturday, I'll have to hear about it from now till kingdom come."

"Son of a mother trucker! I haven't called Callahan! What time is it now?"

"It's after eight, but I don't think you should call him sounding like you do."

I started hyperventilating. "OMG, OMG, OMG."

"Breathe, Jayjay."

"I have to call. Get me the phone."

"I don't think—"

My eyes glared in his direction.

He shrugged his shoulders. "Fine."

Adrenaline surged. "I have to keep it together for all of one minute. Fothermucker!" I dialed Callahan's number from memory and waited.

"Port here."

I held the phone away, trying to clear my throat.

"Anyone there?"

"Yes, it's Jayden. Is Callahan there?"

"Hang on a sec."

"Thanks." Then to Packy, I whispered, "Can you get me some water? The purple cup."

"Hello?"

"Hi, Callahan, it's Jayden." I coughed but quelled it quickly, taking a sip of water from the proffered cup in Packy's hand. "Just calling to say yes to Saturday."

"Are you okay? You sound—"

"It's been a long day." A sneeze threatened, but I squeezed my nostrils closed for a second. "Can I give you my address?"

"Give me a minute. I need to get paper and a pen."

I buried the phone in the bed and sneezed into my elbow.

Packy shook his head.

I shrugged this time. "Yes, yeah," I said to Callahan. I gave him the address, and he repeated it back. "I'm looking forward to it. See you at noon?"

"Yes, and thanks for calling."

"Bye." I hung up and said, "That was a train wreck of formality."

"Yep. You better get your shit together before Saturday."

"Thanks, Patrick. That's oh so helpful."

"Packy to you, missy."

"At least, I got it done. One crisis averted. Now how the frick am I going to turn in my paper and take a test on Friday?"

"I can drop off the paper, and you can call the professor to explain."

I chuckled and coughed at the same time. "He might not believe me unless, of course, he's sick too."

"Oh, then I'm definitely dropping off the paper. I want to check this guy out."

"Don't say anything stup—"

"Not a chance." Packy pulled a box out of my closet and rummaged until he found my crockpot. After filling it with water, he plugged it in.

"There should be a mug in that box too."

"Got it and a box of tissues. Are you hungry at all?"

"No, but I was thinking about Callahan's homemade chicken soup. That always seemed to do the trick." My tears started to fall again.

Packy sat beside me and leaned me against him. "It'll be okay. Have a tissue." He held one out to me.

I wiped at my eyes, willing them to turn off, but they seemed to have a mind of their own. "I can't seem to stop them."

"Don't worry about it. Did you feel sick earlier?"

"No, I just felt really tired riding back here and figured I didn't sleep well last night."

"So you've been sleeping since lunch?"

"Just after that. I typed up my paper for Friday. It's on my desk in the folder—" A coughing fit overtook me, and Packy patted my back. "Okay, okay." I sat forward on the bed. "I need to use the bathroom."

On wobbly legs, I made it to the bathroom and used the toilet. Back in the room, I washed my hands at the sink and splashed my face with water. Once I clumsily removed my shorts, T-shirt, and bra from the day, I pulled a large T-shirt over my head. I felt totally wiped out just from changing clothes, so I returned to the bed and said, "I think I could sleep more."

"Drink your tea and then gargle with peroxide. If your throat gets sore, gargle with a teaspoon of salt in a mug of warm water."

"You're good at this. Have you ever thought about being a nurse?"

"Drink your tea and STFU."

"You learn quickly and—" I sneezed three more times. "Sorry. Now, why do I need to shut the 'eff' up?" I sipped the sweet Chamomile tea.

"I hate blood and guts and throw up, and my family has been pressuring me to get into medicine since I was a kid."

My hand shot up to cover a yawn. "You know what? I have no idea what you're majoring in."

"That, my good friend—"

"Best friend," I said. He smiled at me, causing more tears to fall. I did my best to ignore them.

"Yes, best friend. The reason you don't know is because I don't know."

"When I feel better I'm going to give you shi—crap about that."

Packy rolled his eyes and said, "Looking forward to it."

"Sarcasm much?"

"Be a good patient and drink your tea."

"Yes, doctor." I saluted him and finished the rest of the tea.

He lifted my phone and pulled the cord so that he could lay the phone on the ground by the bed. "Call me if you need me."

"I love you, Packy."

"I know you do." He smiled. "I'm taking your paper. I need his last name and class info."

"It's all on the top of the paper in the right hand corner." I got up again and gargled as he watched, hoping it would make a difference.

"I'll be back tomorrow around lunch time. Hang in there, Jayjay."

"Thanks, Pakster."

Once back in bed, he turned off the lamp and left with my paper in hand.

I pulled my pillow underneath my head. "Toly, if you're listening, please don't let Packy say anything foolish to Travis, and if you could ramp up my immune system, it would be much appreciated. I have to see Callahan on Saturday. I just have to!" I curled up under the covers with a tissue in hand, hoping Toly or any of the other souls in our group were listening. For the life of me, I couldn't remember what Toly called it. "Peeper creepers, help me out!"

CHAPTER SIXTEEN

I slept through most of Thursday and as promised, Packy came to check on me at lunchtime. He brought by a bagged lunch and a supply of lemon wedges, which he stuck in my roommate's fridge. Then he made me more tea with honey and lemon.

By 6:00 p.m., I felt completely slept out. I dialed Packy's room and got voicemail. "Hey Packy, I've risen from the dead. I still sound like crap, as I'm sure you can hear, but I'm awake. Come over when you get this."

I managed to take a shower and put on fresh clothes. It was then I realized that I needed to do laundry before I met up with Callahan. With the paper bag lunch in hand, I settled on my bed with my notes from composition class. As soon as I unwrapped the turkey sandwich and took a bite, I heard the softest knock. I leaned over and opened the door.

Packy waltzed in and sat beside me.

"That was you knocking? Get the frig out of town! You *can* knock softly. I'm in complete shock."

"I thought you might still be sleeping."

"Please knock like that from now on. Pretty please with sugar on top? I guess you didn't get my voicemail."

"Nope. I see you're eating. That's a good sign."

I took another bite of the sandwich and nodded. "Any chance you need to do laundry?"

"I don't love you *that* much, Jayjay."

I chuckled at his incredulity. "I'm not asking you to *do* my laundry. I'm asking if you want to do it with me."

"I'm still good, but I can help you lug it downstairs if you'd like."

"You're the best. Maybe tomorrow after your earlier

classes? Or better yet, maybe tonight because I'm pretty sure I'm not going to be able to sleep anymore."

"The machines will probably be busy tomorrow. Tonight it is. So how are you feeling?"

"Like I was run over by a two-ton truck. I am trying to study for my test tomorrow, though. I'd rather take it than have to make it up. I never did speak to Travis about a makeup."

"I did." He blew on the nails of his right hand and then buffed them on his T-shirt, indicating just how cool he was.

"You've been here for five whole minutes, and you haven't dished? WTF."

"That's still cursing, Jayden."

"Fess and don't keep me waiting."

"He's completely hot, BTW."

I laughed over his abbreviation. "I told you so."

"He said he hopes you feel better and not to sweat the test tomorrow. He gave me a handout that's still with my stuff in the room. I'll bring it by later. That's it. I did ogle him, and he knew it. When you said he was hot, I had no idea you actually meant it."

"You're too funny, Pakster."

"Kind of shocking we have the same taste."

I cackled loudly and then coughed. "We both like men and we both like each other, so why should that be shocking?"

"Good point." He took the chips out of the bag of food he'd brought me earlier and opened the pack. He tilted the bag in my direction.

I shook my head. "Have at it."

"So what's the plan?"

"To get Callahan to talk about himself. Would you get me some water?" I held out the purple cup.

"That seems wise," he said as he filled the cup at the sink. "I don't totally get your stress. He fell for you before, right?"

I took a sip of the water. "That's true, but even when I met him, years from now, he said he would never marry again, never have kids again, and never, ever love again. He was adamant about it."

Packy shook his head and laughed. "You really don't listen to people, do you?"

I chuckled with him. "It's not that. It's just I really enjoyed spending time with him, and then I fell in love. What else could I do but wait for him to love me back?"

"So just like now."

"Yeah, well, except I know him, and he doesn't know me. It makes it more of a sticky wicket to get through." I ate the last bite of my sandwich and crumpled up the wrapper. I aimed for the trash can by the sink and landed it.

"Nice shot! I do think you're missing the obvious when it comes to Callahan."

"How do you mean?"

"*You* know *him*! You know what he likes and what he hates. No one gets that usually. You even know stuff about this time period. You told me he told you lots of stories."

"That's true. He fucked around a lot during this time. Yes, I know I cursed, but even he called it that once or twice. I don't want to be disposable to him."

"Jayjay, just be yourself. It got him to keep your number and to call."

"That's horrible advice!"

"Bite me!" He stood up with his hands on his hips.

I patted the bed beside me. "Please sit back down and just listen. Being myself is how I am with you. I laid out the truth pretty much from the beginning. With Callahan, I have to pretend. I have to pretend not to know the things I do know. I have to pretend to be eighteen, which is easier than it sounds. Cally and I always had this easy banter between us, and it was pretty sexual from the start. On the one hand, I don't want him to dismiss me out of hand because of no sex and him thinking I'm too young. I also don't want to be a wham-bam-thank-you-ma'am and out-the-door-he-goes."

"You might not like what I'm about to say, but I think I'm right. You can't plan this out. You just have to wing it. Let him lead at first like you did the first time. Have fun. Be the fun his life is lacking. Be the friend he needs. Frankly, just pretend he's me with a cock for women."

I rolled in laughter, shoving Packy's shoulder. "Okay, okay."

"You could order alcohol with lunch. That might help too. Where are you going?"

"Tell me what you think of this. He loves lighthouses. Do you think it's too much to suggest we go to St. Marks and have a picnic there? We could pick up supplies at the sub shop or the grocery store. I'm kind of worried if we just have lunch at a restaurant, I'll only have about an hour with him. It might take us that long to get comfortable around each other."

"That's fucking brill, Jayjay."

"Really?"

"Yep, totally. Now you just have to get better."

"I think I'm mostly over the bad part. I just still sound like ... crap."

"Yes, you do sound like shit. No man is gonna want to kiss a sloppy face." He circled his hand in front of my face.

"Come to think of it, I think my mother packed me some cold medicine. Did I tell you that I wouldn't let her help me unpack? It's probably in that same box. Did you see a zippered cloth pouch in there? I think it has flowers on it?"

"Yep, sure did. I'll grab it."

Packy left shortly after and came back later to help me with my laundry. Although I couldn't imagine I would sleep more, I ended up sleeping through the night.

On Friday, I decided to skip my classes. I figured it was best to rest up rather than cause a relapse. I forbade myself from thinking about Callahan and focused on getting ahead in my classes. After my midday nap, I planned my outfit for our date. I chose the yellow sundress Travis liked so much and decided to pull the sides of my curly hair back and straighten my bangs. Butterflies took up permanent residence in my stomach, and nothing I did to distract myself helped.

I only left my room for breakfast and grabbed a bagged lunch at the same time.

Later, Debbie blew in and saw the tissues gathered on the top of my record player. "Good thing I'll be gone for the weekend. I thought I would crash here tonight, but consider me gone."

"There are two messages for you. I left them on your desk."

She rummaged on her side of the room for a bit and then took off without saying goodbye.

Once in bed, I let my mind get lost in all things Callahan. I missed so many things about him but especially his smell. I wondered if I'd get close enough to take in his scent. Would he come back to my dorm room if I invited him? That could be weird. It would be the equivalent of shouting from the rooftops that I'm still a teenager.

Okay gang of onlookers, make sure you're watching over us tomorrow. This is the make or break day, and I need all the help and guidance I can garner.

CHAPTER SEVENTEEN

I ate a quick breakfast in the cafeteria, mostly so I could down some cold medicine that would dry me out. My gut felt like a sailing class practiced knot tying with my stomach and intestines. Fear spread out through my limbs like a spider webbing me up for his next meal.

In our house in the future, we had considered fear the next obstacle to overcome—like a presentation in front of the whole class for Ashley, an interview for me for a new job, or the loss of revenue for Callahan when the economy took the last downturn. "People don't buy insurance or investments when they're struggling to feed their families," he had said. We overcame those fears as a family. Today, I felt our family teetering on the edge of oblivion with only myself to save it or end it for eternity.

When panic pressed in so deep, I contemplated calling Callahan to cancel. Instead, I put on "Changes" by Black Sabbath, turned up the volume, and struggled to take deep breaths.

Incessant banging brought me out of my stupor. I lifted the needle from the album and opened the door.

"You're up early," I said to Packy as he ambled in.

"I wanted to check on you before you left." He clutched my shoulders and asked, "How are you holding up?"

"I'm a mess. It's all too much pressure."

He opened his arms and hugged me to him. "Jayden, seriously, don't do this to yourself." He set me down on the bed and knelt before me. "You have two choices here. You can freak yourself out with the overwhelming responsibility of it, *or* you could see this as the start of the most amazing adventure of your life. You get to spend time with the love of your life. This should be fun."

"Then why does it feel so overwhelming?"

"Because you think you have to be perfect, and there is no perfect. You should keep in mind that your crazy behavior caused him to keep your number and eventually call. And he called back again. It's already happening. It's already working. Trust me, Jayjay, if I could be straight for you, I would. He will see your brilliance too."

"I wish you could come with us."

Packy laughed and smiled. "Me too. Oh, to be a fly on the wall..."

I breathed out a long breath and said, "Thank you. That's just what I needed to hear. Don't go yet." My shorts and shirt quickly fell to the floor and I pulled on the yellow sleeveless dress. "What do you think? Is my hair okay?"

"I'd get rid of the bra and put some mascara on your lashes."

"Okay, brown sandals?"

"Definitely."

Behind my back, I unhooked my bra. Then I rummaged in my cosmetic bag and found the mascara.

"Let me do it." He held out his hand to me. "Most girls use way too much. Oh good, it's brown." With the wand, he lightly brushed my upper lashes. "There, perfect."

After wrapping my purple fanny pack around my waist, I slipped in the mascara, Chapstick, and made sure my license and school ID were in there too.

"Do you have a different purse?"

"It's not exactly a purse. I have a small brown leather pouch with a long strap."

"Get it."

I took it off the top shelf of my closet and handed it to Packy.

"This is much better. Put up your left arm." He slipped the strap over my hand and head and hung it from my right shoulder, across my body.

"It's a bit long."

"No problem," he said and knotted the strap at the top. "Perfect. Now switch your stuff out."

I glanced at my watch and winced. "Ten more minutes."

"You're going to be fine."

After fluffing out my hair, I took one last look in the mirror and lifted the blanket I had set aside for the picnic. We headed out of my room together. As we were walking down the hall, I said, "You have fun today too."

"That's the plan." Packy headed back to his room as I descended the stairs.

I waited on the steps, my heart causing anarchy in my chest. "You're okay, Jay," I whispered to myself. *As honest as I can be*, I promised myself.

As always, Callahan was on time. He got out of the car to greet me. His jeans looked a size too big, and his pale blue, unbuttoned-at-the-collar dress shirt accentuated his startling blue eyes.

Out of my control, I sucked in a breath of air and shuttered as it spilled out of me. I tore my gaze away from his and stared at the ground. "I'm sorry ... I ... I'm just nervous."

He reached for my hand. And in a voice I knew so well, he said, "Don't be. You've given me something to look forward to, and I haven't had that in a long time." With his finger under my chin, he tilted my head up. "You look wonderful."

The blush heated my skin as it swam up my neck to my cheeks. "Thank you."

Maybe I imagined it, but it was as if something in his

eyes spoke to me. "I know you," they said. I smiled and sighed, my confidence growing.

"Where would you like to go?" He glanced at the blanket across my arm, and then with his hand on my lower back, he led me to the tan two-door sedan. He held open the passenger side for me.

I placed the blanket and the purse in the backseat and then wrestled with the seatbelt while waiting until Callahan got into the driver's side to reply. "How would you feel about picking up lunch and checking out St. Marks Lighthouse?"

"Here, let me help you with that." He reached across me and took hold of the seatbelt, feeding it back in and tugging on it again. With the belt in hand, he crossed it between my breasts, waking up my nipples. "Nice." His smile reached his gorgeous eyes, and I wondered how I was going to keep myself from jumping him before the day was over. He settled himself behind the steering wheel. "Great idea. I've meant to check it out."

"Oh, good," I said in relief. "Subs or supplies from a grocery store?"

"Both. I'd like to get some beer."

You hate beer, I thought. Thankfully, I didn't say it out loud. "Make a right and follow it around. What kind of car is this?"

"1980 Mercedes 350 SL. There aren't many in the US. My father gave it to me when—"

Text to self: *She does it again! Foot in mouth. She's going for the record.*

I wanted to punch myself right out. I knew the story of how his father gave him the car as a wedding present. He gave us no such gift when we married. Although I had never seen the car, I should have put two and two together. "It's a nice ride," was all I could think to say.

"Thanks," he said, but the tension had etched his face, making the lines deeper on the sides of his eyes.

In relative silence, I directed him to the sub shop and the grocery store. Frankly, I was scared what might come out of my mouth. Once we were back in the car and on our way across town to the lighthouse, I relaxed a bit.

Callahan pushed in a cassette tape and Tears for Fears' "Shout" began to play—a song I still heard occasionally on the radio in 2015. *A bit alternative for your tastes, Cally.* Bewildered by this young Callahan, I jumped when he asked, "What are you studying in school?"

I suppressed my nervous laughter. "Right now, I'm focusing on my core requirements. I plan to major in creative writing."

"My folks would never have let me major in the arts. To them, those are female jobs, like teaching."

"They must still be stuck in the 50s." *Misogynist much?*

"Like you can't imagine."

I smiled and said with a breathy voice, "I have a very active imagination."

Callahan cocked an eyebrow and glanced in my direction. "Of that, I have no doubts."

I giggled in delight. Here was the Cally I knew. On the surface, he always came across as dignified and conservative, but underneath all of that hid a fun-loving, sex-driven man. I planned to tap into that part of him if I could manage it. The bucket seats in the stick shift car sat close together. I easily laid my hand on his thigh. It reminded me of Travis, and I smiled. His attraction to me gave me the boost I needed to be confident with Callahan.

He looked down at my hand and then back to the road. "You're rather forward for someone your age."

So many responses dared to fly out of my mouth, but I caught each and every one of them before they could escape. I finally said, "I think we'll have more fun if you don't worry about that."

"What should I worry about?"

"How you will afford the gas to come visit me all the time."

A deep, hearty laugh filled the inside of the car.

I struggled to keep back the tears as I laughed along with him. Hearing his laughter, it tugged at my soul. With every atom and molecule that made up my body, I wanted to wrap him up and heal his broken heart. Maybe this was just the start we needed.

We rode out to the coast, driving through the wetlands of the St. Marks National Wildlife Refuge. Lighthouse Road led us to the parking area next to the lighthouse.

"Most lighthouses are automated now, but when I was a kid, I dreamt of being a lighthouse keeper."

Wow, I never knew that. "I can see it for a summer, maybe, but wouldn't you miss other people?" I reached back for the blanket as he grabbed the food and drinks.

"Until very recently, being alone was the only thing I wanted."

Holding back my smile, I hoped I was the *recent* thing.

Together, we spread the blanket out on the grass in the shade beside the white lighthouse, facing the water. We could see a family at the water's edge.

"Would you like a beer?" he asked as he settled down and spread out the food, his knee touching mine.

"Water for me, please. Thankfully, there's a nice breeze off the water."

"Yeah, and the passing clouds help too. Tallahassee is hotter than Gainesville." After he handed me a bottle of water, he used a church key that hung on his ring of keys to open his Heineken.

"That's handy."

"Always be prepared. I learned that from boy scouts."

"Does that mean you're carrying a condom too?"

He spat out the sip he had just taken from his beer. "Good lord, woman!"

"Too much?" I jumped up and wrapped my arms around myself, looking toward the water. *Fuck, Jayden*, I internally berated myself, *don't screw this up, or I'll never forgive you*. Facing him again, I tilted my head and said, "I don't know how to do this right."

After downing the first, he opened a second beer. "What are you trying to do?"

"To get you to like me, to make a good impression. I'm failing miserably."

He chuckled. "You aren't failing miserably. How about not trying so hard? Just be yourself."

I shook my head and sat back down, Indian style. "Trust me, you don't want that."

"Try me."

Not taking the time to think about it, I leaned forward and kissed him on the lips, expecting a quick peck in return.

Instead, he put his beer down and pulled me forward onto his lap, my legs wrapping around his back. He stole my heart as he deepened the kiss. We fell into the dance I knew so well, his taste the salve that could heal *my* very soul. His hands held the back of my head and neck immersing me in his energy.

I had come home again. Tears filled my eyes, which I didn't try to control. Instead, I ran my fingers up Callahan's neck, into his hair, and did my best to merge my body with his. I willed the kiss to last forever, lost in the feel of him against me. His kisses, as always, caused wetness to gather not just on my cheeks.

When he finally pulled away, his brow knitted and he said, "Wow. You have a way with that mouth of yours. You don't kiss like an eighteen-year-old because no eighteen-year-old kisses like that."

I wiped at my eyes, scared he would see. "Oh, you've kissed them all?" I asked flippantly. "Hmmm ... how do I kiss?"

He half smiled over my comment and then answered, "Like you're trying to steal my heart and soul with your mouth."

Worried I was coming on too strong, I said, "Maybe I'm just trying to get in your pants." Recognizing the outline of his arousal, I tugged on his belt.

"That too, but let's slow down and eat." He lifted me from his lap and placed me down beside him.

Still vibrating, I didn't know if I would be able to eat. "That was some kiss, Callahan. Wowsa."

Direct as I always knew him to be, he asked, "Did you leave your bra off on purpose?"

"Packy said I should lose the bra, so I did."

His ears reddened. "The guy from the phone. What's the deal with him?"

Is he jealous? I wondered. I internally did a pirouette like Packy loved to do. "He's my best friend."

"Why was he in your room when you weren't?"

I tried to suppress the grin that threatened to overtake my face. "I loaned him my room so he could ... ummm ... spend time with a friend of his."

"What am I missing?"

"Packy is gay."

"Ohhh," he said with a sigh.

I wished I could take a time out and use my nonexistent cellphone to text Packy.

Jayden to Packy: *All is going well. Really well. I think he was jealous of you! Woohoo!*

"Why do you look so amused?" Callahan asked as he unwrapped his sub and handed me mine.

I squinted my eyes, hoping to drum up a good response. I then recalled my promise of honesty and decided just to go for it. "You seemed a bit jealous, and that's very encouraging."

His smiled turned down into a frown. "I should tell you that—"

I knew what was coming because I had heard it many times before.

"—I will never fall in love again, never marry again, and won't have kids either."

Buying me some time, I chewed a bit of my turkey sub. Last time, I told him how ridiculous that was, but I thought it might be way too soon to say something like that. I swallowed and said, "I can tell something horrible has happened to you, and you haven't gotten past it. Not that I'm saying you ever will. I know some things never get easier to handle, but there is one thing I also believe. You're what? Thirty or so?"

He nodded.

"You could live another fifty years easily. That's way, way too long to go without love. You may not be ready now, but maybe someday. At any rate, I understand where you're coming from."

"This can't be anything more than casual."

Now I was frowning along with him. "Got it." I took a deep breath and watched a Whooping Crane graze along the shore.

"I'm sorry to have killed the mood."

"Yeah, me too."

He pulled me to his side and hugged me briefly.

I smiled up at him, although pain started scratching at the edges of my heart. Impatient as ever, it was hard knowing this was the beginning of a very long row to hoe. *Have fun!* I could hear Packy saying. Easier said than done, Pakster, especially when the one you love doesn't know you from Adam.

"Let's explore the lighthouse. We can finish eating later."

"Okay." I rewrapped my sub and shoved it back into the bag.

He held out his hand to me and pulled me to my feet. Not letting go of me, he led me to the entrance of the lighthouse. As we ascended the steps, Callahan said, "Wow, these stairs are wood. That's unusual."

"What are they usually made of?"

"Metal or cement or maybe stone I would guess."

"Interesting." By the time we made it to the top, my heart pounded hard from the exertion. "Check out this view!" I held onto the railing and looked back at Callahan.

He surprised me by sidling up behind me and grabbing the railing on either side of my hands. With his chest against my back, his scent and energy surrounded me.

I may never wash this dress again. May his smell cover it entirely. I rested my head back and closed my eyes. "This is nice," I whispered.

"Mmmm..." he muttered.

Bravely or maybe stupidly, I spun in his arms, facing him. "Why did you come to see me?"

"I haven't spent much time thinking about it."

"Maybe not, but there's still a why."

"Does it matter?"

"Will you come see me again? If you say you will, it

matters not at all."

"Jayden," he said, stressing the last syllable, a telltale sound of aggravation.

"Oh, no. I know that tone of voice. Never mind." I ducked under his arm, passing another couple, and moved to the other side of the lighthouse. The view was equally stunning.

He came after me and said, "Listen—"

Over my shoulder, I said, "If you don't want to tell me, that's fine."

"I don't want to hurt you."

I furrowed my brow, put my hands on my hips, and then faced him. "What makes you think you can hurt me?"

He sighed heavily. "It's written all over you, Jayden. Your tears when we kissed, for one."

"There's a reasonable explanation—okay an unreasonable explanation for it, but there is one. Just not one I can share at this time."

"Plus, you talked about fate and love, and I'm the wrong man on both those accounts."

"Aren't *you* the one rushing things?"

He chuckled and ran his fingers through his hair. "Let's just say the writing on the wall is very clear and you're young. You still have hope, and I now know what that gets you. I can't give you what you need."

I got pissed. Really, stupidly angry and said, "So let's just fuck, get it out of the way, and you can head on home."

His jaw hung open as I passed and ran down the stairs.

I'm such a fucking idiot. We should have had lunch at a restaurant within walking distance to the campus. That way I could storm off like I really wanted to. I knew I was over reacting, but I couldn't stop myself. Instead, I stomped to the water's edge and watched a school of tiny fish swim in an ever-changing pattern. *Toly or onlookers, help me out! It can't end—*

Callahan's fingers grasped my upper arm and turned me to face him. "Listen, I didn't mean to upset you."

The expression on his face, as if he felt sorry for me, pissed me off some more. "I think you were right." I stepped away from him and headed toward the blanket. "This was a bad idea. You can take me back to my dorm now." Apparently, I wasn't taking *their* help.

"No, wait. That's not what I want."

I huffed through my nose, my palms facing out toward him. "What do you want?"

He again ran his hand through his thick tawny hair, shaking his head. "I knew it was too soon. I'm sorry. I'm still not quite myself."

My shoulders sunk as his pain shot through me, leaving me temporarily speechless. I realized, at that moment, that I had to protect myself somehow so I could stay rational and present for Callahan. He needed me, and I needed to get it together enough to be there for him, no matter how much it might hurt. I took his hand in mine and coaxed him forward into a hug. We fit perfectly together, as we always had. "I'm sorry," I whispered. "Truly. I just want to spend time with you. No pressure." I hoped I could live up to that.

He looked down at me and said, "I'm the one who's sorry. I have a lot of baggage, and it's not fair for me to saddle you with it."

"Let's finish eating." With his hand in mine, I pulled him down onto the blanket. I handed him his sandwich and unwrapped mine. I wasn't at all hungry, but I wanted to try to resurrect the date from doomsville. Part of me wanted to tell him the truth, and another part—Packy's voice really—cautioned against it. Callahan clearly wasn't ready for it—for the truth or me.

As I chewed, I fought against my tears. *Buck up bitches and stay in!* I wished with all of my heart and soul that Callahan had been the one to travel back in time. He would have known just what to do. I was the absolute wrong person for the job.

He startled me out of my reverie when he asked, "What's going on in that mind of yours? Your forehead is all crunched together and your lip and nose are flared."

I wanted to smack my forehead, but instead I tried to relax my face. "I was thinking about how I screwed this up."

"You did no such thing. I mean you're a bit more forward than I'm used to, but it's also rather enticing."

"Enticing is good." I bit the inside of my mouth so I wouldn't break out in a huge grin.

Callahan clucked and then chuckled. "You can smile."

With a beaming smile, I said, "You're like a mine field. I'm not sure which way to step. However, I'd like to figure it out."

He frowned. "I don't mean to be."

"You can talk to me."

"You said that to me the first time we met, that I might need someone to talk to outside of my everyday life."

"And I meant it. I still do."

He swallowed down a bite of the sub with beer and asked, "Why did you say that to me?"

"Maybe for the same reason you came here to see me?"

"Why not date boys your age?"

"That, my friend, is a very long story, and one you won't hear unless we get to know each other better."

"That sounds ominous and possibly intriguing."

"Think more shocking and odd than ominous."

"I'm not sure I can handle any more shock than you already cause."

I cracked up, laughing so hard, struggling to catch my breath. "Oh, that's funny." Callahan had said that very thing to me before, years from now. He'd confessed years later, that I won him over with my unpredictability and spontaneity. He said life with me would never be boring, and it never was. He was our grounding force, and I was the spark. Hearing him say those same words lifted my spirits. Prematurely or not, I thought we might be right on track.

"Something has shifted for you," Callahan said.

"You're very perceptive."

"I'm lost."

"Let's just say I'm pretty confident I'll see you again."

He had no response to that. We sat quietly, finishing our subs. We crumpled up the papers and napkins and shoved it all back into the sub bag. Like we had been a couple for a while, we folded the blanket together and put it, along with the trash and the rest of the beer, behind the driver's seat.

He clasped my hand and said, "Let's walk along the shore before we head back."

My heart swelled with hope. He wasn't ready for the date to end. Frankly, neither was I. I needed another kiss to hold me over until I heard from him again.

Our arms swung between us as we strolled along the water's edge.

"It turned into a nice day," he said.

Please mean more than just the weather! "I agree." On a whim, I kicked off my sandals and waded into the water. "Come join me. It feels great!"

"I don't think we're suppose—"

I walked out of the water and crouched down in front of him, rolling up his pant legs and removing his shoes and socks. Before he could object, I led him into the water. "Nice and cool, right?"

"Yes." He took my curly hair into his hands, and I knew what was coming. His eyes searched my face, and then he lowered his mouth to mine.

I moaned against him, losing myself in his kiss. He twisted the hair at the base of my head, and I grunted, feeling the wetness growing between my folds. I craved his incursion, his cock the perfect fit. I knew I had to wait for that but planned to milk this kiss for all its worth. My hands found the bottom of his shirt and snaked up to his back, touching his warm skin.

He groaned into my mouth, using my hair to tilt my head and deepen the kiss.

I clutched him to me, dueling with his tongue.

He paused, his lips against mine and said, "You taste so good."

"Mmmm ... you too. Don't stop."

Sighing, he said, "I think we have an audience."

Breaking my gaze from his, I scanned the area. "Shi— shoot. Yeah, I guess we should go."

We found a large rock and sat on it so we could put our shoes back on. He used one of his socks to wipe off the bottom of my feet.

"Thank you," I said and slipped on my sandals.

He wiped his feet with the other sock and put his shoes on without the socks.

We strolled, hand in hand, to the car, with my cheeks still flush with arousal. He opened the passenger door for me and helped me in, fastening the seat belt for me.

"Thanks."

We drove back up Lighthouse Road with the windows down.

His hand migrated under the bottom of my dress and grazed my inner thigh, taking me completely by surprise.

Instinctually, I spread my legs, as he traveled upward.

"Wow," he said as he reached my saturated panties. When he had to down shift, he removed his hand.

Feeling emboldened, I asked, "Will you come up when we get to the dorm?"

He didn't answer right away, leaving me to wonder what he could be thinking. Finally, he said, "You said you had other suitors. What did you mean?"

I coughed, choking on my saliva. "You remember that?"

"You're stalling."

"I've spent some time with another man. It hasn't gotten very far at this point."

"How old is he?"

Fuck, fuck, fuck! "Thirty-two."

He glared at me, looked back at the road and shoved the stick shift into fourth gear. Then he said something quite opposite to his normal behavior. "That's good."

"Really? Then why do you look so pissed off?"

We sat in silence, my heart pounding, but I didn't push for a response.

"I'll come up," he said.

As well as I knew Callahan, I couldn't fathom what was going through his mind or why he agreed to come up. Then, it hit me. "You don't believe me."

"Do you make it a habit of throwing yourself at older men? Father issues maybe?"

My mouth hung open, nothing coming out. "Uh ... ugh..." My voice came back to me when my ire reached pinnacle heights. "If you weren't driving this darn car, I'd slap your face. For your information, both of *you* are pursuing *me*. I may have given you my number, but you are the one who called me, and not just when you were drunk. I'm the shocked one now. I never thought you could ever be an asshole. Young Callahan East, I gave you way too much credit. Clearly, you still need ten years of seasoning."

He pulled up in front of the dorm and turned to face me. "What does that mean?"

"It means I wasted the life I had for a fucking fantasy. Don't bother getting out." I released the seatbelt, reached behind the seats, and grabbed the blanket. "Sorry for wasting your time." I got out of the car and ran up the stairs, not stopping until I made it to my room.

CHAPTER EIGHTEEN

As soon as I entered my dorm room, the floodgates opened, and I wailed out my pain. "Toly," I cried, "please send me back, I can't stay here a moment longer." All my hope evaporated, and in its place rested the knowledge that Callahan and I didn't fit together anymore and never would again. I grieved, as I never had before, the loss of Callahan finally a reality. I pulled the covers over my head and buried my face in my pillow, hoping to deaden the sound of my raw, scorching pain.

After a few minutes, I couldn't breathe. I sat up and said in a whispered scream, "I hate you, Toly! You took advantage of me, of my loss, and threw me into the past. Did it leave *you* feeling better? Cause it hasn't worked for me." A stuttered sigh came out of me. I took three tissues from the box and tried to mop up my face, my nose stuffed once more.

If I had been in 2015, I'd have pulled up "I Hate Everyone" by Get Set Go and "Fuck You" by Lily Allen on my cellphone, and maybe even "Something I Can Never Have" by Nine Inch Nails. I'd listen to them over and over.

I thought I heard a sound by the door but dismissed it. At the sink, I splashed my face with water and dried it off, leaving my smudged mascara. At least, I looked how I felt, wrung out and despondent.

A sound at the door again drew my attention. I opened it and found Callahan leaning against the door jam. "Were you planning on knocking?"

"I hadn't decided. You've been crying."

"But you made the effort to find my dorm room? Are you coming in?"

"I owe you an apology."

"I'd say." I widened the door and stepped out of the way.

He tentatively stepped forward and looked around the room. "Have you ever had a boyfriend your own age?"

"I don't want to fight with you. I'm worn out. I'll answer this, and you can be on your way. I had a high school boyfriend my age for two years. Since coming to FSU, I've broken it off with him. Happy?"

"What am I supposed to think?"

Perched on the edge of my desk, I said, "This isn't about my age. It's about your attraction to me that you'd rather not feel. It's easier to focus on my age and not your behavior, which was appalling, by the way. You were right about one thing though."

He sat down on my bed and tilted his head toward me. "What was that?"

"That you could hurt me. You did."

He glanced down at his palms and then back at me. "What I said was completely out of line. You make me want to go against all the promises I made to myself, and I can't let that happen."

"I understand." I nodded.

His eyes narrowed. "Do you really? How could you possibly?"

My heart thumped in his presence. Love and anger fought for possession of the rhythm. *He is not your Cally*, I reminded myself. "Someday, should we ever become friends, I'll tell you. Until then, you can choose not to believe me. For you, it's easier that way."

"The things you say are baffling. Half the time I don't know what you mean. Ten more years? What was that about?"

"In ten years, you might be ready again for love."

He rubbed his thighs, and I thought he planned to stand,

but instead, he remained seated. "There's more to it than that..." he said.

"If we ever become—"

He interrupted me. "—friends. So you keep telling me."

"I'm not sure what you want me to say at this point. Trust me, I was nervous, I just never anticipated it would be so hard."

"What would be?"

As best as I could, I answered with the truth, just not the whole truth. "Being with you and wanting more than you could possibly give. I'm not a very patient person, and I hate walking on eggshells. I end up cracking each and every one."

"I don't doubt that." He leaned back against the wall as if he planned on staying.

Why are you still here? What do you want from me?

"You're scrunching your forehead again. Why don't you sit down next to me?" He twitched his eyebrows seductively, and I almost laughed.

I folded my arms across my chest, hiding my unruly nipples. "I can think of several reasons not to."

Ignoring my comment, he held out his hand to me. I gave in and let him pull me into his arms. With my head against his chest, I sighed into the hug.

"You feel good," Callahan said.

"Yeah, we do fine when we're not speaking."

He laughed, rocking me up and down against his chest. His laughter was the very sound I came back through time to hear.

"I think you might be too young for me, Callahan."

Then he really bellowed. Once he caught his breath, he asked, "Oh, you think so?"

Grinning from ear to ear, I said, "Yep, you still need some seasoning. You haven't been brined long enough."

He pushed me over and began tickling me under my arms.

"Cut it out," I giggled, slapping his hands.

He clasped my wrists and held them beside my head. "If we can stop being so serious—"

"You're the serious one. I'm a barrel of laughs." I struggled to get out of his grip.

"Do I need to tickle you some more?" he said. Words I'd heard many times before.

I shook my head, staring into his intense blue eyes. My heart stopped being angry, and another urge pushed up front and center.

When his mouth lowered to my lips, I let him kiss me. His body covered mine, leaving me laden with his weight and energy. Once he released my wrists, one of my hands found its way under his shirt at the base of his back, and the other traveled to the back of his head, fingers tangling in his hair.

"You touch me in all the right places," he murmured against my mouth.

"Mmmm ... if you turn over, I'll show you I know how to kiss you in all the right places too."

He raised an eyebrow and began to roll over when a knock on the door startled us both.

I sprang up and turned the handle. "Jesus H. Christ, Packy, you have the worst tim— Holy sh— Travis, what are you doing here? Get inside." *OMG, OMG, OMG!*

Travis took in the disheveled Callahan and said, "I thought you were sick. I came to check—"

Here's the perfect scene to write to get the reader to feel, I thought during the madness of having Callahan and Travis in the same room. My heart pounded so fast I could barely breathe. *Lucy, you got some 'splainin to do,* rattled in my head as I held myself up on the side of the desk and tried to catch my breath. I forced air into my lungs and said,

"Travis, this is Callahan, Callahan, Travis. I was sick, but I'm feeling better. I didn't go to any of my classes Thursday or yesterday and took it easy. That seemed to do the trick."

"He's the other guy," Callahan said, his tone incredulous. He stood up with his forehead furrowed and straightened his shirt.

Seeing them together, Callahan stood a good three inches taller, and even with his weight loss, he was far broader across the chest. His anger was palpable to me, and I wondered if Travis could feel it as well.

As if the comedic tragedy couldn't get any worse, another knock sounded on the door, one I completely recognized. I opened the door again.

"You're having a party, and you didn't invite me?" Packy said, looking from Travis to Callahan. Packy stepped forward and held out his hand. "You must be Callahan." He scanned him from head to toe, winking his approval in my direction.

Callahan shook his hand as I mouthed "Help!" to Packy.

Before Packy could even respond, Travis said to Callahan, "Jayden has told me about you."

Cal shot a glare in my direction, his chest rising and falling. Being a gentleman, he shook Travis' hand, his rigid back and jutted chin saying something quite the opposite to me. "I have to guess you're the thirty-two-year-old who's pursuing Britt?"

"Jayden," I said. Holy mother of god, he just called his ex-wife's name. *That can't be a good sign.*

Callahan widened his stance, shoving his hands into the pockets of his jeans and striking a casual pose. His posture read anything but casual to me. "How long have you known Jayden?"

Travis nodded and held up his palms. "I met her just before the start of the semester. How long have *you* known

179

her?"

"The same."

Travis had an odd expression on his face. "She said she didn't know if she'd hear from you, but if she did, she would put us on hold." Then he turned toward me. "Is that why you asked for some space?"

My head spun with all I could or should say. Packy seemed at a loss too, which didn't help me one bit. "Okay, I'm not exactly sure what I should say. I never anticipated your paths crossing."

Packy gave me an encouraging smile.

I continued, "In my defense, I've been completely honest with you both and had no idea either of you would show up here." I pointed to the floor and then I shifted to face Travis, taking his hands. "I really appreciate you checking up on me, and we'll talk on Monday." I led him to the door and hugged him. In a whisper, I said, "I'm really sorry about this."

As he held me, he whispered back, "Are we done?"

I shook my head and stepped back. "I don't know."

"See you Monday then."

Although my gut clenched, I gave Travis a quick smile and stepped back inside the room.

Text to self: *Juggling two men isn't as sexy as it sounds.*

"I should go," Callahan said, although he didn't move from where he stood.

"No, sir, I'm gonna bounce," Packy said. "Come get me when you're done here, Jayjay, and hang in there."

"I'm trying. It's been a crazy day."

"Hardcore, no doubt. Callahan, it's a pleasure to meet you. I hope you come to appreciate our Jayden the way I do." Packy bowed and backed out the door, closing it in front of him.

"Well that was an effed up situation if I've ever been in one." I covered my eyes and shook my head.

"What's the deal with him?" Callahan asked, still standing in his casual/defensive posture.

I plunked down on my bed and closed my eyes. Assuming he meant Travis, I said, "He too is looking for something casual." I glanced up at Cal to take in his reaction.

"Have you had sex with him?" His jaw moved back and forth, the anger showing.

"No. We've made out a fair amount. I did see him naked but chickened out and not because of my age."

"Has he made you come? Have you taken care—?"

"Why does that matter?"

"It matters."

"Once for me. I haven't had the chance to reciprocate." I watched his expression morph, his mouth tightening. "Stop grinding your teeth. You'll end up giving yourself a headache."

"How could you possibly—"

"Psychic?"

He jerked his head, dismissing the thought. "I want to make you come."

"This isn't a contest, and why does it matter anyway. You want casual, and Travis will help it stay that way. Win, win as I see it. Frankly, I thought you'd be relieved."

"Travis won't stop pursuing you, especially now that he's met me."

I scooted to the edge of the bed. "It's not like that between us, and since you don't know anything about Travis, you can't possibly know that."

"I know men."

"I'll take a raincheck. I think it's best if we save it for another time, like when you're not mad at me. I'm feeling emotionally drained, and I don't want to relapse."

"What makes you think I'm mad at you?"

I waved my hand up and down and said, "It's written all over you: back straight, hands in pockets, eyes dilated, jaw clenched. Need I go on?"

"This is the most frustratingly confusing relationship I've ever been in."

Whoa! Did he just say relationship? "Ehhh ... not sure how to respond to that."

"What do you want from this?" he asked, taking a step closer.

"The whole kit and caboodle. However, I'll settle for what I can get, as long as you're nice Callahan and not mean Cal." I preferred Cally, but he was busy being dead in 2015.

He relaxed his shoulders somewhat and said, "I'm rarely mean."

"Well then, I'm glad we have that out of the way. The positive of Travis stopping by is you now know he's real."

He moved right in front of me, staring down. "You didn't mention how good looking he is."

"As much as you hate this word, I'm going to say it anyway. You're my fate. He's merely the holding place."

Callahan shook his head and took my hand in his. "He might feel differently after today."

"Do you?"

He sat down beside me, still holding onto my hand. "I'm feeling stupefied."

"Oh? Discombobulated?" Then, just like old times, a game of ours kicked in, one we also played with Ashley.

"Baffled," he responded.

"Ummm ... oh, befuddled."

"Confounded."

"Perplexed."

"Dumfounded?" he asked.

"Definitely. I have another. Dumbstruck."

"Flummoxed. I'm not letting you win."

I laughed. "Who says flummoxed these days? Flabbergasted would be better."

He smiled. "It still counts. How about stunned?"

I pursed my lips. "Are you stunned? Are you saying I'm stunning?" I shifted to the left and right, posing.

"You're way more than that. Are you giving up?" He shifted his weight on the bed, so he faced me, his knee in front of him on top of the blanket.

"Not a chance. Let's see..." I tapped my lips and then said, "How about thunderstruck?"

"That's a good one. Bewildered."

I slapped my leg. "I was going to say that one."

"Tick tock, Jayden."

Squeezing my eyes closed, I pretended to be thinking. Truly, I willed my tears to stay in place. Callahan had said those very words to me at least a hundred times over the years. *Tick tock indeed*, I thought. "Dazed!" I opened my eyes and smiled. "Trump that!"

"I'm not giving up. How about besotted?"

I removed my hand from his and, staring down, placed it on my lap. "You win."

"Did I say something wrong?"

Besotted is what I wish you were, my Cally. "It's been a long day."

He brushed his hand through his hair and said, "It has been."

After patting my thighs, I stood up and said, "If you want to see me again, call me." I held my hand out to him and pulled him to his feet.

"Will you see Travis again?" He held my elbow to keep

me close.

"Assuredly, I will. He's in one of my classes. What you're really asking is if I'll continue to see him socially. As soon as you're ready for something more than casual, I'll stop."

"We're not practical for many reasons."

"Feel free to list the reasons next time you call."

He chuckled lightly and hugged me to him. "Definitely baffling," he said as he kissed my head.

Enveloped in his scent, I recommitted his smell to memory, hugging him tightly. "Thank you for parts of today. They were nice."

Once we stepped apart, he smiled. "You're welcome."

I opened the door for him, leaned against the jamb, and watched him walk away. I had no idea if I'd hear from him again. The person I needed at that moment lived on the other side of the floor of my dorm.

CHAPTER NINETEEN

*K*nock, knock, knock. "Packy!" *Knock, knock, knock.* "Packy!" *Knock, knock*—

"Settle down, Jayjay."

"You didn't let me finish." I knocked one more time and said, "Packy!"

"You're weird."

"One day you'll see that on a show and think of me."

"If you say so. So, tell me everything!"

I poked my head into Packy's room and said, "Hi, Jamie. I'm stealing Packy for a bit."

"He's all yours."

Packy and I went back to my room and plopped onto my bed.

"I'm ordering pizza," he said.

I handed him the phone. "I can write a check. I'm cashless."

"I got you covered. You're going to provide the entertainment."

"You first. How did it go with Chuck?"

"He's really easy to hang with. He'd never ridden the bus before, so that was a choice experience for him. Some of the people freaked him out."

I chuckled. "I can imagine. How was the art?"

"Some I didn't get at all, but it was cool to hear Chuck's perspective. There was some sweet art there too."

"Any hanky-panky?"

"We made out in the bathroom. I wanted to blow him, but he was scared of us getting caught." Packy shrugged.

"Sounds like a fun day."

He called in our pizza order and then lay back on my

pillow with his hands behind his head and legs over my lap. "Doctor's in the house."

"Shouldn't I be the one lying down?"

"The doctor's tired."

"Ha!"

"So tell me everything, and I'll give you a good head shrinking."

"Overall, the date was a disaster. I can safely say it was the worst rollercoaster ride of my lives."

"That's prophetic. Go on..."

"Prophetic? Ha, ha, ha! It does sort of fit given my foreknowledge. Wait, it's not foreknowledge, it's past knowledge. No word for that, huh? Which reminds me, Cal and I fell into a word game we used to play. It was very déjà vu, only backward."

Packy brushed his hair out of his eyes. "That sounds promising. Did you curse?"

"Well, I was pretty good until he hurt me, and I called him an asshole. I think I might have said fuck or fucker or fucking too."

His eyes opened wide, and he gave me one of his cartoon faces. "Damn, Skippy! You called him an asshole?"

"If the shoe fits and all of that."

"Start from the beginning."

I told him all that I remembered from the day, pausing when the pizza and soda arrived. We sat side by side, eating our dinner.

After Packy had taken a bite of his slice, he said, "Callahan coming up to your dorm room is a great sign, and Travis showing up was just brilliant. Nothing like getting them both riled up and more motivated."

"That's what Callahan said. That Travis will be more interested now, not less."

"I'd say he was projecting. Double whammy. What did you say to Travis when he was leaving?"

"Please pass the liter of coke." I took a sip and then responded, "I apologized to him, and when he asked if we were over, I said I didn't know."

"How does it feel to have two men pursuing you?"

I swallowed and said, "Confusing, complicated, stimulating. I feel like a walking horn dog. I forgot how wet this young body got."

"Ewww, Jayden, I could have lived without knowing that."

"Get over it. Callahan got hard when we kissed, all three times."

"That's great. We expected him to be attracted to your younger self. He looked rightly pissed when I came into the room."

"Oh, that reminds me! He was jealous of you until I told him you were gay. I thought that was a good sign until he started his fucking mantra: no love, no marriage, no kids."

"You knew that was coming."

"Well, yeah, but I thought this would be much easier. I seem to have less patience now than I did ten years from now. Of course, Cal wasn't the walking wounded, and he was more ... stable and grounded, which in turn had the same effect on me. Now we're both just a fucked up mess. He's way different."

"How is he different?"

"He drinks beer and listens to Tears for Fears."

Packy burst out laughing, eyes tearing. "OMG, Jayjay, that's too funny."

"I've never known him to listen to anything other than jazz, oldies, and classical music and the very occasional rock song. My taste in music was far more in line with

Ashley's than Cally's."

"You're right about one thing. We never really grow up, do we?"

"I can only speak for myself and say a definitive no. I had this illusion that I was a grownup in 2015, but back in my eighteen-year-old body and on my own again, I don't feel anything like forty-eight. Twenty-two, maybe, on a good day."

Packy took another slice from the box. "Did you and Callahan make future plans?"

"No. I told him to call me if he wants to see me again."

"Travis?"

"I'll see him in class on Monday, and I have to make up Friday's exam."

"In his office, alone?"

I chuckled, "Probably. Cal asked if I planned to see Travis again. I told him he was in one of my classes, so I'd definitely see him again. I also said that I'd stop seeing Travis if he ever wants more than casual."

"That's funny, the class part. Do you think he'd be pissed that you're dating a professor?"

"I hadn't thought of that. Older Callahan would think it was sexy and a rite of passage. Younger Cal? I have no idea what he'd think." I sighed and leaned into Packy. "The biggest difference between old Cally and young Cal is that young Cal doesn't want to want me. That was never a thing with my Callahan. He said he didn't want a future, but he surely wanted me, as often as possible. Young Cal is fighting with himself and his desires. Maybe I should've waited another year before finding him."

"Like you could have possibly done that? You don't have the discipline for it."

"Yeah, that's probably true. At this point, it is what it is. I'm kind of glad he doesn't live closer. I'd hate to have to see him out with other women."

"That would suck. So now, we wait. How long do you think until you'll hear from him again?"

"If Travis is really a motivating factor then, maybe sooner than later?"

"Does it bother you that he's jealous?"

"Callahan? No, not at all. It's really the only indication that he's invested. If he didn't care at all, I'd think we were doomed."

"Write it all down," Packy said, getting up and washing his hands at the sink.

"I will. Take the leftovers to Jamie and thanks for coming over, Packy. You're the best."

He kissed my forehead and pushed out the door with his hands full.

I stood up from the bed, stripped off my dress and undies and then headed into the bathroom. After a very hot shower, I slipped on a comfy T-shirt and panties. With my spiral notebook on my lap, I wrote to Callahan.

I have no idea when I'll hear from you again. As first dates go, this one was pretty much a train wreck. I didn't count on how my love and knowledge would affect my patience. I can hear my mother admonish me: take a pause before you do or say something you'll regret. At least in the future, you found my lack of filter appealing, most of the time anyway. Cally, I'm not sure I have what it takes to make you mine again. Young Cal is a different animal than you. He's in so much pain, and he doesn't know how to let me in to help. And how can I blame him? I know what you went through before we met.

Would you have counseled me to stay in 2015? In my defense, spending the rest of my life without you seemed impossible. I realize now that I'll never have you back, and that scares the shit out of me. Sorry about the cursing, it just really does.

Young Cal is more edgy and unpredictable. Is it okay that I like it? I thought it would be more like meeting you all over again, but it's nothing like that. Nothing at all. I want him to be my first. You to be my first. Of course, it's not really my first time, although my body might say otherwise. Sometimes it leaves my head so confused.

Toly didn't adequately prepare me for this. He told me empathically that Ashley wouldn't be the same, but he didn't warn me about you. I'm starting to feel like Toly needed me to go back, but for the life of me, I don't know why. Is there a greater scheme afoot than I even realize?

My heart hurts, Cally. How do I say goodbye to you when you're still in my life. It's a twisted wicket, as you would say. Only now, you can't help me sort it out.

I have no idea what to do about Travis. You'd tell me to go for it, but Young Cal doesn't think the same way. His heart and emotions are too raw and broken. I definitely don't want to hurt him, but I most assuredly don't want to hurt myself.

I'm going to stop writing now. I'm just frustrating myself. I love you, Callahan East, and I always will.

I sighed heavily and threw my notebook onto my desk. Once under the covers, I struggled to get comfortable. "Fuck!" I cried out in defeat. I pulled my shirt over my head and tossed it on top of my notebook. Eventually, I settled in and drifted off to sleep.

A soft sound brought me back to the surface. I blinked several times, listening intently. I heard it again and got out of bed. With my arm covering my breasts, I opened the door just slightly. I squinted into the light. "What are you doing here?"

Callahan held up my leather pouch. "Is your roommate in?"

I shook my head, stepped to the side, and flipped on the light as he came into my room. "Did you drive all the way home and then back?"

Taking in my appearance, he scanned me up and down. His mouth hung open, and he seemed to have trouble speaking. He quickly shifted things when he said, "Don't you have a robe? Do you always answer the door half-dressed?"

"First of all, this wouldn't qualify as half-dressed," I said, letting my arm drop as I walked over to my closet to get my robe. "And secondly, I don't usually have men knocking on my door in the middle of the night."

"And thirdly?"

I wrapped myself in my short, pink satin robe and tied the sash. "How did you know? Thirdly, I thought you were Packy."

He cocked an eyebrow and said, "I'm pretty sure you forgot a fourthly."

"Did I?"

"Fourthly, you're undyingly grateful that I drove all the way back to give you your purse."

"Did you really drive all the way home and back?"

"Not quite. I spotted your purse when I was getting gas. I still had another thirty minutes to go. I got something to eat and headed back."

"Holy shit, I mean shoot. Sorry. What I meant to say is thank you. Have a seat, I'll be right back." I waved him toward my bed. By the sink, I put toothpaste on my toothbrush and stepped into the bathroom. I brushed my teeth as I peed. *Holy fucking shit! He's back again. Heart don't fail me now.* It pounded so hard I could feel it pulsing in my throat.

Once back out in the room, I rinsed my mouth and toothbrush at the sink. "I completely forgot about my bag. You didn't have to drive—"

"It has your driver's license—cute picture by the way—and your student ID."

As he sat casually on my bed, I stepped between his legs. "Fourthly," I said, touching the five o'clock shadow on his cheek, "...let me show you just how grateful I am."

He leaned back against the wall with his palms up.

I took hold of his hands and straddled his lap. "You must be tired."

"Not that tired," he said with a raised eyebrow and a sexy smile.

"Good." As I lowered my mouth to his, he wrapped his arms around my back, pulling me in close. With my eyes closed, I caressed his neck and head, catapulting me forward in time. This time, *I* deepened the kiss, trying to force away the pain that tagged along with the pleasure. The odd sensation of twisted emotions marked the difference between my two Callahans.

"You feel familiar," he muttered against my skin, his lips trailing along my neck as he pushed the robe off my shoulder. "Your smell ... I can't explain it." He stopped and lifted my head. "Look at me."

I blinked a few times and focused on his face.

"You're crying again."

"Can we please ignore that? My eyes have a mind of their own." I didn't wait for him to decide. I loosened the sash and tossed my robe aside.

His hard cock twitched against my undies. "Are you sure?"

Instead of answering, I shimmied off his lap down onto the floor and knelt. After removing his shoes, I undid his belt, unbuttoned his jeans and pulled them off with his boxers.

"I guess you're sure."

"From the look of things," I said, staring down at his erection, "so are you." His mushroom head called to me, and I had to answer. I lowered my mouth and kissed the very tip. Then, breathing him in, I buried my face against his cock and balls. My panties flooded with my desire as the need to have him inside me threatened to take over. *Patience!* I admonished myself. *Make this last!* Listening to myself, I cupped his testicles, gently kneading them, as my mouth covered his shaft. I took my time, moving up and down, and caressing him in all the ways I knew he loved.

"Oh god," he groaned. "You can't be— Wait, stop."

I tilted my head up, the tip of his cock still in my mouth.

"My turn." He lifted me up under my arms and laid me down on the bed. "I can smell you and need to taste you." He hooked his fingers on either side of my panties and pulled them off. "Oh, Jesus," he moaned before he immersed his lips in my wetness. He lowered his face against me, his rough bristles prickling my skin.

"Softer," I whispered. For the first time, it didn't feel like my Cally. Callahan had been the first man to make me come from cunnilingus. With my Cally, it never took very long. "Slower."

He tilted his head up. "I'm sorry, you just taste so good."

I sat up, and he did as well. "Will you take off your shirt?"

We unbuttoned it together, and he tossed it to the side. With my hands, I caressed his chest, lightly fingering his nipples in the way I knew he loved. He shifted me on top of his lap again and palmed my full breasts. His mouth lowered to my nipple, and he sucked it just right.

"Oh, yes," I groaned. I lifted my hips and positioned Callahan's cock underneath me. Staring straight into his eyes, I lowered myself onto him, not able to take the full length of him right away.

"Wait!" he cried out.

I didn't give him the chance to stop, and then he didn't seem to want to. "Oh ... ahhh," I grunted.

"Are you okay?"

"Yes. Just give me a second to adjust." My hands gripped his shoulders, and after a few strokes, I was finally able to take all of him, his thickness a surprise every time. His cock convinced me, yet again, that he was designed just for me.

His hands found my hips and, as he controlled the pace, his eye contact remained absolute. "Jesus, Jayden, you feel so good."

"Mmmhmm, so do you."

A look of concern shadowed his face. He paused as his chest rose and fell. "Can you come this way?"

Shaking my head, I said, "Only if you play with my clit too."

"Lean back."

I held onto the edge of the bed and circled my hips against Callahan.

With one hand, he tugged at my nipples, and with the other, he circled my swollen bud.

"Oh, Cal, that feels so good." My hips slammed back and forth against him, wanting him as deep as possible. All the wetness between us helped intensify the incursion.

"If you keep moving like that, it won't take me much longer."

"I'm close too. Oh god, don't stop. Please, Cally, don't stop!" Taking a deep breath, I howled out my orgasm, my sight blurring from the intensity of the release.

"Stay with me. Kiss me."

"Yes."

With our eyes open, we clutched each other close, our lips synchronizing in a dance that I knew so well.

"Don't let me go," he cried.

"Never."

His orgasm contorted his face from a grimace to ecstasy, back and forth, as he shot his come inside me again and again. "Holy heaven of God," he breathed out. Callahan may not curse, but he sure knew how to take the Lord's name in vain.

We both breathed heavily, still embracing. I was scared to let him go.

After a few minutes, he lifted me off his cock and without making eye contact, he said, "No one ever calls me Cally. I need to use the bathroom."

I do. I lay back on my bed, crossing my legs, so his semen wouldn't spill out all over the sheets. When he came out, I said, "My turn." I scuttled to the bathroom, hoping he would still be undressed when I got out.

When I walked back into the room, he was watching me. "Are you staying?"

"As long as I can sleep."

I smiled, feeling lighter than I had in a long time. I turned off the light and joined him on the bed.

He spooned me to him, in the way we'd always slept in the future, skin on skin. "That was incredible," he sighed into my ear.

"I thought we'd take months to get here." I instantly regretted my words when I felt his body go rigid against me. "I know, I know," I said with a slight huff. "No love, no marriage, no kids. Got it."

"Jayden, I don't mean to—"

"Yeah, I know. Let's just sleep." One step forward, ten steps back. That's how it felt to me at that moment. Ecstasy and pain all rolled up into one very messed up Callahan. *I love you, Cally, and hopefully, Cal will let me love him too.* I fell asleep to him lightly snoring behind me.

CHAPTER TWENTY

When I awoke the next morning, the room stood as empty as my heart. Scanning around my space, it looked entirely too orderly. Callahan had folded my discarded T-shirt and had hung up my robe. I didn't immediately notice my panties. My notebook sat squarely on my desk, the cover in place. I felt pretty certain I'd left the notebook on the page I'd been writing on. My stomach dropped, and I scrambled to grab it. *Please don't have read it. Please!*

I flipped to the page I'd been writing on and reread:

I have no idea when I'll hear from you again. As first dates go, this one was pretty much a train wreck. I didn't count on how my love and knowledge would affect my patience. I can hear my mother admonish me: take a pause before you do or say something you'll regret. At least in the future, you found my lack of filter appealing, most of the time anyway. Cally, I'm not sure I have what it takes to make you mine again. Young Cal is a different animal than you. He's in so much pain, and he doesn't know how to let me in to help. And how can I blame him? I know what you went through before we met.

Would you have counseled me to stay in 2015? In my defense, spending the rest of my life without you seemed impossible. I realize now that I'll never have you back, and that scares the shit out of me. Sorry about the cursing, it just really does.

Young Cal is more edgy and unpredictable. Is it okay that I like it? I thought it would be more like meeting you all over again, but it's nothing like that. Nothing at all. I want him to be my first. You to be my first. Of course, it's not really my first time, although my body might say otherwise. Sometimes it leaves my head so confused.

Toly didn't adequately prepare me for this. He told me empathically that Ashley wouldn't be the same, but he didn't warn me about you. I'm starting to feel like Toly needed me to go back, but for the life of me, I don't know why. Is there a greater scheme afoot than I even realize?

My heart hurts, Cally. How do I say goodbye to you when you're still in my life. It's a twisted wicket, as you would say. Only now, you can't help me sort it out.

I have no idea what to do about Travis. You'd tell me to go for it, but Young Cal doesn't think the same way. His heart and emotions are too raw and broken. I definitely don't want to hurt him, but I most assuredly don't want to hurt myself.

I'm going to stop writing now. I'm just frustrating myself. I love you, Callahan East, and I always will.

"Holy fucking shit, you've done it this time." Thankfully, I had torn out all the other pages in the notebook once I typed them up. *What must he think?* A panic attack assailed me, and I started pacing back and forth. "Fuck, fuck, fuck." *What time is it? Shit, just past ten.* "Packy, I need you," I whined.

Breathe Jayden and calm down. Cal must think I'm using him in some macabre fictional story. Now he knows he's my first, but if he doesn't believe the story—and how could he—he must think I'm a lying psycho bitch.

I shook out the contents of my leather pouch and searched my fanny pack. I found $1.50 in change, which was enough for a fritter. I had to get out of my room because it still smelled like Callahan. After shoving all the stuff into the purple pack, I threw on shorts and a T-shirt and raced out of the dorm. Downstairs, I quickly unlocked my bike. I rode until my anxiety's hold loosened its grip and then stopped by The Sweet Shop for my reward.

Inside the shop, I got in line and waited to get my pastry. So lost in my thoughts, I didn't realize Travis occupied one of the tables inside. After I purchased the apple fritter, I sucked in a breath of air when he touched my arm.

"Follow me out back."

"I don't think I can handle this right now."

"Please, just give me a minute."

Never being good at saying no, I followed him outside. "I'm sorry, this really isn't a good time."

"That story of yours, it wasn't fiction, was it."

My breath caught in my throat. I had never been so damn aware of my breathing until coming back to 1985. I coughed and asked, "What makes you say that?"

"I figured you made up Callahan like everything else in your story. After meeting him, I reread your paper."

"It's much wiser to believe it's fiction. Trust me on this."

Travis took my hand, just as I did to him the day before. "Either you're the best storyteller I've ever met, or you're from 2015."

"Whoa, wow. This is too much for me to take in."

"Because you wish it were Callahan that believed you?"

Taking a bite of my fritter, I paused, not sure what to share. Then I told him the truth. "No, I never did tell him. Last night, however, he read something I wrote. I've been keeping a journal—"

Travis let go of my hand. "He stayed all day and night?"

"No. I left my purse in his car, and he brought it back in the middle of the night."

He took a step back and leaned on the corner of the

wall. "Good move on his part."

I frowned. "This isn't a game. It's my life."

"Lives as I see it."

"You really believe me? Toly said I shouldn't share it with anyone." I stared into his deep brown eyes and wasn't sure what to think.

"I read that. Who else knows?"

"Just Patrick. Listen, I don't mean to be ungrateful, but can we take this up again tomorrow?"

"Yes, if you agree to come to my place after school." He kicked off the wall and stepped toward me.

"I'll agree to meet at your office, and we can take it from there. I need to make up Friday's test anyway."

He took my hand again. "Jayden, let me be here for you."

I shook my head. "Everything's so messed up right now. I'll see you tomorrow." I jogged back through the shop, swung my leg over my bike, and tossed the leftover pastry in the outside garbage can.

Back inside my dorm room, I picked up my phone, hoping for the fast ring indicating I had a message. *Yes!* I dialed and listened.

Hi, Jayden, Dad here. Give us a call and let us know how it's going. We all miss you. Beep!

Finding no message from Callahan caused my shoulders to droop. I stripped out of my sweaty clothes and took another shower. As soon as I dressed again, I shuffled across the dorm to Packy's room.

I knocked and said, "Pakster! Craycray at your doorstep." I heard rustling around and then the door opened. I sighed in relief. "I need you."

Packy, in just boxer shorts, said, "I'm starting to feel like a married couple. Should we be rooming together?"

I smiled and chuckled, even though it hurt to do so.

"Wouldn't that be great?"

"I'm not so sure. I don't think you'd let me sleep enough."

"If you need some motivation ... he came back again last night."

Packy's eyes widened. "Which one? Oh, it must be Travis because—"

"Callahan."

"Yikes, trippin'. I'll be over in a minute."

I slogged back to my side of the dorm, kicked off my shoes, and plunked down on my bed.

Minutes later, Packy pushed through my door, which I had left open a crack.

"Dish, bitch."

"Packy, everything is so fucked up. I don't know where to start. Would you believe I also saw Travis today?"

"Jeeze Louise, Jayjay. Lay back and let doctor Packy help. How long did Callahan stay?"

I propped my pillow at the end of my bed and sat with my legs out in front of me. "I honestly don't know. He left while I was asleep. We had sex."

"Holy shit on rye toast! Full on sex?"

"Yep, and technically, this time around, he's my first."

"Oh, Jayjay, this is good news."

"In any other universe, it would be but not the one I'm currently orbiting in. He read this while I slept." I tossed Packy the notebook and waited.

His brow furrowed as he read. "OMG! He didn't say anything? He hasn't called?"

"No. He must think I'm fucking with him or using him for a good story."

Packy nodded. "That's probably a safe bet. And Travis?"

I got up and started pacing. "He believes me now or, at least, is saying so."

"You must be trippin' out of control in that head of yours."

I stopped and faced him. "How'd you guess? That's how I ended up running into Travis. I was having a full on panic attack when I woke—8.9 on the Richter scale, and I had to get out of this room."

"This is probably the one and only time I'd have forgiven you for waking me early."

"Now you tell me." I sat on the bed next to Packy. "I could have avoided Travis and his confession of belief. He said he reread my paper."

"Girlfriend, what the hell are you going to do?"

"Go to Gainesville and wait on the bench for Callahan? Of course, I can't do that unless I go after my classes. Maybe I could get Port's address from his number?"

Packy pursed his lips and moved them from side to side. "You know, maybe Callahan didn't read it and was just straightening up."

I raised my eyebrows. "What are the odds?"

"Slim, very slim."

I punched his shoulder. "Then STFU and don't give me hope."

He held up his palms in surrender. "I'm only trying to help."

"Yeah, sorry, I know. I feel like I can't breathe right, and I don't know what to do."

"It might be time to tell Callahan the truth," Packy said, resting his hand on my arm.

"He's not ready."

"Ready or not and all of that. You can certainly prove it to him. You know his history or do what you did with me. Something from the news?"

"Should I wait for him to call me?"

"Probably." Packy grabbed my shoulders. "I'm not

being a good friend."

"Huh?"

"How was the sex? How are you feeling?"

I chuckled. "The sex was really good, but he needs some direction on the going down bit. He never needed it last time... I felt really connected until it wasn't if that makes any sense. I stupidly said I thought it would take us a lot longer to get there."

"So he emotionally withdrew again?"

"Yeah, and it hurt like hell. It's like I had Cally for a split second and then he was gone again."

"I can only imagine. Sorry, Jayjay." Packy hugged my side and held me.

I rested my head on his shoulder.

"How come he came back?"

"I left my leather pouch in his car."

"That's fucking brill."

"It's only brilliant if I meant to do it," I said with a sigh.

"It's still brilliant to me. Was his cock satisfactory?"

I laughed and nodded my head at the same time. "As brill as ever. He's got it in the thickness department if you know what I mean."

"Too well."

I shoved his shoulder and then snuggled up against him. "Thanks for coming over."

"Again."

"Yes, again."

Before Packy could get the words out, he was already laughing. "You could ask Travis to take you to Gainesville."

"Can you even imagine?" I laughed. "Talk about insanity running amok."

"He does have a car," Packy said, tilting his head.

"Yeah ... no, that's not going to happen." I smacked my forehead and then held my head as if it might float away.

"So then what's the plan?"

I glanced over at him. "Suffer and burn in the hell of my own making?"

"That's the worst idea I've ever heard."

"I'm open to suggestions. Ohhh, I just had a vision of me wearing a placard and instead of panning for money, asking: What would you do?"

Packy rolled over onto his side in laughter. "Jayden, OMG. Instead of saying, 'What would God say,' you should say, 'What would Toly say?'"

"I had another really bad thought."

"Fess, girlie."

"I could announce to the world that I traveled back in time, and maybe Toly would revoke my stay."

In an exaggerated frown, he said, "You would leave all of this?" His hands pointed at his chest.

I hugged him to me. "No, Pakster, I could never leave you."

"Good. Enough of that crap."

"Sorry, I'm just feeling sorry for myself." The phone rang, and Packy and I just stared at it.

"Are you going to answer it?" he asked.

"I'm scared."

"Shall I?" he said, reaching for the phone.

I slapped his hand. "No, definitely not!"

"Well?" He swung his hand, palm up, in front of the phone as if displaying something on *The Price is Right*.

I swallowed hard and lifted the phone. "Hello."

"Is this Jayden?" a gravelly voice asked.

"Uh ... yes. Who's this?"

"Port."

"Oh, fuck," I mouthed to Packy. "Hi, Port. Why are you calling?"

"Callahan is a mess. What the hell did you do to him?"

"What's he saying?" Packy mouthed back.

"Do to him? Sorry?" I held the phone between us so Packy could hear.

"Cal was doing a lot better, he seemed more like his old self, and now he's drunk at ... twelve-fifteen on a Sunday."

"Can you put him on the phone?"

"Look, when I say he's drunk, I mean he's incoherent."

My anxiety ratcheted up again, and it felt like hands were strangling my throat. "Fuck! If I could get there, I would. I don't have a car."

"I could come pick you up."

I sucked in air and said, "In Tallahassee?"

"You're in Tallahassee?"

"I am at FSU."

Banging noises vibrated through phone and then the sound of running water. "Well, you've made a mess. How do you plan on cleaning it up?"

"I don't know."

"He's saying some outrageous shit in his ramblings."

Packy and I looked at each other. "Like what?" I asked, trying to swallow the lump that had lodged in my throat.

"None of it made sense to me. He kept saying that you called him Cally, and he mentioned something like toly and fate. Do you know what a toly is? Then he said something about time travel and a fictionist bitch. He actually cursed."

"Clearly, he read it," Packy said.

"That's so not helping." I shot Packy an angry look.

"Who's that?" Port asked.

"A friend. Listen, I need to talk to him. He read something I wrote, and he's obviously angry and confused over it."

"One thing was crystal clear. He never plans to see you ever again. He said that over and over again."

I broke into hysterical sobs, and Packy took the phone.

"Hi, Port, I'm Patrick, Jayden's best friend. I met Callahan yesterday. We have to figure out a way to get them together again. Jayden can fix things, but only if she has a chance to talk to him."

"Listen, guy, I'm sure you mean well, but I don't think there's any fixing this."

"Then why'd you call?"

"Mostly because I'm pissed off she fucked this up. It's the last thing he needed. He's been dealt a fucked up hand, and *she's* just made it worse."

"Did he tell you that they slept together?"

"Packy! For god's sakes!" I yelled.

He shifted away, so he was out of my reach.

I drew closer, sitting on my hands, so I could still hear.

Port said, "Well ... she's the first since ... uh ... that wasn't just a bar pick up."

"I can tell you really care about him," Packy said. "Convince him to see her again."

"I don't think I can. Shit." He paused and said, "I'll give it try, although I better wait a few weeks until he's found his balance again."

"Take my phone number." Packy recited it to Port. "Let's talk soon." He hung up the phone and laid my head in his lap, letting me cry. He rubbed my back and moved my hair out of my face. "I'm sorry, Jayjay. This really sucks."

"If he hadn't seen my journal, this would all be so different." I hiccupped and cried more.

"It's not your fault. You didn't know he was coming back over."

"I feel so fucking inadequate. Nothing is going right."

"Shhh," he soothed. "It's going to work out. We just have to be patient, which I know is a dirty word to you. As a last resort, you can always write to him, but I agree with Port. You need to give him some space."

I spent the rest of Sunday in a stupor of depression. Just before sleep, I looked over my notes for composition and reviewed art slides for my test on Tuesday. Then Stephen King filled my mind with a story not quite as scary as my own, and that's saying something.

CHAPTER TWENTY-ONE

I awoke shrouded in a mental fog, which stayed with me through breakfast and my first couple of classes. I struggled to pay attention and take notes in composition class, which was starting to feel like the norm. Travis kept trying to get my attention. I, however, did my best to ignore him. I didn't go to his office between classes, and instead, waited until after my math class.

"I wasn't sure you were coming," Travis said when I stepped into his office.

Déjà vu? "I'm emotionally a mess. Can we deal with the test and get that out of the way first?"

He walked over to me and led me to the chair in front of his desk. "You get to drop your lowest grade in my class. I wouldn't worry about making it up."

I took the seat and said, "Thanks, that's a relief." I reclined my head against the back of the chair.

"Tell me what's going on."

"I don't think that's a good idea."

"Jayden, I believe you." He made his way around the desk to his chair.

"So you've said, and it's not that I don't appreciate it, it's just that—"

"That you're in love with Callahan."

"Yes and the whole purpose for me coming back is to—"

"...get him to love you back or again."

I nodded. "And given our history ... you and me ... well? Callahan said you would be more motivated now that you met the competition." I pulled my feet onto the seat to sit cross-legged.

He sat back in his chair. "There's some truth to that. I'd

208

say I'm more motivated by your story."

"How do you mean?"

"How many people do you know who've had your experience?"

I frowned. "Zero."

"Exactly and it gives me hope."

I thought about it for a moment. "You mean soulmates?"

"Yes. Plus, you had yourself a fine time the last time you were in my office. As you said, I can be a brilliant distraction and can help you bridge the gap."

I scooted forward in the chair and said, "Things have changed. Radically."

"Tell me."

Tears started to form in the corners of my eyes. I stared down at my hands and said, "We had sex."

"Jayden?"

I peeked up.

"I assumed. Isn't that a good thing? You mentioned that he read your journal?"

"He told his housemate that he never wants to see me again. I wish I knew what he was thinking. I wish I had a car so I could just show up in Gainesville."

"He lives in Gainesville?"

"Keep up, will you?"

Travis chuckled over my comment.

"I'm sorry." I waved my hand in front of me. "Like I said, I'm not in the best place. Port, his housemate, says I should wait a few weeks."

"I can make the wait easier," he said with a sly smile.

"I have no doubts about that. However, I wouldn't do that to you or myself."

"I can decide for myself."

"I still suggest you choose a new semester student."

He placed his hands on his desk. "That's not happening."

I blew out a lung full of air. "You're a big boy. Listen, I'm going to take off. I appreciate your confidence in me and maybe in a few days I'll feel more like myself again."

Travis came toward me. "If there's ever a way I can help you, I will."

"Even if that means helping me get Callahan back?"

"Even if."

I stood and scanned Travis' face. My gut told me he was telling the truth. "I might take you up on that." I patted his chest, grabbed my backpack, and headed back to the dorm.

Once in my room, I cringed. Debbie was giggling on the phone. I popped my head around and put a pretend phone to my ear. She shook her head, no. *Fuck! No messages.*

I got into bed and stayed there.

Later in the day, Packy dropped by, but I told him I needed time alone. I tried to gain perspective on what had happened, picking apart every conversation and action, struggling to come up with a plan. Sitting around and doing nothing about it caused me to sink deeper into depression.

The next day when Debbie finally flew the coop, I put Journey's *Escape* album on the turntable. I had made it to my Tuesday classes and spent the rest of my time in bed. My bed and I were getting quite close. We had begun to form an unhealthy relationship.

I belted out, "Who's Crying Now," along with Steve Perry when the song came on. Unexpectedly, an errant idea struck me, but I would need help.

Without putting my shoes on, I ran across the dorm and banged on Packy's door.

Jamie stuck his head out, and I was pretty sure I saw

Lenore in his bed.

Good for you! I thought. In the future, I would've high-fived him. Instead, I said, "Oops! Sorry, Jamie. Can you send Patrick my way?"

"He'll be happy that you're up and about."

I smiled. "Thanks!"

Back in my room, I opened my notebook and flipped to a blank page. I made a column for songs Callahan likes and a column for songs Callahan hates. I figured I'd need ten of each.

Having a computer would've made the task one thousand times easier, but I was undaunted. At least, I had something to do.

Likes: "I Feel For You" by Chaka Khan, "Everytime You Go Away" by Paul Young

Hates: "St. Elmo's Fire (Man in Motion)" by John Parr, "Careless Whisper" by George Michael

I heard someone approaching from down the hall, so I opened the door.

"You're out of bed. That's a good sign," Packy said, skidding to a stop in front of my door.

"I'm not technically out of my bed, as I'm sitting right on it. I do have an idea, though."

He sat down next to me and read the lists I had started.

"I'll make him two cassette tapes. I have a few blank ones in the crate with my albums. One with songs he likes and one with—"

"Wouldn't it be more bangin' if you made a tape where all the titles strung together sends a message? You guys seem to be into wordplay."

"Packy, you're brilliant. I'll need your help. I'm not sure how I'll get copies of all the songs."

"I do. I have a friend that has a late night shift for the

campus radio station, WVFS."

"Righteous! Okay."

"What about 'Wake Me Up Before You Go Go'. That would be kind of funny because he didn't wake you—"

"Yeah, I get it, it's just ... he hates Wham!"

"You should put on the radio."

"Good idea." I squeezed him tightly.

"Hey, hey, settle down!" he playfully shoved me away. "Change the station. Definitely no REO Speedwagon. I just thought of one."

"Lay it on me," I said, with my pen poised on the page.

"Don't You Forget About Me."

"OMG, that's perfect. Who sings that again?"

He rolled his eyes at me. "Simple Minds?"

"Right," I nodded. "What about 'One More Night'?"

"Phil?"

"Collins, yes."

"That could work. What do we have so far?"

"'I Feel For You,' 'Everytime You Go Away,' 'Don't You Forget About Me,' 'One More Night.'"

"What about this one? It's Sting, right?" Packy turned up the music.

I kissed his cheek. "Perfect. 'Fortress Around Your Heart.'"

"Add it to the list and switch the stations around. Stop there. What about this? Too romantic for him?"

"Oh, but the words are just what we need. Do you know who this is?"

"I think it's called, 'Do What You Do.' Maybe they'll tell us once it's over."

We listened, waiting.

"Jermaine Jackson?" Packy said. "I wouldn't have guessed that. What about this one? Heart?"

"'What About Love' by Heart. I've added it to the list. I wish we could make a CD instead. It's much easier. You just choose your files and burn the whole thing to the disk. Way faster. We still need to get a hold of all these songs."

"Let me worry about that. Since you now know he likes Tears for Fears, how about 'Head Over Heels'?"

"I'll add it, but I'm not sure if it'll work with the other titles." I copied it to the list.

"How many is that?"

"Eight so far. Let's find twelve, so we can discard a few if we have to."

"Good idea." He looked down at the list. "If he likes Chaka Khan, how about 'Ain't Nobody'?"

"Added."

Packy changed the station and Diana Ross belted out "Missing You."

"Oh, definitely this one. That's ten. Two more."

"What about something from Howard Jones?"

"Ummm ... sorry?"

He looked down his nose at me. "I'll be right back." Out the door, he ran, and a few minutes later, he was back, cassette in hand. "Clearly I need to expand your horizons." He slid the tape in and forwarded it a bit. "His titles are perfect, Jayjay. Check this one out, it's called, 'Like To Get To Know You Well.'"

"Great funky island beat."

"He has other titles too like 'What Is Love.'"

"Excellent. I think we might have everything we need." I smiled broadly. "Should we try to put something together for the top of the cassette?"

Packy moved to the end of the bed and said, "Okay, give me some paper and something to write with."

I tossed him a notebook and pen.

In relative quiet, we both scratched down ideas.

"I think I'm ready," I said, breaking the silence.

He clutched the pad to his chest and said, "You first."

"Okay, how's this? I'd 'Like To Get To Know You Well' and break down the 'Fortress Around Your Heart.' 'Do What You Do,' but please, 'Don't You Forget About Me' because 'Everytime You Go Away,' I'm left 'Missing You'. 'What About Love,' I feel for you? I'm 'Head Over Heels.' Please give me 'One More Night.'"

"That's perfect, Jayjay."

"Thanks! Your turn."

He held onto the notebook and shook his head. "Mine's horrible."

"Come on, don't be a baby. Let me see." I tugged on the top of the pages.

Before I could do anything about it, he crumpled the page and stuck it in his mouth.

"Really? That bad?"

He nodded.

"Go spit that out, and I promise to not read it. Trust me, your saliva is enough of a deterrent."

He hovered over the trash can and spit it out. "This is why you're the one majoring in writing and not me."

"You know, Pakster, you'd make a great therapist."

He chuckled and waved me away as he sat back down.

"I'm serious. You're a good listener, you give great advice and, most importantly, you aren't judgmental."

"I did enjoy my psych class." He flipped his hair out of his eyes in a moment of contemplation. "Anyway, if you're good, I'm going to hook up with Chuck for dinner."

"Amazingly enough, I think I'll be okay. Can you check in with your friend about the songs? Or find out when we can come by to make the tape?"

"I'll see him tomorrow in class."

I stood and pulled Packy up with me. "You're seriously the best friend anyone could ever have, and I have years behind that claim."

We embraced.

"You too, Jayden. Love you, girl."

"Love you back."

CHAPTER TWENTY-TWO

O n Wednesday, when I arrived at composition class, I went to my usual seat in the second row. A card and a single, bright pink Gerbera daisy awaited me. Scanning the area, I didn't see Travis anywhere. *What the fuck is he thinking? Someone else could have found them.* Maybe he counted on me being early for the class, as per usual. Looking to the left and right, feeling very self-conscious, I picked them up and sat down.

Just as I opened the envelope, Travis came onto the stage. Students began to fill in the rows of seats all around me as he smiled in my direction.

Instead of smiling back, I grimaced. For some reason, I felt annoyed. When the card slid out, my mood transformed. I cracked up when I saw the front. A St. Bernard with sad brown eyes wore a knitted cap and a first aid kit around his neck. Inside it read:

No matter the challenge you face,
I'll be right beside you with supplies.
Travis

In the bottom right corner, he had drawn a bottle of wine and two glasses.

When I glanced up, he smiled down at me. I couldn't deny his appeal and the sweet gesture. "Thank you," I mouthed.

He winked and began teaching the class. "Do not forget that your narrative is due on Friday. Write either a personal essay that's very personal or combines reporting and a personal story, or an essay on an observation, or something from your past. A cliffhanger is acceptable. You, my good students, must be the focal point of the story. You can find more about the essay in your syllabus for those who haven't tossed theirs."

The class chuckled, and Travis went on teaching more about writing a narrative.

I managed to stay upbeat through my classes and actually stayed focused. At the cafeteria, I grabbed lunch to go and headed back to the dorm. Once there, I filled my purple cup with water and cut the stem of the flower. It looked nice on the top shelf of my desk.

I still hadn't written my paper for Friday and had other work to get done. The fact that there were no messages on the phone didn't send me for a loop. I had the cassette tape to look forward to, which reminded me to get Port's address. On a whim, I called his place.

"Port's in," he said when he answered the phone.

"Hi, Port, it's Jayden. Is Callahan doing any better?"

"He's gone to work every day this week and hasn't had a drink since Sunday. However, he's still in caveman mode."

"Caveman mode? What does that mean?"

"He's not talking."

"Oh, cocooning. That's what we—I mean, I call it. The reason I called..."

"Yes."

"Can I get your address? I want to send something to Callahan." He paused, and I held my breath. *Just say yes!*

"Listen, I don't think—"

"Help me out here. I know you care for Callahan, and so do I. I think this will help."

He sighed and said, "Okay, but don't make me regret it."

"I promise you, I won't."

He recited his address and hung up.

Next, I had to decide what to write for Friday. Something from the past gave me a whole range of ideas, but I wasn't sure what my heart could deal with dredging up. I missed Ashley so much I decided to write about getting pregnant. Being pregnant with her was one of the biggest joys of my life, something I very much looked forward to repeating. That is if I ever got Cal to come around. I started the paper:

Callahan and Jayden never set out to have children. Given his past, Callahan never planned to be a father. Jayden wanted kids, but she wanted Callahan more. Her mother struggled for years to get pregnant. And like her mom, Jayden's erratic menstrual cycle made it highly unlikely that she would get pregnant.

It took Jayden's mother six years to get pregnant after having her, and that was with hormone shots and the works. The upside, as Jayden saw it, was she didn't have to worry about birth control, like all of her girlfriends. She heard stories of bloating, acne, and depression and felt grateful not to have to do that to herself. She also figured Shannon, her younger sister, would have kids, and Jayden planned to be the best auntie ever.

More than a year after Jayden and Callahan got married, Jayden looked in the mirror and didn't quite recognize her reflection.

"Cally," she called out. "Come here."

"What is it?" he asked.

"Do I look different to you?"

"No. Same ole Jayden," he said and then spanked her butt.

"Hey," Jayden said, chuckling. She grabbed his wrist. "I'm serious. I look totally different to myself."

He gave her an odd look and walked out of the bathroom. Callahan cocooned for a few days, being introverted and not speaking much. Jayden had gotten used to his different moods and didn't worry too much about it. When he came out of it, he usually had something insightful to share. His distance lasted longer than usual, and Jayden began to lose patience.

She cornered him in the den. "Callahan, you have to tell me what's going on. I need to talk to you. Something is going on with me, and I'm starting to get concerned."

"You're pregnant."

"I'm what? No, you must be wrong. I just think I have the flu or a cold."

He gave Jayden a look she'd only seen a few times, and she didn't like at all.

"What? Wait! I can't be pregnant. I haven't had a period in months. Don't look at me like that."

"Like what?"

"Like I've done something to you. Something horrible."

"If the shoe fits..."

Jayden stepped over to him and knelt down beside the recliner. "I'm sure it's just a cold. I'll call my doctor and find out."

"I can't go through this again."

A couple of days later, her doctor confirmed it. Jayden was indeed pregnant. She felt dread and joy in equal measure. On the way home, she struggled to come up with something to say to Callahan. She loved him so much and didn't want to cause him any pain, and yet she knew it was unavoidable.

Jayden waited for him to come home from work. At the dining table, she read her students' papers and graded them. She felt knotted up but kept making herself take deep breaths, not wanting to deny her baby the needed oxygen. She sensed him before he spoke and she tilted her head up.

"So?" he asked.

"I'm pregnant."

"How long?"

"Because I'm so irregular, the doctor won't know for sure until I have a sonogram. She suspects around six weeks. Do you plan to continue ignoring me?" She hated his tortured expression especially since he wouldn't allow her to soothe it.

"Jayden, you told me this wasn't something I needed to worry about. I feel..."

"Say it."

"Tricked."

"So you think I got pregnant behind your back on purpose?"

"Yes."

"Wow. I don't know what to say."

They both stared at each other, at a loss for words.

Jayden broke the silence. "I thought you knew me better than that. I never thought I'd get pregnant, but I will not terminate our baby. You need to decide what you're going to do. Let me know when you do." She gathered her papers and left him standing there.

Remembering the past, tore at my soul. That was the hardest time in our relationship, but fortunately, it only lasted a few weeks. He came around by the time I had the sonogram, where we found out I was ten weeks pregnant. I looked down and touched my stomach, recalling how it felt to have Ashley inside me.

I had to get Callahan back. I just had to.

Just before dinner, Packy poked his head into my room.

"Jack's working at the radio station at 2 a.m. on Saturday and says he's happy to help. Give me those blank tapes you have."

"Two?"

"Yeah, an extra one just in case."

I took out the liner of one so I could write out what I wanted it to say and handed Packy the two cassettes and the song list. "Please tell him they need to be in this order."

"Will do. Up for some dinner?"

"I think I'll pass. I still have half of my lunch sandwich. I'm craving a chocolate shake, though."

"Chocolate shakes and fries! Let's do that soon."

"Deal. Thanks, Packy."

He stepped inside and said, "Who's the flower from?"

"Pretty, right? It's from Travis. That man likes living on the edge. He left it on my seat in class along with a card."

"Let me see."

I pulled the card out of my backpack and handed it to him.

"Oh, I like him. This is too funny. Love the dog."

I smiled. "I almost forgot! I called Port and got his address."

"How's our boy?"

"Cocooning or cave-manning. Take your pick. He's going to work and not drinking, so that's a good sign."

"Hopefully, you'll be able to send the tape out on Monday. Call me if you need me—after noon, of course." He made one of his silly faces and took off.

CHAPTER TWENTY-THREE

By Friday and still no phone call from Callahan, I agreed to have dinner with Travis.

"Just dinner," I said after everyone filed out of class.

"I understand. I can't wait to read your paper. I have yours on the top." His warm smile made him look ten years younger. "Pick you up at the usual spot?"

He seemed so eager I had a hard time not smiling back. "What time?"

"Six. It's a bit of a drive."

I figured he wanted us to be away from the campus. "Okay. See you then."

Once my classes ended for the day and I made it back to the dorm, I piled all my laundry together and hauled it down to the basement, along with Stephen King's *The Shining*. It was no easy feat. That darn hardback book weighed a ton. Thankfully, I found an empty machine and shoved all of my darks in, putting coins into the slot and pouring in the detergent. I started it up and then sat in one of the uncomfortable plastic chairs to wait.

I startled when a young guy in a red T-shirt leaned over my shoulder and glanced at my book. "Better than the movie, right?"

I peered up at a boy Ashley and Packy might appreciate. "The movie scared me plenty. Reading the book alone in my dorm room at night ... far more frightening."

"No roommate?" He slid his hands into his jean's pockets and shuffled his feet.

"Scarce roommate."

"Lucky you. Mine's a complete pain in the ass, and his socks are hazardous waste."

I laughed, and he joined in with me.

"Well listen, if you ever need some company—"

My mouth dropped open for a second and then I said, "I'm truly flattered, but my heart is already taken."

"Well, then, I hope he deserves it."

"Yeah, me too."

His comment left me wondering about Callahan. Cally and I always wished we'd met sooner, but we didn't take the reality of the situation into consideration, just the romance of it. Maybe Cal wouldn't be ready for me for another ten years. It made me sick to my stomach to think that way, especially given that I could have chosen to go back to the very year we met. I had always believed that having choices made life easier. Jayden, back in 1985, no longer thought so.

❤❤❤❤❤

At 5:30 p.m., dressed in my nicest dark jeans and a purple blouse, I picked up the phone and called home.

"Hello," I heard my father's voice say.

"Hi, Dad. It's your wayward daughter."

"I'd say. We were talking about sending out a search party to bring you back home. How's it going up there?"

"Everything's great. My classes are fun for the most part, and I'm keeping up on my work." I perched on the edge of the desk and noticed the time.

"Have you seen Rider at all?"

"No, Dad, we don't see each other anymore. I don't have a lot of time because I'm going out to dinner with some friends, and I have to leave in a few minutes. Are Mom and Sweet Pea around?" As I spoke, I tossed the wilted flower from Travis and cleaned out the cup.

"Mom's listening in now, and your sister is sleeping out tonight."

"Hi, Mom! Miss you guys."

"We miss you too. Did you get the package?"

"Shit, I mean, shoot. I haven't been to the mail center. I plan to go by there on Monday."

"Are you eating enough? Do you have enough money?" Mom asked.

"Everything here is great. I love you guys."

"We love you too," they both said.

"Please call us again soon when you have longer to talk," Mom said. "Shannon will be sad she missed you. You might have mail from her as well."

"Okay, will do. I've got to run. Bye."

Last time, talking to my family felt more like an annoyance. However, this time, it pulled at my heart. Thirty years from now, my parents are both struggling with aging and health issues. Hearing them sound so vibrant made me wish I could hold time static for them. Now that I was back and really forty-eight, I couldn't exactly be myself with them anymore, which was still a far improvement from the ungrateful teen they dealt with the first time.

I pushed off the desk, checked to make sure I had my ID in my pocket, and headed out.

Walking toward The Sweet Shop, half of me wished to be stuck in my dorm room and the other, more controlling half, needed to be out of there. I tread a precarious path with Travis, and I knew it. In some ways, I used him as a security blanket, and it didn't leave me feeling great about myself. I also recognized that he was an adult and had all the facts. It wasn't as if I hid anything from him. However, people don't always make the best decisions for themselves.

Text to self: *Case in point. YOU!*

"Yeah, well..."

"Talking to yourself I see." Waiting for me, Travis

rested against the side of his car. The convertible top was up this time. He held his arms open, and I stepped into them. I missed hugs, and his were great. "No dress this time? You're denying me a view of your sexy legs."

"Strategic."

He chuckled. "Ready to go?" he asked, opening the passenger door for me.

Inside the car, I strapped myself in, thinking of Callahan's finicky seatbelt. *Please be okay, Cal.* I shook off the sadness and asked, "Where are we going?"

"It's a surprise."

"Uh ... okay." I sat back and tried to relax, relieved that Travis didn't put his hand on my leg.

He pulled out of the parking lot. "So, I read your paper."

"And what did you think?"

"It was good. It definitely met the assignment criteria, and I felt it. I will say your words are more powerful when written in first person rather than narrative. So what ended up happening?"

I scrunched my forehead. "How do you mean? With Callahan now or then?"

"Then."

"He begrudgingly went to the sonogram with me, and he transformed when he saw Ashley on the screen. I also pointed out that my mother never miscarried. It just took her years to conceive me and then my sister."

"And that was it?"

I shifted to face him. "Oh, he hovered a lot, sometimes too much, but I understood. There were no complications with the pregnancy, and against his wishes, I had a natural childbirth."

"What did he want you to do?"

"C-section, all nicely scheduled with an epidural. We

had a big row over that."

"I bet."

"I said I was unwilling to live in the past—his past—which is kind of funny when you think about it because that's exactly what I'm doing now. Anyway, I wanted to be awake and present for the birth. After we had Ash, he expressed his gratitude for being there for the birth, even though it scared him. I honestly believe that if I had opted for the surgery, he'd still have had to carry around some of his demons. He was a different man after that. More at ease. I think he forgave himself, although he had nothing to do with the cause."

"What was wrong with his first wife?"

"Preeclampsia. Unfortunately, hers started early, and even with all the bed rest, she lost the baby."

"That's very sad."

"Yeah, and the now Cal is still very steeped in it. I should've come back ten years later."

He glanced at me and then said, "I disagree."

"Why, because we met?"

A smile played at his lips. "I'd be lying if I said that wasn't part of it. I meant it for his sake. He doesn't know it, but you're exactly what he needs."

I opened my mouth and then closed it. "Uh, how so?"

"As someone who went through a divorce and completely lost hope for a while, you have an astonishing way of bringing hope back." His eyes shined in my direction.

"Please don't fall in love with me. I'd hate to give you your hope back and then steal it away again."

He belly laughed. "You are very bold, Jayden." He patted my thigh and said, "Don't worry about me. I'm happy to be a part of your journey. I've started writing again."

"You have?" I clapped. "That's exciting. What's it

about?"

"You."

"Me?" I rubbed my forehead and swallowed hard. "How so?"

"It's a love story. *The Resurrection of Hope*. The main female character is named Hope."

"Clever title. As you know, I'm writing my own story."

"Don't worry, it's not your story. Let's just say you're my muse, and she was desperately needed. I haven't felt this good in years."

"That's great." It felt amazing to have a positive impact on someone's life, especially since I had anything but on Callahan.

"Were you really a teacher?"

"High School English. I bounced around over the years to different schools. The petty politics associated with teaching made it more challenging to like."

"Preaching to the choir on that."

"I'm planning to avoid it this time around if I can." Looking out at the scenery, I didn't recognize the area. Lots of water and trees lined the sides of the road. "Where are we heading?"

He glanced over and said, "Ever been to Cedar Key?"

"I haven't. How much longer until we get there? There doesn't seem to be much out here."

"Nervous?"

"Is part of your story dumping Hope into the Gulf of Mexico?"

Travis cracked up and smacked the steering wheel. "You know, Jayden, you sure do have a twisted mind. That'll come in handy in your writing. Our dinner tonight is to celebrate my awakened soul."

"It's interesting because this time around, I'm more

aware of how I impact other's lives. Last time, I didn't think what I did mattered to anyone. Not until I'd met Cally, and we had Ashley. The only exception to that was my sister Shannon. Do you really feel like you're more awake now?"

"Aren't you?" he asked.

"Let me think about that one. I still don't quite get why you believe me. Knowing Callahan is real can't be—"

"There's more to it, but you weren't in a good place the last time we spoke of it."

"Tell me, we've got time."

"It was more than one thing that led me to consider you were telling the truth. Callahan mentioned his ex-wife's name. When I reread the paper, you had written her name, Britt. There was no way, given your brief encounter in Gainesville, that he would have mentioned her or anything about his life. He also confirmed that he met you around the same time I did. How could you be so desperate and in love with him that fast? It certainly doesn't fit with the personality I've observed."

I smacked my forehead. "Fuck, I forgot he called me Britt. That's a really bad sign."

"To the contrary, it's a very good sign."

"How do you figure?"

"Britt is someone that really mattered to him, and he called you that. I'd say, he's way more invested than he even understands."

"Travis, I sure hope you're right." I stared out the window at the passing scenery.

We rode in companionable silence until he pulled up to the Island Hotel & Restaurant.

"Please tell me you didn't get a room."

A warm grin puffed out his cheeks. "I hadn't considered it."

"Phew." I exaggeratedly swiped my forehead. "Of course, ordering room service in a hotel room is something I've rarely done. It was always cheaper to go down to the restaurant. I've had breakfast in a hotel room before but never dinner."

"Let's do it. We can eat and snuggle and watch something on the tube. I promise not to pressure you, and we don't have to spend the night."

I thought about it for a few minutes and decided to go for it. It could be fun, and Travis promised to behave. "Okay, let's, but no hanky panky."

"Deal."

I waited in the car while Travis checked in. Excitedly, I took in the 1800's hotel and surrounding trees. Instead of waiting, I got out of the car and made my way to the beach. The ocean breeze, palm trees, and the ever-changing sky greeted me. I imagined Cally here with me. The quaint charm somewhat reminded me of St. Augustine, Florida.

"There you are," he said, jingling the key to the room and holding a bottle of Sauvignon Blanc, already uncorked, in his other hand.

I followed him back to the hotel and up to the second floor. The room held a queen-size bed and had space for two chairs and a table along the far wall. The claw-foot tub and sink shared the main space. The toilet lived behind a wall with no door. I started second-guessing my decision.

"I can see your expression, Jayden. I keep my word."

"Okay, let's order and then see what's on TV." What was it I always said to Ashley? *There's no point in making a choice if you're going to constantly second guess it.* I decided to enjoy myself.

"What do you want?" he asked as he gathered two water glasses he found next to the sink.

"Seafood? You order." I sat on the edge of the quilt-covered bed and flipped on the TV with the minimalist remote, muting the sound. After Travis had finished ordering and handing me a glass of wine, I said, "TVs are different in 2015, and so are the remotes. We had four different remote controls."

"What for?"

"Most won't make sense to you. We had DirecTV, which had a bazillion channels and worked via satellite. We also had a remote for our DVD player. Think VHS player of the future. It's a different and better format, but I think that might be on the way out too. The third remote controlled the TV so we could switch between things and change the settings and the last one was for Amazon Prime. Really long story on that one. It's a cool system that streams different shows and movies."

He scratched his head and said, "Dare I ask about the TVs?"

"At your own risk." I chuckled. "Most tube TVs are a thing of the past, like this bad boy in front of us. They become flat screens and people subscribe to cable, which you know about, or satellite to get programming. Many people just watch their shows and movies online. A word to the wise, invest in technology. That's the way to go."

"That's a lot to digest. So cellphones are a real thing, like you said in your paper?"

"Totally real and it changes people and how they live. People get lost in their phones. Think mini computers with many more features and applications than you can fathom."

"Do you think technology makes the world a better place?"

I took a sip of wine and contemplated his question. "That's a great and complicated question. The wine is yummy, thanks. Listen, I have to pee. Will you step out onto the balcony?"

"I've heard someone pee before."

"Not me. Please?"

He stood up. "Okay."

I quickly peed and flushed and then washed my hands at the sink in the room.

As Travis came back inside, a knock sounded on the door.

"Where do you want it?" a tall young man asked.

Travis looked to me and I said, "On the bed, please." I slid off my shoes and sat Indian style in front of the huge tray. "Oh my god, Travis! You ordered enough food for eight people!"

He paid and tipped the young man and shut the door. "I hope you're hungry."

"Starving." I lifted one of the metal plate toppers and said, "What's this?"

"Escargot."

"I'd pass this over to you, but the plate is hot."

He shook his head. "You have to try one."

"No, really I don't."

"You're telling me in all of your ... how many years?"

"Forty-eight."

"That you've never—"

"I can wait another hundred years for that."

He pointed at me. "I thought you were adventurous. Trust me, it's no different than you eating the butter clam that's currently in your mouth."

I chewed and swallowed. "This in no way takes away from your sex appeal, but right at this moment, you feel like the brother I never had."

Travis shoved my shoulder, and I shoved him back, the both of us laughing. We both lifted a piece of garlicky bread and clinked them together like champagne glasses. "Too bad you aren't gay. I think you and Packy would hit it off."

He harrumphed. "We're talking about you, Jayden. Try one. Didn't you get Ashley to try new things?"

"Fine, way to go..." I kidded, "...throwing Ashley in my face."

"Open up." He held out a tiny fork dripping with butter.

I chewed it, making funny faces.

"Well," Travis demanded.

"I guess anything drowned in butter tastes good."

"Good point. Now tell me about how technology has changed the world."

After taking another sip of wine and swallowing the bite, I said, "The best part of it is that it brings the world together. I guess that's probably the worst part too. It enables the crazies to group together. I think the younger generations are losing the ability to interact in person now that it's so easy to do it virtually. I love being able to look up anything. That's a treat. Think of the biggest library in the world but at your fingertips."

I paused and took another bite of the seafood feast in front of us. "When Ashley started driving, I loved that we had our cellphones to stay in touch. It really reduced my stress knowing when she arrived safely to places. On the other side, it's hard for people to unplug. Between all the shows, movies, and games, life is filled with solitary distractions."

We ate in silence for a while until I said, "Oh, you'll love this!"

"What?"

"eBooks! I was really slow jumping on that bandwagon, but I grew to love it."

"What is that? Some kind of book, clearly."

"You have a device that can hold hundreds of books.

Instead of turning a page, you swipe the screen with your finger. I still borrow books from the library because sometimes I want to hold a real book, but it's more convenient for traveling and waiting for appointments."

"Sounds very interesting and exciting. Did you try the crab dish?"

"Yes, I've tried a bit of everything. I need to slow down and save room for the decadent looking chocolate cake." I looked up and noticed some of the characters on the screen. "Dallas? Is that show still on? I will say that TV is much better in the future. There are so many more selections, which is a great thing. Unless if, of course, you have a hard time making choices." I lay back on the pillows. "Oh, I'm stuffed."

Travis moved the tray to the table and climbed back onto the bed. We lay there, him, I imagined, thinking about the future and me thinking about the past. He wrapped his arms around me with my head resting on his chest. My mind floated to the last time older Cally and I were together.

We had saved up for our trip to Barbados for three years. We wanted to splurge and not have to worry about money. Callahan found an incredible mansion B&B in Barbados. We lay naked on the beach for days, had gourmet food prepared for us, and explored the island town.

On the actual day of our anniversary, as I drank coffee sitting in the chair by the window while looking out at the ocean, Callahan pulled out his sketchpad and pencils and began to draw me. Naked underneath my robe, I pulled the fluffy white material off the one shoulder that faced him. I had my feet up on the seat, and my coffee cup rested on my lap. He wanted to capture my just-fucked look, although he would never call it that. My messy, long, curly hair draped along my back, and my cheeks were still red from our play.

"You look radiant," he said.

"Thank you," I said, smiling in his direction.

"Don't move! That's perfect. I just need to get one of those flowers we saw on the other side of the road. Hang on and don't move!" He jumped up from the bed and left the room in a flash.

That would be the last time I saw Callahan alive.

I waited in the still silence, as he demanded, reminiscing on the previous days of our trip and my stellar orgasms from the morning.

Screeching tires and honking horns shattered my peaceful existence. My stomach twisted in such acute pain it caused me to double over. No, no! It can't be. Still in my robe, I slipped into my flip-flops and walked out onto the balcony to look for him.

When a staff employee ran by, I yelled to him, "What's happened?"

"A man was hit by a car."

I felt the wind knocked out of me, and time slowed to a crawl. I ran back into the room, although it felt like slow motion as if every single detail registered to my brain: the messy bed to the right, the billowing white curtains over the window, a pile of dirty clothes by the bathroom door.

I threw on some clothes and rushed outside. By the time I made it to the site of the accident, a crowd had gathered. Still clutched in Callahan's hand was the pink flower for my hair.

No one had to tell me he was dead. I forced my way through the onlookers and sat down on the street next to his lifeless body. People yelled at me, but I didn't take in any of their words. I held onto him and screamed, "Cally, come back. You have to come back." My sobs continued as part of me died along with him.

Hands finally lifted me away and placed me into the

ambulance with him. Our anniversary forever marred.

It took two days to cut through the red tape to get his body home. Shannon flew out and held me all the way back to Florida.

My heart broke again as I lay in bed with Travis. He held me close, soothing my back. Somehow, he knew not to ask any questions. He allowed me to weep and sob uninterrupted.

At some point, I drifted off to sleep.

Later, I awoke as Travis attempted to lift me off the bed, like a bride going over the threshold. "What the fuck?" I fought his hold.

"Sorry," he said, setting me down on my feet. "I thought I could get you out to the car without waking you. It's really late."

I rubbed my eyes and took in my surroundings. "Oh. Sorry, I must have been dreaming. Where are my sandals?"

He handed me my shoes, and I slipped them onto my feet. Over by the tray, he collected the large, uneaten slice of chocolate cake.

My cheeks flushed when I recalled I had broken down in his arms. "I'm sorry. I didn't mean to make tonight a downer."

"No apologies necessary."

At the sink, I rinsed my mouth with the provided mouthwash. Then I shuffled around the partition and peed as he waited. I figured that if he could see me lose myself in grief, he could listen to me pee.

Once I'd finished and washed my hands, he smiled at me and led me back to his Saab.

"Did you sleep too?" I asked.

He started the engine and drove out of the parking spot. "Not as long as you, but yes. Do you want to talk about it?"

Noticing the clock in the car, I said, "Is it really three in the morning?"

"Yes. Thankfully, tomorrow is Saturday."

"Oh shit, sorry." I giggled slightly.

He smiled over at me. "So tell me."

"Earlier tonight, or I guess it's technically yesterday now, you asked me if I was more awake since I've traveled back."

"Yes, and you never answered me."

I sighed. "I'm not sure I'm more awake, but I'm definitely more emotional this time."

"That's understandable."

"Is it? Tonight I was thinking about the last time I saw Callahan alive. It ripped my heart open to relive it again. It was one of the most romantic days of our life together. It was our twentieth anniversary, and the sex just before floored me. Even after twenty years together, he still managed to shake things up and surprise me. We were so connected when he left this world. It's still hard not to feel like only half of me is here. Sometimes, I wish I wasn't so awake."

"I can only imagine what you're going through."

I reached out with my hand and took his. "You've been an incredible friend. Thank you."

"It's been my pleasure to get to know you better, and I appreciate the wake-up call."

I leaned against the passenger door and closed my eyes. It felt good to have a positive effect on Travis, especially since he freely gave me support and understanding.

Reliving the past did give me another idea. I hoped I would be able to find what I needed.

CHAPTER TWENTY-FOUR

Travis insisted I take the chocolate cake. After a warm hug and promises to stay in touch, I headed up to my room.

I unlocked the door and yelped as I entered, almost dropping the dessert.

Packy popped up in my bed, his chest rapidly rising and falling. "Fuck, Jayjay."

With a hand on my hip, I said, "What are you doing in my bed and how did you get in?"

"Your roommate let me in because I was worried about you. You told me you were going out for a platonic dinner."

"Shit, sorry, man. I didn't mean to worry you. Are you up for some dessert?" I held out the cake as an apology.

He swiped his hair out of his eyes and said, "Count me in."

"Let's wash our hands since I don't have any forks to eat it with." I gathered a clean hand towel for us to use as a napkin.

We sat, devouring the cake, side by side on the bed.

"This shit is really good," Packy said. "I forgive you for scaring the crap out of me. Dang, Jayjay, I think you almost gave me a heart attack."

"Same for me. I strolled up to my room in a daze and didn't expect to find someone in my bed." I filled Packy in about my night with Travis, and he shared his time with Chuck. After I licked the frosting off my fingers, I said, "It seems like things are moving forward with Chuck. How do you feel about him?"

"I was going to ask you the same question, although I have a few more. Chuck is my longest ... fuck-friendship."

"In the future, they're called 'friends with benefits' or 'FWBs.' Could it be more than that?"

He wiped his mouth on the towel. "From my end, maybe, but not from his. He'll never come out. He'll marry a woman in the end."

I hugged him. "Sorry. That kind of sucks."

"It's perfectly fine. I'm a hot young stud and have plenty of time. I'm not sure I'm the settling down type anyway."

"Hmmm. Maybe not."

"So tell me, how do you feel about Travis?"

I glanced to the ceiling, thinking. "He's a great man, and I really like him, but at this point, I don't see it being anything more than a friendship."

"And if Callahan doesn't come around."

I swallowed hard. "Then I might reconsider."

"He's incredibly hot."

I smacked his shoulder. "Give me more credit than that. Dude, give him more credit than that. I think, once he gets over his ex-wife, he'll make someone a great husband. I don't know if I'll ever marry if Cal doesn't come around."

"That's ridiculous. What about Ashley?"

"I don't have to marry to have her. I just have to get pregnant."

He seemed to be thinking. "We could have a baby together."

My mouth fell open. "Whatcha talkin' bout Willis?"

Packy fell out in laughter. "Damn, girl. You are so funny sometimes. I don't mean I will stick my penis in your vagina." He mimed along with his words. "I just meant we could raise her together."

"Wow. Wowsa. I thought you didn't want kids. I'm not even sure how to respond to that. I love you, Packy, and I might take you up on that if Callahan—"

"I still think he'll come around. So what's your new idea?"

"Along with the tape, I plan to send Cal a sketch pad

and Prismacolor pencils. I hope I can find the ones he used in the future. I'm not sure his brand was made in 1985, but I'm going to see."

"Chuck might know."

"Oh, good idea. Please ask him when you see him next. They're color pencils."

Packy cleaned his fingers using the towel. "We're hanging out tomorrow."

"Great. Are you going to your room or staying here tonight?"

Packy yawned. "My bed *really* is much more comfortable."

"Uh-huh. Night, Pakster."

"Nighty-night."

Once alone, I brushed my teeth, peed, and stripped off my jeans and top. Sleep found me as soon as my head touched the pillow.

❤❤❤❤❤

It wasn't until Sunday that I heard from Packy again. I picked up my ringing phone and heard, "Suicide hotline, how can I help you?"

"Silly boy, that only works if *I* call *you*."

"It's still funny."

"Whatever, man. So what's up?"

He huffed. "I've got the tape and Chuck suggested checking out Utrecht Art Supplies. It's car-ride far, though. He said to take—"

"Let me get a pen. Not everyone has a perfect auditory memory like you do."

"Ready ... get set ... gooo—"

"Okay, ready." I wrote down the directions. "Thanks, Pakster. Can you drop the cassette by so I can listen to it?

Now I just need to sort out a ride. I have to get out of this room anyway. Cabin fever is getting to me."

"I think it's called impatience, not cabin fever."

"That too. I hope the store takes checks. I'm still cash-poor at the moment. Want to come?"

"I'll take a pass. I think I'll skulk down to the cafeteria, grab some lunch, and crash again."

"Another late night with your FWB?"

"Yep."

"Please thank Chuck for me when you see him."

"I will. Good luck on your search."

"I hope I won't need it." I hung up the phone and then scoured my desk for Travis' number. Finding it, I dialed his home.

"Hello?"

"I hope I'm not disturbing your writing."

"I'm ready for a break."

Damn, he's sweet. "How would you like to be my knight in shining armor? I'm only calling because you—"

"You need my help?" he asked, enthusiasm threading his words.

"I need a ride to an art supply store, and I was—"

"Meet at the usual place?"

"Just like that?"

"Just like that."

Thank you, thank you, thank you!

Text to self: *You have incredible taste in men. You've come a long way since high school.*

With the directions, my checkbook, and IDs, I set out on my mission. The hot sun beat down on my shoulders as I walked, but I didn't care. I waited on a parking stump until Travis arrived.

"Get in." His Miami Vice shades gave me a chuckle.

However, the stern expression on his lips didn't. He leaned across the seats and held the passenger door open for me. Once I was inside the car, he pulled out quickly.

"Uh, is everything okay?" With the top down, the wind of our departure blew through my hair.

He tilted his sunglasses up. "I think Professor Baxter might have seen us."

"Oh, shit. Are we in trouble?" I scanned the area behind us to see if I could spot anyone looking in our direction.

"I'm not going to worry about it like you will."

I scrunched my eyebrows and then laughed. "That's probably true. The place is at the crossroads of Magnolia Drive and Mahan Drive. Do you know where that is?"

"We're on our way there now."

I squinted against the hot sun. "I don't know what I did to deserve you. Thank you so, so much for taking me."

He smiled at me and kept driving.

Once we arrived, Travis opted to stay in the car. I ran in and found an employee to help me. "Can you show me your drawing pencils? I'm looking for a color pack by Prismacolor."

A young girl led me down the aisle to a large selection.

"Holy shit! You have them." I clapped and jumped up and down.

The girl's eyes widened.

"Oops. I'm sorry. I just didn't know if I'd be able the find the right ones." I chose the pack of pencils I wanted and said, "Sketch pads?"

"This way." She waved at me to follow her.

Once done and back in the car, I settled into the seat and sighed. "That was much easier than I thought it would be. They took a check too. Luckily, I brought both of my IDs because they required two forms of identification."

Travis squeezed my thigh and then drove out the parking lot. "Where to now?"

"If you wouldn't mind, are there any office supply stores around here? I need to get an envelope large enough to fit the sketch pad, pencils, and a cassette tape."

"I don't mind at all. I planned to get more paper for my typewriter while we were out." He made a U-turn and headed in the other direction.

Once parked at the office supply store, I stayed in the car, and Travis went inside to shop. As he said I would, I worried about the other professor. I felt horrible that Travis might get in trouble over our friendship.

Text to self: *Worrying is a misuse of imagination, as you've told Ashley a boatload of times.*

I could hear Packy saying, 'Write it all down, Jayjay, write it all down.'

"What's with the odd expression?" Travis asked when he got back in the car.

"The professor."

He cracked up at me and patted my thigh again. "Don't sweat it. Now where to?"

"Back to school? I need to figure out what I'm going to write to Callahan. Plus, I still haven't written on the cassette sleeve."

He paused. "I could draw something for you if you'd like."

I shook my head rapidly. "Worst idea ever! My particular art falls in the chosen word and not in any other art form. Trust me when I say, you'd hate my attempt at drawing, and my singing is even worse. I can hear it now, 'Did you draw that so and so? No? Oh? Who did?' That would go over so, so well."

"You're probably right."

Changing the subject, I said, "When do I get to read

your book? Shouldn't you get back to your writing? I know when I'm on a roll I don't like to take too much time away from it."

"I'm procrastinating," he said, rubbing his chin.

"Are you stuck? Maybe I can help."

He pulled his head back and then gave me a sheepish smile.

"What?"

"I'm waiting to see what happens."

"Uh..." I blinked my eyes, trying to understand what he meant. "Oh, no. Move along doggie. I told you to find another semester distraction."

"I'm done with that."

I lowered my shoulders. "Travis, please. Don't do this."

I'm such an idiot.

He started the engine and drove out onto the road. We rode in silence until we arrived back behind The Sweet Shop.

After removing his seatbelt, he pivoted to face me, taking my hand. "All I'm asking is that you take me into consideration if things ... if they don't go as planned."

"Please don't put me in the position of hurting you. I couldn't stand it." I got out of the car and grabbed my stuff. "How much was the envelope?"

His sad expression hurt my heart. "Don't worry about it."

I went around the car to his side. "I'm sorry. I should never have—"

"Shhh. You're doing everything right."

Then I understood. He would go home and write some more. "Okay, Travis. Thanks for the ride." I tried to force a smile, but I think it came out more like a grimace. *Let it go.* I needed to focus on getting everything together for Callahan, so I could mail the package out tomorrow between my classes.

When I stepped into my dorm room, Debbie said, "The phone has been ringing off the hook."

My heart rate soared in hope. "Oh yeah," I said, pretending calm. "Who called?"

"Messages on your pillow."

I dove onto my bed and held them up to read. The first one read: *Professor Jenkins called. Debbie clearly needs a course on taking a message.* I shouted, "What did Jenkins want?"

"Doesn't the note say—"

"No."

"I'm such a scatterbrain. You have no class on Tuesday. Maybe Thursday too."

The next note read: *Shannon called.* I missed adult Shannon, almost as much as I missed Ashley. I flipped to the next one. *Jack? Who the hell is Jack?* "Did Jack say anything?"

"Ummm. He said something about one of the songs. I didn't actually get it."

Motherfucker! She better leave soon so I can listen to the tape. Why didn't I pack my headphones? Note to self: Have Mom send them.

The second to last message was from Packy: *Did you get it?* The final one read: *I'm sorry. Travis.* Everyone called but the one person I wanted to hear from the most.

Callahan, I hope you're okay.

I removed the items from the plastic shopping bags, laying everything out on the bed. The cassette tape sat on top of the turntable. "Are you spending the night?" I called over the partition.

"That depends on Darin."

"Trouble in paradise?"

Debbie exhaled loudly. "Something like that."

I lay back, trying to remember this day last time but,

with my emotions in turmoil, I couldn't focus. *Dammit.* Instead, I would concentrate on writing what I wanted to say on the first page of the sketchpad.

Dear Callahan,

I know you were very upset when you left my room, and I can only imagine what you read left you confused and angry. There were so many scenarios in my mind of how I would finally tell you, and you reading my journal was never one of them. I have so much I want to say, but it needs to be said and explained in person.

I will leave you with this:

In a week or so after you receive this package, Hurricane Gloria will land in New York with 130-mile-per-hour winds.

A couple of days after that, the first of the five cyanide-laced Tylenol victims will die.

I know how you hate Howard Stern. You'll be happy to note that he will be fired from WNBC just a day later.

I wish I had more uplifting events to share, but I didn't watch the news much in 1985 the last time around.

None of this will make much sense to you, but in the future, we are married and often talked about how great it would have been if we had met ten years earlier than we did. After twenty years of marriage, your death devastated me, so I came back in time to meet you ten years earlier. Only, I never considered the realities of meeting earlier in our lives. It was easy to get lost in the romance of it all. The only thing I could imagine was ten more wonderful years together.

I'm so sorry for any pain I've caused you. With all

my heart, I had hoped to do just the opposite. I'll be as
patient as I possibly can be but, unfortunately for both
of us, I'm a bit limited in that arena. Please don't write
me off. I need you as much as you need me.

   I love you and always will,
   Jayden

As soon as I finished rereading what I wrote, the phone rang again. Debbie answered. She whispered into the phone, hung up, and said, "I'm out of here." She hoisted a bag over her shoulder and took off.

I breathed a sigh of relief. Just then, my stomach roiled, and I ran to the bathroom, just in time to throw up into the toilet. *What the fuck?* I hadn't eaten anything for breakfast or lunch, so I figured I wasn't quite over my cold yet.

After rinsing my mouth, I rode over to the cafeteria and gathered a meal to go. Back in my dorm room, I ate while I listened to the tape. The food left me feeling much better. I fast-forwarded from one song to the next, hoping to figure out the one song Jack couldn't find.

It turned out my roommate stressed me out over nothing. He'd recorded all the songs in the right order and, in addition, he had written all the song titles and artists on the sleeve. I decided to use the song list for the cassette and to tape my message under the letter to Callahan.

I shoved everything into the envelope and addressed it.

Tomorrow couldn't come fast enough.

CHAPTER TWENTY-FIVE

On Monday, in composition class, Travis and I acknowledged each other with a nod, but otherwise, it was pure business. On my side, I didn't want to draw any unwanted attention to our friendship. On his side, I couldn't be sure. Maybe he was still perturbed with me. I put the thought aside and focused on the course work.

Between Sociology and my math class, I hurried to the mail center. I found enough change in my backpack to pay the postage to send Cal's package first class. The woman behind the counter told me it should take a day or two. Using my mailbox key, I opened my box and found a letter and a slip for picking up my box from home. Back at the counter, I retrieved the package.

After my math class, I met up with Packy for lunch.

"Who's the box from?" he asked when he approached.

"From my folks."

"What's in the box?"

I circled my palm over the unopened box a few times and said, "My psychic impressions tell me that my favorite baked nut balls covered in powdered sugar reside in a red box tucked right against a framed photo of my family. Under the photo resides a box of Swiss Miss hot chocolate. On the other side, will be the more practical gifts: a new package of undies and socks. The *pièce de résistance,* cash taped to the bottom of the goody box."

"You must know you have to open it in front of me now."

I gave him an austere look, and he put his hands together, pretending to beg.

"Fine." I handed it over to him. "By the way, the envelope is on its way, shipped out to Callahan. Thanks for asking."

"I'll carry the box for you?" He tilted his head down in mock shame.

"Damn, I'm hungry," I said, as we shuffled through the line. "I have to stop skipping breakfast. It's making my stomach all wonky."

"You are looking rather peaked." He stuck out his tongue and winked.

I playfully slapped his arm.

"Actually, you look pretty darn fine. If I didn't know better, I'd think you were getting laid."

"Don't I wish! I'm just so excited to have the package on the way. I feel like I should walk around with my fingers, toes, and eyes crossed for good luck."

Packy mimicked my description, waddling like a duck with my box under his arm.

"Then again..." He made me laugh so hard. "...maybe not." I pushed my tray down the row and slipped my hand around his arm. "I'm still craving a chocolate shake and fries. Let's make a date for later in the week."

"Me too since you mentioned it. How will we get to Whataburger? Call Travis again?"

"Shhh," I hissed with my eyebrows arched high. I searched the area, and no one seemed to be paying any attention to us. "How about a ride on my bike?"

We made our way to a table in the back, my box occupying one of the empty seats.

"You're kidding, right?" Packy asked and then shoved his chicken sandwich into his mouth for a huge bite.

"I figured we would get there faster, and I finally got some cash, so I'm treating."

"You're going to pedal *and* pay? Morally and ethically I can't say no to that."

"Funny you."

He gave me a smug smile.

"Can I have a chip?" I asked.

"Help yourself, but only if you open the box and then fill me in on your—*Travis,*" he whispered, "—outing." He swiveled his tray in my direction.

I popped a chip into my mouth. "Have at it," I said, pointing to the box.

Packy ripped up the packing tape and opened the top. Staring down at the contents, he laughed. "You know, Jayjay. You should be enjoying this more."

"Yeah, yeah, I know what you mean. If losing Callahan weren't in the mix, I'm pretty certain it could be a fuck-ton of fun."

"I'm having fun by proxy." He lifted the red box and turned it over. "Cash, as you said there would be."

"That's my Mom's doing. She's worried I don't have enough money."

"Sweet lady," he said as he sat back down. "And *Travis*?" he whispered.

"I'm no longer sure he believes me."

Packy pulled his head back and appeared to be contemplating my words. "What gives you that idea? I mean you said he made the connection with Callahan's ex and rereading and all of that. Why the sudden doubts?"

"He's writing again and using me as his muse, so he says, but I think he's writing about me and what I do and what I share."

"Can he do that?"

"Morally and ethically?"

"Now who's the funny one? No, I mean legally."

"If he changes enough of it, he can. It would be hard to prove, and that takes money anyway. I think he believes I'm in love with Callahan. I also think he's counting on him never coming around. I don't know. Maybe I'm just being paranoid. I don't think I've completely recovered from my cold, and all the stress is leaving me feeling—"

"Feeling?"

"Discombobulated." I couldn't help thinking of Callahan and our word game. "I feel like I'm off a step. I'm having a hard time putting it into words. I guess the farther away from my old life I travel, and the more time I spend here, I'm not me anymore." I shook my head. "I don't know what I'm saying."

He sipped a straw full of coke and said, "I think I get it, Jayjay. It'll take time to sort all of it out. I'm counting on Callahan. He will pull through this." He downed the rest of his sandwich and chips. "Listen, I have to head out to class soon. Let's touch base later."

"Thanks, Packy. Have a good day of classes."

He stood, swinging his head to get his hair out of his face and took off.

I sat for a bit, nibbling on my chef's salad and wondering if I would make it through myself. In my backpack, I found my journal and pen. I moved my salad to the side and wrote.

There are still moments when I expect to wake up with you sleeping next to me, Cally. Mornings are the worst, although I never let myself linger. I can only imagine I dream of you at night, of us and our life together. I know I have no right to complain. My best friend Packy, who you've heard of in stories from my first time at FSU, is even more incredible this time around. I'm certain my sanity would have flown the coop if he wasn't here to make me laugh until my sides hurt. He's been tremendous, and I know if you both met, you would totally hit it off. He's really the only person who I totally trust like I trust you.

I'm going to share something I might not even share with Packy. I'm scared. It might be more apt to say downright terrified. I'm sure we could come up with many more verbs to express it. If you don't come around, fail to open my package, or don't care what you read, Callahan, I really won't pull through.

Ashley would tell me to find my lady balls, and you would tell me to buck up and be strong. Do you know why those things worked before? Because I had you both in my life. As much as I love Packy, and even having his friendship at my side, I'm not sure I can live this life knowing I'll never have you again. I'm not stupid. I know the 1985 Cal won't be entirely like you, but I can't help wishing that Cal might get there over time.

A tickle up the back of my neck alerted me. I searched around the large cafeteria to see if someone was watching me.

Across the expanse of the dining room, a man with gray hair and a darker mustache I didn't recognize appeared to be staring in my direction. He seemed to glare down his nose at me. When I met his gaze, he frowned and pivoted on his foot in the opposite direction.

Who the hell was that? The mysterious Professor Baxter?

As if I could handle another stressor added to the top of the pile, the hits just kept on coming. I put away the journal and zipped up my backpack. With the food tray in hand, I discarded the rest of my meal and headed to the Williams Building that held the English department. I approached the first older person I could find there. She wore a blue sweater and had spectacles hanging around her neck on a silver chain.

"Excuse me," I said.

"Yes?"

"This might seem like an odd question but can you please tell me what Professor Baxter looks like?"

The woman's forehead creased. "He should have his office hours listed on his door."

"Is he an older gentleman with a mustache?"

"No, dear, quite the opposite. Young, clean-shaven, and a bit full of himself if you ask me."

Instead of the information putting me at ease, it did quite the opposite. "Do you know a professor with gray hair, a dark mustache, and long in the nose?"

She seemed to chew on her bottom lip. "No, I'm afraid that's not ringing any bells."

I touched her forearm. "Thank you for your time."

On top of my handlebars, I balanced the box from my parents for the ride back to the dorm.

When I walked into my room, I said, "Is anyone home?" A welcome silence bounced back to me. I tossed the box onto my bed and rested my backpack on my desk. I checked the phone for messages and found none. In the backpack, I rummaged for Travis' syllabus, which listed his office phone number. I dialed and waited.

"Professor Stratford speaking."

"Hi, Travis. Do you have a minute?"

"For you, always."

"I might just be paranoid, but an older man was staring at me in the cafeteria today. Do you know a gray-haired man with a dark mustache? I thought it might be Professor Baxter, but I now know he's a young teacher." I kicked off my shoes and sat in the chair at my desk.

"Interesting. I'll look into it."

"That's it?"

"That's it. Nothing for you to worry about."

I heard a knock in the background.

"Come in and take a seat," he said.

"Thanks!" said a high-pitched voice.

"Interviewing, I see. Good luck." I hung up the phone before he could say anything.

With force, if necessary, I planned to extract the mystery man and Professor Baxter from my pile. I felt a mixture of relief and irritation that Travis decided to move on. Thankfully, it was mostly relief. *Maybe I'm PMSing. That would explain so much.*

On the bed, I reopened the flaps of the box. I tossed the package of undies and socks to the bottom of my closet, which I would deal with later. From under the red metal box, I untapped the five twenties my mother placed there. Then I indulged and allowed myself five nut balls. Damn, those were yummy. After licking the powdered sugar off my fingers, I placed the family portrait on the top of the desk.

Remembering the letter in my mailbox, I opened Shannon's envelope.

Dear Jayjay,

    I love sleeping in your bed. I'm glad you didn't get mad. I like getting a letter from you. Can you write some more?

    I don't really no what else to say.

    I miss you,

    Shannon

With the phone at my side, I called home expecting and getting voicemail. "Hi Mom, Dad, and Sweet Pea. I love the package and your letter, Shannon. When you're talking about knowing something, it's the K know not the N no.

Dad, Mom? I'm doing great. I think I'll get all A's this semester, so don't worry. Have I said thank you? Thank you for everything. I plan to make the most of the college experience. Love to you all."

I moved the box off my bed and lay back. For once, I didn't have homework to tackle and felt like I needed a time out. I wish I could just lose myself in my favorite romantic comedies or cooking shows. For better or worse, I could use some of the distractions from 2015. As Tom Petty and the Heartbreakers sang, "The waiting is the hardest part." I rummaged through my crate of albums and put that song on.

CHAPTER TWENTY-SIX

By Thursday evening and no phone call from Callahan, I cajoled Packy into calling Port. I didn't want Cal to end up answering the phone and hear my voice.

"Please don't use any of your funny voices."

Packy harrumphed. "Give me some credit." He pretended to be pouting.

"I'm sorry, I'm just so anxious. Pretty please?" Holding the phone, I dialed the number and then handed it over to him.

"Hello?"

"Can I speak to Port?"

"One sec."

"Was that Callahan?" I mouthed.

Packy nodded. "Yeah, hi, Port. It's Jayden's friend Patrick." He tilted the phone so I could better hear the conversation.

"What can I do for you?"

"Did Callahan get the envelope?"

"Yes, and it's sitting unopened on his dresser."

I shot up and said, "Fuck!"

Packy waved me back. "Is there anything you can do to get him to open it?"

"I'm of the mind to let him do it in his own good time."

"Fuck, shit, fuck, shit, fuck!" I muttered to myself.

Packy said to the both of us, "At least we know he has it, and he hasn't thrown it away."

"That's not exactly good news, but I guess I'll have to live with it," I mumbled. At that moment, I wanted to punch my pillow but refrained.

"Thanks, Port. Do us a favor, will ya?"

"What now?" he grunted.

"If he doesn't open it or ends up tossing it, would you please let us know?"

"When I know, you'll know."

"Thanks, dude. Much appreciated. Talk to you later."

"Okay, bye."

Packy hung up the phone and said, "*Sooo* we wait some more. Sorry, Jayjay." He sat up suddenly and grabbed me by the hand. "Let's go get those shakes and fries."

"Good idea. I might become homicidal if I don't burn off some of my disappointment."

He placed his hands on my shoulders and looked down at me. "Jayden, I get the impatience, but I think you're looking at this all wrong. He has it, we now know, and he's probably waiting for the right time."

"Right time? Really? I think you're just trying to cheer me up. Who gets a package and doesn't open it up?"

"Someone who might not be ready to know the truth?"

"Fine. Let's go." I gathered my fanny pack, clicked it around my waist, and made sure I had money in it.

Outside, Packy balanced on the seat, and I climbed up on the pedals. "Fuck, Packy. This is harder than I thought it would be."

"Once you get going, it won't be so bad. I'm a twig."

"Uh huh. Feels more like one hundred thirty-five pounds of cement."

"That's one hundred forty-five to you!"

I made it about five blocks before I gave up. "Let's walk."

"You know, Jayjay, we could've done that from the start."

I rolled my eyes. With one hand on the handlebar and the other on the seat, I walked the bike the rest of the way. "Did I ever tell you about the man in the cafeteria after we had lunch on Monday?"

"Staring gray dude with the funky mustache?"

"Yeah, him. Travis never mentioned him again. On the other hand, he won't stop mentioning that we have to get together so I can inspire him."

Packy chuckled. "I'm sure he wants your ... in ... spir ... ation." He swiveled his hips for emphasis. "That old dude might have been looking at someone else. The cafeteria is packed at that time."

"Yeah, maybe. I've changed my mind about Travis."

"Oh?"

"I don't like being a project, and he makes me feel responsible for his lack of writing. I'm thinking about dropping the class. I just don't want to stress out my parents needlessly."

Packy scratched his temple. "I'm holding out for Callahan. Once he shows up, you can blow off Travis for the rest of the semester. Let him write his own story."

"Your faith in Callahan is sweet."

"Jayjay, my faith is in *you*, not him."

Still holding on to the handlebar, I hugged Packy's side with my free arm. "If only you were straight."

"If only you were a dude."

We both cracked up as we walked our way around to the drive-thru window.

I ordered, "Two chocolate shakes, extra chocolate and extra thick and two large orders of fries, and please pack a bunch of ketchup and napkins too. Thanks. Wait! Make that one shake and one malt, thanks." To Packy I said, "You prefer malts, right?"

"You remembered! This is too fun!" He smiled and poked at the corners of my mouth to get me to smile too.

I paid, and we strolled to the second window and waited. "I'm salivating! Maybe I'm low on calcium. In 2015, I take a bunch of supplements."

"Supplements?"

"Oh, you know, vitamins, calcium, something for cholesterol, etcetera."

"Is getting older as miserable as it seems?"

I glanced away and thought about it. "In some ways that's true. The aches and pains suck. And watching my parents grow old is very sad and frustrating. You know, I look in the mirror now and don't recognize myself because I'm young. Unfortunately, it works the same way when I'm older. I often looked at myself in the mirror and was surprised. 'Oh yeah, that's what I look like now.'" I chuckled.

We collected our frozen beverages and fries. Packy took one handlebar of the bike, and I held the other with the bag of fries clutched in my hand. Too busy sucking on our straws, we didn't talk for a bit.

Packy broke the silence. "So tell me, Jayjay, so I don't commit suicide at thirty, in what ways is getting older better?"

"Sharing your life with another, having children, seeing everyone you know grow and change. It's pretty darn cool."

"Yeah, I think about kids sometimes, but that'll never happen."

"Hey, not true, man. In the future, gay couples can marry and adopt."

"No way, I don't believe you."

"It's true." I held up three fingers in a scouts honor pledge. "I think the older you get, the less you worry about what other people will think. It's rather freeing."

"I think I was born that way."

"Yeah, Pakster, you were definitely born with a leg up in that regard." I took another sip of the shake and enjoyed the coolness trickling down my throat.

Without missing a beat, Packy said, "I can pee easier that way."

"OMG!" I choked in laughter.

He shot me an exaggerated smile. When we stopped cracking up, he said, "I hope I keep my hair."

"I've heard it's based on your mother's father."

"Good god, I hope not."

"Bald?"

"A cue ball."

"Sorry, dude."

Back in my room, sans roommate, we huddled on the bed and chowed on the fries and shakes.

"That was perfect," Packy said, rubbing his belly.

"For me too." I sighed. "I'm not looking forward to the weekend."

"There's a party Saturday ni—"

"Thanks, I'll pass. Stephen King and I will get chummy."

"Alrighty then. I'm off. I have studying to do."

"Thanks for the company, Packy."

"My tummy thanks you. Later gator."

Alone in my room once again, I did some homework and studying. At bedtime, my good friend Stephen K. scared the crap out of me until I drifted off to sleep.

CHAPTER TWENTY-SEVEN

On Friday, I found a note on my seat in composition class.

Jayden,
Come to my office between classes. I have
something to share. I miss our talks and time together.
Travis

I tucked the note into my backpack and pulled out my supplies for taking notes in class. Although it wasn't my first choice, I planned to go to Travis' office after I got something to eat.

Over the last week or more, my ability to enjoy my classes grew. I participated more in sociology than I did the first time, having a greater perspective on many of the social issues. After math class, I rode over to the cafeteria.

With my grilled chicken sandwich and a side of broccoli in hand, I found an open table in the usual spot. I pondered the upcoming weekend, which felt like a bed of coals I had to cross. Dread was an understatement.

About halfway through my meal, a similar tickle crept up my neck. I dropped my sandwich and quickly wiped my hands and mouth. As I panned the large space, my heart stopped when my eyes connected with the man watching me. I shot up and ran toward him. I would not let him get away.

"You're here," I yelled, when I jumped into his arms.

Callahan caught me in a tight embrace as my legs wrapped around his waist.

Neither of us caring where we were, we locked lips.

At that moment, the air flowed freely to my lungs once

again. I felt myself filling up. Once we broke apart, into his hair, I breathed, "You opened it."

He set me down on my feet and said, "Port said he would kick me out if I didn't."

"You should know straight off that I'm in love with your roommate."

He smiled and chuckled, looking gorgeous in a tighter pair of jeans and a short-sleeved, plaid button-up shirt. "What is it with you and older men?" he asked.

My tears mutinied again, but this time in joy. "Wait here." I stepped away and then thought better of it. "Never mind, I'm not letting you out of my sight. Come with me." I tugged him along to the table and my belongings. "How did you find me?"

"I ran into Patrick on my way into the dorm." Callahan took my backpack from me and swung it over his shoulder as I dumped the rest of my lunch.

We walked hand and hand back toward the dorm.

I squinted up at him through the sunshine. "There's so much I want to say and ask, but mostly, I just need to be in your arms. I'm scared." Hope and fear battled for dominion.

"Why are you scared?"

"I'm stuffed to the hilt with so much hope. Like a helium balloon filled to the max, I'll burst if popped and will not safely float back to the ground."

"Stop for a second and breathe, please. Your face is getting all red."

I patted his chest and searched his blue eyes. "Are you real?" I was so wrapped up in the moment, I didn't see Packy approaching.

"He seems real to me," Packy said. "I think our Jayden is in shock." He stepped closer. "It's a good thing you showed. I thought I'd have to take drastic measures."

"Like?" Callahan and I asked simultaneously.

He pulled up the short-sleeve of his T-shirt and flexed his biceps.

I slapped my thigh and cracked up. "You're lucky Patrick is gay, or I might have traded you in."

Callahan frowned.

"Oops. Too soon to kid?"

"Too soon for everything, but I'm here anyway."

"Right." I quickly hugged Packy and whispered, "I hope I don't fuck this up."

He whispered back, "Relax and don't try so hard."

"Yeah, yeah, I know you're right. Would you mind collecting my bike on your way back from classes?"

"No problem."

I gave him my combination. "Thanks."

Callahan and I strolled, still holding hands, back to the room. It nearly killed me to take my time. I wanted to run and slam the door closed behind us.

Once inside my room, I said, "So?" The tension between us felt awkward. Part of me just wanted to jump him again. That worked out fine last time, but we had to get past the hard conversation, and maybe, we could move forward from there. After I couldn't take the silence for another second, I asked, "Shouldn't you be at work?"

"I have plenty of sick days accumulated." He walked over to the desk and lifted the family portrait. "This wasn't here last time."

Should I stand or sit? Why do my hands feel so big? It feels like there is no right place to put them. A wave of nausea hit my stomach, and I did my best to breathe through it. "Uh, yeah, I just got it in a package from my folks.

He turned the chair at the desk around and sat down, waving me to him.

I sauntered over to him with confidence I didn't really feel and stood close.

As he fiddled with the edge of my dress, he brushed his fingers lightly against my thigh and asked, "So you came here last time?"

"Yes." I gasped softly, my heart pounding faster over his touch. "I dropped out my second year."

"Did our paths cross?"

I shook my head. "Not for ten years and not in Tallahassee. We met on the beach in St. Augustine."

Using his other hand, his fingers trailed up my arm, giving me chills.

I touched his thick tawny hair and said, "Do you believe me? I mean, it's okay if you don't, I just— Why did you come?"

"The events you listed haven't happened yet."

"You didn't answer my question, but that's true." I closed my eyes and searched my memories for something I could give to him. "You like baseball. On Sunday, the St. Louis Cardinals set some sort of record. I don't recall the details."

"I wasn't asking for another example. Why didn't you tell me from the start?"

I touched his cheek and said, "Patrick warned me against it, and honestly, when I saw you in Gainesville, you seemed so sad. It seemed like the wrong time."

"And then at the lighthouse?"

I shrugged. "I wanted us to get to know each other first. As Patrick would say, 'save my bag of crazy for later.'"

"I believe you." Just then, he scooped me up into his arms.

"You could've said that first." I sighed into his embrace, trying to let go of the tension that surfed my bloodstream. "Why is it so easy for you to believe me? Even Patrick asked me to prove it to him."

He drew my hand to his heart. "I felt you here. And your smell—I can't explain it—it feels like home."

I closed my eyes, feeling them well up again.

He held me tightly, cupping the back of my head as the tears resumed their fall.

I loved that he always seemed to need to touch me. I felt reassurance from the contact. "But if you believed me, then why did you freak out after you read my journal? I'm confused."

"When I read it, at first, I didn't know what to make of it. I thought you were using me for some macabre story. I had opened myself up again, something I promised myself I would never do. It was easier to be angry than deal with the implications."

Implications? "What changed your mind?"

"The pencils. Although I don't believe in fate, I also don't believe in coincidences, and you bought the only ones I like to use. Port doesn't even know about my drawing. I also listened to the tape on the way. That was an interesting way to get my attention. I don't want you to think I've changed my position—"

No love, no kids, no marriage, I thought and then said the same aloud.

"Well, no kids or marriage."

I felt stuck somewhere between elation and disappointment. Love ... well, that was, at least, a start. "I hear what you're saying."

"But you plan to ignore it like everything else?" He held me away from him, scanning my face.

I chuckled softly. "Something like that. How will this work?"

"I thought about that on the way here. We can see each other on the weekends when it works for both of our schedules."

"And phone calls during the week?"

"That shouldn't be a problem."

I should have been ecstatic, but something twisted in my stomach. Something felt wrong, but I couldn't place it.

"Are you okay?" he asked. "You look a bit flushed."

"Yeah, I think I'm still just in shock."

"Let's lay in bed and talk. I have so many questions." He got on the bed, his back against the wall, and rested on his side with his head propped up on his hand.

I lay on my back, staring up at him. "This feels very familiar to me."

"How so?"

"We often talked just like this in the future. Especially about Ashley."

The smile left his face. "Who's Ashley?"

"Our daughter. Well she was our daughter and will be again if you ever change your mind about having children."

He sat up and ran his hand through his hair. "I can't and won't do it again."

"We had zero complications and having her relieved you of a lot of what you still carried around with you ten years from now."

"Jayden, if you push this, we won't work."

"Okay. Let's talk about something else."

He lay back on his side and said, "Tell me about the day we met in the future."

"Back then or—how should I say it—forward then, I taught high school English, and it was winter vacation. Breeze, a fellow teacher and housemate, decided we needed to take a road trip. As her name implies, it was easy to get swept up in her ideas and adventures. She liked to drive until she felt like stopping. We ended up on St. Augustine beach. I'd never been to a beach you can drive on and was impressed.

"Men typically paid attention to her. Having come to the States from Brazil, her exotic looks garnered her endless choices in men. However, when you approached our blanket, your eyes locked on me. Well, my legs first and then my eyes."

He ran his hand over my thigh and down my leg. "I've always been a leg man."

"You liked other parts of me as well."

"No doubt about that." His hand burrowed under my back, and he pulled me to him. Once his lips touched mine, all of my angst fled as I melted against my Cally. At least, it felt like him.

This time, when Cal kissed me, I didn't tear up. Me being me, I worried that it wasn't a good sign. With mental force, I shoved away the thought and dissolved against him. My body caught fire with the passion he infused in me. My nipples strained for his touch and the desire to be penetrated overwhelmed my senses.

He led me on a journey of lust, the chemistry between us feeling more volatile than with older Callahan.

As if he heard my thoughts, he pulled away and asked, "How is it different this time around?"

I rolled onto my back and brushed my hair out of my face, staring at the ceiling. "I ... I'm not sure how to answer this."

"The truth works."

Words I had heard before many times, so I just spit it out. "You're more intense and edgy. You, ten years from now, are settled in yourself, calmer, more staid. You're volatile in a way I've never known you to be. I had hoped to be more patient now, but that hasn't worked out well. Somehow your older, more grounded self, grounded me too." I blushed when the next thought floated across my mind.

"What, Jayden?"

I blew out a breath of air and answered, "Our chemistry is electrifying and powerful."

He smiled. "Are you saying it's more intense now?"

I nodded repeatedly. "Yes. It's weird for me because, in a way, it feels like cheating on the you in the future. I never counted on that. I never counted on most of what has happened. I mean, I didn't think it would be a cakewalk because of where you are in your life now, but I had no idea of all the ramifications. Toly—he's the entity that sent me back—never really warned me, other than to say you might not believe me and there were no guarantees we would be together again. I just couldn't imagine my life without you. I was so distraught that I leaped before looking down.

"I know you don't want to hear this, but I miss Ashley so much. She was my age and about to set off to college. And you, Callahan, I miss you. I miss everything about the life we built together. If I had been in my right mind, I don't know if I would have jumped." I put my arm over my eyes, and unwillingly, I started to cry again.

"I can't be the person you knew."

"I know. I really do. Patrick has told me to get to know you as a different person, and I'm trying."

Cal moved my arm and wiped my cheek. Looking down at me, he said, "I understand it's hard for you. We are coming at this from very different places. You want everything, and what I want is very limited. I can't just ramp up to your speed."

"I get it. It's just ... it hurts. I know I have to deal with it myself. I'm doing my best. Thank you for coming. Thank you for giving us a chance. It's a start. So where do we go from here?"

In response, he trailed his finger over my covered nipples, causing them to flare with heat. Our eyes connected, and I gasped, seeing his desire reflected back to me.

"I don't share well with others," he said.

"Neither do I."

The phone rang, startling me. I didn't move to get it.

"You should answer it."

"I don't think so."

He pushed my shoulder and rolled me out of bed.

"Fine!" I picked up the phone and said, "Hello?"

"You didn't come to my office," Travis said.

My stomach dropped. "Callahan showed up, and I forgot about it."

"That leaves me feeling great," he said, sarcasm coating his words.

"Look, everything is different now. Do I need to drop the class?"

With a scowl on his face, Cal shifted into a sitting position.

"No, of course not. Enjoy yourself, and I'll see you in class on Monday," he said and hung up.

Fuck! I peeked over to Cal. His rigid back and clenched jaw said it all. "What?"

"He's your professor?" he spat out the words.

"Clearly, you're angry. I'm not sure why, but let me just say I haven't so much as kissed him since you and I were together."

"So you seduced a professor and me?"

With my hands on my hips, I said, "Not this again. I had met him before classes started and before I went to find you in Gainesville. We've been over this before. *He* pursued *me*. Don't you see? He doesn't matter anymore."

"I'm not sure—"

"Cal, you're going to have to start trusting me, or there's no point in moving forward. You forget I'm forty-eight wrapped up in an eighteen-year-old container. I would think it would be more offensive if I dated eighteen-year-olds. Creepy really."

He ran his fingers through his hair. "You're extremely frustrating."

I stood in front of him, not willing to give an inch.

He took me completely by surprise when he grabbed my wrist and wrestled me down onto the bed. He held my arms above my head and raked his eyes over my body. With his free hand, he undid his belt and popped the button on his jeans. As he kicked off his shoes and pants, his eyes burrowed into my soul.

I was about to be the recipient of angry sex—a first for me. My blood boiled in hunger, craving his incursion. "Please, please, now."

He yanked my panties off and tossed them on top of his discarded pants. He pushed my thighs wide and used the tip of his cock to draw across my wetness.

"Oh god, yes. Take me." He did as I begged and plunged straight into my core.

"Oh, Jesus," he grunted while he pounded in and out of me.

I tilted my hips, so he banged right against my clit, causing my wetness to spill onto the bed, but I didn't care. "Oh yeah, take me. Give it to me! Make me yours!"

He paused, still staring at me and said, "You *are* mine."

Oh, I am! Cully, he's a Neanderthal, and I love it. "That's … what I've been … trying to tell you."

Some of the tension in his jaw relaxed, and he let go of my hands. He resumed his penetration with less aggression. He circled his hips, hitting all the right places, sensuously raising my need and arousal.

My hands trailed up under his shirt and played in the smattering of hair on his chest.

"Oh god, that feels so good. You're so wet, Jayden."

"Mmmhmm. You make me that way." I then clutched his ass and kept rhythm with him.

Our fervor continued to climb until he flipped me over, so I straddled his cock. "I can play with your clit this way."

I stripped off my sundress and leaned back, grasping his thighs, and opening myself further to him. "Yes, please, touch me."

And he did. He touched me just as I needed, using his thumb to circle my arousal. "You're so sexy. Come for me. I want to watch you come for me."

I rode his cock as he met me with each thrust. "I'm ... almost—oh, yes—almost there."

"Give it to me."

And then I did. I broke into a million pieces, like confetti, exploding into the air. "Oh, Cally, please don't stop. Oh my god!" I cried.

"Shhh," he said, chuckling. "Your neighbors?"

"Fuck them," I said, without apologizing for my language. I leaned forward and whispered in his ear, "That was outstanding." Older Cally never took me with such force. I had a feeling I would experience a different variety of sex with Cal. Angry sex, make-up sex, and hopefully, loving sex too.

Once I recovered, I clutched his chest and swiveled my hips as I rode him up and down.

He palmed my breast and tugged my nipples, still maintaining eye contact. "You're beautiful. So beautiful and baffling. I'm not sure— Oh Lord, oh Jesus, I'm coming," he shouted.

I laughed with joy. "Now who's being noisy?"

He grunted and laughed with me, breathing heavily.

I collapsed onto his chest and hugged him to me.

His hands lifted my face, and he kissed my eyes, then the tip of my nose just before he devoured my lips. He buried his hands in my curly hair and kissed me as if I were the air he needed to breathe.

I struggled against letting the fear of his departure inundate the now. *Maybe I could kidnap him and make him stay forever.* I chuckled into his mouth.

He poked my side and said, "What's so funny?"

"I was thinking about kidnapping you and never letting you leave."

"Deranged."

I immediately knew what he wanted. "Demented."

"Crazed."

"I'm not going to let you win this time. Insane."

"You do realize you're calling yourself insane," he said.

"Now who is stalling? Tick tock, Callahan."

"Unbalanced. You thought you had me, but no. I have tricks up my sleeve."

"Speaking of sleeves, off with the shirt."

We sat up so he could finish undressing.

I cuddled up next to him. "That's much better. My turn. Hmmm. Perturbed. Top that!"

"Let's see... Off kilter."

"Nope, that's two words. Try again."

"So competitive."

"They're actually *your* rules. YOS's rules."

"YOS?"

"Your Older Self."

He cracked up, slapping his thigh. "Oh, that's funny but good too. We need something to call *him*."

"Is that weird for you?"

"Extremely."

I kissed his cheek. "You've had more than enough time to come up with another word. Are you giving up?"

"Definitely not. Disturbed. I'd say you *are* disturbed."

"Thanks. Let's check the list: sexy, beautiful, baffling, deranged, and disturbed. You've got your hands full."

"Don't I know it. Are you giving up?"

"Not a chance. Unhinged," I countered.

"Hmmm. You might have got me on that one. Is brainsick one or two words?"

"Darn it! One word and that works." I playfully shoved him. "Mad."

"Oh, good one. I forfeit. I want to get back to kissing." He pushed me over and covered my body with his. His lips suckled mine, and then he tugged on my bottom lip with his teeth.

My lust caught fire yet again, and I needed more. Unfortunately, both of our attentions drew to the door. "Wait!" I cried. "Give us a minute." I tossed him his clothes and grabbed mine, pulling him into the tiny bathroom. "Okay," I shouted.

Cal climbed into the tub/shower to dress while I used the toilet, wiping up all the excess come. I threw on my dress and undies and took Cal's hand. "Do I look okay?"

"Scrumptious."

I smiled up at him. "Time to meet the roommate," I whispered. When we walked back into the room, Debbie's eyes opened wide when they lit on us.

"Hey, Deb, this is Callahan."

"Uh, hi. Wow, he's—is he your boyfriend?"

I looked at Cal and then back at Debbie. "Something like that."

Cal stepped behind me and wrapped his arms around me. "She's mine."

I glanced up and smiled.

Debbie seemed uncomfortable. "I'll be leaving again around dinner time." She walked to her side of the room.

"Okay," I said, shooting a glance at my messy bed.

"I'm going to use the restroom," he said, and kissed my head. Once he went into the bathroom, Debbie rounded the corner.

"You've been holding out on me."

"How do you mean?" I asked, as I first washed my hands and then straightened out my bed.

"He's gorgeous and possibly old enough to be your father."

I almost burst out laughing, but did my best to hold it in. "He's not old enough to be my father, Deb. I promise you. It's not like you and I talk a lot."

"That's true. I thought you were a fag hag, though."

I couldn't help myself. She raised my ire. With clenched fists, I said, "Those terms become very politically incorrect in the future." Then I remembered the current time and culture I presently resided in. "But it is true that I love Patrick. He's one of the greatest men I know."

"I didn't mean to upset you."

"Don't worry yourself about it."

When Callahan came back into the room, I said, "Let's get out of here for a while."

"Great. I haven't eaten anything since breakfast."

We put on our shoes and then hand in hand strolled outside. "What are you in the mood for?" I asked.

"A burger would be great."

"Patrick and I went to Whataburger yesterday, and I sure wouldn't mind another shake. It's within walking distance, but it's hot as ... ummm ... heck out today."

"You seem to have a thing about cursing in front of me. I really don't care one way or the other. Port curses like a sailor."

"What?" My mouth hung open in shock. "Callahan hated cursing."

"I'm Callahan."

"I'm sorry, yes, YOS hated it."

"Well, I don't. Let's ride to the place."

CHAPTER TWENTY-EIGHT

My head spun as I directed Cal to the burger joint, which was a very short car ride away. He went through the drive-thru, and we sat in a shady spot in the car with the windows down.

I sucked on the straw of the shake while pondering all that had happened. "YOS and I never had angry sex. Not that I'm complaining, it was smokin' hot. You know, technically you're my first."

As he chewed his burger, his brow creased. "You're on something, right?"

"No. I'm very irregular like my mom, and it's hard for us to get pregnant."

"But you had Ashley. YOS was fine with it?"

"Not exactly. At first, it was challenging. He felt like I did it on purpose, which was far from the truth. I had resigned myself to not having kids because you, I mean YOS didn't want to. He said he couldn't risk having another child, and I respected it."

"So what changed?"

"He went with me to the sonogram and did a complete one-eighty. Ashley became real to him. He was sometimes an overprotective bear during the pregnancy, and we fought about the birth. The thing is, and I'm not pushing my agenda but letting you know, Ash is a sure thing. My pregnancy with her was perfect and without complications. Toly promised me she would be my first child."

"Why didn't you have more kids?"

"I never got pregnant again, and we didn't want to force it. I didn't have Ash until I was thirty and then we were like the three musketeers, and I loved our family as is or was.

You were a tremendous father. Shit, I mean YOS was. He was hard on her when it came to school and being responsible. There were times he was too hard, in my opinion, but she turned out incredible. She even grew to appreciate him pushing her to do better."

"I can see you loved her. I have a feeling that'll be our breaking point."

"Yes, it does seem that way." Although I'd have given up having kids with older Cally, I wasn't willing now. No way would I live my life without Ashley in it.

"What are you thinking? You're doing that thing with your forehead and nose."

I tried to relax my face. "I was thinking about Ashley and how I can't give her up this time. Not even for you."

"A sticky wicket if I've ever heard it."

My shoulders dropped. "Yeah, it sure is."

"Seems to me we should just enjoy each other as much as we can in the meantime."

"That makes logical sense. However, knowing myself as I do, I won't be able to stop myself from wanting more. Wanting it all, as you said."

"So what do you want to do?"

"More angry sex?"

He laughed with his beautiful smile, and it warmed my heart. I didn't know how long I'd have my new Callahan, but at that moment, I vowed to figure out a way to enjoy him to the fullest.

He swallowed and asked, "How and why were you able to come back?"

"Toly said it was because we're soulmates, and you weren't set to die and that one of our watchers failed to keep you from crossing the road when you did. I think he called them sentinels."

"I got hit by a car?"

"A fast speeding car on our twentieth anniversary."

"Jesus Christ."

"Yep, so maybe you can understand why I leaped before really thinking it through. A huge part of me truly believed I had gone insane and none of this..." I spread my arms out, palms up. "...would really happen."

He gripped the steering wheel. "But it did."

"I probably should have gone back to the year we first met, but we had fantasized about meeting sooner and—"

"You mentioned that in your letter. Do you regret coming back to now?"

"No, Cal. I'll admit, I've had my moments, but when we're together, I never do, I never could." I stroked his cheek and then laced my fingers around his neck, pulling him down to me. When his lips touched mine, I let my heart open fully. *I'm sorry, Cally, but I love Cal too.*

"Wow, you sure know how to kiss."

"Yeah, so do you. I know it's too soon but, Cal, I love you and not just because you're young Callahan. Please ... just let me love you. You don't have to love me back."

He moved his car seat back and then lifted me across to his lap. "I never thought I'd feel this way again. For as long as it lasts..."

"For as long as it lasts."

His arms held me tightly as I sunk against him. The familiar feeling of his energy surrounding me soothed my worn-out soul.

"This feels so good," I said.

He coughed and cleared his throat. "For me too."

I peeked up and saw tears in his eyes, which caused my eyes to fill as well. *Please let me have the patience to love him. My sad, damaged Callahan. Maybe if we can just assuage each other's soul, it will be enough.*

I wanted to say so much, but I just said, "I'm here."

He kissed my head and said, "Thank you." He released the embrace, and I scuttled back into the passenger seat. "This burger isn't half bad."

"That's good. Want some shake?" I tilted the straw in his direction.

"No thanks."

I refused to let the awkward tension take over. "So next weekend? Will Port be cool if I spend it at his place?"

"I'm sure he'll be thrilled. He's sick of me moping around."

"Oh, good. What about today? Are you planning to go back?"

"I didn't pack anything because I wasn't sure how this would go."

"Hmmm." *Did he really come to say goodbye?* "How did you think this would go? Worse or better?"

"Worse, much worse."

I frowned. "Why did you come then?"

"I had to see you again, so I would know for sure."

"Know what?"

"If all that you said is real and if the intensity is still..." He rubbed the side of his face.

"Still?"

"You incite all these different emotions in me. Ones I've rarely had to contend with."

I searched his blue eyes for the answer. "Like?"

"Jealousy, passion, anger, and fear to name a few."

"That's a lot."

"Yes. Yes, it is. And you keep pulling me to open more. Feeling vulnerable is the last thing I want."

"Ouch. Then why are you still here?"

He scratched his head and appeared to be thinking. "Let me ask you this. Did YOS believe in fate and soulmates?"

I shook my head. "Not before he met me and not right away. However, it became undeniable. We had a one-of-a-kind marriage, and we knew it. We never took it for granted. He was my rock. He made me a better person—stronger, braver, more settled and content. Without him by my side in 1985, I don't quite feel like myself. With him, I felt safe in our messed up world."

"Safe huh? I'm not sure I'll ever feel that way again."

"YOS felt safe with me too. But let me be clear about something. I have no interest in retracing our steps. That's part of why I came back to now. I thought if I went back to the time we first met, I'd have to play a part as I tried to do exactly the same things to get you to fall in love with me. At the time, it seemed the worse of the two reinsertion times I considered.

"Plus, I have all this knowledge about what will happen. I don't plan to become a teacher again. I plan to write novels and maybe bartend or wait tables to accumulate money to invest. If you have any money saved at this point, I know of a few sure things. I haven't looked for a job as of yet, but it's on my agenda. I want to start saving soon.

"When I dream of us being together again, I don't see you selling insurance and investments."

"What do you see me doing?"

"Whatever the hell you want. Draw and paint. Volunteer. Invest in other people or businesses. YOS had so many ideas of how he would have spent his time if he didn't need to work for a living."

Callahan sat there, staring out the window in front of him.

I waited, sipping on my shake. After a while, I became antsy. *Breathe*, I told myself. I rolled the window down more, hoping to catch a breeze. Part of me fantasized about getting out of the car and walking back to the dorm, leaving him sitting there, just like at the lighthouse. I wished I knew the right thing to do or say. I felt stymied.

He crumpled the paper from the burger and tossed it into the bag it came in, then shifted to face me better. "Everything you said sounds like a dream."

Nodding, I hoped he would continue.

"We can't have the future you imagine for us."

I crossed my arms and glared at him. "Why not?"

"There're at least a hundred and one reasons—Ashley being the biggest. The idea of investing money in the volatile stock market, which I've set aside for buying a house, doesn't seem like a wise move."

"You either believe me, or you don't. I'm now leaning toward don't. I thought Travis believed me, but I now think it was a ploy to get me to talk so he could use it in a book."

"That sounds familiar."

"Fuck that shit. What you read was from my journal where I wrote to YOS. I had planned to let you read them all at some point. However, you got to it before I had a chance to explain. Being with you is like riding an unruly rollercoaster. Let's make a deal, okay?"

"What?"

"Let's not talk about the future anymore. It sets you off and, in turn, it hurts me."

He reached out to me. "I don't want to hurt you, Jayden."

I searched his eyes for the truth. "I believe you."

"No more talk about the future, but I do have one question. How are my parents in 2015? How did they deal with my death?"

I touched his arm and said, "I'm sorry to tell you, they both died before you."

"How?"

"You're mother died of breast cancer in 2012. Your father died shortly after. Your sisters believe he died of a broken heart and followed her to heaven."

His eyes seemed to dart everywhere at once as he grimaced. "I'm not sure how I'm supposed to feel."

"I don't think there's a right answer."

"And my sisters?"

"They're all alive and well. Sissy is divorced but kept your parents' house in the settlement."

"Did you get along with my sisters?"

"Uh, not exactly. It's not that I didn't get along with them so much as I just found their religious pressure unpleasant, and they constantly made a point of passing on unwanted information from your mother. Your parents didn't like me at all."

"That's not surprising."

Outraged, I pursed my lips and smacked his knee. "What's that supposed to mean?"

"You're too progressive and proud."

"You mean I'm a whole person that is unwilling to kowtow to misogynistic bullshit."

He laughed. "Yes, exactly." His full smile dissolved my anger and tugged on all my sensitive parts. "Should we head back?" he asked.

I scanned around us and found the parking lot mostly empty. "We have more time to kill before Debbie leaves." I yanked his belt, trying to release it until he caught my hands.

"What are you doing?"

"Don't stop me and you'll find out." I twitched my eyebrows and winked.

He lifted his hands in surrender. His cock seemed to

know my exact intent. Once out of his jeans and through the hole in his boxers, he felt hot to the touch.

I buried my face against him and inhaled our merged scents. "Oh, you smell like both of us."

"Jayden, I don't think—"

"Don't think. Just let me have this."

He raised his eyebrows and tilted his head. "Okay."

I licked and suckled until he became fully erect. I palmed his balls as my head bobbed up and down.

"Jesus, woman! If ... oh, god ... if you didn't ... oh, oh."

"Yes?" I paused.

"If you hadn't told me you knew me before, I would've wondered how you know all the right places to touch me."

"How's this?" I stroked his cock with one hand, fondling his nuts with the other. Then I slipped one hand into my panties and fingered my wetness.

His eyes dilated watching me, and when I brought my finger closer to him, he opened his mouth and licked off my come. "Oh Lord, Jesus Christ." He swelled, and I knew it wouldn't take him much longer.

I lowered my mouth over the head and suckled as I ran my hand up and down his shaft in the perfect Callahan pace. Knowing what he loved gave me the confidence to seduce him over and over again.

He groaned and grunted, finally shooting streams of come into my mouth. Struggling to catch his breath, he said, "What did I do to deserve that?"

I licked my lips. "I live for and time traveled to hear you laugh and see you smile again. And..."

"What?"

I blushed. "You're virile and sexy, and it's hard for me to be around you and not want to jump you. That is when you're not pissing me off. In this case, even if."

He sighed and rested back into the seat. "You're something else. You're the first woman to swallow my orgasm."

"They missed out. You taste delicious." I smacked my lips and licked them to emphasize my point.

"You're one of a kind, Jayden."

I winked again. "And don't you forget it."

He fastened his pants and said, "Shall we head back?"

"Let's." I put on my seatbelt and asked, "Have you ever considered going back to school for art or something else?"

He turned the engine and pulled out of the parking lot. "No. What would be the point?"

"The obvious. You don't enjoy the work you do."

"I never said that."

"No, you haven't. YOS did." I didn't bother giving him directions back to the campus. Callahan had an internal GPS and only had to drive to a place once to remember it.

"YOS is becoming the bane of my existence."

"That's one way of looking at it. You might consider another."

He glanced at me. "What might that be?"

"Insight into your own life. He *was you*, Callahan."

"I can't wrap my head around that. He doesn't sound like me."

I bit my lower lip, thinking, but I came up with nothing. "It's your call. Just make sure you're not taking your position out of stubbornness."

"Stubborn isn't a good word to use with me. It was one of Britt's favorites for me."

Yes, I know.

"But I imagine you already know that."

"Yep, I do." *If the shoe fits.*

Once we arrived back on campus, he jumped out of the

car and came around to open my door. "Thank you," I said as I grabbed his proffered hand.

"Should I come up?"

"I don't think my roommate has left yet. What time is it?"

"It's almost five."

"You don't want to be traveling back during rush hour, especially on a Friday. I think my mother packed me an extra toothbrush."

He smiled at me and took my hand as we walked toward the dorm. His mood swings left me reeling. My Cally had such an even and mellow persona. Cal, on the other hand, ran hot and cold—better than the faucet in my room. When he smiled, the world was set right again.

I knew I trampled on a precarious road by giving him so much power over me, but I couldn't help it. Stupidly, his volatility caused me to swoon.

Text to self: *Knowing what is good for you and doing it are two very different things.*

Don't I know it.

As we entered my room, I had an epiphany. I loved two men: Cal and Cally. Although technically they were the same person, the ten years between them really defined them as different and unique. I peeked around the desk and found it devoid of Debbie.

"Listen," I said, "I promised to check in with Patrick. Will you be okay alone for a few minutes?"

"Sure." His sexy smile made me want to climb all over him again.

I straddled his lap for a steamy kiss before leaving.

Once we parted, he said, "At least I know you'll still find me attractive when I'm old."

"YOS was never old."

"Can I read the rest of your letters to him?"

My gut warned me to do otherwise, and yet I had always planned to let him read them. "Okay." I gathered the printed pages from the side drawer of the desk and handed them over. "There are some papers I wrote on the stack as well. Oh, wait." I tore out my latest letter to YOS and gave it to Cal. "That one goes last."

"Don't look so worried."

Worried is my middle name! I waved goodbye as I left the room, which he didn't see because he was already reading my deepest thoughts. I flounced down the hall over to Packy's room. I knocked and called out, "Pakster, are you in?"

He cracked the door and stuck out his head. "Where's the man?"

"Sitting on my bed, reading all my letters to Cally."

"Is that wise?"

"Don't start."

"You're a mess." He tugged me through the door over to his bed.

"Keep the compliments coming. You're helping so much."

Packy touched my shoulder, and his look of compassion transformed my attitude.

"I'm sorry. I just don't know which way is up anymore. Would you believe Cal doesn't care about cursing? WTF?"

He clapped his hands and cracked up. "You ... oh, you worry about the silliest things. Are you having any fun?"

"Yes, lots." I blushed. "In between the arguing."

"You're so funny, Jayjay. Please tell me you got laid again."

Mimicking Packy, I blew on my nails and then rubbed them on the upper part of my dress. "Pakster, I blew him in the car while parked at Whataburger."

"Shut up!"

"I kid you not, and we had amazing sex earlier. I thought we were heading for a second round, but then Debbie showed up. She was shocked to meet Cal and actually called me a fag hag. I wanted to slap her, but I refrained."

"And what's wrong with being a fag hag?"

"Fag is a very inappropriate word in the 2010s. Plus, I found it insulting to the both of us."

"Then on my behalf, I thank you. So back to Callahan. Other than sex, how's it going?"

I shrugged. "You know how you thought I had an advantage because I know Cally. I have to throw all that shit out the window. Ohhh, Packy."

"You're blushing again. What is it?"

"We had angry sex. I wasn't particularly angry, but he was. OMG, it was good. His emotions are explosive."

"You're smiling, Jayjay."

"I like him."

"I can tell. I'd like a chance to know him too."

I hugged him. "I want that too. Come over for pizza later?"

"Are you sure you want me there?"

"There's only so much sex and arguing a girl can take."

He shoved my shoulder. "Lighten up, girlfriend. It's happening."

"At least, he dropped one of his mantras."

"Love?"

"How'd you guess? He says we should enjoy each other for as long as it lasts. Ashley will be the breaking point. We did sort of make plans for next weekend. I'm going there. I think he's going to pick me up, but we haven't solidified that."

"Let me see if I can borrow the car again. I wouldn't mind going home for the weekend."

Excited, I jumped up. "Why don't you ask Chuck to come with us?"

"My parents aren't the most liberal of people. Hmmm, I'm going to contemplate that."

"I'm going to get going. I'm scared to leave him alone too long. He could get pissed and take off."

"I understand."

I hugged him. "Love you, Pakster."

"Love you, you fag hag."

Chuckling, I stuck out my tongue and then left his room. I paused before my door, taking a few deep breaths. Upon entering, Cal glanced up for a second and then continued reading. On the bed, I sat down next to him and waited.

Tears trailed down his cheeks and his voice cracked when he finally spoke. "You really loved YOS."

"With all my heart, and I still do." I wiped his cheeks and stared into his eyes. "I love two men."

"Jayden," he uttered, clasping my wrist. "I've been so caught up in how this affects me. I hadn't realized the pain you've been in. Your loss."

A sob tore out of me.

He scooped me up into his arms and whispered into my hair, "Thank you for sharing your letters and papers with me." He held me as I spilled out all my pent up pain and fear. In his embrace, it felt as if both my Callahans had me wrapped up in their arms.

After a while, my tears subsided and at that moment, I really thought we had a fighting chance. "Thank you." When I glanced up, it appeared he had been crying with me.

He moved me off his lap and reached for the box of tissues. We both used them surrounded by the silence. With his arm, he leaned me against his side and rested my head on his shoulder. For once, the silence didn't bother me one bit.

Shifting us to face each other, he asked, "So Travis read your papers?"

"Yes, just the papers."

"He didn't believe you after the first paper, right?"

"Yes, that's true. Would you have?"

He shook his head. "Doubtful. Part of me still hasn't wrapped my head around it."

"I understand."

"I believe you do," he said, holding my chin. "I wish I brought your package with me. I'd love to sketch you in the light of the window, just as you look right now." He wiped away the new tear that fell.

Fighting all the emotions that threatened to take over, I said, "I invited Patrick to come by later for pizza. Should I call and cancel?"

"Definitely not. After reading what you had to say about him, I want to get to know him. Travis, on the other hand, I'll take a pass."

"I'm with you on that."

"You mentioned that you aren't sure if Travis really believes you."

I sighed. "I don't know what to think other than he seems to think he needs me for inspiration. None of that matters anymore."

"How so? Isn't he still your professor?"

"That's all he is to me now. I told him from the start that he was a holding place, and as I said, I haven't done anything sexual with him since our first date. We did have dinner together last weekend, but I ended up crying about you—well YOS, about the day he died." I huffed when I saw Cal's expression. "There is no one else, just you."

He moved his jaw back and forth and said, "You probably already know this, but Britt cheated on me."

Hearing his words felt as if someone knocked me over and forced the air out of my lungs. I shook my head rapidly, feeling violated. "Cally never told me!"

"Jesus," he said, running his hand through his hair.

"How could he not tell me?" Tears pooled in my eyes and poured down. "I feel..."

"What?"

"Angry at him. Furious. Why wouldn't he tell me that? He told me everything else about that time. What it was like having Britt on bedrest and the fights you would have and how she thought she knew better than the doctors and Jesus fucking Christ, why wouldn't he tell me that?"

He tried to hold me, but I moved away and started pacing.

"I thought I knew everything about him. Please explain to me why he would have kept that from me."

Cal held out his hand to me. "Jayden, I don't know. Maybe he didn't think it was a relevant part of the past? It happened toward the end when everything was falling apart. I thought we were trying to put our life back together, but she needed to be far away from it all. She wasn't the type who liked to deal with her emotions and tended to bury herself in something else. She hated me crying about it and was unwilling to get help to grieve."

"I feel like throwing up." With my head in my hands, I drew air in and out of my lungs.

"I don't mean to minimize what you're experiencing, Jayden. I told you because ... because you understand my pain."

"He never seemed worried I would cheat on him."

"Come," he said, waving me over to him.

I sat on the edge of the bed, one knee up with my other foot on the floor.

"I don't think he consciously omitted it. For us, the pain

stems from the loss of Katy and of the life we thought we would have."

"Okay." I shook out my hands, trying to let go of the surge of anger. "This isn't about me. It's supposed to be about you. I'm sorry for how I reacted. I'm sorry Britt acted out that way. My track record precedes me or procedes me. That's not even a word."

"I know what you're trying to say."

"I couldn't and wouldn't ever cheat on you."

He stood and pulled me up with him. His hug relieved some of the confusion I felt. "I believe you, love."

Just then, an entirely different emotion filled me up. He called me love! I smiled up at Cal.

"What? What just happened?"

"You called me love."

"I did?" he asked with a raised eyebrow and his sexy smile.

"You did."

"Well, I'm not taking it back."

"Good." I stalked over to the closet as my mood totally transformed. Rummaging in the box that my mother packed, I found the extra toothbrush. I held it up. "For later."

"Is that an invitation?"

"Please spend the night. I love sleeping in your arms."

"I enjoyed that as well. I accept."

I clapped and bounced up and down a few times. "I just realized something."

"What is that?"

"I have to focus on now and leave the past and the future in their rightful places, within reason. I do plan to try to change your mind about investing."

"I'll try to stay open to listening."

"Awesome!"

We settled back on the bed, with my head in his lap. As

he played with my hair, he asked, "Can I ask you a question about you and YOS?"

"Okay."

"Did you often do to him what you did to me earlier in the car?"

"No, never."

Cal opened his mouth then quickly closed it again.

"I mean, never in the car. Often, yes. It was a big part of our sex play."

"I figured that's what you meant. Why then?"

I glanced to the left and then back at him, smiling. "Because I wanted to."

He chuckled. "I've never had a lover like you."

"Is that a good thing?"

"The very best."

My smile beamed. It felt as if it could light up a stadium.

"And me?"

"You'll get there," I brayed.

"Hey!"

Giggling, I said, "You're a passionate lover, and our chemistry is off the charts. You do everything incredibly—"

"But?"

"My clit is sensitive. When you lick, I prefer slower and softer."

"YOS had me on that."

"Yeah, well, he had ten years on you."

He puffed out his chest and said, "I'll do much better next time. After Patrick leaves, you'll see."

"You're on." I winked and became aroused, knowing what was coming. Me!

He took me completely by surprise when he said, "It's good you came back earlier."

"Oh, Cal, I'm not sure there's anything nicer you could

have said. I'm glad too."

Then he kissed me again, and I felt the difference. He was falling in love with me. In his arms, I thought the world might be righted once again.

CHAPTER TWENTY-NINE

*B*ang, *Bang, Bang.* "Jayjay." *Bang, Bang, Bang.* "Jayjay." *Bang, Bang, Bang.* "Jayjay."

"What the heck?" Cal said.

I hopped up and answered the door with my hands on my hips. "Sheldon never knocks so loudly."

Cal scratched his head, and I thought to explain but decided against it.

Packy did anyway. "She says it's from a show in the future."

"It's called *The Big Bang Theory*," I elaborated.

"Is that a sex reference?" Packy asked.

"Science. It's about a group of science nerds."

"Huh." Packy took a step toward Cal. "Okay, then. Callahan, it's good to see you're still here. That's a good sign."

"Thank you for being such an amazing friend to Jayden."

Packy shifted his posture and rested his hip on the desk. "How do you know that?"

"She talks about you to YOS in her letters."

"YOS?"

I stayed out of it.

Callahan leaned forward and said, "Your Older Self. That's what we're calling older Callahan."

"That reads Jayjay all over it. It's brill. She usually refers to you as Cal or Callahan and YOS as Cally. It makes so much sense. Thank you for having me over when you could be—"

Then I butted in. "Why don't you order the pizza? Should we get two? Cal's favorite is mushroom, onion, and sausage." I looked in his direction for the affirmation.

293

Cal nodded, his eyes shining.

"It's pretty cool when she does that, isn't it?" Packy asked.

"Most of the time," Cal said, and then we all laughed.

"Does that pizza work for you, Packy?"

"You know I'll eat anything."

"Great. Please order me a small veggie pizza, no peppers. Thanks."

He picked up the phone and placed our order.

I climbed onto the bed and snuggled up next to Callahan.

Packy turned the desk chair around to face us. "So how are you handling everything?"

"I think Jayden would say, not well."

I didn't chime in, waiting to hear the rest of it.

"I don't feel ready for her and yet, here I am. Honestly, there is no place I'd rather be. But, I worry it's folly even to try."

"Thesaurus?" Packy looked at me.

"Stupid," I answered.

"Gotcha. Sometimes we have to let go of how we expect things to unfold or what we plan or what we think we want and open up to what's in front of us."

"That's pretty profound, Pakster."

"Jayden here has me thinking about becoming a psych major, which I never considered before. If I've learned anything about Jayjay's resurrection and what she's gone through in coming back, it's that change is inevitable, and if we truly want to be happy, it requires risk. It also requires incredible flexibility of purpose. There's one more thing."

"What's that?" Cal asked, holding me close.

"One person can make a huge difference in your life if you let them. Oh, and I forgot! We never really grow up. We may become more disciplined and less reactive, but our personality stays the same."

Cal turned his attention to me. "Do you agree with that?"

"For me I do, but I'm not sure about you. I mean you're clearly still Callahan to me, but the recent pain you've endured changed you. Maybe as you get older, you revert back? I'm not sure." I kissed him and then faced Packy again.

"So what's the plan then?" Packy asked.

I glanced at Cal, and he looked at me. "You first," he said.

"To have as much sex as humanly possible. I might just piss him off so we can have angry sex again."

Cal's eyes opened wide. "You told him about that?"

"Oops, sorry. There's not much I keep from Packy. If it helps any, I was bragging on your behalf. What's *your* plan, Cal?"

"You didn't completely answer the question," Cal said.

"Are you sure you want to know?"

"I do," Packy said.

I squinted my eyes at him and pursed my lips.

"I do too."

"Fine, just set me up to put my foot in it. You asked for it. I plan to have Cal fall madly and deeply in love with me. Then I hope he takes my advice and invests in the stock market, with my help. Then I hope he quits his job, which he won't admit he hates or maybe he doesn't quite hate it yet. Then he will sweep me off my feet, and we will live happily ever after. How's that sound?"

"Sweet and romantic," Packy said.

"Diabolical," Cal uttered. A knock on the door sounded, and he got up. "It's on me."

"Thanks."

"Great," Packy said, rubbing his stomach. "I'm hungry."

After Cal had paid the pizza delivery guy, I said, "You still have to answer."

"Food first."

"Fine, fine."

"You know what else I've learned from Jayjay?" Packy asked, munching on a pizza slice.

This can't be good.

"What?" Callahan asked, taking a slice for himself.

"Fine, never means fine."

"Oh, yeah, I learned that from my mother ages ago."

I harrumphed. "Male bonding, it's so sweet. Your turn, Callahan."

"I can't say I really have a plan. I think I do, and then it flies out the window."

I walked over to the sink and got some water. "You mean like coming here today to say goodbye?"

"Wait a minute—" Packy interjected.

"Jayden, that's not what I said."

"So explain it to us." I got back on the bed and awaited his response.

"I wasn't a hundred percent sure what to believe. Were you playing me? When you lose your internal compass, it's hard to trust anyone. I didn't want to believe her. But when I saw her sitting there writing in her notebook, I wanted to..."

Packy leaned forward in the chair. "What?"

"Draw her. I hadn't felt that in a long time. Then she looked up, and her smile transformed her features and dissolved my plans. She's ... so real. The idea that she sought me out to hurt or play me left, and so did *some* of the fear. It's still easier to believe the worst."

"Would you believe you became the optimist between us?" I chuckled.

Cal laughed. "That's pretty hard to believe."

"It's true. At least, it was. Maybe we'll get to see."

"Maybe," Cal repeated.

"That's a start," Packy said.

After we had finished eating the pizza, I offered my coveted nut balls to the guys. "This shows how much I love you both. I'm sharing my yummy balls with you."

"That sounds all kinds of wrong," Packy said, popping the dessert into his mouth.

"Wow, these are good," Callahan said, reaching for another.

"My mom makes them especially for your birthday every year. She knows ... she knew how much you loved them. YOS did. You know what I mean."

"Well, YOS and I, at least, have that in common."

We all laughed.

Once I cut them off so I could save a few for myself, Packy stood, and Cal followed him to the door. They hugged goodbye.

"It was good to meet you," Cal said as he patted Packy on the back.

"Same. Be good to Jayden. She deserves it."

As I walked Packy back to this room, I asked, "So, what do you think?"

"I think he's further gone than he even realizes. I see how he watches you, Jayjay. He seems younger and much more relaxed than the first time we met."

"Well, Travis was there, pissing him off."

He rested against his door and said, "It's more than that, and you know it."

"I'm trying to stay away from the deep end. You know, keeping perspective and all of that."

"Just be you, Jayjay. It's gotten you this far."

"Thanks, Packy. Listen, next time we talk, remind me to tell you what Cal told me that Cally never did. Thanks so much for coming by." I hugged him tightly.

He unlocked and opened his door.

"Have fun at your party Saturday. You'll be happy to know no cops show up to that one."

He flung his hair back and smiled. "I like having you around."

"The feeling's mutual."

"Later days and better lays," he said, just before he shut his door.

Smiling, I strolled back to the other side of the dorm and found Cal waiting for me on the bed. "What did you think of Patrick?"

"I like him, and I can see why you care about him so much."

"That's awesome. I had hoped you'd like him. I'm looking forward to meeting Port."

"He's a curmudgeon."

"Grumpy maybe, but he's not old, is he?"

"He acts like it sometimes."

"Consider me warned. I like a challenge."

"Evidently." He pulled me to him and gave me a soft kiss.

"Do you need to call Papa Port?"

Cal laughed. "I probably should, so he doesn't think I'm dead on the side of the road." He stood up and dialed. "Hey... Yeah, I'm still here... No, no, it's good... Yes, I plan to stay over." After a long pause, he continued speaking, "Listen, don't worry... No, really... Yes, I know... I hear what you're saying. It's all good... Yeah, I'll be back tomorrow... Yes, Port, I know... Okay, bye."

"That didn't sound good."

"He's just worried about me."

"Did you show him the package?"

"No, Jayden, I'm much more private than you are."

I frowned. "Was that a slight?"

He sighed. "I'm sorry. It does bother me a bit.

However, it's what makes you so..."

"So?"

"Open, honest, genuine."

"Maybe someday you learn to appreciate that as much as my oral skills."

He toppled me over and tickled my sides. "I already do."

"Surely a start."

Then he kissed me, and we sailed the current of budding love. His taste and the soft caresses of his lips helped to put the pieces of my heart back together. He paused, smoothing my hair away from my face. "So beautiful," he murmured. Then he sucked my bottom lip, causing my wetness to grow. "I want to taste you again."

As he rolled onto his side, I lifted off my dress and pulled down my panties. "You don't have to ask me twice."

He chuckled. "I'm going to take my time, so just lie back, and enjoy."

With Cal, I felt a confidence in my body that Cally gave to me. His love for my big nipples, full lips, wide hips, and more gave me a new perspective of myself. *Thank you, Cally.*

Cal bent my knees up and out and said, "Hold your legs for me." Then his blessed tongue licked up from the base of my opening, all the way to my most sensitive spot.

"Ohhh," I groaned. "So good."

He tilted his head up, smiled, and went back to work. His tongue softly explored my folds and plunged into my center. "Jesus, you taste good."

"Hmmm." I patted his head and pushed him down again.

Laughing, he lowered down and imbibed more of my come. His finger slid into my core and found my G-spot.

"Oh, oh, Cal ... you learn quickly." My back arched over the intensity. "So, so good. Mmmm."

Then he focused his tongue on my clit, using his finger to

stroke my insides. Gently, he swirled around my swollen arousal bringing me higher and higher to the edge of release.

He paused. "How am I doing?"

"Other than stopping, perfect."

He shook the bed with his laughter and thankfully resumed his dancing tongue against my clit.

"Mmmm," I moaned. I let my legs fall to the side and began pulling and twisting my nipples.

It drew his attention. "Jesus Christ, woman. You're the sexiest lover I have ever known. Do that next time you ride my cock."

"Shhh," I murmured, pushing his head back down.

Once he resumed and steadily licked my clit, I flew back up and out into the universe. The contractions racked my body, squeezing his finger and sending more wetness over his hand. Euphoria flooded my bloodstream, and for the very first time, I blessed Toly for sending me back.

"Wowsa, Callahan. You've redeemed yourself."

He sat up with his chest puffed out. "Better than YOS?"

"Hmmm ... at least as good as."

"I'll take it."

"Fun fact: YOS was the first to make me come that way."

"And now, I am."

"Yes, you are." I sighed a long breath of contentment. "This is the best I've felt since returning. I have you to thank for that. Ummm..." I said, staring down at the bulge in Cal's jeans. "Looks like your friend needs some attention."

"Are you up for more?"

I giggled. "He sure is. Let's let him out to play." I started unbuckling his belt, and he helped me undress him.

Once naked, he scooped me up and laid me crossways on the bed, with my legs hanging off. "Pull your legs back like before." Still standing, he leaned over me and fed his cock through my swollen folds. "It won't take me long. Hearing your moans and groans was a total turn on."

"I'm yours. Take me."

And he did, over and over again.

"As hard as you need, Cal."

He increased his pace and pounded into me, the wetness sloshing with each penetration. "Oh, Jayden," he cried out when he finally released his come into me. His expression of lust and release engrained itself on my psyche. He looked down and said, "I've made a mess."

"Want to shower? It's rather small, so we'll have to take turns."

"I have nothing to change into."

"Good thing I prefer you naked."

He glanced to the other side of the room.

"Roommate won't be back until Sunday evening."

"You first."

I gathered an extra towel for Cal and tossed it over to him. Inside the bathroom, I set the temperature to what I wanted and got in. I bathed quickly and left the water running. "You're turn." At the sink, I flossed and brushed my teeth, parted my wet hair, and then shuffled over to the closet to get my robe. I yawned, pleasantly exhausted from the day.

While I waited, I tried to read from *The Shining*, but my mind kept wandering. Callahan was in my shower, in my dorm, planning to spend the night. For a moment, I couldn't remember feeling so satiated until I thought about our final trip together. Those days of lingering in bed, making love and enjoying the island sat at the pinnacle of our life together. Our love kept growing and deepening to such a sweet place. With Cal, I had to set my expectations to something realistic instead of the where Cally and I left off.

"Whatcha thinking about?" Cal asked as he walked out of the bathroom with his towel slung around his hips.

"Damn, Cal, you're hot." I ogled the V that dipped under the towel.

He shook his head, chuckling. "You want more?"

"No, not tonight. I was just appreciating all of this." I waved my hand up and down.

"The feeling is mutual."

"Thank you. I left your toothbrush on the sink."

After he had brushed his teeth, he said, "Off with the robe. Let's cuddle."

I put the book away, stripped off my robe, and climbed into bed next to Cal.

We sighed in unison when he spooned me to him.

"Sleep well," he said.

My heartbeat caught, and then I replied as I had in the future, "You too." *I love you.*

CHAPTER THIRTY

B linking several times against the light that cascaded from the window in the room, I scanned my space. No Callahan. He had straightened up again, hanging my robe and folding the towel he used. My heart dropped until I spied a piece of paper on my desk and scrambled to get it. On the front, I found a sketch of me sleeping. He had done it in pen ink. I smiled from ear to ear. Turning it over, I read the note on the back:

Jayden,
    I woke at 6 a.m. wide-awake and felt inspired to draw you. It was incredible to create again. It's been a while.
    Port and I have plans for today, so I decided to head back and not disturb your sleep.
    I'll call you later.
    Callahan

I used the bathroom and jumped back in bed with the sketch, holding it above me. In his depiction, my messy hair lay across my cheek, my lips slightly pursed, my closed eyes relaxed, and my shoulder out from under the covers showing the dip in my clavicle. I loved it. I wondered how he could have seen me in the dark. Maybe he turned on the lamp, or maybe the light coming from under the door provided enough illumination. With one of the corkboard pins from the back of my desk, I pinned it to the wall beside my bed.

Snuggled under the covers once again, I drifted back to sleep. I didn't wake again until lunchtime. My stomach clutched in hunger, motivating me to get up and get dressed.

I knocked on Packy's door to see if he wanted to eat too.

"Give me a minute," he said through the door.

"Sure." I sat down against the hall wall and waited.

When he finally opened the door, he said, "Where's the man?"

"Back to Gainesville." I stood up. "He again stole out early in the morning. This time, however, he left a note and a sketch of me."

"Definitely progress."

"He said he would call me later. I guess we shall see. I'm starved." I tugged on Packy's wrist. "I don't recall being so hungry last time."

"How many times did you have sex yesterday?"

"Uh, good point."

"You don't need to blush on my account."

I shoved his shoulder. "Walk faster."

"Settled down, girlie, the food will still be there."

Inside the cafeteria, I loaded my plate with eggs, bacon, toast, and potatoes, then grabbed a cup of coffee with lots of cream and sugar.

"You weren't kidding. You usually eat like a bird."

"Caw caw!"

"What the hell was that horrible sound supposed to be?"

"My bird call. Was it really that bad?"

"I wouldn't let her rip in mixed company."

I laughed so hard I almost dropped my food-laden tray.

As soon as we settled at a table, Packy asked, "So, what was the thing I was supposed to remind you about?"

I shoveled a few mouthfuls of eggs and sipped my coffee. "I want your opinion."

"Fire away."

"Damn, this all tastes so good. Can you pass the ketchup?"

"Sure. So?" He handed it over to me.

I took a couple more bites of food and then said, "Cal

told me that Britt cheated on him. Cally never told me that. At first, I felt ... like ... I don't know, like I didn't know Cally as well as I thought I did. Then Cal said he probably didn't think it was relevant because it was at the end of things. However, it still matters to Cal, hence his jealousy. Cally was never jealous."

"I'm siding with Cal on this one. Cally hadn't gotten over the loss of his child, but he married you. I doubt he left it out purposefully."

"Okay, thanks. That's what I was hoping you would say. Is Chuck going to the same party tonight?"

"Yes, I'm thinking about asking Jamie if he plans to stay over at Lenore's again. He wasn't in the room last night. I think Lenore's roommate is gone for the weekend."

After swallowing, I said, "That sounds fun. I hope it works out. Have you asked him about next weekend?"

"I will tonight."

"Cool." I had a few more bites of food and then pushed the tray away. "My eyes were way bigger than my stomach." I sipped my coffee and waited for Packy to finish his meal.

"Dare I say you seem calm?"

"I think he's falling in love with me."

"Yeah, so do I."

"Hey, Pakster, any change with you and Chuck?"

He shook his head and took a sip of his soda. "I touched his shoulder the other day when we were out together. He went ape shit over it."

"Sorry, dude."

"Like you, I know what I'm getting myself into. At least, with you, I'm pretty sure Cal will come around in time."

I placed my coffee cup on the tray. "Are you having fun?"

"Yeah, it beats the one-night stands. He has a great sense of humor, and when we're alone, it's great. When we're out, he stiffens up."

"Deep in the closet."

"He might be walled in *behind* the closet."

I chuckled slightly. "I'm sorry we're both dealing with complicated relationships."

Packy leaned back in his chair. "What are your plans this weekend?"

"Waiting for Cal's call."

He slapped the table making our trays bounce. "You're too funny."

"I have some studying to do, math homework, etc. Oh, shit!" I lurched forward and held my stomach, as a wave of nausea assaulted me.

"What?"

"My stomach just cramped. Do you think I could still be sick?"

"You've been dealing with a lot of stress lately, so yeah. Why don't you go to the clinic and get checked out."

"Ohhh. Yeah, I'll do that on Monday. I have to run. Can you take care of my tray?"

Packy stood. "Of course. Let's talk later."

"Okay." I waved and hurried through the cafeteria and across the quad back to my dorm room. Prostrate on my bed, I groaned. My stomach grumbled and bitched at me. "Sorry I ate so much." I flipped over onto my back and took a few deep breaths. The nausea seemed to pass.

When the phone rang, I didn't want to move and wake up my stomach again. I sat up anyway and leaned forward to retrieve the phone. "Yeah?"

"Are you okay?" Cal asked.

"Hey, you!" Energy jetted up my spine. *He called!* "Yeah, I'm okay. Breakfast didn't sit well with me."

"Maybe it was last night's pizza?"

"I guess it could be. What are you up to?"

"Port has a bunch of guys over, and we're drinking beer and playing pool. They plan to order pizza again, but I'll pass on that."

"Has Papa Port settled down?"

"He seemed relieved that I came back early."

"I miss you, Cal."

He covered the phone, and I couldn't hear what he said. "Sorry about that. Yes, I miss you too. A lot."

"That's great!" My unruly stomach seemed to heal itself instantly. "Thank you so much for my sketch. I love it."

"It felt amazing to draw again. I hadn't realized how much I missed it."

"How were you able to see me?"

"The light from under the door. I sat on the floor and drew it."

"I want to be awake next time."

"Deal. Listen, I need to get going."

"Port's shooting you dirty looks?"

"How did you know?"

"Please warn him that he's going to like me."

Cal laughed, and I could feel his smile through the phone. "I will, love."

"Thanks so much for the call." Once we hung up, I danced around the room for a few minutes. *I'm in love, I'm in love, I'm in love.* Then I ran into the bathroom and threw up. *Motherfucker that sucked.* I felt amazingly better after giving up breakfast. I studied for a bit and then went out for a bike ride. The warm day didn't deter me. I thought about stopping for an apple fritter, but I didn't want to chance a run-in with Travis.

Although my stomach didn't seem to be cooperating, I felt elated. Cal and I were moving forward far faster than I ever expected. *He misses me!* It doesn't get much better than that. Plus, he liked Packy. That could have been a deal breaker. I planned to have Packy in my life for a very long time.

The weekend seemed to fly by. Callahan called two more times to say hi and to confirm we were on for next weekend.

CHAPTER THIRTY-ONE

B ecause I felt so much better, I didn't go to the clinic on Monday. On Tuesday, I got up too late to have breakfast and again felt sick after eating lunch. I broke down and went in.

The clinic had plastic chairs against the wall. I took a seat, filled out the paperwork, and waited for my turn.

A middle-aged woman, with short blond hair, waved me over. "What can we do for you?"

"I'm not sure really. I find if I skip breakfast, I get sick to my stomach when I eat lunch."

She looked up and away and flared her nostrils, which left me with the impression she thought I was a stupid teenager. "So eat breakfast?"

"It's never happened to me before. I used to skip breakfast in high school, and I never felt sick."

"How many times has it happened?"

I thought about it for a minute. "Three or four times. It started happening after I got sick."

"It could just be remnants of the cold. Let's draw blood just to make sure it's not Mono or something else."

"Okay, great. Thanks."

I ran into Packy on my way back to the dorm. "I went to the clinic, and the woman treated me like I was a dumb kid."

"Get used to it again. Shit happens. They can't see your insides. What did she say?"

"She thinks I'm not quite over my cold. She took blood. In the meantime, I'm not skipping breakfast anymore."

"It's the most important meal of the day, so they say."

"Yeah, those 'they' are know-it-alls."

He smiled. "How's Callahan?"

"He seems excited about the weekend, but he keeps warning me about Port."

"Are you worried about meeting him?"

"Not in the slightest. I know how to tame grizzly bears."

"That I don't doubt. I'm off to class. Later gator."

"Later."

On Wednesday, I found another note on my seat in composition class.

> *Come see me today. I have a question.*
> *T.*

Ugh! I decided to get it done between classes, so there wouldn't be much time to linger.

After class, I found my way to Travis' office. I knocked on the door and waited.

"You showed."

"I'm here." I shrugged. "What's up?"

"How are things going with Callahan?"

"Is that why you asked me here? I need to leave in a few to get to my next class."

He perched on the edge of his desk. "No. I wanted to know if you'd be willing to meet my ex-father-in-law."

"Why would I do that?"

"I showed him what I was working on, and he wants to meet you."

The puzzle pieces fell into place. "He's the man with the gray hair and dark mustache. No, absolutely not. I can't believe you had the audacity to tell someone I don't know about me and my circumstance."

"Yes, that's him. He only thinks you're a creative storyteller. He's in publishing, so you might want to change your attitude."

Everything about it felt wrong. "I'll think about it. I've got to run." As I tromped my way to my next class, I pondered what Travis' motivation might be. Was he really trying to help me, or was something else going on? I didn't know what to make of it.

❤❤❤❤❤

After dinner, as I worked on my next paper for composition class, the phone rang.

"Hello?"

"Hi, love. Did you have a good day?" Cal asked.

"Overall it was good. Travis wants me to meet his ex-father-in-law, which seems odd to me. He says he's in publishing. I'm—"

"I'd prefer to come with you if you go."

"You'd do that for me? I mean, wow. I'm not sure I want to go, but that's really great to know. How was your day?" I lay back in bed and twirled the phone cord around my finger.

"Thank you for letting me know about Travis. I'm certain he hasn't given up." He cleared his throat. "Enough about him. Today was a good day in sales, and I thought about you when I left the office to get lunch."

"Crazy pizza snatching girl?"

He chuckled. "Exactly. Two more days. What time do you plan to leave?"

"We were thinking about heading out after we eat lunch. What time will you be home?"

"I plan to leave a bit early to get the place ready for you."

"That's sweet, Cal, but you don't need to straighten up on my account. Besides, YOS was always clean and neat."

"So am I. I just need to do a bit of shopping. Port and I

are going to grab some dinner. Talk to you tomorrow?"

"Great. Thanks for the call."

"My pleasure. I'll be thinking of you."

"Me too. Bye."

I finished the first draft of the paper and then looked over the art slides for tomorrow's upcoming test.

Packy poked his head into the room. "Any news from the clinic?"

"No, I haven't heard anything yet. She said it might take a couple of days."

"BTW Chuck is flaking on this weekend. It'll just be us."

"We'll make it fun. Maybe we can all hook up for dinner one night. That way you can meet Port too."

"Sounds good. Okay, I'm off to study. Leave the door open or closed."

"Closed is good."

❤❤❤❤❤

On Thursday, I aced my art history exam, and even though I barely ate breakfast, I felt fine. I figured my body had finally kicked my cold. I stopped by the computer center and typed up my paper due on Friday.

Back in the room, Debbie made a quick appearance and took off again. She was gone even more than I recalled.

Since I wouldn't be doing homework over the weekend, I pushed to get it all done after my classes. I had a math test on Monday I wasn't sweating and a Spanish test the following Tuesday. I had three articles to read for Sociology and another chapter to read for composition.

Halfway through all the work, my phone rang.

"Hello?"

"Can I please speak to ... Jayden Cooke," asked a male voice I didn't recognize.

"This is Jayden."

"Can you please give me your birthdate?"

"Not until I know what this is about." I sat down on the edge of the bed.

"Your blood work test results are in."

"Oh, why didn't you say so?" I gave him my birthday. "So?"

"Two things. The first is your white blood cell count is slightly elevated, which probably means you are getting over a cold. The second is ... you're pregnant."

"That's not possible." I stood up and started pacing. My heart thumped like a cartoon character's did. It pounded so hard it stretched my chest.

"I have the test results right here. You're definitely pregnant."

I stopped by the side of the desk and rested my forehead on the partition's edge. "But it's too early for me to have morning sickness."

"That's probably due to the cold you had."

This can't be happening! "Can I come back in to redo the test?"

"Blood tests rarely give false positives. I do suggest you come in and review your options."

I dropped the phone and crumbled to the floor in shock. How could this happen? I had plenty of sex last time and didn't get pregnant until I was twenty-nine.

A little voice in my head said, "Yes, but you weren't having sex with Callahan."

"That's horseshit!" I yelled at the sink. "Toly said it would be the same as before."

That tiny little voice, which wouldn't shut up said, "That's true, but you weren't having sex at eighteen."

I can't go to Gainesville now. Fuck! I have to go. I

can't end our relationship over the phone. Motherfucking, goddamn shit!

I picked up the phone and dialed Packy.

"Patrick's Lingerie. Today's special, Freudian slips."

"Packy ... it's all fucked up," I blubbered.

"Chuck, keep studying. I have to check on Jayden."

I tried to level my voice. "I didn't realize Chuck—"

"I'm already on my way." The phone clicked off.

I crawled over to the door and opened it a crack. Not bothering to get up, I scooted over and rested my back against my bed.

"Why are you on the floor?" Packy asked as he blew into my room. "Take my hand." He pulled me up, and we sat on the bed together. "Now tell me what has you in such a state?"

"Can I ... stay at your house this weekend?"

"What the fuck are you talking about? Did Callahan cancel?"

I shook my head. "I can't say the words."

"Is this about Travis?"

I shook my head again.

He appeared to be thinking. "The blood test?"

I nodded.

"Are you seriously ill?"

"I wish."

He jumped up and yelled. "Holy shit! The rabbit died?"

"Are you ready to be a dad?"

"Does Callahan know?"

I shook my head through the tears.

"How did this happen? I mean, other than the obvious?"

"I didn't think I could get..."

He knelt down in front of me. "Knocked up..."

"Yes, until I was much older."

"Come here, Jayjay." He held his arms out to me.

I fell apart in his embrace. "Cal and I ... were ... we were making ... progress. This annihilates any chance."

"You can't be sure that's true. Maybe he'll come around like Cally did."

"Fuck me, we should've used condoms."

"Ya think?"

"He'll never forgive me, and now Port will have a real reason to hate me."

He pulled my hair back and brushed my cheeks. "First things first. You're keeping the baby, correct?"

"Yes, of course, it's Ashley."

"When's the baby due?"

"Uh... When did I go to the lighthouse with Callahan?"

"Almost four weeks ago?"

I shook my head. "Almost three weeks ago." Using my fingers, I counted off the months. "Mid-June?"

Packy clapped. "That's perfect. If Cal doesn't come around, we can move into an apartment and stagger our classes as they are now. We'll have the summer to get everything sorted."

"Packy," I sobbed. "You ... are too young."

He stood up and crossed his arms over his chest. "Are you saying you don't trust me with your kid?"

I took his arm and pulled him to me. "No, of course not. I just don't want to fuck up your life."

"Then STFU. Here take one, no take five." He held out the box of tissues to me.

Although my tears continued to fall, I dabbed at my face and blew my nose. "I love you, Packy."

"I know you do. We'll get through it."

"I don't even know if I can be pregnant and stay in the dorms. Oh god, my parents. My father is going to lose his mind, and my mother... Oh Packy, this is sooo fucked up."

"Breathe, Jayjay, and don't stress out. It's not good for the baby. You've been through this before, and you're young and healthy. You'll be even better at it this time. If you stay calm, it'll help everyone else around you stay calm."

With every effort, I got myself together and wiped away the last of my tears. "Packy, Ashley is on her way. Maybe this means I'll have more children this time. I'm going to do my best not to freak out. That is *after* I speak to Callahan. I'm going to miss him so much."

"Of course, you can stay at my house in Gainesville. The only problem with it is that it'll give my folks hope. Should we tell your parents that we're a couple?"

"It's still early, and I won't show for a while. Once we have it all planned out, then I'll talk to my parents about it."

Packy rose to leave. "Okay. I'm going to run back to my room and tell Chuck to go back to his frat house."

"Please don't. I'm wigging, but I'm going to be okay. We can talk over dinner or even tomorrow. Ashley isn't going anywhere anytime soon. I need to think about what I want to say to Cal tomorrow, and I still have homework to finish. Thank you. I know those words aren't nearly enough, but thank you so much for being you. You make my life so much better."

"If you're sure."

"I'm sure. Please don't tell anyone."

"Of course not."

"Thanks."

After Packy left, I sat on my bed and stared at my closet, not seeing anything. My mind hopped around so fast it was hard to keep up. Then I touched my belly and remembered being pregnant the last time. Ashley loved when I played music. Her favorite was Sting. *I'll have to get his CDs from this time period.* I wondered how different she would be without all the technology. At least she would have a loving dad, regardless of how everything panned out. Although it was only a small part, I felt some excitement over meeting Ashley again. Knowing that I had Packy on my side, I would be okay. I definitely needed to get a job. I would start looking on Monday.

Somehow, I managed to finish my schoolwork. In my closet, I took out a small suitcase and packed for the weekend. *I'll have to go clothes shopping soon. At least, I'll be able to wear my dresses for a while longer.*

At the desk again, I pulled my notebook in front of me and started to write.

I guess the chocolate shakes should have been a sign. Ash loved her chocolate shakes. Just when I thought Cal would come around, I had to screw it up and get pregnant. Is this just some big game to Toly and his horde of onlookers? Cally, I wish you could show up for an afternoon so we could talk. I don't mean to minimize Packy. He's been incredible. I thought he was great last time, but I had no idea just how amazing he is. Is it fair for me to change the course of his life? I don't question it about you because you said you wanted me earlier, and I believed you. It would have been nice if you let your younger self know that too. Cal's going to think I did it on purpose, just like you did. He doesn't have the ten extra years to get past the deepest pain the loss of your baby caused. Tell me, Cally, what should I say to him?

I waited for some inspiration to strike. None came. What happened to the team who should have been sending me guidance? *I don't hear anything!*

When Cal called that night, I tried to keep it brief.

"I'm all packed and ready to go. I finished up all up my school work, so I'm free this weekend."

"Perfect, because I have some plans for us."

"Oh, yeah?"

"It's a surprise."

My gut twisted, but I kept my voice upbeat. "That sounds great. Listen, I'm going to go and get ready for bed. I want to be well-rested for tomorrow."

"Sounds like a good plan. Can't wait to see you."

"Me too. Sleep well, Cal."

"You too, love."

I hated playing the part, but I couldn't have the conversation I needed to have over the phone. That would be almost as bad as texting. Almost.

In bed, I tossed and turned for what felt like hours until I finally fell asleep.

CHAPTER THIRTY-TWO

On Friday, we had a short quiz in composition, and I turned in my finished paper. As it would happen, on the day I wish my classes would take forever, they sped by.

I met up with Packy in the cafeteria.

"How are you feeling?" he asked as we moved through the line.

"Sick to my stomach. There's no right way to let Cal down. It's like I lured him to open up just so I could chop off his head." I put fries and a small salad on my tray.

"I doubt he'll see it that way."

"That's exactly how he'll see it, and Port will curse me until the end of time."

"Hang in there, Jayjay, and focus on what Ashley needs. That should help keep you centered."

We carried our trays over to an empty table.

"That's good advice," I said as I sat down. "Hopefully, I can follow it."

After we finished lunch, we trudged with our bags in hand to the car.

"Damn, it's hot out," Packy said when we got into the black car he again borrowed.

"Thanks for driving. I think we'll survive with all the windows down. I brought some water for the ride."

"Good thinking."

Once we were on the road, the drone of the tires on the pavement lulled me to sleep.

The jostling of my shoulder woke me up.

"We're almost there."

"Fuck!" I stretched my neck and tried to get my bearings. Then I searched my fanny pack for some gum.

"Want a piece?"

"Sure."

I unwrapped a slice and put it in his mouth. "The butterflies in my stomach are multiplying and flapping like crazy."

"I can only imagine. Do you want me to come in with you?"

I shook my head. "I think it'll be better if you stay with the car."

Packy pulled into the driveway in front of Port's house. "Hang in there, Jayjay. Stay strong and be as nice as you can be. Expect him to be angry."

"Don't worry, I do. Okay... Here goes nothing." *Or everything.* I stepped up onto Port's wrap-around porch and stared at a much larger house than I expected. *Lady balls.* I shook out my hands and bounced a couple of times. Glancing back at Packy, I saw his thumbs up. Moving past my fear, I knocked on the door.

The door swung open, and Callahan embraced me, lifting me off my feet. "I'm so glad you're here!" He looked amazing.

"You got your hair cut." I touched his hair.

"I did. Where's your bag?"

"It's still in the car. Can I come in for a minute?"

"Of course. Is everything okay?" He took my hand.

"Let's talk inside."

Past the foyer, Port sat on the couch watching TV.

"Hey, Port," I said, struggling to sound calm and neutral. "Cal, do you mind if I talk to Port for a moment?"

He smiled. "Not at all." He gave me a wink of encouragement.

Port stood and led me to the billiard room.

I expected him to be a big towering man that matched his

deep voice, but instead, he had a compact, wiry physique.

"Why do I have a bad feeling?" he asked.

"Because if you didn't like me before ... you're *really* not going to like me now."

"Now what?" He crossed his arms over his chest.

"I hope someday Cal and I get past this, and you and I can actually be on the same side. I'd really like to have the opportunity to get to know you."

"But?"

"I'm about to give Callahan some news, which in his eyes makes us incompatible. I believe he's already falling in love with me. And just so you know, I love him with all my heart and I always will. He can change his mind at any time."

"You're not going to tell me what it is."

"That's for him to share if he decides to. I'm pretty sure this is going to cause a tailspin, and I wanted you to know ahead of time. Trust me, if I could avoid it, I would, but that's not possible."

Port stared at me, not speaking.

"Well, I guess I better get it over with."

"Don't call me asking for any more favors. I'm regretting the ones I've already done."

"I'm sorry for that." I ambled out to find Cal waiting on the couch. "Can we go to your room?"

"Sure. It's so good to see you. It's been a long week."

I tried to smile as he led me into his room and over to the bed. I spotted a gorgeous bouquet of flowers on his chest of drawers. "Flowers?"

"Should I be worried?"

"Please sit. I have to tell you something that won't be easy to hear." I held onto my arms, fear seeping in from every pore.

He slowly lowered down, sitting on the edge of the bed. His jaw tightened, and his back straightened. "Did you sleep with Travis?"

"Good god, no. I could never, would never. Callahan, I'm completely and utterly in love with you."

"Phew," he breathed out. "You had me scared."

"You'll think this is worse."

He took my hand and held it. "Tell me." His sweet, loving look tore away at my soul. I might not ever see him look at me that way again.

I'm sorry, Ashley and Cally.

I knelt down, praying this wouldn't be the last time I saw my Cal. My heart broke as I forced out the words. "I'm so sorry to hurt you like this, and truly, I never thought it would happen. If I did, I would have been smarter about it." I took a deep breath and forced out the words, "Cal ... I'm pregnant."

"What?" He dropped my hand and shot up off the bed.

I stood and followed him. "I went to the clinic because I wasn't feeling well and they took blood."

"Jesus H. Christ." He clutched his head as if it might explode. "When?"

I knew what he was asking. "The first time."

He looked up at me, and I hardly recognized him. Fear and anger transformed his face and posture. His tight fists at his sides scared me.

"Please, Cal. I didn't mean for this to happen. I assumed it wouldn't happened again until I turned twenty-nine, like last time. I had no idea. I love you so much, and I truly believe ... no, I know we can have a wonderful life together. Please don't let this be the breaking point. I can't imagine living my life without you."

"How could you do this to me? You had me believing we had a shot at some kind of—"

I took a step closer and risked putting my hands on his chest. "We still do, Cal. I know the timing is not ideal but—"

He grabbed my wrist. "No, Jayden. You think I'm going to be like YOS and just change my mind. No kids, Jayden. I could never survive going through it again."

"But you wouldn't have to. That's what I'm trying to tell you."

"You don't know that any better than you knew you couldn't get pregnant now. That's what I get for going against all the warning signs." He crossed his arms and turned his back to me.

A sob ripped from my throat. "Please, Cal." I fell to the floor, broken. As I cried, I struggled to get it together. I used the edge of the bed to lift myself back up. "I love you, Callahan, and I will forever and always. Take the time you need and please know, I'll be waiting for you. I'm yours."

He remained stoic and didn't respond.

"I'm going to go." I paused, hoping he would ask me to stay. As I walked out of his room, I heard what sounded like a punch against a hard surface along with mumbling and cursing. I wanted to go back inside and take care of him, but I knew that was the last thing he wanted. Once outside, I made my way to the car, my tears continuing their ritual flow.

Packy caught me up in his arms and led me to the passenger side door. "It'll be okay, Jayjay. Just give it time." He helped me in, then got into his side, and quickly drove away.

I stared out the window and took in the blurry scenery around me. *I'll never be the same. I came here to rid myself of the loss of Cally, and now I have the great privilege of grieving for two Callahans.*

Packy reached over and rubbed my back. "It's not far now."

"Won't your parents be concerned that you're bringing a weeping woman home?"

323

"Trust me, they'll just be glad you're female."

I laughed for a second and then cried some more.

When we arrived, it turned out Packy's parents hadn't yet made it home from work.

I had the chance to collect myself and wash my face.

He then led us to his room, and we dropped our bags there. His room reflected his personality. Posters of punk and rock bands covered the wood paneled walls. He had a collection of snow globes on a row of shelves. In his open closet, I spied a few leather jackets.

"You wear leather jackets? I've never seen you wear one."

"Uh, Jayjay. It's summer."

"Right. I don't know what I was thinking. Where will I be sleeping?"

"We can sleep together in my bed, or I can crash on the couch in the living room if you'd rather."

"Don't be silly. We managed to sleep in our tiny twin beds together. I'm certain we'll be fine in yours."

"So, how are you doing?"

"I feel like shit, really. It went as I expected. Oh, and you should know, we can't expect any more favors from Port. I think he wanted to strangle me as much as Callahan did. I don't mean to be a pain, but do we have to stay two nights?"

He put his arm around me and led me into the kitchen. "Nope. We can head back tomorrow or right now."

"Don't your parents know we're coming?"

He shook his head.

"What the fuck, Packy?"

"I just show up. They don't seem to mind." He flashed me a cheeky smile.

"What if they had something planned?"

"What? Like a big orgy or something?"

I laughed hard, clutching my stomach. "Stop making

me laugh. I don't want to feel good."

"Silly girl. It's my job to make you laugh."

"You should know you're very good at it."

He pointed his thumbs at himself. "I'm the best."

I chuckled again. "Yes, you are. I have to meet your folks now. Please, let's go back tomorrow. I'd say early, but I know who I'm dealing with."

"That's a good thing."

We had dinner with Packy's parents. As odd of a duck as Packy could be, he had very normal parents. I thought my mother and father would like them. Just as Packy warned, they were so thrilled to meet me. I hoped they still felt that way when they found out Packy and I would be raising Ashley together.

CHAPTER THIRTY-THREE

Weeks went by and still no word from Callahan.

My body began to change in subtle ways. My breasts became more sensitive and filled in more. I gained a few pounds from eating for two. This time, I didn't worry about the weight gain and enjoyed the extra calories. I made sure never to skip breakfast and avoided the perils of morning sickness. I seemed more emotional too, but other than Packy having to suffer my mood swings, I managed to adjust my expectations.

Although my life had turned upside-down, classes carried on, and I did my best to focus. Somehow, I believed that if I aced my classes, it might make the sting of the pregnancy less potent to my parents. I still hadn't told them and planned to put it off as long as possible.

I got a job working in the cafeteria. As jobs go, it sucked. At least, I could easily ride my bike there, and they allowed me to work around my class schedule. I saved every penny I earned.

Packy and I had started checking out apartments in the area and hadn't decided on one yet. With neither of us having a car, we decided we wanted our place to be within walking and biking distance to the campus.

After I had gotten off from work, Packy and I set out to see yet another apartment.

"What was wrong with the last one?" I asked. "It had great light in the kitchen, and it wasn't that far of a walk to the campus."

"It was too small, and the security deposit too large," Packy said. "I have a good feeling about this one."

"Uh-huh. That's what you said about the last three we

saw. I'm starting to think you're Goldilocks. We need to choose, Packy. I'm sure the ones closest to FSU fill up the fastest."

"Let's check out a few more and then decide."

I couldn't figure out why he kept putting me off. "I'm willing to see two more and then we have to pick."

"Okay, deal."

"Are you sure you haven't changed your mind?"

"STFU, Jayden. I'm already in love with Ashley. You, on the other hand..."

I playfully punched his shoulder, and he shoved me back. "Hey, dude, lady with a baby," I said, pointing to my belly.

"Lady with the baby should be nicer to the guy with the presents. Come on," he said, taking my hand and leading me up the steps to explore the potential apartment.

"Presents? Did you say presents? I *love* presents."

"Technically, they're not for you. They're for Leelee."

I clapped my hands together. "Let's look fast and get back and her nickname is Ash, not Leelee."

"I thought you would see it my way, and she's Leelee to me!"

❤❤❤❤❤

Once we got back to the dorm, Packy made me wait in my room. I finally heard him shouting through the door. "Coming," I yelled.

Packy came inside, carrying three poorly wrapped packages.

I bounced on the bed and held out my hands.

"I wrapped them myself," he said, handing them over to me.

"I can tell." I winked at him and began tearing open the one on the top. Inside, I found a pink onesie with embroidered words on the front, "Mommy adores me." Placing the other packages to the side, I jumped up and hugged Packy. "I love it! It's perfect."

He lifted the next package and said, "No, this one is puurfect."

I ripped off the paper and opened the second box. There, I found a white onesie that had a cute kitten on it and read, "Puurfect in every way." It came with a matching blanket. "You weren't kidding. It is perfect, Packy. What's in the last one?"

"Check it out."

Opening the last of the boxes, I pulled out a T-shirt that read:

YES, I'm pregnant
NO, you can't touch
Now give me some CHOCOLATE

"I was hoping to find one that said, 'now give me a chocolate shake,' but they didn't have that. This was as close as I could find."

My tears spilled out of my control. "Thank you so much, Pakster. You're the very best of people I know. I honestly can't imagine my life without you and all your support. You're helping me be excited about having Ashley again."

"Still no word from Callahan?"

"I'm pretty sure that ship has sailed. I'm going to have to start charting my own waters."

"Did you sign up for a sailing class next semester? Cause you have the jargon down."

"No, silly." I pulled my shirt off over my head and put on the one Packy got for me. "It's big, which is good. I don't see wearing it until I show."

"That's probably wise. Have you told your roommate yet that you're moving out?"

"It's on my to-do list alongside telling my parents. I did inform housing. I guess it's happening. Now we just need to pick out our apartment and give our security deposit. I think I have enough saved for my half."

CHAPTER THIRTY-FOUR

O n Monday as usual, I rode into campus and locked up my bike. I found my seat in the second row of composition class and waited for Travis to take the stage. He hadn't given up trying to persuade me to meet up with his ex-father-in-law. I kept putting him off in the hopes that Cal would come around and eventually go with me.

I felt someone sit next to me, which drew my attention. "WTF, Packy? What are you doing here and why are you up before noon?"

"I heard through the grapevine that today's class shouldn't be missed."

I opened my mouth to respond, but then Travis took the stage and diverted me.

"Today we are veering off the syllabus, and I'm introducing a new module: How to instill passion and romance into your writing."

Packy raised an eyebrow and then returned his attention to Travis.

"What the fuck is going on, Pakster?" I whispered.

He shrugged.

I looked around the large space, and it seemed to hold more students than in previous classes.

"Passion is an intense emotion that's barely containable. It can stem from anger, love, or desire. Okay class ... share something you're passionate about."

A few hands shot up around the room.

"You in the green shirt?" Travis said, pointing toward the back.

"Chocolate. I'm passionate about chocolate."

The students laughed.

"Although I agree it's an amusing choice, it doesn't quite qualify. You?"

"I'm passionate about cars."

"Folks, passion is a barely controllable emotion. Unless you're so enamored by chocolate and cars that you will shun other activities in favor of waxing your car or gorging on candy bars, I think what you're expressing is more a keenness than passion. Anyone else?"

A guy in the fourth row, called out, "I'm passionate about sex. I can't get enough and think about it all the time. Does that qualify?"

The class cracked up and awaited Travis' response.

"Yes, in *your* case, I'd say that qualifies as passion. Your writing assignment for this week is on the board. Five hundred words expressing romance and passion, which the reader can identify and feel. You can write about cars or chocolate if you believe you can convince me of the passion you have for it. Passion can incite a person to behave outside of what is normal and, at times, in dangerous ways. Our horny friend here..." he said, pointing to the guy in the fourth row, "...might take risks he might not otherwise to fulfill his passion."

"Like?" A few students asked.

"Unprotected sex, unsavory partners, etc." Travis perched on the edge of the desk and continued, "The other component of the writing assignment is romance. As you may see, passion and romance can be intrinsically tied together. Romance is often an expression of passion."

I took out my notebook and began to write down the new assignment.

Travis continued, "For a clear example of passion and romance, I have a guest coming out on stage." He waved someone forward.

A male voice cleared his throat, and I glanced up from my

paper and coughed, trying to force air back into my lungs.

Packy took my hand and held it.

"The floor is yours," Travis said, stepping to the side of the stage.

Callahan strode forward under the lights and gazed down at me. "Love, like passion, takes risk. The most intense love affairs can rip your guts to shreds or can take you to the greatest heights. That's where the risk comes in." He took a step closer. "I'm sorry it's taken me so long to come to my senses. I had to become so miserable without you to realize what you already knew. You, my love, are the greatest thing that has ever happened to me. You take me as I am and only ask for the same in return. You are the bravest, most honest person I've ever known. If you give me another chance, I promise to be by your side for the rest of our lives."

Tears filled my eyes and shed down my cheeks. Glancing at Packy, I saw he too was crying.

Callahan went down on one knee and pulled a box out of his pocket. "Jayden, love of my life, will you do me the greatest honor of becoming my wife and lead us on a journey of romance and passion."

I stepped up to the stage, and two guys helped to lift me up. Once I stood in front of him, I said, "Yes, of course, I will. I love you, Callahan."

"I'm completely and utterly in love with you too." He took out the engagement ring and slipped it onto my ring finger.

My eyes remained locked on his face the whole time. Callahan was finally mine again.

He scooped me up into a hug as I wrapped my legs around his waist. "I never want to let you go," he said.

The entire class stood and applauded exuberantly.

"Don't, Cal. Don't ever let me go."

He set me down, not letting go of my hand.

I caught a glimpse of Travis as we descended the steps from the stage. He smiled in my direction, and I knew he had the ending to his story. I couldn't help feeling grateful.

Packy joined us, carrying my backpack. "Nice job, Cal. What do you think of the ring, Jayden? I helped him pick it out."

Pivoting on the spot, I said, "You did?" For the first time, I held up the ring and took a good look at it. Not just one but two diamonds kissed on the diagonal, and the ring had a flowing ribbon design.

"Read the inscription," Packy ordered.

I pulled off the ring and read, "From Cal and YOS." My tears resumed. "I'm a blubbering mess. Damn hormones. I love it. It couldn't be more perfect."

"That's what we thought," Cal said. "How would you feel about Packy living with us and helping with Ashley? Since we'll all be going to school, it'll make it easier on all of us."

"What? How long have you all been planning this?"

"He's been relentlessly harassing me for weeks." Cal smiled over at Packy.

"Had you stopped wiggin' out sooner—" Packy chided.

"It's just been the last couple of days, love. We think we found the perfect apartment for all of us." Callahan lifted my chin and kissed me. "I've missed your lips."

"I'm sorry, my head is spinning. Are you saying you quit your job, you're going back to school—"

"Starting in the winter, yes."

"You're moving to Tallahassee, and we're all living together?"

"She's finally caught up," Packy said.

Text to self: *Wait until the end of the story before jumping to a conclusion.*

"Holy shit." *Toly, I'm sorry for all the bitching!*

"You're going to need to cut down on the cursing when Ashley gets here," Cal said in that parental tone I recognized.

"I knew YOS was in there somewhere." I playfully shoved Cal.

We all laughed.

I ditched the rest of my classes, and Cal and I stayed in bed, making up for lost time.

EPILOGUE
DECEMBER 2015

My parents nearly disowned me when they found out I was pregnant. Fortunately, Callahan won them over. We married in December during the winter vacation from school. Port was Callahan's best man, and Packy was my maid of honor. Port finally decided I wasn't the devil incarnate.

Packy ended up majoring in psychology and becoming a marriage and family counselor. I had to wonder if all of the counseling he gave me led him in that direction. Not being sure what he ended up doing the first time around, I would never really know.

He became my savior yet again when, unbeknownst to me, he kept calling Callahan after I told him I was pregnant. I can only assume he used his charms as a budding therapist to bring him back to me. Neither has ever shared the tenor of their conversations, and frankly, all that matters to me is that it worked.

Packy also coordinated with Travis so Cal could propose to me during composition class. According to Packy, Travis was very game to assist.

Just like my love for Cal is one of a kind, so is my friendship with Packy, and it still is to this day. He lived with us until he graduated with his Bachelor degree in Psychology. He got into a graduate program in Atlanta, and as we pinky swore, we stayed in touch. The bond he formed with Ashley is still strong today. Five years ago, Packy got married, and a year later, they adopted a baby girl from China. Cal and I visit them as often as we can.

In March of 1986, we sunk all the money we had into Microsoft's IPO. After our windfall, we diversified and stayed financially solvent.

Ashley, not quite the girl I knew the first time, but ever so loveable, became a sister ... twice. Cal and I had two more girls.

Instead of celebrating our twentieth anniversary in 2015, we're celebrating thirty years together surrounded by our children and grandkids. Packy and family even flew out.

My parents are still hanging in there, and Shannon and Del never got to the point of considering divorce this time around. I can't pinpoint the exact reason, but I suspect that remaining close and making sure she put in the effort to stay connected with Del helped.

I don't regret all I went through to get my Cally back. I just didn't realize how much my life would change. He's still the grounding force, and I'm still the gal who leaps before she looks. It works for us.

Travis ended up getting fired from FSU for inappropriate conduct with students, which to me was a shame because he actually was a good professor. He did publish *The Resurrection of Hope* to some acclaim. I never heard if he published again.

Our bedroom and much of the house is covered with Cal's drawings and paintings, which I love. After a while, though, I had to convince him to find a subject matter other than me.

We opted not to tell the kids about my time travel, but we did instill in them the importance of finding your soulmate. If I had to guess, I would say all three have. At the very least, they have loving relationships that stand the test of time like their mother and father.

Cal still teases me about the time when we were still in college, and Packy talked us into getting high. I thought I saw Toly up in a tree, winking at me. (I believe it really happened.)

If you're wondering if I ever wrote my story, I did. I hope you have enjoyed it.

Thank you so much for reading *The Second First Chance*. If you enjoyed my writing style, I have other books available.

Bound by Your Love Series (erotic romance)
Stuck in Between
Bittersweet Deceit
Blue Persuasion

My Body Trilogy (dark, erotic, suspense)
My Body-His
My Body-His (Marcello)
My Body-Mine

Co-Authored with Dana Bennett (romance)
The Demarcation of Jack

ACKNOWLEDGMENTS

The inspiration for this story stems from my deep abiding love for my soulmate and husband, Dana Bennett. We've often wished we had met ten years earlier, and I have often fantasized what might have been. Although the characters in this story are not us, the love they share mirrors our own. My husband is not only my first reader, but also my biggest supporter. Without him, I'm not sure I'd go on writing. Having him in my corner is priceless.

Luckily for me, I have other great supports. My test readers, once again, have helped to make this story the best it can be. A huge hug and thanks go to Tami C., Debbie R., Sara S., Ann P., Kim L., and Thanos P. My mother, a test reader too, has continued to cheer me on and encourage me to keep at it. Thank you!

I feel so fortunate to have connected with my editor, Harper Jewel. Not only do I love her work, but I really like her too. She's done an incredible job as I'm sure you will agree.

The cover artist, Happi Anarky, created my vision for the cover, and I am so impressed with her work. She's a true artist with whom I know I'll be working with again.

A huge thank you goes out to my loyal readers. You give me the biggest reason to keep creating and getting lost in the journey with my characters.

Blakely Bennett grew up in Southeast Florida and has been residing in the great Northwest for over ten years. She graduated from Nova Southeastern University with a degree in psychology, which accounts for her particular interest in crafting the personalities, struggles, and motivations of her characters. She is an avid reader of many genres of fiction but especially enjoys erotica and romance. Writing has always been her bliss.

Blakely is married to a wonderful, loving, and supportive husband, who is also a writer, and who helps to keep her grounded. She is a mother, a communitarian, a lover of music (it is always on while she is writing thanks to Pandora), and a good friend. An advocate of love and female empowerment, she is also a facilitator for a women's group. She loves to walk and hike for exercise, and finds that, since moving to Seattle, Washington, she is now one of those crazy people who walk in the rain.

The Second First Chance is her eighth novel. Her other novels are the Bound by Your Love Series (*Stuck in Between, Bittersweet Deceit, & Blue Persuasion*), the dark erotic suspense My Body Trilogy (*My Body-His, My Body-His (Marcello)* and *My Body-Mine*) and the co-author of the contemporary romance, *The Demarcation of Jack*, which she co-wrote with her husband, Dana Bennett.

www.blakelybennett.com